WHAT PRICE MAGIC . . . ?

These days you can buy anything if you just know the right places to shop. Even true magic might be yours if you can find a reputable supplier and come up with the price. But what price is right and which is just too high to pay? Now you can find out in stories where the magic may prove bright or dark, and the purchaser might get far more than was bargained for:

"For Whom the Bell Tolled"—When he purchased the bell from a young woman in desperate need of cash, he never dreamed how it would transform his entire magic shop. . . .

"Dime Store Rings"—Sometimes it's hard to tell whether the magic is in the gift or the giving. . . .

"The Assassin's Dagger"—She was the top troubleshooter for Abracadabra, Inc., a firm which had bought magic shops all over the world. But when she was called in to deal with what might be one of the legendary Assassin's Daggers, she might just be walking into more trouble than even she could handle. . . .

D0556104

The Magic Shop

Edited by
Denise Little

DAW BOOKS, INC.

DONALD A. WOLLHEIM, FOUNDER
375 Hudson Street, New York, NY 10014

ELIZABETH R. WOLLHEIM
SHEILA E. GILBERT
PUBLISHERS
http://www.dawbooks.com

First Printing, February 2004
2   3   4   5   6   7   8   9

ACKNOWLEDGMENTS

CONTENTS

INTRODUCTION

by *Denise Little*

MAGIC is a subject that fascinates us all, no matter what our personal beliefs. In every society, from the most primitive to the most advanced, magicians flourish— whether in the guise of shamans or street performers or highly paid headliners in Las Vegas. Even the most skeptical among us will suspend our disbelief in magic at least long enough to watch a magician make a tiger appear out of nowhere—all the while trying to figure out how the trick is done.

I think that we watch magicians at work because somewhere deep in our hearts there's a part of us that wants to believe that magic really is possible—that the lady was actually sawed in half and magically restored, that the doves which appeared on the magician's gloved hand really materialized out of thin air rather than crawling from a handy pocket in his sleeve.

Folk magic, too, is alive and well in the world—even in skeptical Western society. Whether it's a lucky rabbit's foot on a key chain, a souvenir *gris-gris* picked up on a trip to New Orleans, or a voodoo doll with a vague resemblance to a former lover or coworker, most of us have bought a charm of some sort or another at some point in our lives, often as a joke . . . though not always. We want magic in our lives— and we're willing to pay for the privilege of having it.

In nearly every city of any size there's a magic shop, usually a cluttered and dusty specialty store in a side street located a little way off the beaten path, though these days some have gone nicely upscale, with fabulous displays of crystals and wands and tarot decks and big glass jars of aromatic herbs as well as the more traditional paraphernalia. I used to walk by just such a shop in New York on my way to work. I always wondered who shopped there, and what they hoped to buy.

It seemed to me that buying magic would be a chancy business: if it worked at all, it wasn't likely to be predictable. In fact, if it worked spectacularly, the purchaser might be in for a BIG surprise. If magic *was* real, I decided, then all sorts of odd things would happen to the patrons of a magic shop. Some of those things, I was quite sure, would change the life of the buyer forever—though never quite in the way said buyer had planned.

My musings on the nature of buying magic got steadily more involved in the years that I walked past that magic shop every day. There was a story in it, I was sure. I wasn't alone in my thoughts—when I mentioned the idea to several writer friends of mine they were intrigued, too. So you are holding in your hands the results of our speculations on the nature of magic shops. You'll find tales by many of your favorite writers and some who are new to you, a collection of stories of the changed fates and challenged minds of the amazed consumers—both mundane and magical—who dared to shop at a Magic Shop.

EVERY LITTLE THING
SHE DOES

by Susan Sizemore

Susan Sizemore lives in the Midwest and spends most of her time writing. Some of her other favorite things are coffee, dogs, travel, movies, hiking, history, farmers' markets, art glass, and basketball—you'll find mention of quite a few of these things inside the pages of her stories. She works in many genres, from contemporary romance to epic fantasy and horror. She's the winner of the Romance Writers of America's Golden Heart award, and a nominee for the 2000 Rita Award in historical romance. Her available books include historical romance novels, a dark fantasy series, The Laws of the Blood, *science fiction, and several electronically published books and short stories. One of her electronic books, the epic fantasy* Moons' Dreaming, *written with Marguerite Krause, is a nominee for the Eppie, the epublishing industry's writing award. Susan's email address is Ssizemore@aol.com, and her webpage address is:http://members.aol.com/Ssizemore/storm/home.htm*

"COULD you help me? Please?"

Trevor responded to the touch of panic in the female voice, though he couldn't help but notice what a very pleasant voice it was, apart from the panic, that is. He looked up, and the woman standing on the other side of the glass counter was . . . enchanting. He was used to things being enchanted, but the idea of *someone* being enchanting . . . well, it simply didn't make any sense, and he pushed the notion away between one blink and another.

"May I help you?" he asked.

She looked around the dim and crowded shop as though she thought for a moment that he must be speaking to someone else. When she decided that they were the only ones in the place at two on a Tuesday afternoon—he did do most of his business in the wee hours of the night—she addressed him once more. "I already asked if you'd help me." She smiled when she said it, as though to imply that she was not being at all sarcastic when referring to his absentmindedness. She had a most . . . charming . . . smile. He *sold* charms, that sort of magic was not supposed to be bestowed lightly, and for free.

"You're a mundane," he said.

"How can you tell?" She didn't stop smiling, and her eyes were a twinkling, bewitching green.

"Not a pentagram or ankh in sight," he told her. "You're wearing a suit." A short, pink suit. "And high heel shoes," he added when she noticed him noticing her legs.

"Come on, I'm sure some witches dress like this."

"Not to do business with me, they don't."

"I'm taking a long lunch."

"You are an ordinary human being."

"I'll bring a broom the next time, all right?"

"What are you doing in my shop?"

"Are you always so rude to people who ask you for help?"

"Usually." He pointed toward the door. "Listen, we don't do tarot readings in here, there is nothing tie-dyed among the merchandise, and the term New Age is an insult. I think you want—"

"Good," she interrupted with an emphatic nod. "Just the man I'm looking for. I need your help, Mr . . ."

"Adam. Trevor Adam."

Her smile somehow managed to brighten, which caused

Trevor to blink behind the thick lenses of his glasses. "What a wonderfully British name to go with that lovely accent!"

He did not have an accent. He sounded just like any man born and raised in the shadow of Stirling Castle. There was nothing lovely about it, was there? "I'm from Scotland. I come from a long line of Scots sorcerers. I don't suppose the name Hepburn means anything to you."

"Other than Katherine and Audrey, no."

"They were a clan of evil magicians. My ancestors defeated them in magical battle." And why was he telling her this? Was he trying to impress this mundane woman who hadn't even told him what she wanted yet? Not that he'd given her much chance, now had he? "What do you want, woman?"

"You. I mean, your help. You see, it's my house. I'm new in town. I only moved in last week." She fidgeted as she spoke, twisting her hands together. Trevor couldn't help but notice that she wore no rings.

"House? Madam, I am not—"

"Don't call me madam." She chuckled. "Of course with all the bedrooms in the old Pantaseres house I suppose I could turn it into—"

"Pantaseres? Did you say Pantaseres?"

"Yes. Is it serious, doctor?"

Trevor braced his palms on the top of the display case. "This is nothing to joke about, young woman."

"I know. I'm the one living there. Along with . . . things."

"How the demons did a mundane end up in the Pantaseres house?"

"I bought it. From a realtor. I suspected the price was too good to be true, but the place enchanted me the first time I walked in—"

"Of course it did. No doubt the dark entity reached into your mind and made you buy the place."

"Actually, I rather think it was the low asking price, small interest rate on the mortgage and no points on closing that influenced me more than any dark entity. I like a bargain, Mr. Adam. May I call you Trevor?"

"Dark entities know how to manipulate our weaknesses."

"Do tell."

Trevor lifted his chin proudly. "Do you wish my aid, or to mock me?"

"I would never mock you, Trevor." She gave him *that* smile again. "Maybe tease a little, but never mock."

"Who are you?" he asked. "How did you find me?"

"I am Amanda Brewster. Not Amy, not Mandy, but simply Amanda."

"Of course," he acknowledged her introducing herself. It was nice to see an American with a certain sense of formality about names. Then he was surprised when Amanda held out her hand, as if she expected him to shake it, or perhaps kiss it. "Of the Brooklyn Brewsters?" he inquired, rather than explain that an adept of his talents and training did not willingly touch anyone but those with whom he was intimately involved. Intimacy had not been part of his life for some time.

She looked puzzled for a moment, then her features lit with a brilliant flash of humor. "I haven't seen that movie in years. I forgot the crazy family in *Arsenic and Old Lace* is named Brewster. You have a sense of humor, Trevor."

"Upon occasion."

"Don't get huffy with me. Not when I need your help."

"Yes, of course. How did you find me?" he asked once more as he rolled down the turned-up cuffs of his white shirt and buttoned them. Such informality was all very well and good while alone in the magic shop, but hardly proper while speaking to a possible client. He did not take on outside assignments very often. In fact, he was well aware that he'd settled into a comfortable rut doing research and dealing in very esoteric merchandise to a very exclusive clientele. He had not felt any call to adventure recently—not until he looked into Amanda's fascinating green eyes.

"I found you by a very circuitous route," Amanda answered.

"That is how it is usually done."

"First I complained to my realtor about the strange things

that I was seeing and feeling in the house. Actually, first I considered seeing a psychiatrist about hallucinations and paranoia—but frankly, Trevor, I know the difference between insanity and a cursed, haunted, magically infested house. *I'm* not crazy. The house is nuts."

"A bold realization for a mundane. Go on," he urged.

"The realtor was not sympathetic. He had a rather 'you get what you pay for' attitude, and I suppose he's right, up to a point, but there are ethical questions involved. I'm digressing, aren't I?"

"Yes." Trevor had been enjoying listening to her and watching her so much that he'd hardly noticed. "Go on."

"I don't believe in wallowing in indecision and self-pity and letting situations overwhelm me. If there's a problem, I find a solution."

"Admirable."

"But not as easy as it sounds, of course. Even I wallow occasionally. I am only mortal—the same can not be said for you, I take it?"

Trevor kept his expression and voice bland. "I told you I come from an interesting family."

"You mentioned sorcerers. I heard the term 'paladin' mentioned in connection with you when I researched the sort of help I needed. Imagine my delight in finding out that the man I need lives right here in town." She looked at him with touching earnestness and admiration in her green eyes. "I could use either a sorcerer or paladin—both—right now."

Trevor cleared his throat and rather diffidently tilted his head and touched his ear. "Yes, well . . ."

"Please?" She looked around the crowded, rather dingy shop. "Besides, you could definitely get out more."

Trevor bridled a bit at the implications and said stiffly. "I will think about it. Where can I contact you?"

"At home," Amanda answered promptly. "I can give you my phone number, cell phone, work number, email address, pager, PDA—"

"At home!" He very nearly leaped over the counter with

the impulse to protect her. "You can't possibly be staying at the Pantaseres mansion!"

"It's my house. I'll admit that I put my dogs and cats into a kennel, because I was beginning to fear they might get eaten . . . and they were acting really weird. One of my cats started talking like the little girl in *The Exorcist*. Changing his brand of cat food did not help. And Murphy, that's my Irish setter, the people at the kennel are worried because his eyes are still glowing. Gambit and Rogue, those are the greyhounds, well, they—"

"Enough!" Trevor shouted. He held his hands out before him. "I'll help you." He looked around the crowded shelves and cabinets of the shop. "I have to gather some things. I'll meet you at the Pantaseres house this evening."

Her smile brightened his life again. "Fantastic! Around seven? I'll make dinner."

Of course it occurred to him that she might be a demon sent from the nether reaches of hell to trap his soul, bend his will to hers and take over his mortal existence, but she could certainly cook.

She'd also come up with some rather clever innovations in the effort to exist with a certain amount of comfort in a place known in the occult world as the Dark Storm Nexus. It was a place where anything could happen, and fifty years ago an arrogant, undisciplined wizard had shown the utter, foolish audacity to build a house here. No one knew what had happened to Mingo Pantaseres. Some said he'd been carried straight to hell for his presumption in trying to control the Nexus. Others said that he'd run away and ended up tending bar in a broken-down roadhouse in the Arizona desert. Some said he ended up in a madhouse. Others that he'd built a fortune in the real estate business by continuously reselling the haunted house after each new owner fled in terror.

Whatever had happened to Mingo, the problem of the house remained. Every now and then some brave soul took it upon him- or herself to try an exorcism, or a new cult leader chose to perform dark ceremonies out in the back garden. Trevor was certainly not above providing the necessary herbs, grimoires, incense, and other paraphernalia for the fools who approached the Pantaseres property. After all, he did have a business to run. He'd never thought to approach the place himself. He liked being a shopkeeper, and had hated being a wizard. As for being a paladin, he preferred a quiet life. A cup of tea and a good book in the evening was much more his idea of a pleasant time than standing about with a heavy magical sword in a thunderstorm whacking at a flame-spitting demon. He really hated the flame-spitting ones. Dragons were the worst.

He sighed now, wondering how Amanda had so easily talked him into helping her with her house problems.

"Pie," she said, turning to him with her bright smile. "I made peach pie."

"The crust. Fantastic," he said after he recovered enough from the first bite to speak. He was practically quivering with pleasure.

"It's the hellfire," she answered. "When the oven opened up onto a fiery pit I was concerned at first, but I've discovered it's perfect for baking. I made focaccia yesterday that'll knock your socks off. I'll make you a roast beef sandwich with it to take home."

"That won't be—" She gave him a look that told him not to mess with the cook. "Thank you. I'd like that. Assuming I make it home, that is."

The teasing glint came into her eyes. "Are you saying you'd like to stay over?"

"I am saying I might not make it out of here alive."

She waved a hand at him. "Oh, don't be so modest. You'll do fine."

Her confidence somehow bolstered him, which was distinctly odd since he knew she had no idea what she was talking about. During a preliminary tour of this extremely haunted property he had noted her taste in books tended toward business publications, cookbooks, and popular fiction when the contents of a bookcase spewed from the shelves to forcefully attack him. There had not been a single magical grimoire among the attacking horde, thankfully.

He had not had time to work a counterspell before Amanda pushed him to the floor and used a broom to beat the wayward publications into submission.

"Bad books!" she'd shouted. "That's no way to treat a guest! You'll all end up in a garage sale if you keep this up."

The books had kept still after that, but Trevor could feel them sulking as he helped Amanda shove them back into the case. "You shouldn't be so—stern—with your library. Words have power, you know," he cautioned her.

"Words have the power you give them," she'd answered. When he'd stared at her in shock, she smiled, and said. "Have I just insulted one of the laws of magic?"

"Trampled it into the dust, more like."

"Guess I'm a hopeless mundane."

Then she'd invited him into the kitchen for dinner and whatever shock or disapproval he'd been feeling had dissipated in the warm glow that rose in him with every bite of shepherd's pie, a pear and cheese salad, and now, warm peach pie covered with a dollop of vanilla-flavored heavy cream.

"This was delicious," he said, rising to his feet after he finished the pie. "Now I must get to work."

"Wouldn't you like a cup of coffee first? Or a cup of tea? There's boiling water coming out of the tap at the moment. I know there's a hint of sulfur to it, and it's an odd shade of green, but that's better than yesterday. I suspect the stuff trickling out yesterday was blood, but I didn't feel up to confirming that guess. Still—"

"There are spells to be performed, Amanda," he interrupted what he realized was nervous chattering. "A magical battle to be waged."

She looked anxious for the first time since they'd met. "Well, I'd hate to see you get hurt."

She would? How nice. Her words added to the warm glow he felt whenever he looked at her. "I'll be fine," he told her. He wasn't sure that all would go well, but reassuring her made him feel better, especially when she smiled at his words.

She stood and rubbed her hands briskly together. "Fine, then. Time for us to gird our loins and face the beasts in their den of iniquity, and all that. What, what."

"What?"

"I'm trying to sound all brave and stiff upper lip here, Trevor."

"I . . . see. It sounded rather silly, actually."

"Well—"

"And no loin-girding for you. Facing evil is my job."

"Facing evil is everyone's job, darling. You get to handle the magical kind."

He considered this for a moment, then came to the conclusion that she wasn't insisting on engaging in spell-to-spell combat with the creatures of the Dark Storm Nexus, but she wasn't going to stay out of the way either. "You'll be standing right behind me, I suppose."

She nodded. "With a first-aid kit and my cell phone with 911 set on speed dial. Just in case I need to call the fire department again," she hastened to add. "I'm sure you won't need any medical help, but I always believe in being prepared."

"Wise to take whatever precautions you feel necessary," he told her. "Help me clear the table, will you?"

"You aren't planning on helping with the dishes right now, are you?" she asked as they carried used plates and utensils and set them on the counter next to where the green geyser rushed into the sink.

Steam boiled up out of the deep sink to fog Trevor's glasses. While he took the time to carefully clean the thick lenses, he answered. "Let's save the dishes for later. Right now I need the table to set up my equipment." When he put his glasses back on he noticed that she was studying his face intently, with her head tilted thoughtfully to one side and a slight smile on her face. "What?"

"Nothing." She cleared her throat, and went back to the

table. "The sooner we get this over with the sooner we can get on with our lives."

"That's the spirit," he agreed. He picked up the duffel bag he'd placed by his chair when they sat down to dinner and took out the necessary ritual implements. He stepped back when he was done. "Light the candles, will you?" he requested, then turned his back to her.

"Certainly." He heard her moving about while he proceeded with his preparations. "Trevor," she said after a few moments. "You've taken off your shirt. And tie, and awful tweedy jacket," she added when he turned around to face her. His skin went hot as she looked at his chest.

"It's necessary for the ritual," he told her. He cleared his throat. "Actually, the ritual should be performed while sky clad."

"You mean naked?"

"*Um* . . . yes. But I thought I'd save you the embarr—"

"No, no. That's fine. I'm not the embarrassing sort. You do whatever you have to do to make the spells work correctly. Remember, I'll be right behind you. Of course, if you'd like me to stand facing you, I'd—"

"Stand over there." He pointed to a spot near the door that led to the backyard. "And be quiet," he added. "And if anything goes wrong, run."

"How will I know if anything goes wrong?"

"A fire demon will be eating me."

"I suppose that would be a fairly obvious sign."

"*Shh.*"

Much to his surprise, she actually did as he told her: kept out of the way and let him get on with the task at hand. After he finished undressing, he used athame, salt, and holy water to set a protective circle. He sprinkled a thin layer of earth onto the white tiles of the kitchen floor and stepped onto the dirt. He then invoked the help of the guardian spirits of good against the evil forces of the Nexus. After that he cut a thin line across his palm and let several drops of his own blood fall into the silver goblet filled with a mixture of herbs and wine. He took one sip of the powerful mixture, then used the rest to paint the proper magical symbols on the chakra power points on his body, whispering a combination of prayers and spells while he worked.

When he was done, he spoke one Word of power, and the symbols began to glow silver, then the silver light spread out and enfolded his body. He stood with his feet planted on the earth, arms stretched out to the air, gaze fixed on the water running from the tap; the fire from the pit that had once been an oven warming his naked back. When the silver light had turned into a suit of silver chain-mail armor, Trevor took up the paladin's sword lying in the center of the table and shouted for all the evil of the Nexus to come forth and do battle.

After that he became quite busy, and, frankly, everything went to hell.

"What hit me?"

"Everything in the kitchen. And I think a gargoyle dropped on you at one point. Not a real gargoyle, but a stone one, like from a cathedral. It must have weighed a ton. Then there were the dragons."

"I hate dragons."

"You shouted something to that effect at the time."

"Then what happened?"

"You cut off their heads. I'm afraid you got a little singed doing it, though."

"Something does smell likes it's burning. Is it me?"

"Not anymore, dear. I always keep a fire extinguisher in the kitchen."

"Wise of you. I can't see."

"There's a bandage over your eyes."

"Why?"

"Something to do with the concussion, I think."

"A concussion."

"From the gargoyle, maybe. Possibly from the refrigerator."

"*Ah.* Of course. The refrigerator. Tell me, am I dead, or in intensive care?"

"You were dead, but the EMTs managed to resuscitate you. You were in the ICU unit for a while, but you're healing surprisingly quickly for a man with so many burns, broken bones, and internal injuries, so you've been moved to a regular room. The attending physician says she knows what you are and how magic works, so she's going to send you home in the morning to make room for really injured people."

"I'm really injured."

"Yes, you are. I'm very proud of you."

He sighed, which made his ribs hurt. "Did I win?" he finally remembered to ask.

"Of course you did." He felt Amanda's lips brush gently across his forehead, and it did wonders for his very serious headache. "And I'm going to take very good care of you."

She was going to take care of him, Trevor thought as he drifted back off. That sounded nice.

"Woman, I do not need to be taken care of."

"Well, excuse me, Mr. Grumpy."

He was *not* grumpy. He would admit that perhaps he was a bit irritable, but that was only because skin beneath the remaining casts on his left arm and right leg itched. His wounds had healed quickly since he'd been out of hospital, but for the itching.

As if the itching wasn't bad enough, there was the matter of change. He looked around his quiet little shop and let out a grunt of disgust at the realization that he barely recalled what the place had looked like not two weeks before. Dingy, he supposed, and drab, dark and mysterious. Just the way a magic shop ought to look. Dull, of course, and the emptiness had seemed a bit lonely sometimes, but he'd had his books to read and spells to practice. It had really been quite pleasant, hadn't it? And he missed it. Of course he did.

Now the curtains were thrown open, the shelves dusted, a bright rug was laid before the door, a group of comfy chairs were set around a low table, and carafes of tea and coffee rested on the table, along with cups and a plate of biscuits. It was all very homey and inviting. Amanda had hung crystals in the windows, and a wind chime tinkled every time someone walked in the door. And people kept walking in the door! And leaving with purchases. The place was actually beginning to turn a profit, and somehow that seemed wrong. It wasn't as if he minded making enough to live on, his wants were few, after all, but. . . . He simply couldn't get used to the idea of the differences Amanda had made while he was laid up. Frightening differences, really, not that he was frightened, of course.

It was not that he did not cope well with the idea of change; a man in his profession needed to be flexible and prepared for anything. It was sudden change to his personal life and space that he'd always approached slowly and methodically, and—and not at all, really. It made him grumpy to realize that he was staid and stodgy and totally bowled over in the face of the Whirlwind Amanda.

"I am not grumpy!" he announced.

"Yes, you are."

"Am not."

"Would you like a cup of tea?"

"No!"

He had not shouted; he had merely spoken loudly. At least it was loud enough to disturb the white Persian cat occupying his lap. It got down and stalked away, tail and head held high. The cat was Amanda's. Amanda had a petting zoo's worth of pets. She'd brought this particular member of her menagerie to the shop because she claimed having a cat in a magic shop added to the ambience.

"That is not ambience," he muttered, dusting white hairs off his pants, "it's shed fur."

"What did you say?" Amanda asked. She was sitting on one of the comfy chairs. Her laptop computer rested on the table.

"What are you doing?" he countered.

"Inventory spreadsheet," she answered.

"I see." He didn't, really. All he knew was that she was being managerial again. With his stuff. "Must you?" he questioned. She looked up from her work finally and stared at him. He could see the hurt in her eyes, but he couldn't keep from saying again, "You don't have to do this."

"You won't let me pay you for saving my house," she reminded him. She waved at the reorganized shop that represented his reorganized life. "This was the least I could do."

"I think you've done quite enough."

"Fine. Let me write you a check."

"Paladins don't take money," he said. "For tax purposes," he added, trying to make a joke of it.

He'd hoped she'd smile. She hadn't smiled in days, and he missed it. Maybe it was because he'd been so grumpy. . . . No, no, this whole situation was not his fault.

Amanda rose to her feet and crossed her arms. "I do not take charity," she announced.

"Not charity," he countered. "Chivalry."

"You are so old fashioned."

"I thought you found that charming."

"I do—I did—I never said that. Oh, never mind!" She flipped the lid of the laptop shut, picked up the cat, and said, "Come on, Cyclops, we're out of here."

When she left he didn't hear the sound of the wind chime tinkling over the thud of the slamming door.

"Fine," he said. "Good riddance." Now he could get back to his regular life.

One day passed. Two. The last of the casts came off. He was finally able to have a proper scratch, but that didn't help his mood any. On the third day he closed the curtains and brought a funereal dimness back to his shop. The darkness suited his melancholy quite nicely. On the fifth day he found himself longing painfully for a piece of peach pie. On the sixth day he noticed that a thin coating of dust was settling back onto his books and shelves and very nearly took a cloth to them before sternly stopping himself.

He would not let *her* influence him. He wasn't lonely, he told himself, and woke to a miserable, restless night after dreaming about her smile. He told himself smiles weren't everything. By the twelfth day he'd stopped looking up eagerly every time the shop door opened and told himself he was going to take down that stupid chime.

On the thirteenth day he couldn't hear the chime for the loud *thud* of the door slamming. The sound certainly got his attention.

He'd barely looked up when Amanda marched up to the counter and declared, "Trevor Adam, you call yourself a paladin?" She put her hands on the lovely curves of her hips and glared.

He rose to his feet and glared back. "I certainly do, Miss Brewster."

"Then how come my house is still haunted? Infested?"

"Really?" This time he smiled. "You have monsters?"

"Lots of them. I want your help or my money back!"

She needed him! He almost jumped with joy. She. Needed. Him. All right!

"I don't charge money," he reminded her. "But—I would like a piece of pie."

"I was thinking a large layer cake with white frosting would be more appropriate."

"I see. You think I'll work for cake."

"And a new black suit. I have one picked out for you."

"*Hmm*. You think I should work for food and clothing. How about room and board?"

"I have something in mind."

"What sort of monsters?"

"Dragons."

"I hate dragons."

Her hands were still on her hips. "You want me, you have to fight dragons."

"Indeed." He didn't deny wanting her. "What sort of dragons?"

"Little ones. About the size of cigarette lighters. In the back garden."

"You realize, of course, that it might be impossible to completely exorcise the creatures that inhabit the Dark Storm Nexus?"

She nodded. "Yes, I realize that. But since I have no intention of moving, you'll be a useful fellow to have around."

"So that's the room and board you're proposing."

"You could use that term if you like."

She was a woman who believed in solving problems and controlling her own destiny. His, too, apparently. Which was quite all right. "I hope you're planning on telling me when and where the wedding is."

She smiled, and his world became perfect. "In the back garden," she told him. "But you have to get rid of the dragons first."

Trevor sighed in token resignation, and said, "Yes, dear."

TARNISHED LININGS

by P.N. Elrod

P.N. "Pat" Elrod has written over 16 novels, including the on-going Vampire Files *series for Ace, the* I, Strahd *novels, and the* Quincey Morris, Vampire *adventure book. She has coedited two anthologies with Martin H. Greenberg,* A Time for Vampires *and* Dracula in London, *and is working on more toothy titles in the mystery and fantasy genres, including a third Richard Dun novel with Nigel Bennett.*

THE SKINNY kid with the too-black greasy hair and baggy pants slouched over to the front counter and smirked at Caitlin. "Hi. Wanna go out with me?"

She looked up from the Tarot cards she'd been pretending to read. "What?"

He kept smirking. The two other customers in the small shop turned to stare. "You heard. Go out with me."

"No, thank you." Caitlin shuffled the cards, willing him to wander off.

Instead he leaned on the counter, giving her a good view of his spotty skin and weirdly vacant gray eyes. "Why not?"

"You're not my type, sorry." She left out the detail about him being young to the point of illegality, and even if they'd been the same age she'd have still turned him down. Caitlin liked hairy Sean Connery types, not underweight Goth wannabes. This kid hadn't gotten the look right, anyway.

It was her third day at The Cauldron, and she'd enjoyed

the change from her usual freelance computer work. The clientele were eccentric by some standards, but generally cheerful, trouble-free sorts. But the moment this kid had oozed in—it was the only way to describe his hesitant, shifty-eyed entry—Caitlin pegged him as a potential shoplifter and kept him under watch. She suffered no illusions that the displays of crystals, drums, incense, candles, books, and other more esoteric items held much interest for him. He was a young teen with time to waste and probably not enough money for the mall's video arcade.

"But you don't know me," the kid insisted.

"The answer is no." She pointedly read from the instruction book that had come with the Tarot deck.

He chuckled as though she'd been witty and drifted over to inspect some locally made dream catchers dangling from the ceiling.

Creep, she thought, shuffling. A card fell out. She made note of it—the Knight of Swords, reversed—and looked up its meanings, one of which had to do with the rapid comings and goings of a troublemaker. How fitting.

He caught her glancing at him and leered. So that was it. He'd interpreted her frowning watchfulness as flirting. God, how dumb can a person get?

"C'mon," he said, oozing back. "I know you like me."

Pretty damn dumb, apparently. She pointed at the door. "Out." Her other hand closed around the can of pepper spray she kept within reach under the counter.

The two other customers, regulars from the nearby university wearing matching sports bras in the school colors, stepped up and faced him. The girls were taller, very fit, and looked like they could bend him in half the wrong way without much effort. When he tried to move past, they blocked him, standing shoulder to shoulder with identical hostile glares.

"Store's closed," one of them stated.

"Closed?" He pretended surprise. "No, it's not."

"Closed to *you*," said the other. "Out or I'll introduce you to the Goddess Castrata."

"*Huh?* Who's that?" His playful, I'm-too-cute-to-be-hurt charm didn't work on them. It turned to instant rage as they herded him out the door in very short order. He rapped on the front window at Caitlin and smiled, then slouched off, hands in the pockets of his low-riding pants. If those drooped any farther he'd be showing that smile, too.

Caitlin breathed vast relief. Until he was gone she'd had no idea how hard her heart had been thumping. "Thanks."

"Our pleasure," said the first, relaxing from her guarded stance. "Who was that jerk?"

"No idea. Could be from the high school."

"Then he missed the sign out front about them not being allowed in until after four. Some of the dippier kids steal stuff. From *this* place, if you can believe it. He's probably cutting homeroom or detention or something."

"Little shit," the second girl muttered murderously. "When a girl says no, she means *no*."

"Maybe he's mentally impaired." Caitlin tended to give people the benefit of the doubt, unless they pushed her too far.

"Or on drugs. Where's Bear? He can put an end to that kind of crap."

Bear, otherwise known as Bernie Ernstein, was the rather large owner of the shop. "He had a family emergency; I'm filling in for him as a favor. Should be back in a week." Caitlin introduced herself.

"I'm Raven," said the first girl, who had appropriately dark hair and a tattoo of that same bird on one nearly bare shoulder. "This is Hower."

"Hower?"

The second girl, a chubby-faced blond, stuck her hand out. "As in 'Hower you'?"

Caitlin chuckled and shook. "Fine, thanks. That's easy to remember."

Hower nodded. "Every other girl in my school was named Jennifer, I had to go for something different. My parents are *soooooo* mundane."

"I hear that a lot. You're both into the New Age thing?"

Caitlin knew enough about the various types of pagans, Wiccans, witches, shamans, and the like to understand that some were occasionally touchy about the nomenclature. She always made her queries neutral, seasoned with an ingenuous expression.

With that opening, Raven and Hower readily gave her the headline version of their spiritual beliefs and how much they liked The Cauldron.

"Bear always has the best stuff," Raven enthused. "Makes his own incense—Raindrops is my favorite, it's so romantic." She bumped her hip against Hower, who rolled her eyes and playfully returned the bump. "But you're out."

"I'll look in the back," Caitlin offered. She went through a doorway curtained off by a faded yellow-and-black batik hanging and searched the incense bin. The thin sticks were bundled together in labeled plastic bags to preserve their scent, but it was still a fragrant task. She'd just closed her hand on the right one when the kid's voice drifted in from the outer room.

"Just tell her Greg's here," he was saying.

"You were told to leave," said Raven, forbidding in tone. He snorted contempt. "No, I wasn't."

Caitlin felt her heart go into overdrive, then made herself settle down. He was just a smart-ass kid wanting attention. His home life must be hell for him to be so earnestly seeking abuse. *Not* her job to play therapist. She came boiling out of the back and hurled her most ferocious go-to-hell look at him.

"Hey," he said, breaking into a big smile. "There's my best girl."

"You. Go." She pointed to the door. "Before I call the cops."

"C'mon, just go out with me. We can have fun."

"The lady said no." Hower grabbed his arm and spun him around while Raven opened the door. Push-pull and Greg went staggering onto the sidewalk, catching his balance in time to keep from falling. He started to charge back like a lemming, but Raven slammed the door and threw the bolt.

Greg cupped his hands around his face, looking in, tapping the glass. Smiling.

Willing her goose bumps to smooth out, Caitlin clawed for the phone behind the counter and held it up warningly. Greg shook his head, snarled, then moved away.

All three women sighed in relief.

"Thanks again," said Caitlin. Adrenaline flooded her, made her shake.

"You got yourself a fledgling stalker," Raven pronounced ominously. "We were over by the bookshelves and he slipped right in again. You better call the cops, make a report. We'll be your witnesses."

Caitlin didn't want to draw negative attention to Bear's shop but changed her mind when she noticed her Tarot cards were no longer on the counter. "That little bastard!" she exclaimed.

"He *stole* them?" asked Hower. "Oh, my goddess! What a dope!"

Furious, Caitlin phoned the police, using their non-emergency number. Denton, Texas was a small town, and it was a slow weekday. A patrol car soon parked by the shop's curb. A large country-boy officer came in, looking walleyed, obviously aware that this store was ground zero for witches in Denton County. Maybe he expected an army of cackling Snow White-style crones in black hoods to leap out brandishing wands and poison apples. He settled down at the sight of Caitlin in her innocuous work shirt and jeans and the two grimly smiling, well-endowed college girls. He listened to the story of Greg's weird behavior, noted his description, and promised to keep the street on his regular patrol pattern.

"How much was stolen?" he asked.

"The cards were worth about twenty. I'd just gotten them, too." Caitlin could replace the deck easily enough, but the violation rankled.

"If he comes back, phone 911," he advised. "Don't take chances."

She nodded in agreement. This was about what she'd expected, though she recommended that the cop check with the nearby high school about truants named Greg. Beyond that, no more could be done.

Raven and Hower had other ideas. As soon as the cop left they asked if Caitlin had a black candle she was willing to burn. She took this to mean it would be her purchase. The candle display had sold out of blacks; she went behind the curtain and nosed around. Up on a high shelf, she finally found one, the type where wax was poured into a glass container. It had a strange oily scent and a taped-on label: Protection. There was no price tag, but the other seven-day candles were only three dollars. *Why not?* she thought, taking it down.

"Perfect," said Raven when she saw it. "We're gonna whip you up a protection spell."

Mouth shut and mind open, Caitlin watched as the girls held the candle between them. They closed their eyes and hummed to get the same note, then began to chant in a decidedly non-English language. Putting the candle on the floor, they walked in a clockwise circle around it, their elbows raised, palms together in front. Caitlin wasn't certain what they were invoking or praying or whatever it was; the ceremony put the hair up on the back of her neck, though she was touched by their concern. When they were done and the candle lighted and placed on the counter before her, she thanked them again.

"I'm not too into this stuff, but don't you usually say something at the end about 'harming none'?" she asked.

Hower sniffed. "Not for *this* spell. If that thief comes back, the Rule of Threes is gonna be the Rule of Tens on his skinny ass."

Caitlin understood that rule: whatever you did, good or bad, would come back on you three times over. It sounded like an excellent precedent to live by for any religion. No wonder most of her customers were such nice people. "Don't you worry about rebound?"

"This is a protection thing. Like putting up razor wire. If

he insists on throwing himself on it, it's not our fault. We built that into the spell."

All that in one little black candle? Its flame danced, then settled and grew strangely tall. "People have been sued for setting booby traps."

Raven showed white teeth. "You find a court anywhere that can prove intent to harm for lighting a candle and saying a prayer. Unless it's arson—which this isn't." She and Hower laughed. "I think I've seen that kid before. The wanna-bes who wear pentacles and black T-shirts to scare their folks tend to look alike to me."

"They want the magic but don't want the real study involved," Hower added. "They watch a couple of movies and believe the special effects. They think it's all about casting spells, not a spiritual path for life."

The phone rang. It was Bear.

"What's going on?" he asked, voice tight. "Who's messing around in the shop? What's happened?"

Caitlin was not the sort to dither, but this was unexpected.

"Someone's doing magic in my place," he clarified.

She felt cold all of a sudden. "Oh, jeez. You *know*?"

"What kind of witch would I be if I didn't?"

Catching Raven's eye, she passed the phone over. "It's for you. It's Bear."

Raven was delighted. She gushed about the good deed she and Hower had done, explaining the motivation behind it. "I'm sorry we were in your space here, but I didn't think you'd mind." She listened some more, said "*uh-huh*" a few times, then, "Okay, we'll be careful." She hung up. "He was kinda pissed."

"Because of the spell?" Hower asked.

"Yeah. He said not to do anything like that here again. The protections he has up are enough."

Caitlin was unsettled that Bear had even *known*. Was that telepathy or something else?

"It's an etiquette thing," Hower continued. "We got excited about helping you with the creep and forgot it's not polite to do workings in another witch's space. Not without permission. He seemed to think no harm was done, but for us to back off in the future."

Hower breathed out relief. So did Caitlin. Though aware of the existence of things metaphysical, she was quite content to give them a wide berth. Her life was busy enough; dabbling in Tarot cards was as far as she wanted to venture into supernatural realms. But she would have gladly embraced the ability to throw lightning bolts when Greg suddenly turned up again, interrupting Raven's and Hower's intense debate about spell protocol.

He pushed through the door, grinning when he saw Caitlin. "Hi. I'm back, what d'ya think?" He pointed to his forehead where he'd inexpertly drawn an upside-down pentagram with permanent ink marker. "You like it?"

"Where are my Tarot cards?" she demanded. In those raggedy-hemmed bags with legs he wore he could hide a dozen decks.

"Huh? What do you mean?"

Caitlin was ready to show him exactly what she meant, but Raven and Hower were faster, bracketing him, then going through his pockets. He submitted to the search without a word, his face gone to stone.

"He must have ditched them," said Hower.

"Where are they?" Raven wanted to know.

"Where's what?" I'm-too-cute-to-be-hurt returned. He'd worn it out.

"You idiot. You just stole Tarot cards from a *witch*. You wanna die?"

Caitlin chose not to contradict Raven's lead. She tried to look witchy. Whatever that was.

Greg continued with the obtuse act. "She's no witch, where's her warts? You gonna put a spell on me? You lesbo."

"Oh, dear, he thinks *that's* an insult. You're coming with us."

"Where? The cops?" For the first time a hint of worry showed.

"Worse than that. We're gonna take you shopping." So saying the much taller Raven put an arm hold on Greg, and she and Hower hustled him to the next store over, which sold comic books.

I owe you two a really good dinner, Caitlin thought. *And I'm going to have words with Bear about hazard pay*. She'd been told he'd cast a number of protection spells on the shop over the years to guard against catastrophe and theft. Presumably it included slugs like Greg. On the other hand, perhaps those spells were working since Raven and Hower were on the spot to deal with Greg.

The black candle burned brightly, the flame nearly five inches tall and strangely unwavering. She wondered if that meant anything special, then placed it out of the way as a new customer came in. Her two unexpected bodyguards and weird Greg didn't return, though the cop dropped in.

"Any more trouble?" he asked.

She related an edited version of·the latest encounter. He thought it extremely funny.

"Are those angels?" He pointed to some porcelain figurines under glass. "You got crosses, too? I thought this was only for witches."

"The Cauldron caters to all tastes," she cheerfully informed him. He bought an angel for his mother's birthday; she gave him the employee discount. Bear would have done the same. The cop left, happy.

Minutes to closing time, Raven and Hower returned, grinning.

"What a day!" Raven exclaimed. "We hit every store on the street with bozo boy."

Caitlin trusted that was not a literal description of things, though she wouldn't put it past them. Their enthusiasm was admirable.

"He's *persona non grata* in this town," said Hower. "When we went into a camera store the guys there took his picture and made photocopies. Here's yours." She pulled a sheet from a plastic shopping bag. The image, apparently enlarged from a disk camera shot, was not of the best quality, but recognizably Greg.

"The pentagram's gone," she observed.

"Their photo program blocked it out. Aren't computers great? We figured he'd wash it off and went for a gene shot so it wouldn't distract from his face. Boy, was he mad."

"Isn't this illegal?"

"Must be, but there's no caption that says 'shoplifter'; the merchants just know to look out for him. This was the funnest day I've had in ages."

"You guys like Italian?" asked Caitlin. "My treat."

"Cool!" they chorused.

She made arrangements to meet them at Bari's around the corner in thirty, allowing her time to close the register and run to the bank with the receipts. A fun day for them, a tiring one for her. The idea of ending it with new friends and a plate of eggplant parmigiana made up for the stress. There were silver linings in clouds after all. If Greg hadn't been such an oaf she'd have gone straight home to channel surf over a TV dinner.

Lights out, she locked the door, walking quickly along an empty sidewalk to the lot where her car waited. She kept an eye out for Greg, and had the pepper spray in one hand. Because of the shop cash in her purse she'd have been this alert and aware regardless; he was just one extra factor to juggle.

Then she had to juggle him as a reality. He came lurching toward her, red-faced, sweat patching his T-shirt, and his vacant eyes flushed with fury. He'd been crouched in the shadow of a dumpster where he commanded a view of the whole lot. Waiting.

"You bitch! Why didn't you *stop* them? I thought you *liked* me!"

To her horror, he drew a small gun from a pocket in his shapeless pants. He aimed it at her.

Better to be a moving target. She sprinted back to the street, nearly falling at the flat *popping* sound of gunfire, then running faster, heart clogging her throat.

"Goddammit, you fucking bitch! You come back here!"

Like hell I will. She aimed for one of the campus apartment buildings, and its possible cover. It wasn't far, but she had short legs and wasn't in her best shape. She didn't look back, dashing across the street, making the opposite curb barely in time to avoid a big black delivery van hurtling down out of nowhere. It would shield her for a few precious seconds . . .

Then close behind she heard a really terrible meaty *thump*.

Instinct said to keep running, but foreboding got the better of it. She ducked behind a fat tree and glanced back.

Yeah, Greg was still there. All over the street. The van didn't stop. It tore down the road—in total silence. When it reached the stoplight at the corner it began fading, going transparent. It continued fading until nothing remained.

She stared openmouthed at the place where it absolutely wasn't.

Oh, shit.

The aftermath was bad. Shaking too much to use her cell phone, she beat on the nearest door and with barely subdued hysterics got the startled tenant within to make the 911 call. The country-boy cop was the first one on the scene, the first of several who questioned her. Yes, the kid had shot the gun. No, she didn't see the van's plates; no, she didn't notice any writing on the side. It was big like a UPS truck, but black. No, she didn't see the driver.

She left out the last bit about the vanishing.

Raven and Hower saw the commotion on their way to the restaurant and found her in the crowd of cop cars, ambulance, onlookers, and flashing lights. They got permission to take her away and soon she was back in The Cauldron drinking a paper cup of water Raven urged on her. Little registered with Caitlin; she'd shut herself down on purpose. She would emerge to deal with things, but for the time being it was better like this. About two minutes after the water hit her gut she ran to the rest room and threw up. Perversely, she felt better. Seated in the front where the shop's wide window showed all the street activity, she told the girls what had happened. She told them everything, this time detailing the unbelievable last part about the truck.

"Are you *sure*?" Raven asked.

"Yes. That thing was solid as a brick, but silent. It hit Greg, then vanished like a ghost."

Both exchanged looks but made no comment. Outside, the ambulance people loaded something into their vehicle. The cop came back to give Caitlin his card. She was to come to the station tomorrow to make a formal statement.

"What about his family?" she asked.

"We'll take care of that," he said, then left.

"Gawds," said Hower. "Where's the candle?"

"I left it in the rest room sink. Fireproof." Caitlin found a tissue and blew her nose.

Hower retrieved the candle, holding it like a bomb. The flame was still unnaturally tall in its glass. "It's only supposed to protect, not go all *Terminator*. We have to reverse this."

"It conjured up the truck?"

"I don't know. Conjure might not be the right word, but *that* should *not* have happened." She gestured at the street.

"Did you put anything extra into the spell?" Raven wanted to know.

Hower shook her head, but her color had gone green. "Nothing on purpose. I was just really, really angry. Was that bad?"

"You *know* how emotions add to the potency of a spell. We have to find out what went wrong."

"You really think we killed him?"

"Until another explanation occurs to me, yes."

Hower looked ready to cry, but got herself under control.

"Couldn't you just blow the candle out?" Caitlin suggested. God, she was tired.

"Not as simple as that," said Hower. "The spell is still up and running, so the intent behind it will continue. We were specific about a time limit, so that's a plus."

"So for the next seven days if someone is stupid with me they could get killed?" Caitlin felt sick again.

"Maybe. Anyway, you don't blow these candles out, it's disrespectful. You use a snuffer."

"No, you pinch them out," argued Raven.

"You can't pinch them out when they're burned down to the bottom of the jar."

"So you let them go out on their own."

Caitlin cleared her throat. "A little focus, please?"

They settled down, chagrined.

"You two do whatever it takes, but put a chill on that whammy."

"Okay," they chorused.

Cross-legged on the floor with the candle between them, they joined hands, shutting their eyes. A few minutes later the phone went off. Caitlin got it.

"Hello, Bear," she said wearily. Only he would be calling this late after hours. "Yes, they're at it again. They have to, something really awful happened. . . ."

She gave him the basics. He promised to cut things short with his family and hurry back. He was in mid-word of instructions for her, which included locking the store and going home for a week, when the line went dead.

"*Uh-oh,*" said Raven, staring at the candle, which had begun to give off thick gray smoke. "It's not supposed to do that."

She and Hower hastily backed away as the smoke thickened, coalesced, assumed human shape. Very shortly a young man with a smiling, yet decidedly evil face floated above the candle. He seemed made of gray fog, then took on color, going solid. Red hair, a white T-shirt with the Cheshire cat printed on it, and torn jeans, he'd have blended in at any of the college mixers—except for the glowing red eyes and horns. He landed softly on the bare linoleum, his purple high-tops causing a puff of sulfur-smelling smoke to billow up.

"Okay," he said in a bored voice. "What is it now?"

Raven recovered first. "Who are you?"

"A demon, what'd ya expect?"

"I mean, what's your name?"

"*Uh-uh*. I tell you that and you'll have me under exclusive contract." He flashed a pointy-toothed grin and wandered around the shop, alternately laughing and sneering at the stock, but not touching anything.

"He's a real demon?" asked Caitlin. She edged over to the display of crosses and angels.

"Yeah. Not too impressive, is he? Talk about your cliché looks."

"Hey!" The demon glared at Raven. "I resemble that remark!"

"Oh, be quiet. Hower, this is your doing, isn't it?"

She looked supremely unhappy. "I was just really, really angry. I didn't think it would put that much strength into the spell."

The demon laughed. "But you did it in *here*. This is one big magical hot spot, girlie-girls. Bear has some doorways you didn't know about. He keeps them shut tight most of the time, but you two warm-fuzzies-aroma-therapy-earth-goddess-is-tops-tree-hugging-crystal-cuties managed to kick one open using that summoning candle."

"Summoning?" Raven stared at the candle, horrified. "You mean that thing was loaded? With *you*?"

"Just primed to suck in any handy demon to do your dirty work. Too bad for me I happened to be hanging in the area when it did. I was all set to go feast off a five-car pileup. Had to settle for bimbo-boy's anger, instead. What a comedown. I'm starved."

"Bear's into black magic?" asked Caitlin.

"There's no black or white, just energy," said Raven. "Like electricity. It can kill or cure depending how it's used."

The demon snorted contempt.

"All right, there's more to it than that, but some perfectly legit and otherwise nice magicians, wizards, whatever, occasionally have a use for a demon. *Not* something *I've* ever done."

"I'm really, really sorry," said Caitlin. "I didn't know the candle was dangerous."

"You and a few billion other souls, baby-cakes," said the demon, winking.

"Are you saying that I'm damned?" Her voice went up.

He licked his eyebrows with a suddenly forked tongue. "And what a tasty morsel *you'll* be."

"Caitlin, don't pay attention to him, he's feeding on the fear you're throwing." Raven fixed him with a cold eye. "Okay, you, I'm calling you off. You're going to go back to wherever you came from and cease and desist. Your job here is done."

"Not for another week, it ain't." He peered out the front window. "*Mmm*, boy, you can still smell his anger hanging in the air. I love teenagers, all that formless rage, despair, and hopelessness, nothing like it. When they finally cut loose—come and *get* it!" He rounded on Caitlin. "But *you* spoiled things. He wasn't supposed to go postal for another month, then he'd have taken three of his classmates with him. *Then* I could have visited *their* families. . . . You cost me decades of steady feasting! But, hey, when I get called in, I obey orders no matter what."

"I want you to stop," said Raven.

"Except *that* order. Sorry, chickie. There's rules to this game. If you can't trouble yourself to learn them. . . ."

"But I didn't *know*—" Raven caught herself. "Never mind. You will tell us how to stop you."

"Trade."

"What sort of trade?"

"Oh, souls, life energy, the usual."

"If we give you a soul, you'll stop?"

"I prefer a life. A good one. More satisfying. Souls are cheap, but throw me a well-beloved life and you make a delicious hole in all the lives around it. Nothing like a course of grief and anguish from the survivors."

"He wants us to kill someone?" Caitlin got one of the larger crosses from the display and slipped it on, along with a pentacle and a Thor's hammer.

Raven shook her head. "He wants us to think that. He's after life energy, but if we find him a reasonable substitute he has to agree. Isn't that right?"

The demon shrugged. "If I can feed off it, we can make a deal."

"Okay. So if I give you energy, you cease the protection thing and return to wherever you came from."

"You left out the 'and harm none' part," said Caitlin. "It goes in this time."

The demon quit the floor, floating up to perch lightly on a tall drum in a corner.

Caitlin stared, then got mad. "Get down from there!"

Surprisingly, he did so. "Some gratitude. I saved you from three in the lungs, rape, and a cheap funeral, and *this* is the thanks I get?"

"You could have just tripped him. You didn't have to kill him."

"Where's the fun in that? I suppose *you'd* have gotten him into therapy and forgiven the little shit."

"Shuddup. Raven, what kind of energy will get rid of him?"

"There's a very powerful one, but I don't think Hower's in the mood."

Hower stopped looking green and flushed red. "You *can't* be serious."

"You wanna give him life energy instead? Or a soul?"

"What are you talking about?" asked Caitlin.

They looked at the demon, then at her. "Sex energy," they said in unison.

Caitlin shut her mouth.

The demon cackled. "Oh, yeah, baby! I'll go for *that*! Nothing like a few hours of foreplay to get me all charged!"

"But he'll be watching," Hower protested.

Raven shrugged. "Call it a learning experience. Next time I try not to be so damned helpful with the magic and you chill out with the anger. And we *both* take care about our tools and *where* we do any workings in the future."

*   *   *

Caitlin was grateful she didn't have to participate, though the demon gleefully invited her in. The girls assured her that since it had been their spell, they were the only ones needed to undo it. She locked the shop from the outside, leaving them to work out where they would . . . effect things. She didn't want to know. If a death hadn't been involved she'd have found it comical.

Her cell *bleeped*. It was Bear. In a *bad* mood. She caught him up on what had happened since the demon's entrance cut off the shop phone.

Bear eventually made sympathetic noises when she began to cry. "Not your fault," he told her over and over. He promised to sort things out as soon as he got back.

But Caitlin was certain things were as sorted as they would get. One angry, dysfunctional kid was dead. Only one. Not himself and three others. Not herself with them. So why didn't she feel better?

Silver linings could be a bitch.

FOR WHOM THE
BELL TOLLED

by Jody Lynn Nye

Jody Lynn Nye lists her main career activity as "spoiling cats." She lives northwest of Chicago with two of the above and her husband, author and packager Bill Fawcett. She has written twenty-two books, including four contemporary fantasies, three SF novels, four novels in collaboration with Anne McCaffrey, including The Ship Who Won, *a humorous anthology about mothers,* Don't Forget Your Spacesuit, Dear!, *and over sixty short stories. Her latest books are* Myth-Told Tales *and* Myth Alliances, *collaborations with Robert Asprin in his* Myth-Adventures *series, and* The Lady and The Tiger, *third in Jody's* Taylor's Ark *series.*

"AND WHEN I cleared away all the boxes of figurines, I found this bell," Annabel Crane told Charles. "Do you want to buy it?"

Charles Roxton rubbed his long hands together. He restrained himself for only a moment before reaching for the little artifact. He felt its smooth bronze patina under his fingertips, rubbing the ornamental engraving lovingly. The metal tingled against his skin. "You say your aunt couldn't possibly have afforded all those Hummels, but when she died she had over seven thousand of them?"

"That's right," Annabel said, seeming to melt toward him a little at the sound of his plummy English accent.

It was one of Charles' best assets, a smooth bit of London in the midst of rough-spoken New York City. He liked her voice, too: a warm, smoky contralto. She was a very attractive woman, he realized, with those glorious sapphire blue eyes surrounded by a forest of lush, black eyelashes, and the way her dark hair curled on her shoulders was positively provocative. He tried to look suave and Hugh-Grantish, but he had too much chin, and his light brown hair was too fine to lie in those handsome waves.

"She said the bell called them to her. Only ones she didn't have, and only by mail order. She was kind of shy and didn't like having to go into stores. She wanted one of everything. *I* think she must have had the whole collection. After she died I kept waiting for bills to come from the vendors, but none ever did. The Hummels must belong to her—to me, now—after all. And the bell, but I don't want it. It makes me feel creepy. I mean, that's why I brought it here. I thought you might know what to do with it."

Called them, a greedy little voice popped up in Charles' mind. What a treasure! The magical curio shop he had begun with such hope five years ago could use such a helpful artifact. But he wasn't a fool: it could be a fake. He'd seen thousands of convincing shams, even inadvertently bought a few.

"I'll have to authenticate it," Charles said, setting it down firmly on the counter between them.

"Oh," Annabel said, sounding disappointed. "I hoped you could just buy it. I know you're not supposed to sound desperate when you're selling something, but I need the money. Auntie's death left me in a financial hole. She left me the house and all her possessions, but no cash. I can charge the funeral expenses, but I need something to live on for a couple of weeks until I can sell the figurines." She fixed him with hopeful eyes. Charles had to surrender.

"I think we can come to an arrangement," he said, rising. "Let me check my books." But he knew what they'd say.

There was far more in the minus column of Spells 'N' Stuff's ledger than in the plus column. But he wanted to help this young woman. She was the kind of girl he'd have been crazy about, if he hadn't had to focus so hard on making a living. Torn between trying to impress her and wanting to get his hands on a true artifact for a reasonable price, he studied the figures for some time before deciding which bill he wasn't going to pay that month. "I can give you $200," he said, a little lamely. It was a weak offer if the item was legitimate, princely if it turned out to be Auntie's sickbed bell that she had used for summoning soup and aspirin.

But Annabel seemed relieved. "That'd be *great*. Thank you *so* much. I really appreciate this. You don't know how much it means to me."

But he did. With the greatest of reluctance Charles opened his cash box and counted out the bills, feeling the knell with every one he put down. Slowly, he gathered them up, squared the corners, and offered them to Annabel.

"Thanks," Annabel said again, folding her hands around his. She looked up into his eyes, and his mouth went dry. "If there's anything I can ever do for you. . . ."

How attractive she was, Charles thought. It was on the tip of his tongue to ask her if she would like to have a cup of tea with him. He opened his mouth, and stammered on the first syllable. She blushed, and hurried out of the store.

Charles watched after her, a picture in his mind of two hundred greenbacks with wings fluttering away.

He sat up late into the night in the room behind the showroom that doubled as storeroom and efficiency apartment, thumbing through his collection of dusty research books under the single bulb of his reading lamp. Those thick, leather-covered tomes had been the impetus for his beginning to collect magical artifacts in the first place.

Once he'd read about fabulous treasures like the great beryl scrying ball and the staff of Merlin, he wanted to touch them for himself, find out what lay behind their power. Charles imagined himself as a latter-day John Dee, delving into the mysteries of the unknown in the midst of the great cities of the world. But whereas Doctor Dee had rich patrons like Queen Elizabeth I to support him, Charles had only the savings he had put by from his former job booking rooms for the Trusthouse Forte hotel chain. He could always get another position in the hotel industry, but he'd almost certainly have to leave the United States. He loved America and wanted to stay, though he missed his family and friends back in the U.K. It was his dream to be wealthy enough to pursue his studies, but he was practical by nature. His solution had been to operate a magic shop. What artifacts came through his hands he could choose to keep or sell.

Unfortunately, in his present circumstances he had little choice but to sell what he bought, for as much profit as he could squeeze out. If this bell proved to be real, he could interest a moneyed patron in buying, and at least stake himself to a few more months of security. Was he clever enough to get a good price? There was no way he'd settle for as little as he'd given Annabel. He had overhead to consider and a long, dusty time in between honest magical items.

Charles felt a pang as he looked up and stared at the front door. What if he couldn't find a buyer? He loved his little shop. A high-class magical boutique was what he had started out to create. But rents in New York were so high, he hadn't been able to find a building near the upper class condominiums. Paying out so much for basic expenses, he couldn't afford many good pieces. His shelves were embarrassingly sparse. He could have filled the space with trashy trinkets and fakes, but he preferred not to. There were so many frauds out there. They gave him a bad feeling, and what he knew about the law of rebound persuaded him he shouldn't pass them along to unsuspecting buyers. That did not fit in with his lofty ideals.

He examined the bell's braided silver and gold clapper. By the object's ornamental rim and thinly but evenly hammered metal, it appeared to be four hundred or four hundred fifty years old, approximately of the era of Doctor Dee. That was good: it meant that there was a possibility of finding documentation. Charles located no references to a

collectibles-summoning bell among his own books. He
thought about emailing some of his European correspon-
dents but changed his mind. What if the bell turned out to be
an ancient hoax they'd all already passed on? No, he'd figure this one out alone.

He turned the little object over in his hands. The clapper
tinkled pleasantly against the inside. At the top of the bell
was a metal loop. So it wasn't a hand bell, but designed to
hang up. Who had made it, and why? Annabel had said her
aunt had used it to amass Hummels, her passion. A modest
wish. A pity the aunt had died without passing on the means
of activating the bell. He didn't want to be stuck with a
shopful of china knickknacks, but a box or two of esoteric
impedimenta would do his soul, and his bottom line, some
good. He ran his fingers over the smooth, thin bronze, making it sing lightly. A few more things like this would set him
on his feet.

With regret, he wrapped the bell in its cotton batting and
put it away in its box.

Four days later, Charles unlocked the front door of Spells
'N' Stuff and propped it open, spreading his doormats on
both sides of the threshold. Summer in New York was hot
and sticky. The streets melted into viscous goo that got
tracked in onto his narrow floorboards. He dropped the outside mat, then snatched it up again as he caught a glimpse of
brown paper beneath it. A flat package the same color as the
sidewalk lay there. He picked it up and turned it over. There
was no address. Had someone dropped it on the way to the
post office? He looked up at the sky. Clouds were gathering
in the west. If he left it, it would be ruined by the coming
rain.

He took it inside, intending to look for paper to put up a
notice in his window to let the owner know to come in and
ask for it, but as soon as he crossed the threshold the paper
fell open, and its contents flowed over his hands. A mandala,
painted on silk, Charles thought, excitedly turning it over
with care. How beautiful, and how rare. The delicate yel-
lowing of the white fabric meant that it was ages old.

He'd heard of things like this coming out of Tibet in the care of monks to prevent them from falling into the hands of the Chinese government. Naturally there were communities representing every country and nearly every culture in the world in New York. He had met Tibetans and Nepalese in the course of searching for merchandise for his shop, one of them would help him find the owner.

But no one came forward to claim the mandala. In fact, a few days later, he found another package on the doorstep, this one containing a set of dusty old books. Charles put up a notice about those, too, but found himself inexorably drawn to read them. To his delight, they were Latin texts written by a medieval herbalist, with cures and spells listed for each plant. They were well and clearly written. Their style gave him a surprisingly clear picture of their author, an older, witty man of means who believed in magic as a gift of God, not as an evil apotheosis. Charles longed to make the books part of his own collection, but he couldn't do that until the owner turned up. He came up with an offer that he thought was more than fair and set it aside. If only the owner were willing to sell!

The next day the UPS driver stopped by with three parcels. Each of them had come from a different state. They contained a pair of blue velvet shoes, a small bronze lamp, and a cheap paperback book entitled *Satanic Love Spells*. When he phoned to inquire about the mystery deliveries, the company was unable to provide him with any clue to their origins. No address or other identifying mark could be found on any of them, inside or outside.

Charles decided that since the parcels had been sent to him anonymously he could do what he liked with them. In his ledger he marked down a fair price, vowing to pay back if the owners ever came forward. He threw away the book, earmarking ten cents if the donor came forward to demand payment, and put the other items in the back room until he could analyze them. He thanked his lucky stars, whatever they were, and looked forward to discovering the items' function and finding a buyer for them. Perhaps the website he had on the Internet had begun to attract attention, though he would rather have had customers than suppliers.

He had no time to do more than a cursory scan of the usual sources, because over the course of the next week UPS, the postal system and every delivery service in New York started bringing him packages of all shapes and sizes. At first only a few came, but on Thursday alone over a hundred parcels arrived. Not only that, but his doorbell was constantly jangling as people came by the twos and threes, then the dozens with their own offerings. No one wanted to buy anything, which dismayed him further, but they all wanted to give him something.

"Ma'am, please," Charles protested to the woman who paid no attention as she laid out vintage components for stage magic tricks on his counter. "I can't pay you for these now. Please take them away."

She looked at him in surprise. "But I want you to have them," she said. "They belonged to my late husband. I don't care what you do the moment the door closes behind me, but I want them out of my house. Take care of them, destroy them, or pass them on. I don't care if you give me a dime. I hope you get a million dollars for them, but Al drove me nuts with his crazy little tricks for fifty years. I don't want them in the house any longer."

Charles would have protested further, but the *jingle-jingle* alerted him just in time to see the huge African-American man slipping out after leaving something enormous and hairy by the door. It was a stuffed buffalo head with glass eyes and mysterious sigils painted on the horns. By the time he turned around the woman was gone, and three small boys were piling paperback astrology books on the counter from a cardboard box on the floor.

What was going on? Charles wondered. A horrible thought struck him: had someone hacked his website and put out a call for any old kind of junk, no questions asked? He shooed a teenage girl and her carved broomstick out of the door, put up the CLOSED sign and flew to the back room to check the Internet.

He almost died of impatience waiting for the connection to go through. In the meantime he could see shadowed figures outside the front door pounding on the glass. He *willed* them to go away. At last he brought up his home page. Nothing out of the ordinary. Not even a message on his chatgroup function. He went through a web search of his name and the name of his shop, but there was nothing. That left only a spam campaign, but he had no way to trace that until someone complained. Nor had he any reason to think someone wanted to start one, unless there was a religious fundamentalist group out there who believed that inundating him with the works of the devil would be the way to drive him out of business. If the object was to make him insane, it was working.

By the end of the week the shop had filled up like a gigantic saucepan overflowing with rice. The little showroom was packed to the walls with dowsing twigs, a stuffed owl, crystal balls; books, staffs, wands, even a scepter or two; swords, knives, and athames; astrological charts, astronomical charts, charts of the higher and lower planes; magic rings, bracelets, and brooches of mixed utility or none at all; necklaces, belts, garters; more shoes, items of clothing, and hats than a Goodwill shop.

Charles kicked his way to the door on Saturday morning, wondering if he should bother to open it or not. He was worn out trying to keep people from giving him things. He'd begged, pleaded, even threatened, but nothing could stop them. If he threw something away, another item took its place—usually two. He had wanted to fill in his stock, but this was overwhelming. He had to laugh, bitterly. He'd been living on baked beans on toast to pay for the bell and a few small odds and ends, and now he couldn't move his feet for all the artifacts he was amassing free of charge.

"Roxton, open up!" The voice and fist on the door had to belong to his landlord. Charles racked his memory. Yes, he had sent up his rent check. He hurried to let Mr. Stehl in, who stared around the shop in amazement.

"There's a pile of boxes outside . . . holy murder! What's

all this? You switch places with the city dump? We got fire laws in this city, y'know."

Charles was alarmed. He grabbed the parcels out of his landlord's arms and hastily put them on top of the nearest pile. "No! It's a . . . practical joke someone is playing on me. *Heh, heh.*"

Stehl looked unconvinced. "*Heh, heh.* Well, you get this cleaned up, you hear me? I don't want to get a call from the fire marshal."

"No, of course not. I'll take care of it at once."

A practical joke, that was it! Charles decided, as he let the landlord out. This had to be an elaborate practical joke. Most likely it had been perpetrated by the owner of the silk mandala. If that person wanted his property back, all he had to do was ask for it!

Inevitably, there were boxes on the stoop, seven in all. Deciding that it would be better not to open at all for the day, he brought them inside and locked up. He had no choice but to bring them into his already cramped living quarters.

That night, he sat cross-legged on the bed with a book in his lap and an artifact in each hand. The only way to get rid of the items was to identify them and put them up for sale at once. If that meant sleepless nights, so be it.

So much of what he had accumulated was trash. Even worse, getting rid of the stuff was difficult. The bin at the rear of his building was always full. The restaurant on the other side of the alley, which was supposed to use their own receptacles, inevitably ran over with unsavory slop and spoiled food. Charles never ate there. He was forced to amass the discards near the back door and sneak out under cover of darkness to the dumpster farther up the alley.

Gradually, he discovered a few treasures hidden among the dross. A tarnished silver ring with a watery gem set his palm a-tingle as soon as he picked it up. The best way to figure out what an item did was to use it, but putting on magical jewelry had its own perils. Still, Doctor Dee wouldn't have hesitated. . . .

By morning he was bleary-eyed but feeling more optimistic. The deluge couldn't last forever, and he had half a dozen items that he could say with reasonable certainty were valuable. The pair of brass candlesticks would have been priceless in medieval Germany, from which they had come, because once lit, candles set in them would not blow out. Perhaps he could offer them to a woman who gave a lot of dinner parties. But the most magical item was the silver ring. It gave off a strong aura, but he was unable to discover it listed among the great treasures. He spent several hours with it on his hand, and discovered that it did not make him invisible, nor allow him to fly, nor help him to read unknown languages, but every time he began to feel the urge of nature he found his hand pointing invariably toward his lavatory. Not everyone would understand the utility of a bathroom-detecting ring, but it might be invaluable to a person who traveled a lot. It was with optimism that he opened for business.

And discovered more boxes on his doorstep. Charles looked out at the bleak day and felt his heart sink. There must have been dozens of containers, piled any which way. Charles eyed passersby and wondered whether, if he closed the door again, friendly New Yorkers could be counted upon to steal them. A patrol car rolling up the street slowed as it came near his shop. The cop in the driver's seat peered out at him. Hastily, Charles grabbed the nearest box and smiled nervously at the officer. The officer nodded sharply and looked away.

He had no more room. He asked the neighbor upstairs as she was coming back from church if she could hold on to some of the parcels temporarily.

"I'm not a warehouse, sweetie," the elegant *Puertoriqueña* said, peeling off her white gloves.

"It's Sunday, Sofia," he pleaded. "Nothing will be available until tomorrow."

With a kindly look, she relented. "All right. One day, then you have to find somewhere else."

Very early Monday morning he started calling around. The prices that were being asked for storage were outrageous. It was ironic that the items he was trying to find storage for would solve his cash flow problem, but he was spending all his time just finding places to put them, let alone catalog or sell them. He just barely had time to put each into a general category when another load took precedence. He found a warehouse all the way out in Queens that was reasonably cheap. He made a quick visit to be certain that it was dry and secure before coming back to load up boxes in the pickup he borrowed from the grocer at the end of the street.

Rounding the corner into the alley he stared. More cartons were piled up in the alley beside the ones he had packed.

His patience was exhausted. All the way through the horrible Monday morning midtown traffic he fumed. He was normally intimidated by driving in Manhattan. So inflamed was his temper that no taxi got the better of him, no pedestrian had a living chance of cutting him off. The warehouse owner in Queens tried to extort an extra fee for taking possession in the middle of the month, but Charles looked so forbidding that the man backed up a pace, almost dropping the cheap cigar from the corner of his mouth. None of these small victories soothed Charles.

He could hardly squeeze back into the shop for the new boxes that had arrived in his absence. He had no choice but to rearrange everything to make room to walk. It took him hours and left him tired, sweating and red-faced. By midnight he was ready to walk out of the building without a backwards glance and throw a lit match over his shoulder as he left.

Charles' hands were shaking as he consolidated all of the rings, bells, amulets, and bracelets in the glass case near the cash register. He badly needed a few hours' sleep, but perhaps if he set the alarm he could identify a few of the really big pieces for sale before he was overwhelmed by the next tide. He stroked the silver comfort-relief ring as he set it on the faded maroon velvet liner. But no one was coming to buy! He clenched the box containing the bronze bell in his

fist. Why in heaven's name couldn't there be a few customers, even *one* person who wanted to *buy something*? Inside its wrappings the bell let out a tiny ping as if in
sympathy.

He heard the doorbell ring. Suddenly consumed with
rage at the imposition of people dumping their garbage on
him Charles flew to the door, and flung it open to see a short,
dark-haired woman with a large parcel in her arms. She was
going to leave it on the doorstep! Not another one!

"What are you doing?" he demanded. He was preparing
a string of invective to blast at her until he realized the parcel in her arms was a purse. She clutched it to her chest in
the face of his fury.

"I'm sorry," she said. "This is a place where you can
buy . . . magical stuff?"

"Why, yes," he said, drawing back in horror at how he
must have looked. He smoothed his hair back with one hand
and did his best to resume his natural polite expression,
"Yes, it is. Do you need something?"

She melted with relief. She pressed her fingers into his
wrist, her eyes wide with appeal.

"Oh, yes, I do. I—I've been so frightened. There's this
guy at work I reported for slacking off, so he hates me. I
think he's been following me. He leaves garbage on my
stoop, and creepy things like that. I haven't got evidence that
I could get a restraining order from, but he just scares me. I
don't believe in guns, and karate's not for me. You wouldn't
have something, like, *supernatural* I can carry around with
me for protection?"

Charles smiled, his handsome face relaxing. "Madam, I
believe I can show you an attractive selection of protective
amulets."

Rita Barber was his first real client. She liked her bronze
Celtic knot pendant so much that she brought a gaggle of her
friends to meet him. Not that all of them found precisely
what they were looking for on their first visit, but they were
very impressed by his shop, his assured manner.

"And we just love your accent, honey," her friend Cyrene

Jackson said, flirting her brown eyes at him. "Just keep on talking!"

More people noticed the comings and goings, and stopped in out of curiosity. Some of them even spent money. Heartened by his first-ever successful week, Charles made a list of their requirements, certain he would get what they needed in anonymous shipments sooner or later. He could now afford a storage facility large enough to hold the overflow of goods that started to come in.

Wednesday morning, he flung open his door with an eager heart to see . . . nothing. No shipments came that day or for the next week. He was almost annoyed. Fate must despise him, he thought. No goods, no customers, then goods but no customers, now customers but no goods!

Charles decided to make the best of the situation and identify what he had on hand. If Rita's friends didn't need what he had in stock, surely there were others who did.

At last he had time to unpack and peruse the myriad dusty old tomes that had arrived during the deluge weeks. Among them he was delighted to find a small early-Victorian monograph on bells. Out of curiosity, he thumbed through it. A cornucopia design on one page matched the decoration on the lip of the bell that Annabel Crane had sold him. When Charles bent to read the paragraph accompanying the illustration, he laughed out loud. He looked around for an audience, but met only the glass eyes of the stuffed owl.

"Doctor Dee would have pitied me. I have not been thinking like a scientist. It's not a curse or a joke. It's the bell that's been doing it all along. It has been trying to help me!"

The owl didn't reply. For the first time Charles felt a pang that no one was there to share his triumph. Now that he had such a treasure, he ought to use it. He took out the bell and held it in his long fingers, tentative for the first time. Because it did not look very impressive he had underestimated its value. The bell brought to its possessor anything that he or she desired, "without stint" as the book put it, "and at the sound of its ring the world must do its bidding." He must have made a wish without knowing it, unlike its previous owner, who'd known exactly what it was for.

With a pang he thought of the dead woman's niece, and wondered how Annabel was getting along. Then he pushed all thought of her from his mind. He must be very careful what he was thinking about when he asked the bell for help. He knew a good deal about karma. Nothing came free of charge. There was always some kind of a price to pay. He must strive to maintain a balance in what he asked for and what he gave back.

Call magical items to me, he thought, handling the bell, *but only ones of quality, that I'll be able to sell. Nothing of a deep-black dye,* he added. *I don't want anything used only for evil. If any of the donors is doing this unwillingly and wishes to be paid, make certain I get that information. I do not,* he thought with a shudder of the twisted steel pen stained with blood he had just buried with a banishing ceremony in the nearest park, *need to meet them.*

Over the course of the next few weeks the flow of goods began again, but far more slowly. Now that he had the time to handle objects, Charles began to enjoy his studies again. With careful use of the bell, which he now mounted above the swinging door of the shop, he put out a silent call for items that Rita and her friends wanted. When they were happy, they told *their* friends. Without any further advertisement the magic shop became a kind of open secret among the *cognoscenti* of the Upper West Side, a divine tingle of something sort of spooky but not dangerous. They knew Charles would take care of their needs but not let them go too far, like a doctor of sorcery.

Once in a while he changed the aim of the bell to bring him new customers. He wanted to meet interesting people but only the kind who weren't out to rule the world or harm children or animals, and who paid their bills. In the middle of what should have been a good week he had been stiffed by a client with a bad check for a very large amount, which set his cash flow back a few months. He didn't want any more of that. During "client-calling," the inflow of goods stopped, but traffic in the shop increased. And his satisfied clients came back even while he was in an item-attracting phase.

With the time to read, he learned a lot about magic. He never dreamed there was so much responsibility involved in casting a spell. He'd once had a rather grandiose idea that magic was all art. One learned the words and movements, added a few imperious gestures, and you could do what you liked. Instead, he came to know how subtle magic really was: the touch of a hand, concentration upon intent, the ringing of a bell. He passed along his knowledge to his clients, a lesson with every piece sold. A few of them didn't like the lectures and walked out while he was talking, but Charles felt it was important that they knew. He realized that *he* was responsible if they did something wrong or evil, since he had facilitated their action. Rebound again.

As he became more prosperous, Charles began to add to the shop's repertoire. Without having to put out a magical call he started to attract local practitioners. He allowed psychics, leaders of meditation, and auric cleansers to hold seminars or see clients in his back room. People came and went all day long, chatting in groups over the jewelry display or having lively debates over a deck of cards. Spells 'N' Stuff became the site of a big, unrelated community, almost a family.

The store was busy all the time. Charles ought to have been happy. And yet, at bottom he felt unsatisfied. In the midst of all the whirl of success it took him a while to realize that when the bell rang for the last time each evening the door closed with all of New York on one side of it and him alone on the other.

He was lonesome. It was ironic that he had begun his business with the aim of making enough to fund his private studies, but at the end of the day he discovered he didn't like being isolated. Now that his shop was a going concern he had time to focus on the world around him. All those happy people walking away from his shop, concentrating on one another, left him envious.

Rita noticed it first. "Charlie," she said, one day while picking up an astrological chart she'd commissioned for her daughter-in-law, "we've all been wondering. Do you have a significant other anywhere?"

Charles felt a little taken aback. "Why do you ask?"

"It sucks to be lonely," Rita said forthrightly. "You're such a nice young man, but you don't seem to have anyone special around here. Does she—or he—travel a lot, or are they back in England?"

"I . . . don't have anyone," he said, but he hesitated, remembering Annabel Crane's sapphire-blue eyes. "No, I . . . no, actually, I don't have a significant other."

"There's someone," Rita guessed, probably by the expression on his face. "Is she pretty?"

Charles felt his cheeks go pink. He dropped his gaze to the counter. "Very."

"But she doesn't know you're alive, is that it?" Rita asked. "I know what your problem is. You're too shy. You need something to break the ice. If I can help, let me know."

Charles stared after her, not really seeing Rita, but another face: Annabel's. He had never really stopped thinking about her, though it had been many months since the day she had stopped by. In a very real way he owed his success to her. That day had changed his life.

He had felt a special spark between them, like nothing he'd ever experienced before. Had she felt it, too? How foolish he'd been to have been focused upon mere money. But all this mooncalfing was academic. She hadn't left an address. New York was so big, and any intelligent woman had an unlisted telephone number. He could pay a web-search database for her personal information, but if she didn't want to be found he would feel horrible. She knew where the shop was. Chances were good that if she had not come in since then it meant she didn't want to. Or did she? She seemed to be as shy as he.

The bell jingled over the door as the mail carrier leaned in, whistling, and dropped off the day's post. Charles' eyebrows climbed to the sky as he looked up at the source of the sound. *The bell.* Yes. *It* could bring her to him. Before he knew it he was on the ladder beside the door, unhooking it. He turned the sign to CLOSED, and locked the front door, taking his prize into the back room with him. He sat down at his desk with the bell between his hands.

But he stopped short, his conscience battering at him, before speaking his wish. Did he have the right to ask? He had read numerous accounts of magically compelled love. It never worked out, and rebounded unfortunately upon the spellcaster, as rightly it should. But Rita was correct: being lonely . . . sucked. What if Annabel was as lonely as he?

He knew he was going to ring the bell anyhow. Very well. The only correct way to use it would be to construct the wish so that it did not compel her, but reminded her of him. He wanted to find out, now that he was no longer in dire financial straits, if he and Annabel could learn to like one another. He told the bell very severely that he wanted to give a relationship a chance, but only, *only* if it was her free will to do so. If she was compelled there could be no love, and certainly no trust. He would rather give up everything and go back to genteel poverty if he couldn't have trust.

"She must not come to me if she won't trust me," he said aloud. "Call my true love to me."

He rang the bell. The sound filled his ears and rebounded off the walls of the shop. Nothing happened immediately. With a feeling of being let down and a little silly, he put the bell back in its place and retired hastily to his room to read.

It was quiet all the rest of that week. No deliveries came. Rita called to say she wasn't coming in to get her book on candle magic until the following week. Her brother had come in from San Francisco, and he was stuffy about her bad habit, as he called it. Charles said he understood.

Then, late one afternoon, he was on a ladder dusting behind the vials of werewolf hair and bat's blood, when the front door opened, causing the bronze bell hanging over it to jingle. He didn't have time to turn around before he heard that soft, smoky voice.

"Hello, Charles," Annabel said shyly.

WINTER PHOENIX

by India Edghill

India Edghill's interest in history can be blamed on her father, whose favorite authors were Will and Ariel Durant. Her interest in the ill-fated Romanovs can be traced to sitting through Doctor Zhivago *and* Anastasia *too many times, which led to reading far too many books about the lost Anastasia. Never satisfied with the life story of the best-known pretender to the identity of HIH the Grand Duchess Anastasia Nicolaievna, India has succumbed to the temptation to provide a different outcome to the events of the night of July 16/17, 1918. Her short fiction has appeared in* MZB's Fantasy Magazine *and* The Magazine of Fantasy & Science Fiction, *as well as in various anthologies. She is also the author of* Queenmaker, *a historical novel set in the court of King David.*

ST. PETERSBURG. AUTUMN 1916.

Although she did not know it, she bought her future on a whim, purchased all her tomorrows upon the very last day her family ever shopped in the city that once had been St. Petersburg. It was rechristened Petrograd now, the city's two-hundred-year-old name converted to reflect a world forever altered by war. The war that was never over by Christmas; the war that dragged on and on, one year, two years, three, pulling lives and sanity into a dark whirlpool of destruction and death.

But there had still, for a while, been time to enjoy one-self, however briefly; time for visits, and shopping, and small frivolities. That day, their youngest aunt took the four of them for an afternoon away from bandage rolling and hospital rounds, an afternoon of strolling along the splendid Nevsky Prospekt, with the promise of shopping in the exotic Gostinnar Dvor, the domed bazaar in which one might discover glorious treasure trove. But before they reached that exotic market, they turned into an intriguing side street. And there, shoved in between a jeweler's barred window and an antiques emporium, like a slim book forced into a crowded bookcase, stood a crimson door beside a show window so narrow it was a mere sliver of glass. The name inscribed upon the window, in flaking golden letters, proclaimed it to be the *Magazin Magii*. The Magic Shop.

For a moment they stopped and stared, caught by strange glints and gleams through time-dark glass. Then their Aunt Olga started on again, and her older sisters began to follow, and she said, "No, wait," and put her hand on the heavy door, her gloved hand ghost-pale against the door's dull dark red. Her sisters paused, then trailed in behind her; she had known they would, for they did almost everything together, like four white swans.

The *Magazin Magii* was long and thin, as if it had once been a hallway in an ancient house; its heavy air smelled of incense and dust, and its wares caught the eye in jumbles of glitter and gilt. Gold-tipped wands clustered in a Chinese umbrella stand; crystal balls balanced on dragon's-foot holders. Black-glassed mirrors reflected clouds and stars. Icons hung from velvet-draped walls, and bright cards scattered across glass tables: images of swords and queens, moons and mages.

"May I help you?" The shopkeeper came forward, flowing slowly, like a tired serpent; muffled in embroidered robes and cashmere shawls. It was impossible to tell the figure's age, or even its sex. It paused, studying them, its eyes pale and blank as winter snows.

"Ah," it said, and then, "Yes, of course. You are welcome, Your Imperial Highnesses. Let me see what I have for you."

They glanced at each other, three of them intrigued and delighted; never in their lives had anyone been less than delighted to see them, less than kind. But she, the youngest, who saw so much more than was ever there, so much more than she ever wished to see, veered away and began turning over the careless playing-cards as her sisters chattered, asked eager, guileless questions.

"Do you offer magic games?"

"Do you have blessed icons?"

"Do you sell love potions?"

They barely waited for the mumbled answers, swiftly distracted by the curious objects, the bizarre wares spread before them.

As her three sisters scattered, hunting through the crowded shop, she drew off her white kid glove, fingered a small coiled bangle of plaited straw that lay upon a locked glass case. The shopkeeper shuffled over, and she fumbled for a reasonable question, something appropriate to ask one so steeped in magic and mystery.

"Do you tell fortunes?" she asked at last.

A long pause; pale eyes blinked once. "Not yours. No. Not yours."

"Why not mine?"

The keeper of the *Magazin Magii* simply gazed at her; understanding the silence, she looked away, as if distracted by a spangled scarf, its thin silk a drift of glitter and darkness. Her fortune. Her future. Glitter and darkness. . . .

"Glitter and darkness." The shopkeeper's words came slowly, echoing her thoughts. "Remember that fortunes are made, not told."

Gathering her courage, she turned back to meet the shopkeeper's distant eyes. "So I shall make my own fortune, then?"

"Everyone does. What else would you buy?"

Sensing clouded meaning behind the simple question,

she looked about her, taking in the shop's fanciful offerings. "What will you sell me?"

The shopkeeper unlocked the glass display case and fumbled within its cluttered depths, then offered her a gilded walnut shell. She took the object doubtfully; the gold was thin, the shell itself showing through in places.

"What is it?"

"It is whatever you need. A tear. A dream. A smile."

"A smile?" Surely she, the family's *shvibzik*, its prank-playing imp, needed no help to smile. But the sense of mystic purpose behind the shopkeeper's simple words drew her. Father Gregory possessed the same eerie power; a force that awakened her nascent awareness of the worlds beyond.

Curious, she took the golden shell, weighing it in her hand, and then opened it. A pinch of multicolored glitter wafted over her fingers; save for that, the walnut shell was empty. She looked at the heavily swathed shopkeeper.

"A time may come when you will need a smile, Your Imperial Highness. Do not waste it."

She thought of many rejoinders, and made none of them. But her bare fingers closed over the time-dulled walnut shell, and when they left the *Magazin Magii*, her three sisters happily carrying a dozen packages of white cardboard tied with red string—presents for themselves, for their parents, for their little brother Alexei—the walnut shell holding the magic smile was the only thing Her Imperial Highness Anastasia Nicolaievna took away with her.

TSARSKOE SELO. MARCH 1917.

The dying world roared, a whirlwind of chaos. Gunfire and shouting; shattered glass and bloody snow. Pain and darkness. Endless night—Gasping for enough breath to call out, she struggled with the sweat-soaked sheets tangling her body; clawed at wet cloth bonds with desperate hands. "Mama!" she cried into the darkened room. "Mama!"

A cool hand pressed her brow. "Mama?" she asked, sensing even as she spoke that it was not.

"No, *shvibzik*. It's me, Marie. You had a nightmare."

She stared up into her sister's worried blue eyes. "No, not a nightmare. It—" Even as she began to explain, she knew she could not, not to Marie, so blithely prosaic. But Mama believed in visions and in miracles; this time Mama *must* listen to her. "I must speak to Mama, Masha. It's important. I *must*."

But Marie was shaking her head. "Mama's resting. You don't want me to wake her, do you? You know Mama hasn't slept for two days."

Mama had not slept because four of the five Imperial children suffered through the high fever and sore eyes of a severe attack of measles, and of course Mama insisted upon nursing them herself. Only Marie had so far been spared, and tonight the air surrounding Marie glowed dull crimson, occult prelude to the disease's assault.

"You've got them, you know. The measles," she explained, and Marie smiled cheerfully. "No I don't," Marie said. "Do you want a cold compress for your poor head?"

"No. I want Mama." She must tell Mama what she had seen, must warn her; there was still time—

"Mama's sleeping," Marie reminded her firmly, and laid the compress upon her burning forehead. Then Marie held a glass to her dry lips. "Drink this, and then I'll call Lili Dehn and we'll change these wet sheets. You'll feel better then, *shvibzik.*"

Despairingly obedient, she drank, and almost at once fell back into sleep. And when Anastasia woke again, it was too late to speak to Mama about anything at all.

EKATERINBURG, SIBERIA. JULY 1918.

Since the empire's newest rulers had nailed up the tall wooden fence, Anastasia could no longer see past the yard's mud to the town beyond. The fence was for their protection, the Imperial Family had been told. Just as were the guards with their greedy eyes and battered weapons.

"We must take great care of you. There are those who would not be as kind as we are."

No one argued with these guards. Mama and Papa submitted with pious resignation to all the indignities their newest jailers inflicted upon them. The dedicated men who had guarded the Imperial Family during its imprisonment in Tobolsk were gone now, dismissed by the ruthless Urals Soviet. Anastasia knew some of those men who had cared for them were now dead. She had seen their doom reflected in their hopeless eyes.

Just as she had seen her family's doom; fever-dream turned reality. That ruthless clairvoyant gift had become hers the day Father Gregory had first entered the Imperial nursery and looked into the young Anastasia's deep blue eyes. The *starets'* uncanny gaze had woken something slumbering within her; since that long-ago day, Anastasia Nicolaievna had seen too much and too far when she looked into the worlds surrounding her.

After her first childish attempts to share the futures shown her, she had learned to suffer knowledge in silence. No one believed her; no one *wanted* to believe her, not even Mama, who truly believed in holy men and visions. Who believed in miracles, and in Father Gregory.

Especially Mama. For Mama did not wish to know what Anastasia knew that first day of Gregory Rasputin's invasion of their lives: that baby Alexei would never become Tsar after Papa. Never. . . .

So Anastasia had ceased revealing tomorrows no one wished to know, the futures no one wished to see. The only future she could not summon was her own. When she stared at herself in mirrors, only her square-jawed, stubborn face was reflected back.

Unseeing, Anastasia stared at the painted window barring her view into the outside world. In the hot little room behind her, pen nibs scratched across rough paper like dutiful mice: her sisters writing their diary entries as Mama had decreed. A low murmur of voices drifted from the larger room across the hall: Papa soothing Mama, or Mama coaxing Alexei to rest. Thump of hard boots upon the stairs: the Bolshevik guards, vigilant as starving wolves. No sound at all came from the world raging beyond the window. Here in Ipatiev House, within the whirlwind's heart, all was calm.

For this moment. Blowing on sun-hot glass, Anastasia created mist which vanished instantly. Lacking other entertainments, she had sat at the window since luncheon, breathing transient patterns into being. It was a poor occupation for an energetic girl, but the family was permitted only half an hour's walk in the yard each day, and even staring at a whitewashed window was preferable to writing optimistic lies upon the blank pages of her diary. Mama always read her daughters' thoughts, and Mama must not be permitted to know Anastasia's truth.

For Mama would only cry, and expect her daughter to weep as well, and Anastasia had never been a girl for tears. Even now, knowing what she did, she endured with dry eyes.

Her sisters cried during the long nights, smothering the sound in their thin pillows. Her mother cried during the day, her tears liquid chains binding the family closer to her than ever. Papa could not bear to see Mama weep, each diamond-clear tear a reminder of his failure to protect his wife, his daughters, his fragile son.

Knowledge of failure ate at her father, armed each unforgiving minute with wolf-sharp teeth. Once her father had possessed ultimate power and her family had glittered bright as untouchable stars. Now that power was gone, torn away.

Thrown away. But that truth, too, could not be spoken. Bending her head, Anastasia breathed again upon the windowpane. Beyond that painted glass lay a world she could no longer imagine; a world altered beyond recognition.

Fortune's wheel had spun into being a world in which her father no longer ruled an empire, and she was no longer a princess. When men looked at her now, it was no longer with awe-tinged respect. Young as she was, cloistered as her parents had kept their four daughters, Anastasia still knew what glowed in the guards' eyes when they stared at her and her sisters.

Desire, and greedy hunger. Lust.

Another truth that must never be uttered. Words possessed power; to speak them might summon ultimate disaster.

Since honest work held no interest for their guards, the painting over of the windows had been done in arrogant haste. Whitewash had splashed untidily, creating a monochrome pattern of arcs and swirls on the glass. Anastasia began to trace the careless brush strokes, moving her finger with great deliberation, consuming as much slow time as possible with her self-ordered task. It was important to bind time, marshal its relentless flow to purpose, however humble.

As she traced random curves, rays of dying sunlight burned against the window, stained the whitewashed glass blood red. Behind her, her three sisters continued their obedient scribing, marking each long day with pious thoughts and hopeful platitudes. Occasionally, one of her sisters sighed.

The world holds its breath, and we wait. Unlike the others, she knew what they waited for, what would demand them. Her Imperial Highness Anastasia Nicolaievna didn't need her mystic gift to see this future. The image of what must come burned dark and clear as the guns the guards carried as they stalked the hot, crowded rooms of Ipatiev House.

And in her pocket, waiting, lay the gilded walnut shell, and its hidden smile.

THE KOPTIAKA WOODS. JULY 1918.

Someone called a name; called over and over with the urgency of one seeking a lost child. Her name? Did they summon her?

Before she could decide, she felt hands upon her, shifting her body. Pain stabbed through her head, hot and fierce; she cried out and a hand pressed her mouth, muffled the sound.

"Hush, you must be silent. Do you understand?"

A man's voice, young and rough and urgent. An unknown voice. "No noise, you understand?"

She opened her eyes and stared into his. Her sight was blurred; his face wavered in the dawn light. Cautious, wary of further pain, she nodded, and the pressure on her bruised mouth eased.

"Are you too hurt to move? We must go, quickly."

She didn't know how badly she was hurt, or why. Perhaps her rescuer knew. She groped for words. "Why? Who are you?" Small words, little more than hoarse whispers, as if some endless time had passed since she had last spoken.

He stared at her, his mouth frozen half-open. She waited, absorbing the hot knowledge of pain and gathering courage to move, as he had said she must.

At last he swallowed hard. "Don't stare at me like that. Now come, please. We have a long way to go before you will be safe."

Try as she might, she could attach no name, no memory, to his broad plain face. But his voice was kind and his hands gentle as he released her from the sharp embrace of briar and thorn.

Once she stood free of the untamed hedge of briars that had sheltered her, she looked through white-hot bursts of pain at the world surrounding her. She stood between a massive thicket of wild rose and a dirt road whose mud bore the deep marks of a heavy vehicle; beyond road and roses stretched endless forest, candle-lit by pale slender birches.

"Come," said her rescuer, "we will go into the trees. The road is too dangerous."

Why? But her head throbbed with such pain that the question was driven into the echoing darkness where her memories lay hidden. And since she knew no one and nothing, there was no reason not to do as he urged. Obediently, she let him put his arm around her and help her stagger away from the road and the tire tracks that scarred the road's muddy surface.

She looked back only once, when he at last let her stop to catch her sobbing breath. The dirt road had vanished behind them, hidden by birch trees that blazed like sword blades in the rising light.

* * *

His name was Ivan, he told her; a common enough name. She had been injured—he would not tell her how—and he had stumbled over her while hunting beside the road through the birch forest. Her name was . . .

"Anna . . ." An odd hesitation, a waiting pause, as if there should be more. Then he repeated, "Your name is Anna." This time his voice held only assurance, and she accepted the name, and the story, as her own. For the lingering heat of pain ate her strength, and so she hoarded her energy. It was more important to keep walking south than it was to question, and to think—or to remember.

For uncounted days Ivan kept them away from roads. They walked through timeless forest until at last he thought them far enough away—*From where? From what?*—to chance the road again.

Travel was easier on the road.

As they journeyed, she walked away the bruising and the stiffness that had hampered her. Gradually the deep wounds through her hands healed, and the bloody gash along her temple. Only her head still troubled her, pain stabbing blade-keen when she least expected hurt.

South, always south, away from soldiers and pain and darkness. She knew Ivan's dream for them, now. He had told her as they walked through one of summer's long white nights.

"America. We will go to America, Anna. There we will be free, we will be safe."

America. Golden land; new world. Haven.

"There is no war there. No Bolsheviks. No—" An unspoken word whispered on the night wind and was gone. Ivan stopped and took her pierced hands in his work-roughened ones; his callused fingers traced the scarlet lacework of her healing wounds.

"In America a man who works can be whatever he chooses. In America we can both be free."

"Free." She tested the word, weighing it against her

empty past, seeking meaning in the concept. Out of the darkness that owned her memories, phantom images rose: a tall fence, a muddy yard, a door closing forever on the world beyond. . . .

The images faded back into her lost past, intangible as smoke. Only a great longing remained.

"Anna? Would you like to go to America, Annoushka?"

"Yes," she said, the word solemn as a holy vow. And then, "Yes. I would like to be free."

South, and always south. Whatever lay behind was forgotten now, buried deep. She learned to smile again, and sometimes she even laughed, teasing Ivan for his overly gentle care of her.

"I will not break in your hands, Ivan Petrovich. I'm not made of glass!"

At first he only stared at her when she joked and teased and laughed, as if she were mad, or he were. Later he began to smile back, hesitant, as if his smiles might offend.

Later still he laughed when she did, and they walked hand-in-hand through silver summer nights.

So they fled southward, through endless fields of sunflowers and wheat, along roads that ran like rivers of golden dust toward the Black Sea. No one paid them any special attention. One more young man and one more young girl amid the stream of refugees fleeing the terror in the north; why should they be noted more than any others?

And if the young man wore a threadbare tunic that might once have been a uniform, and the young girl bore crimson scars upon her hands, and upon her face, why, that was no rare thing these days. Prey ran before the wolves, and no man cared to question another too closely.

In silent pain she burned, then froze, then burned again. In the fire's heart she dreamed; flashes of nightmare horror: *Sharp flat noises and blows hard as the diamonds sewn into her clothes. Clutching hands and slicing blades. Yelping as a small frantic dog tried hopelessly to protect its young mistress. Blood pouring hot over her hands and face; screams haunting her ears. Weight falling upon her body. Soft hair spilling, warm and wet, over her face. . . .*

"No!" she gasped, and woke to quiet darkness.

Late in the glowing autumn, they found a lonely railway station. There they waited three days for a train from the north to arrive. The train was already over-full when it pulled in; with all his strength, Ivan forced her aboard and crammed himself after her, winning them precious space in the narrow boxcar. There they stood and waited until the train rolled south half a day later.

They stood all the way to the Crimea, and took it turn and turn about to sleep braced in each other's arms.

SEBASTAPOL, CRIMEA. AUTUMN 1918.

In refugee-crowded Sebastapol, Ivan somehow found them a room at an inn. Not a large room, but one they owned for themselves alone for the space of a few nights. A room barely large enough to hold a narrow bed and a washstand. A room with one small shuttered window and one mirror.

The mirror too was small: old-fashioned, bounded by wood that once had been painted gold. Now all that remained of that long-ago splendor was hints of gilt lurking in the depths of curves and arabesques. The glass itself was mottled and discolored with age. Looking into that time-worn glass was like peering at one's reflection in a summer pool. She was drawn, only half-willing, by its uncertain surface. What did she look like? For the first time, she would know her own face.

And perhaps—her lost past?

But all that looked back at her from the greenish depths of the looking glass was a stranger; a young woman whose blue eyes were shadowed and whose mouth was tightly closed over unknown secrets. Nothing more was revealed to her.

Still, the scar across her face was not as bad as she had

feared. Only a line of fading crimson slanting upward from her cheekbone, transmuting at her temple into a blade-thin streak of white lancing through her soft brown hair. There were those who had suffered far more; were marred hideously and forever. She had seen them on the roads, tragic figures, as she and Ivan traveled south.

She accepted the mirrored face as hers; it was the sort of face a young woman called Anna might possess. And staring at the image of Anna in the ancient glass, she knew that if she had once been anyone else, Anna no longer wished to remember that lost reflection.

In their little room, Ivan revealed at last the jewels that he had carried to safety with them. A dazzle of unset diamonds; a string of cloud-cream pearls; a gold crucifix edged with emeralds. He spilled the gems across the thin wool blanket covering the bed and then looked at her.

Waiting.

She scooped up a handful of diamonds and sifted them through scar-stiff fingers. The gemstones fell like blazing tears onto the rough blanket. She looked from the diamonds to Ivan, puzzled. "We are rich, then?"

His cautious look vanished; he smiled, and touched the white hair starring her temple. "Yes, *doushenka*. We are rich."

"And now, Ivan Petrovich?"

"And now we go to America, Annoushka." That was the first time he kissed her. A gentle, awkward brush of his lips over hers, a caress instantly withdrawn, as if he dared greatly, and feared rebuff.

She stared up into his honest eyes and knew deep in her bones what he desired of her. She remembered nothing before she had wakened to his urgent voice calling her out of sleep into pain and life, but that blank history no longer mattered. She owned other memories now: Ivan's gentle care of her; his endless kindness.

And from some distant past, she remembered love.

That was what Ivan wished for, the thing his eyes told her

he dared not dream of obtaining. But somewhere on their long journey south, somewhere between one weary step and the next, her frozen heart had warmed. She was ready, now, to wake, and live a new life.

"America," she said, and moved into his hopeful arms.

He stared down into her eyes with as much awe as if he embraced a star. Then he swallowed hard, and his arms tightened around her. "I will serve you always, Annoushka. I will love you forever. I swear it."

That was the second time he kissed her. And then it did not matter that the bed was narrow and the blanket thin, for they kindled their own warmth. Afterward, she slept cradled in his arms, and for the first time since he had freed her from the cage of thorns beside the muddy road, she did not dream.

In Sebastapol, Ivan transformed some of the jewels into treasure far more precious than mere gems: traveling papers for them both. This was easier to accomplish than it would have been during the reign of the last Tsar, before the Revolution. But now the Tsar was dead. *Bloody Nicholas is dead, with all his family!* the Reds boasted. Sebastapol was the refugees' lodestar, the gateway to freedom. What must be had could be bought at a price.

Their jewels, carefully husbanded, bought them out of Russia, carried them across the Black Sea to Constantinople. While they rested in that ancient city, they learned the Great War, ravager of nations, at last had ended, ended in grief and in silence and in brooding hate. The Armistice, with its dear-bought peace, made their own journey easier. All the world seemed on the move, and again they passed unnoticed among the restless crowds.

From Constantinople, that city balanced so precariously between East and West, they took another train. This time they sat upon a bench. And this time they journeyed north, instead of south.

PARIS. CHRISTMAS 1918.

Paris is a great city, but each great city embraces many

lesser cities within its limits. Their Paris was not the Paris of the aristocratic émigrés, that glistening dreamworld as lovely and as false as Fabergé blossoms caught in a crystal vase. Theirs was the Paris of the frugal poor, of those who make each penny work hard for its keep. Ivan sold only those he must of their hidden jewels; only enough to thriftily feed and clothe and house them.

And to secure their passage to America. For this Ivan committed extravagance: the purchase of third-class tickets, granting them beds of their own, rather than steerage, the cheapest fare of all.

The ship that would carry them to America would leave from Cherbourg in the New Year. Until then, they rested, waiting in the City of Light.

On their last night in Paris, they went to Christmas Eve Mass at the Russian Orthodox Church. Midnight Mass; chanting and candle flames; muted jewels and sweet, thick incense smoke. She stood, head bowed, beside Ivan, and let joyous noise wash through her, seep into her bones. Christmas Eve, a time for solemn rejoicing. Tomorrow would be Christmas Day, a time for—

Presents and parties; white furs and diamonds bright as snow. . . . Frowning, she shook her head and Ivan reached out and grasped her hand. With the touch of his warm flesh the wistful ghost-images that shimmered before her vanished into the hot gleams of a thousand candle flames and the pressure of a thousand eyes.

But that was foolish; those who filled this church did not look at Anna Nobody. Why should they? All eyes were fixed on the blazing gold of the icons above the altar, the swinging gleam of the censer, the blue clouds of incense smoke.

If hard eyes watched her, judged her, they did so only in the shadowed maze of her imagination.

He waited for them at the wide church door; a tall man armored in a well-tailored greatcoat and an indefinable air of command. As they passed out into the night, he stepped into their path, forcing them to halt.

"Highness?" His cultured voice cut the midnight air like a rapier's blade. "Anastasia Nicolaievna?" He was looking straight at her. Staring straight at her. Speaking straight to her.

Beside her, Ivan's body twitched as if the word were a bullet hitting his flesh; his broad hand clenched over her stiff fingers. But he did not try to evade the man who had stopped them. And he said nothing; took refuge in the silence of endurance.

"Yes, it *is* you. I watched you during the service, and was not sure. But now. . . ." The tall man paused, frowned. "Don't you know me, Anastasia Nicolaievna?"

Silently, she shook her head.

"Prince Ygornin; your cousin Sergei. Don't you remember?" Now he saw her scars, her badges of suffering and change, for the first time. He reached out and pushed back her head scarf, stared hard at the scarlet line across her cheek, the slash of silver through her light brown hair. "My God," he breathed, and then, "It's a miracle, a true miracle. We were told you all died at Ekaterinburg. How did you escape?"

Worshipers pushed past them, hurrying home on Christmas Eve. Stone-silent, she turned her head and looked at Ivan. As if releasing her, his fingers slid away from her clutching hand. Although Ivan did not speak, she saw the story clearly reflected in his faithful eyes. A summer night, a cool summer night—

—*but it was hot in Ipatiev House, sickeningly hot. The cellar room reeked of blood and cordite; bodies lay like broken dolls scattered across the blood-drenched floor. Men dragged the bodies out of the cellar into the barren dirt of the yard. There a truck waited, its engine growling loud in the black night's silence. The men lifted bodies, tossed them hastily into the back of the waiting truck. Forcing himself to the task, Ivan lifted a girl's body and saw that it was Anas-*

*tasia's. In his arms she moaned, the sound faint as a dying
baby's wail.*

*Blood soaked her jacket and blouse and skirt; blood
soaked her soft hair. But she was not dead. Not yet. . . .
Scarcely daring to draw breath, Ivan rolled her into the
truck, trying to be gentle with her, laying her upon the limp
corpses of her sisters to cushion her wounded body. Then he
climbed in after her.*

*Loaded, the truck drove out through once-barred gates,
into the empty streets of Ekaterinburg, and then into the
countryside beyond. Ivan knew they headed for old mine
shafts hidden deep in the forest. But country roads were only
hard-packed dirt, and summer rain had turned dirt to soft
mud. The truck slowed and stopped more than once, trapped
by sodden ground. At last the truck's wheels stuck in a
muddy stretch of road shadowed by hedges of wild rose and
blackberry. The only light came from the truck's head-
lamps—and those pointed forward, toward the mines and
their shafts sunk far into the cold earth. The truck paused,
wavering as the swearing driver rocked it back and forth to
free the vehicle from the grasping mud. And during that vital
moment, Ivan pushed her body off the truck and she fell hard
into darkness. . . .*

"*No,*" she said, reaching in the midnight chill for Ivan's
hand. In vain; he had slowly moved away from her. Imper-
sonal as a stranger, or a servant.

Or a guard. . . .

Prince Ygornin smiled, and moved closer. "So. You will
be well rewarded, man. You have saved the last of the Imperial Family. You have saved our beloved Grand Duchess
Anastasia."

"*No,*" she said again. "*No. It is not true.*" Could not be
true; she would not let it be true.

"It is true; I knew it the moment I saw you in the church.
You are the Tsar's daughter. You are Anastasia Nico-
laievna." The prince's voice was firm and certain. "Tsar
Nicholas is dead"—here the prince crossed himself—"with

all his family, all save you. God spared you to be our hope. Our cause will live again in you."

The prince sank down upon his knee and kissed her blade-marred hand as if it were a holy relic. "Your Imperial Highness." Then he looked up and as she looked into his eyes the ground seemed to slide beneath her feet like a giant serpent, treacherous and cruel.

For she knew that look. She had seen it before, in the eyes of the guards at Ekaterinburg. *Desire, and greedy hunger. Lust.*

A look unlocking her lost past. Harsh memory flooded her, poured through her mind like heart's blood.

Mama crossing herself. Papa jumping up, shoving Alexei behind him in one last useless gesture. Jimmy barking, and a guard clubbing the little spaniel into silence. The rolling noise of trapped thunder as guns fired and the horrified look on a young guard's face as bullets struck and bounced off diamond-lined corsets. Olga and Tatiana screaming. Gun butts and blows and herself dropping to the floor. Bayonet blades piercing flesh and bone. Marie falling, glossy brown hair slick with crimson and wide blue eyes staring amazed into Death's. . . .

The deadly future she had watched unfold on the blind surface of a painted-over window; a future now frozen in her eternal past. She moaned and pressed her scarred hands to her head, but the images would not vanish. *The stairs. The cellar room. The men with guns. The door closing forever.*

The pain.

"Your Imperial Highness?" The prince peered at her, appalled, as if she were an exhibit in some perverse museum.

They are dead. All dead, all, I thought I too would die. . . . For she had seen no future for the Grand Duchess Anastasia beyond that cool July night. But she lived.

"No," she gasped. *"No."*

"It's the shock," Prince Ygornin decided, rising inexorably to his feet. "A doctor. We have one who served your father the Tsar." Still he stared at her, his eyes seeking to devour her. Just so had the Bolshevik guards once stared, seeking to possess. But their lust had been purer; they had desired only her body. Prince Ygornin sought her lost soul, had dragged that fragile entity back from darkness to suffer in the light.

And more, he would use her to make others suffer. *"Her Imperial Highness the Grand Duchess Anastasia. Martyred Nicholas' daughter. The last princess."* The smoke of battles swirled in the prince's eyes as Ygornin waved the resurrected Anastasia as a standard to rally the retreating Whites. She watched herself exalted as a living icon: the exiled princess. An icon fed with blood and souls.

"The Bolsheviks burned the bodies and threw them down a mine shaft. Bloody Nicholas is dead."

Icon of a church that had been toppled and burned.

"Your family will be overjoyed to see you again, Highness. The whole world will rejoice."

Yes; there is Grandmama and my cousins and—

But they all thought her dead. Had accepted her death as one of many. *They fled and left us. And my English cousins abandoned us. Refused us sanctuary and left us to the mercy of the Bolsheviks.*

Prince Ygornin held out his hand, an imperious invitation. "Come along now, Anastasia Nicolaievna. Your people await you."

My people. Her father was dead, and her frail brother Alexei, and her three sisters. Five lives, and now she, the youngest daughter, was heiress to the Imperial myth. One hand moved, automatically patterning the cross over her body. The other closed over the small gold-and-emerald crucifix Ivan had incautiously given her to wear to Mass; the jewel rescued from the mud surrounding the Four Brothers Mine.

"They will call it the Four Sisters now. . . ."

And with a burst of clarity, she saw, not the future, but the past. Four sisters in matching white dresses chasing each other through summer sunlight at Livadia; four identically clad girls skating on the frozen pond at Tsarskoe Selo. Four girls who had been so sheltered, so protected.

So smothered; so guarded from reality by their overly loving parents. Treated as eternal children, too young, too tender, to face even a pampered life alone.

"OTMA" was how they had signed their gifts, their cards, their letters. Olga, Tatiana, Marie, Anastasia: four sisters molded into "OTMA." One perfect entity. As if each girl possessed no life of her own, no individual spark of mortality.

No prospective suitor had ever passed their parents' iron tests of suitability. None ever would. Mama and Papa could foresee no more desirable future than an endless echo of the past; the family together always, bound by fearful love. Their son and daughters remaining forever young. Forever children.

Four princesses under glass, kept unchanging as butterflies in amber. Ornaments of a dreaming world that could not waken even to foresee its own destruction.

But the dream had ended, that pretty world destroyed as if cursed. Now her three sisters slept forever under cold earth, and she stood awake and alone.

She need only hold out her hand to be drawn once more into the old world. To dwell forever within a glittering fairy tale of dreams and ice, shielded from harsh reality by barriers of custom and convention as thick and unyielding as glass. For an eternal heartbeat she saw herself reflected in Prince Ygornin's gleaming eyes.

Before an empty throne, she accepted homage from a timeworn aristocracy. Aging men and women kissed her white-gloved hand, blinded to reality by the jewels bound upon her hair, upon her wrists, upon her throat. In a timeless ballroom they watched avidly as the Grand Duchess Anastasia waltzed in endless circles forever.

Her Imperial Highness' future, exposed by Prince Ygornin's covetous eyes. Slow rebellion kindled. Why must she become that Fabergé princess, an illusion entrapped forever in a fantasy of white lace and pearls and other people's dreams?

Have I no dreams of my own? Mama and Papa, Alexei and my sisters, they are all dead. Grief cut through her, keen

as shards of glass. And mingled with the grief and loss, a
baffled anger. *They are dead; must I be dead too?*

Guilt at such heresy slashed her; she crossed herself
again and looked from Prince Ygornin to Ivan. She knew
him, too, now. One of the guards Commissar Yurovsky had
set to watch the Imperial Family in the House of Special
Purpose. A young man who once, when Yurovsky's all-
seeing eyes were turned elsewhere, had dared to smile at
her. A smile. Humanity, and hope, offered in a dead world
where there had been neither.

And knowing what the unknown guard had risked with
that shy smile, she had smiled back. . . .

Gentle Ivan, who had known all along that he cherished
the Grand Duchess Anastasia, and whose honest eyes said
now that he knew he could not hold her. A princess did not
marry a pig-herd, save in fairy tales. Not even a pig-herd
who had received a magic smile—and so had saved the
princess from endless sleep.

*Fortunes are made, not told . . . someday you may need a
smile. Do not waste it. . . .*

She had not wasted her smile; magic or not, that smile
had saved her life.

And now a prince awaited her. The proper fairy-tale ending for the lost princess, an ending so much more appropriate than the truth.

The last princess rescued from reality's gutter, raised
once more to Imperial heights. No matter that those heights
owned no foundation now, that her throne would be built of
gilded cardboard, her court composed of the hopeless, the
failures.

Of the cowards who had run, leaving their Tsar and country to the ungentle mercies of the Bolsheviks.

But I am not dead; I live. I wish to live. What would happen if she denied the future she saw? Could she create her
own world in its place?

Glitter and darkness. . . . She slid her hand into her coat
pocket; her fingers grasped the walnut shell lying deep
within the warm fabric, last souvenir of her gilded past.

"Your Imperial Highness?"

"You are mistaken," she said at last. "I am not the Grand Duchess Anastasia." Holding her breath, her fingers closed cold over the hard edges of the walnut shell, she prayed silently for another miracle. *It is whatever you need. A tear. A dream. A smile—*

—a future. A life created of her own will and desire. *Please. My own world. My future, not theirs. . . .* There was an inaudible snap as the ancient shell shattered under her frozen grasp.

Disbelieving, Prince Ygornin studied her with keen hunter's eyes. "Your Imperial Highness is overwrought," he announced. "It is understandable. The doctors—"

"No," she repeated, more firmly now. The edges of the broken nutshell bit into her fingers, sharp as memory. "Your Highness is wrong. I am not the girl you wish me to be."

The prince stared at her now, seeking reassurance. Seeking to see the girl who had descended into the cellar of Ipatiev House. But that girl was gone, fled into the dead past, leaving only smoke and ash.

Memories and ghosts.

She stood firm, and waited, and saw the moment when the prince's certainty turned to doubt. "You are not—?"

"Did I say I was? Do I look like a Grand Duchess to you?"

Shaken now, the prince slowly shook his head, forced by her will to believe as she wished. "No. No, of course not. Now I see. But the resemblance, it *is* extraordinary."

Yes, a resemblance; that is all. A whim of chance. A trick to fool the eye. Let me go.

"But—who are you?" The dying breath of hope.

Without looking, she reached out, and Ivan's fingers wrapped hard as truth around her hand.

"My name is Anna," she said, and turned to Ivan and smiled. And with Ivan beside her she walked away from the church door, away from Prince Ygornin and the fatal promise of the past, into the dawning hope of Christmas morning.

THE MAGIC KEYBOARD

by *Laura Resnick*

Laura Resnick, a cum laude *graduate of Georgetown University, won the 1993 John W. Campbell award for best new science fiction/fantasy writer. Since then she has never looked back, having written the best-selling novels* In Legend Born, The White Dragon, *and* The Destroyer *with more on the way. She has also written award-winning nonfiction, an account of her journey across Africa, entitled* A Blonde in Africa. *She has written several short travel pieces, as well as numerous articles about the publishing business. She also writes a monthly opinion column for* Nink, *the newsletter of Novelists, Inc. You can find her on the web at www.sff.net./people/laresnick.*

SHE STARED at the empty page. She gazed at the blank screen. She watched the blinking cursor. . . .

"*Arrrrggggh!*"

Ethelfreda Feldsnitch picked up her computer monitor and flung it out the window into the humid night air. Or, rather, she tried to do so.

Unfortunately, Ethelfreda was an underpaid mid-list writer who couldn't afford protein-rich foods and who never bothered to exercise, so she was sort of scrawny and weak. The monitor, a refurbished bargain acquired in a Dutch auction on eBay, was nearly as large as her twelve-year-old hatchback car, and so she was unable to lift it.

So Ethelfreda settled for flinging the keyboard, instead of the monitor, out the window. The keyboard was lightweight (and liberally stained with coffee), and it sailed out the window like a cruise missile.

"*Arrrrrggggh!*" cried the passing stranger in the street who was hit by a keyboard falling mysteriously from the sky.

Ethelfreda slammed shut her window, flung herself on the bed she had acquired in Goodwill's post-Millennium sale, and wept bitterly. Her mystery series, featuring a spunky Belgian cat who dressed like a nun and solved murders in Victorian London, had been canceled due to poor sales. The poorest sales in the entire history of the publishing house, in fact. Since there was no chance of another publisher buying additional books in the series, this put serious pressure on Ethelfreda to come up with something new if she wanted to save her career. Something marketable. Something someone actually might want to read.

So far, things didn't look promising. Ethelfreda's first attempt at a new mystery series featured a precocious suburban parrot who helped his golf-pro owner solve poisoning cases. After reading it, Ethelfreda's publisher suggested she consider returning to college or marrying well as a perfectly respectable alternative to writing for a living. Ethelfreda was no quitter, though, and so she came up with yet another series. After reading the submission, her publisher changed their phone number and issued a restraining order.

However, Ethelfreda was less discouraged by this than one might suppose. By then, her literary agent had convinced her that mystery series were a career dead end, anyhow. She should instead, he said, be focusing her efforts on writing an action-packed blockbuster thriller. When she handed him a manuscript about intrigue, betrayal, and espionage set in a geriatric sewing circle in Bakersfield, he developed a sinus condition that forced him to cut back his client list, and he kindly wished her all the best luck in finding representation elsewhere.

Since then, Ethelfreda had been collecting rejection slips

while her meager bank account dwindled into a black hole of debt. Not only was her fiscal solvency destroyed by this succession of crushing disappointments, so was her creativity.

Ethelfreda had finally gone dry. Now she was a blank wall, an empty well, a barren field. *Maybe she was just a lousy writer,* she thought as she stared at the blank screen day after day. *Maybe selling three books in her mystery series, after years of trying to break into publishing, had been a fluke,* she told herself as she doodled aimlessly on her note pad hour after hour. Maybe she'd never sell another word. Never *write* another word. Never even have another story idea.

Tonight, this certainly seemed likely. She would certainly never sell another book if she couldn't write one, after all, and the encroaching despair had now robbed her of her ability to compose even a sentence, never mind a whole novel.

Tormented by hopeless misery, Ethelfreda feel asleep, facedown on her soggy pillow, while someone in the street called an ambulance for the stranger who'd been hit by a flying keyboard.

Dawn dawned, as dawn does, and Ethelfreda awoke with a puffy face and a terrifying realization: She'd have to go get a job. Now that she wasn't even producing new material, there was no chance of her generating income and paying her rent. So she'd have to—egad!—go back to working a *day job.*

Understandably, Ethelfreda shuddered and cowered under the covers for a while. Eventually, though, the desire to keep living under an actual roof asserted itself, and so she got up.

She donned her nicest clothing, which were hand-me-downs from her mother, and ventured out into the world in search of employment. She remembered that Magicks R Us, the magic shop at the end of the street, had a "Help Wanted" sign in the window. In fact, the sign had been in the window as long as she could remember. She'd never been in the place, but she'd looked through the dusty window before. It was a murky, dark, cluttered little shop which didn't seem to keep regular hours. Ethelfreda had no interest in magic or retail, but at least this place was close to home, which would save wear and tear on her ancient automobile, and it looked like the sort of place where her hand-me-downs would meet the dress code for employees.

There was no one in the shop when she entered it. Not even, it seemed, a proprietor. The dusty shelves were densely packed with jars of herbs, spices, minerals, amulets, and pickled animal parts.

"Good God!" Ethelfreda cried upon realizing she was staring into a jar of little eyeballs swimming in preservatives.

A confusing array of items competed for space on the walls, floors, and tables. Medieval-looking weaponry, large bushels of dried plants, urns and boxes and vases, Tarot decks, lion and leopard claws, gargoyles, icons and idols, old bones, and—

"*Aiyee!*" Ethelfreda realized she was looking at a shrunken human head.

She whirled away and bumped into an enormous bookcase, packed to overflowing with hundreds of volumes. Since books were not among the things which could frighten her, she started examining them. Grimoires, spell books, treatises, ancient manuscripts in Latin, books by German alchemists, tomes about French wizards . . . and an enormous stack of *People* magazines.

A voice right next to her said, "One has one's little weaknesses."

Ethelfreda gasped, dropped the issue with the cover story about Tom and Nicole's divorce, and gaped at the woman who seemed to have materialized out of nowhere. "Where'd you come from?"

"Oh, nowhere." She was redheaded, probably over fifty, plump, and very attractive. She dressed with flare, used makeup skillfully on an interesting face, and smiled at

Ethelfreda with cool charm. "I'm sorry I startled you. I'm Mrs. Gotti. Welcome to my shop."

"Mrs. Gotti?" Ethelfreda's jaw dropped.

"No relation."

"Oh."

"People ask all the time."

Recalling her mission, Ethelfreda said, "I saw the sign in the window. I'm looking for a job—"

"A job?" Mrs. Gotti shook her head. "No, I don't think so."

"Oh, but I am. I—"

"No. I think what you're looking for is in here." Mrs. Gotti opened a cabinet in the enormous bookcase. Inside, there was a tumbled array of writing implements.

Ethelfreda blinked in surprise. "How did you. . . ."

"Know that you're a writer?" When Ethelfreda nodded, Mrs. Gotti said, "You have that pale, physically unfit, financially desperate, and emotionally downtrodden look about you. It's unmistakable. Only writers ever look like that."

"I see."

"What you need," Mrs. Gotti said, rummaging through the writing implements in the cabinet, "isn't a job selling things you don't understand to people you can't help for wages you can't live on."

"Well, when you put it that way. . . ."

"What you need is . . . *Ah-hah!*"

"*Ah-hah?*"

Mrs. Gotti held up a quill pen and stared at it consideringly. "Yes, I think *this* might be what you need."

"A pen?"

"Try it out. If you don't like it, bring it back."

"I don't understand. Why do I need this?"

Mrs. Gotti placed a manicured hand over her ample bosom as she gazed at Ethelfreda. "Did I misunderstand? Am I mistaken?"

"About what?"

"You're suffering from writer's block, correct?"

Ethelfreda's breath came out in a rush. "Wow! How did you—"

"You have that look."

"Oh."

"And if your work were going well, you wouldn't be seeking a minimum-wage job in retail. Am I right?"

"Completely."

"So, as I said before, take the pen home, try it out, and if you're not satisfied—"

"With what?"

"Why, with the magic, of course."

Ethelfreda stared. "It's a magic pen?"

"Yes."

"For writer's block?"

"Yes."

"You're putting me on."

"No."

"Oh, right. And how much does this *magic* pen cost?"

Mrs. Gotti smiled. "Why don't you take it home for a free trial," she suggested. "If you don't like it, return it free of charge. If, however, you want to keep it. . . ."

"You trust me to come back and pay you for it?"

Mrs. Gotti shrugged. "You live in the neighborhood, don't you?"

"How did you know that?"

"It's the sort of neighborhood even a writer could afford."

Ethelfreda felt conflicted as she stared at the pen's drooping feather. "I really don't think this will solve my problems."

"Take it home. Try it." Mrs. Gotti put the pen in her hand. "What have you got to lose?"

"Miss Feldsnitch! What a pleasure to see you again," Mrs. Gotti greeted her a few days later.

"Please, call me Ethelfreda."

"No, thank you. I couldn't possibly." After a pause, she added, "Your mother must have really hated you."

"She did," Ethelfreda admitted. She pulled the pen out of

her bookbag. "I have to thank you, Mrs. Gotti. This pen has changed my life. It's a miracle!"

"It's working for you, then?"

"I'm producing the best work of my life! In fact, if you don't mind reading a few pages. . . ."

Mrs. Gotti's smile was brittle. "Of course. There's nothing I'd like better, during the all-too-brief span of time we call life, than to wade through your unpublished prose."

Ethelfreda, whose mother's rampant hatred had made her immune to subtler forms of rejection, smiled and pulled the first chapter of her new manuscript out of her bookbag. "I want your honest opinion after you read it," she said as she handed it to Mrs. Gotti.

"Of course, dear. I can hardly wait to . . . to. . . ." Mrs. Gotti frowned as she read the first paragraph of the hand-written work.

"What's wrong?"

"'It was the best of times, it was the worst of times. . . .'" Mrs. Gotti looked up. "I've read this before."

"You're kidding! Damn. And it's such a great opening, too." Ethelfreda sighed. "Oh, well. I'll have to revise that part. But the story . . . I'm so excited about the story!"

Mrs. Gotti said, "Let me guess. French Revolution, two men who are physically identical, one of whom finally redeems himself by dying in place of the other?"

"Yes! And when he does, it's a far better thing—" Ethelfreda frowned. "Wait a minute. How did you know?"

"You've never read *A Tale of Two Cities*?"

"No, I'm not a Danielle Steel fan. But what does that have to do with—"

"My God, you don't even know who wrote it? Where were you educated? Mars?" Mrs. Gotti snatched the pen from Ethelfreda's hand.

"Hey!"

"The pen *is* helping you write a magnificent novel. Unfortunately, Charles Dickens already wrote it." She glared at the pen and added, "And to think I didn't believe the dealer who told me it once belonged to him."

"So you're saying the pen writes the book, and it doesn't matter who's holding it?"

"Not at all! The pen inspires the person holding it, coaxes their best work from them. Dickens was so prolific, though, he may have worn out this one."

"Well, it's certainly no help to me if I can only use it to write a book which you say has already been written."

"I don't *say* it's been written, it *has* been written. Go to a library once in a while, for God's sake!"

"So do you have any magic pens that *weren't* owned by Dickens?"

"I do, but you don't want it. The last three owners all used it to write brilliant but despairing nihilistic novels which drove them to commit suicide before the books were even published."

"I'm not that desperate yet," Ethelfreda admitted, "though I'll get there if things don't start improving for me soon."

"It's a shame you didn't come here until a few days ago. Only last month, I had a magic pen with an incredibly illustrious history of provenance. Jules Verne, J.R.R. Tolkein, Marion Zimmer Bradley. . . . Ah, the stories that pen could inspire. Amazing!" Mrs. Gotti shrugged. "But I sold it last month to a desperate epic fantasy writer. The poor woman had a particularly haggard, hollow-eyed look."

"I'm a mystery writer. Do you happen to have an Agatha Christie pen lying around?"

"Not even a Dorothy Sayers pen, I'm afraid. Mystery pens go fast." Seeing how disappointed Ethelfreda was, Mrs. Gotti said, "I do have a typewriter that might suit you, though."

"A *magic* typewriter?"

"Of course. Mind you, though, it's very old-fashioned. A heavy, black, manual typewriter. Not electric. You might not want—"

"I'll take it."

"Well?" Mrs. Gotti asked when Ethelfreda came to the shop the following week.

"Well, the story's good. No doubt about that. Appealing characters, vivid setting, clever plot. . . ."

"I hear a 'but' coming."

"But I realized after a few days that I was writing about a warm, sympathetic, tall, blonde, widowed woman who used to be a schoolteacher and who is now a successful mystery writer. She lives in a small town in Maine, on the coast, where she's friends with the local sheriff and chess partners with the local doctor. She solves—"

"She's Angela Lansbury."

"Well, Jessica Fletcher."

"Damn!"

"Was this old typewriter used by one of the scriptwriters for the show or something?"

"No. You know the old typewriter you see Jessica typing on in the show's opening credits?"

"It's *this* one? Wow."

"My supplier obviously didn't cleanse the energy before sending it to me."

"Now what?"

"Well, another pen has arrived since your last visit."

" 'Call me Ishmael,' " Mrs. Gotti read.

"Sound familiar?" Ethelfreda asked sourly. Even she, admittedly weak on nineteenth-century literature, recognized *Moby Dick* when she wrote it.

"I don't understand this," Mrs. Gotti said. "Herman Melville never owned this pen."

"I think this pen is a plagiarist. It's got me writing another book, too. *Catch-22*."

"Well, to look at the bright side, at least you're writing, right?"

"And I'm enjoying it," Ethelfreda admitted. "I'm doing the best writing of my life. I'd just like to write something original."

"My dear, that's what every writer says to me."

"I mean, something I can sell as my own work." She sighed. "I'm getting discouraged, Mrs. Gotti. This magic writing implement business doesn't seem to be working out well. I noticed the sign is still in your window. 'Help Wanted.' I'd really like to apply for that job now. Seriously."

"Oh, I don't need any help, my dear. I just keep that sign in the window to encourage people to come in when they're down on their luck. When it's time for them to open their minds to whatever I can offer them."

"Sneaky," Ethelfreda commented.

"But effective. Anyhow, you mustn't give up. I think I finally have the perfect implement for you." She opened the cabinet in the bookcase so Ethelfreda could see what lay inside.

"A magic keyboard?" Ethelfreda perked up. "Wow. A *keyboard* . . . that would be great! All this work on a manual typewriter, all this writing with a pen. It's exhausting! Makes me wonder how all those writers produced all those novels before computers ever existed."

"I don't understand these things myself, but if you know how to use a keyboard—"

"I'll take it."

Six months later, Ethelfreda stopped by the shop and offered to treat Mrs. Gotti to lunch.

"Ah," Mrs. Gotti said. "The advance has obviously arrived for the novel you sold."

"I feel I owe it all to you."

"Nonsense."

"It's true! I've been producing the best work of my career ever since I bought that magic keyboard from you. I wrote a book, it was good, I got an agent, she negotiated a major deal for me with a new publisher, and I'm writing the next book. If it weren't for you, none of this would have happened."

"In that case, I hope we're going somewhere expensive for lunch."

"I just worry what I'll do if anything ever happens to the keyboard," Ethelfreda confided.

Mrs. Gotti shrugged. "You'll go to the computer store and replace it, of course."

"They don't sell magic keyboards, Mrs. Gotti."

"Neither do I."

"But you sold me—"

"My dear girl, that is not a *magic* keyboard, and I never said it was. It's the one you threw out the window the night before you first came to my shop."

"What? No!"

"Yes."

"But I—wait a minute, how did you even know I threw it out the window?"

"I'm the one who called the ambulance for the poor fellow it hit in the street below. He's fine now, by the way. When you showed up here the next day, I knew you had to be the one who'd done it."

"It's *my* keyboard?"

"You didn't need a magic implement, dear. You needed to believe in yourself. I gave you back the keyboard when I saw that you were ready to write without magic."

"Then why didn't you tell me the truth?"

"Because I could see that *you* didn't know you were ready."

"So it's really not magical, then?"

"It's really not. Yet you have written a wonderful novel and are now writing another. You see? It's in you, not in the implement."

"I see." Ethelfreda thought this over. "In that case, can I have my money back?"

OFF KEY

by ElizaBeth Gilligan

ElizaBeth Gilligan is a happily married mom of two teens and the Keeper of the Vast Menagerie: eight cats, one dog, frogs, newts, and over a hundred guinea pigs (daughter's homeschool genetics project). She has been writing ever since she figured out how a pencil worked. Her mother reports that ElizaBeth declared as early as the age of two that she was going to "make books" when she grew up. Her first and second short stories appeared in DAW anthologies. As a novelist, she aspired to one day find a place in the DAW family and, to her great delight, 2003 saw the release of her first book, Magic's Silken Snare, *in the* Silken Magic *series by DAW.*

When she's not writing or working on one of her various projects, she leads an on-line research group for writers and hangs out at sff.people.lace.

"OH, IT isn't that bad," Marva teased from across the table.

Sarah looked down at the grainy, yellow, congealing puddle of tofu and eggplant curry and tried to work up an appetite. Her only option was the salad: two slices of yellow tomato, some slivered carrots, and sprouts—she had seen samples of it in the occasional sandwich box brought in for business luncheons with California clients. Sarah never expected to find herself in a situation where she actually preferred alfalfa and clover to everything else on her side of the table. Clearly, letting her twin Marva order for her only compounded the error she made by letting her choose the restaurant.

"At least try some of it," Marva urged.

Sarah pushed the plate away. "I've long outgrown the urge to actually *eat* mud pies. Why on earth. . . ."

Behind Marva, Sarah watched as a tall lean man with wavy brown hair and a face and body to die for entered the restaurant. He was dressed in a gray Armani suit, a crisply pressed white shirt, and an azure tie which matched his heavenly blue eyes—none of which she could see just at this moment because he'd turned back to hold the door open for his companions, two women and a man. He glanced around the restaurant and ushered his guests toward the hostess. He made eye contact with Sarah. He grinned and gave her a friendly salute.

"You know him?" Marva breathed. "Who is he?"

Flustered, Sarah quickly took a bite of the unfortunate curry. "Oh, just someone I work with," she said and then closed her eyes. She swallowed. The tofu, which Marva had promised was cooked to absolute perfection, slid, sluglike, down her throat.

"Well, whoever he is, he's the dog's *meow*!"

"Cat's *meow*," Sarah said automatically. The brown recycled paper napkin muffled her words. She had it pressed to her lips as a precaution as she concentrated on keeping the "curry" she'd swallowed inside and south of her hand-stitched silk collar.

"*Huh?*" Marva stared openly, watching the hostess escort the man and his guests to another section of the restaurant. "What?"

"The phrase is 'cat's *meow*.' "

Marva waved her hands vaguely. The silver rings of porpoises and opal-eyed cats adorning her fingers glinted briefly in the sunlight. "What*ever*! He transcends species!"

Sarah dropped her napkin onto her plate. "C'mon, let's go!"

"*Ooh*, are you going to introduce me?" Marva licked her fingertips and pressed down the ever-wayward silver-blonde lock in the middle of her forehead.

"No. Absolutely not!" Sarah slipped three twenties under her plate—enough to cover the tab and leave an outrageously generous tip—then grabbed her sister by the arm and all but frog-marched her out of Chicago's latest dining debacle. As was the way of things, within a week people would have to make reservations days in advance.

A strong northerly breeze swept between the buildings. Needles of cold, remnants of a nasty winter, blew through Sarah's flesh. Forced to battle fabric and wind just to get into her suit coat, Sarah switched her purse from hand to hand. Marva, as usual, was oblivious. Well, she wasn't actually oblivious, she was staring into the restaurant, no doubt trying to catch sight of Edward.

"So," her sister said, turning. "Just who exactly is the eyeful? I know he isn't your beau."

Miffed, Sarah snapped "And how do you know that?"

"Well, for one thing, I'd have heard about him before. For another thing, the family knows you have no time for men." Marva looked back into the restaurant, shielding her eyes from the sun.

Sarah snatched Marva's free hand and gave it a pull. If she didn't do something right now, Marva would set aside all sense of propriety and lean against the window, like a child salivating over a pastry. She'd probably leave nose prints. Or worse. "I still have a little time before I need to get back to the office. Why don't you take me to that shop you keep talking about?"

"Really?"

That got Marva's attention. The look on her pixielike face was comical: her green eyes opened wide and her lips formed a perfect "O."

"Sure!" Sarah said. Anything was preferable to having Marva commit another of her famous social gaffes that never turned out the way they should. Marva was, well, Marva.

"Oh, this will be so *neat!*" Marva grabbed Sarah's hand and jumped into the street, waving down a taxi. "Just you wait!"

And there, like magic, without a screeching of tires or blare of horn, was a yellow cab. Marva always had a way with things, Sarah thought, as she allowed her sister to bundle her into the warm interior of the car.

Marva looped her arm through Sarah's, laying her head back on the seat. "So, why didn't you want me to meet your friend?"

"He's not my friend. I barely know him. We just work together. That's all!"

"Then why are you blushing?" Marva asked. She grinned knowingly, then leaned forward to direct the cabbie to the shop she'd been trying to get Sarah to visit for weeks.

Sarah used the opportunity to glance at her reflection in the window. She *was* blushing! That would never do, especially not in Marva's company.

"Why don't you go for him?"

Sarah started. Marva watched her intently. Sarah sighed. She could never hide anything from her twin. Marva would pursue the subject until she was satisfied she'd gotten every detail out of her sister.

"He's married," Sarah said.

Marva snorted. "Right. Try again, Squeak."

Sometimes Sarah longed for a little of Marva's chutzpah. Didn't her Bohemian sister ever hear the voice of caution? Feel a shred of compunction? Demonstrate a drop of discretion? Or had Sarah managed to leave the womb with both their shares of reserve?

Marva seemed to live her life without that nasty recriminating inner voice that was Sarah's lifelong companion, cautioning her before she spoke or acted.

On cue, Sarah's little voice reminded her that she should watch what she wished for. Marva had neither a savings account nor a retirement plan, much less health insurance. Marva's portfolio consisted of pressed flowers and sketches of her lovers, instead of carefully distributed investments in real estate, stock options, CDs, and IRAs.

Sarah told her inner voice to shut up. She had her hands full with Marva.

"Here it is!" Marva leaned forward and waved a bill through the narrow slot in the safety glass.

The cabbie took his money and swept up to the curb, splashing a curtain of muddy brown water onto a pair of pedestrians. The driver didn't get out of the car, offer them change, or seem in the least bothered by the hostile hand gestures he was getting from the damp, dirty people on the narrow walkway in this little street well off Chicago's beaten thoroughfares.

Sarah pushed the door open and ignored the driver's complaint as it scraped the sidewalk. She offered her sister a hand, bobbing her head apologetically to the grumbling couple as they turned back toward their day. She wondered what had brought them to this lonely stretch of side road where they'd been splattered.

She looked up and down the street. Cars were parked bumper to bumper along the side road, water from the ongoing drizzle beaded up on their roofs and hoods, dripping off them onto the street. As far as Sarah could tell, her sister had dragged her to some real backwater section of town this time. She could still hear the blare of traffic and the noise of the city, but it seemed very distant—oddly so, in fact. The only taxi she saw was the one disappearing around the corner.

"Marva, I still have to get to work this afternoon. Where in the hell are we?"

Her sister just smiled. "Don't worry so much. I'll get you back to the office in a 'timely manner.' "

Apparently, Sarah's expression reflected her doubts.

"Really I will," Marva said. "Just trust me, okay?"

Reluctantly, Sarah nodded. This was fast working on becoming something much longer than the two-hour lunch she'd scheduled. It was the second time in minutes that her sister had asked her to "just trust" her. Prospects for the afternoon weren't looking good.

"So," Sarah said, resigning herself to her fate, "where's this shop?"

Her sister grabbed her by the hand and pulled her ever farther from the Chicago she knew. For the most part, this block seemed to be the back end of larger corporate buildings. A little florist's shop with its wares spilling out onto the sidewalk gave the drab gray street its only color. She wondered how it stayed in business. There wasn't a pedestrian in sight, other than themselves. The two splattered victims of the cabbie were long gone. This odd alley was what Sarah expected a ghost town to look like, not a Chicago downtown side street—it was eerily quiet, barely touched by the muted, distant sounds of the city surrounding them. The street felt as though it was somehow separated from when and where it actually was.

Marva took her hand and led her the short distance to the flower shop. Beside it, wedged between the smooth slate-gray granite walls of the modern skyscrapers like an out-of-scale child's toy, stood a boxlike building only a few stories high. Someone had painted it electric blue, with trim in lime green. It was so close to the floral store, it almost appeared to be a part of it, a neatly wrapped gift box to accompany the blooms the florist specialized in. A driftwood sign hand-lettered in silver hung in the window of the old-fashioned door, reading simply "The Shop."

Sarah searched the windows. No neon signs of pentacles, palms, or "psychic" blazed in or near them. That, at least, was an improvement over some of the other shops Marva had dragged her to see. On the other hand, she didn't need to ask her sister if this was the place. Once they'd passed the flower shop, it was their only option. The little store, despite its bright colors, was unassuming, as though designed to be missed by all but those seeking it out. Something about that felt comfortable to Sarah. She walked in without Marva's coaxing.

A bell jangled over the door. Sarah looked. It was an ornate bell suspended above the door by scroll-shaped iron. She noted that not just the bell was old-fashioned. There were no security wires tracing the door or, for that matter, any of the windows she could see from the entryway.

The Shop smelled of sandalwood and cinnamon—spicy, unique, and subtle.

In the far corner, an auburn-haired woman sat curled in an armchair, reading. Two cats were draped over her shoulder and sprawled in her lap, and a moppetlike dog curled at her feet. At the sound of the bell, she looked up, wriggling her nose so that her glasses shifted up. She smiled, nodded, and returned to her book. The little dog rolled its eyes to watch them. The cats displayed no interest in anything other than preserving their respective perches.

The store was larger than Sarah had imagined from the outside and looked more like a comfortably cluttered living room than a hub of mercantile activity. Shelves covered the walls; most of them contained books interspersed with bizarre odds and ends: statuettes; miniature cauldrons; mortars and pestles; crystals of various size and shape; and candles of every hue, size, and style, plus tapers and pillars, formed and in glass jars. Nestled on a table near a window were plants—herbs, Sarah guessed. On the shelves along the floor were rows and rows of apothecary jars. Sarah knelt, scanning the carefully penned names: Deer's Tongue, Devil's Shoestring, Ditany of Crete. Farther down the shelf, a container of bright red powder drew her eye. She picked it up, reading the label: Dragon's Blood.

"Let me guess, Marv, this is Instant Dragon," Sarah teased.

"Actually, no."

The sisters turned as the young woman divested herself of both cats and dog.

"It isn't even supposed to be real concentrated blood from a dragon. It's made from the resin of a palm tree." She took the jar and put it back in its place between Dogbane and Dutchman's Breeches. "You didn't come looking for herbs, so how may I help you?"

Sarah blinked and looked at her sister.

"I've been in before. Last week, remember? I bought—"

"I remember," the woman said, but Sarah held her attention. "What brought *you*?"

Sarah began to feel an itch in the middle of her back now that she was being studied so carefully. She managed to maintain composure and not wriggle like a schoolgirl. "A cab," Sarah said, then swallowed the chuckle. She shrugged to hide the fidget. "My sister keeps talking about your store, so I came along."

Determined to regain a little control over the situation, Sarah took another assessing look around. It really did look like a comfortable parlor more than anything else, but with a little bit of promotion, its whimsical charm could sell very well.

"You know, with a little advertising—" Sarah began.

The auburn-haired woman smiled and nodded. "So. You are a businesswoman, are you?" She turned and strolled away, pausing by a coffee table to rearrange decks of cards.

Sarah followed. Five years in trademarks and copyright research didn't invalidate her degree in advertising. The store would be a small client for the firm, but a new client nonetheless. "Well, we're all businesswomen to one degree or another, aren't we?" She fished around in her coat pocket and produced a business card.

In exchange, the storekeeper flared out one of her decks of cards and offered it to her. Sarah drew a card automatically, then stared, confused, at the picture of embracing lovers. She returned the card.

"You have a nice store here, but you could probably improve your profits," Sarah tried again.

The storekeeper took down three candle tapers and held them out. "Which would you pick: the red, the pink, or the green?

"Green—no, red, no—" Sarah shook her head, flustered. "I don't want a candle."

The shopkeeper shrugged and returned them to the shelf.

As she turned back, she held out a basket of objects glinting gold and silver.

"What are these?" Sarah peered into the basket. There were hundreds of keys of all different sizes and some in the oddest shapes she had ever seen.

"I call them Keys to Success. Would you like one?"

Sarah shook her head. The items in the basket looked fascinating. One so-called key was a swirling golden orb, another a disk. Sarah couldn't help but wonder at the locks these fit into.

"*Oooh*, these are cool, Sarah," Marva murmured from beside her. She reached into the basket and fished around, like a child playing with the wind outside the moving car. She hooked something and drew it up into the light.

Marva held out her find. A silver fish lay across her palm, folding to conform to her wriggling hand.

"What kind of key is that?" Sarah asked, picking it up by a fin. The fish was made of tiny articulated scales; most of them silver, but a few gold.

The shopkeeper shrugged and smiled. "It is the key to your sister's success. Each has an individual metaphorical meaning. You choose."

"No, that's all right." She glanced at her watch and gasped. "Marva! The time! Ohmigosh! I've got a meeting! I've got to go."

"Shall I ring it up?" the woman asked Marva.

"Yes, please." Marva handed Sarah the basket and followed the shopkeeper to a curtained corner of the store to make their transaction.

Sarah tried to contain her impatience. As she turned her wrist to look at the time again, the catch broke. "Damn!"

The watch fell into the basket of "Keys." If Sarah didn't know better, she'd have sworn it had been sucked into the very depths of the basket.

Rummaging through the basket, trying to find her watch was like trying to grasp a tiny bit of eggshell in a bowl of eggs. The watch slipped out of her grasp time and again. She sat down on the edge of the couch, plunked the basket onto her lap and began her search in earnest.

Mother had given each of them an heirloom timepiece upon college graduation. This was hers.

"Did you decide to get one, too?"

Sarah looked up to find Marva and the store clerk standing over her. "I've lost Momma's watch."

"Well, of all places!" Marva exclaimed. She bent over the basket, too.

The shopkeeper reached down between them, sinking her hand deep into the basket. When it surfaced, Sarah's watch, entangled with a skeleton key, lay on her palm.

"I'll get a cab," Marva said and darted out the door.

Sarah looked at the mess she'd made. She had thoughtlessly been taking out handfuls of trinkets in her retrieval endeavors. "I'm really sorry about this." The gold skeleton key clung to the watch. Frowning, Sarah tried to jiggle the key loose, but it was thoroughly snarled in the antique beadwork of the wrist strap. "This is so embarrassing."

"Why?" the storekeep asked.

Marva leaned her head in the door. "Gotta cab, but he says he won't wait!"

"Damnation," Sarah grumbled. She put the basket on the coffee table, shoved her purse onto her shoulder and tried to concentrate on disengaging the two pieces.

"Take it," the shopkeeper said.

Sarah looked up, surprised. "What?"

"Take it. It's my card," she laughed and closed Sarah's hands over the watch and key.

"Oh, at least take some money for it."

A car horn blared loudly.

"Sarah!"

"Go on. I have your card. We'll be in touch."

Sarah typed in a search topic and hit return. While she waited for the computer, she stared down at the key. It looked like a perfectly ordinary skeleton key to her, well, except for being made of gold and. . . .

She leaned closer. There *was* something more to the key. She turned on her desk lamp and pulled out her magnifier. Letters, written in legalese-sized fine print. She wiped away accumulated grime that made the writing illegible. Then she pulled out her makeup kit, selected a brush and dusted the key with blush powder. With any luck, this would do the trick. She blew the powder from the key's surface and squinted into the magnifying lens. Powder remained in the grooves and red letters stood out against the gold:

> *Whosoever invokes this key,*
> *the doors now lie open*
> *and the paths to succeed set free.*

A shock wave of electricity blistered through Sarah's hand, making her drop the key and jump back. The little skeleton key now seemed to have a life of its own as it rattled and shivered across her desk. Tiny sparks of green and blue, red and gold went up in showers that rose high enough that residents of the other cubicles might see the display. Fissions of power emanated from the key like waves of heat, enveloping and smothering her.

The key sent off one final display of fireworks, more spectacular than the first, bursting forth in kaleidoscopes of color. And then, just as suddenly as it began, it ended. The key performed one last spasm of dance before falling silent and unspectacular back onto her desk. The tension in the air broke and Sarah was able to breathe again.

With shaking hand to her heart, she peered over the walls of her work space. The problem with Cubicle Hell was non-existent privacy. Except for the single bank of overhead and security lights always left on, she appeared to be alone in this part of the building. She looked at her watch. It was well after nine p.m. At least there were distinct advantages to working late . . . not that she suspected anyone else had had the occasion to hide the results of a dancing, explosive key.

"Sarah?"

She screamed, one of those long piercing screams that

you can't stop even when you know there's nothing to be afraid of.

Edward raised his hands apologetically and stepped back. "Sorry about that, I thought you heard me coming."

"*Uh*, no—I—" Sarah stopped and drew a deep breath. She didn't think her heart would ever beat normally again. She started to speak, stopped and glanced over at the key on her desk. It had begun to glow again. She moved to stand in front of her desk and palmed the key. It thrummed in her hand, sending electric vibrations up her arm. "No, *uhm*, Edward, I didn't. You surprised me. I'm, I'm sorry for screaming like that."

"I guess, staying late, you get used to having the place to yourself," he said.

"Y–yes," Sarah said. She blinked hard and swallowed. She had now said more to Edward McGuinness—the man she and Marva had seen in the restaurant—in these few brief moments than she had since he joined the firm as the new wonder boy over a year ago.

"Do you always stay this late?" Edward asked.

Sarah shrugged. "I don't pay much attention."

"Nobody waiting at home for you?"

She shook her head, too surprised by the question to be offended. She licked her lips nervously. "And there's no Mrs. at home waiting for you?"

Edward smiled. "No, I'm all alone in this cold, cruel world."

Sarah laughed.

"Really," he said. He leaned against her cubicle wall, folding his arms.

The key in her hand tingled. Had he seen the confabulation? "So," Sarah murmured, "what brings you to this end of the building?"

"Honestly?" he asked, eyebrow rising suggestively. He sighed and pushed away from the cubicle wall. "I was hoping to take you out to dinner first."

"First?" Sarah was intrigued. "Before . . . ?"

"I thought, possibly, that if we went to dinner, something casual, perhaps tonight—"

"Edward, are you asking me on a date?" Sarah worked hard at keeping her jaw off the floor.

"If you say yes, then absolutely," he grinned winningly.

Sarah's heart melted under his smile. "But?"

"But?" Edward said. He shrugged and stared down at his shoes. "The people I took to lunch—you saw us at the restaurant?—well, they're from a law firm, Keyes & Rhodes. I've brought them on as a new client. They'd been with another agency before and were very dissatisfied."

"And this involves me how?" Sarah asked. The key quivered in her hand.

"I want you on my team," Edward said.

Sarah laughed. "I can't imagine how I could contribute. I've spent the last five years in trademarks and copyright." The key felt icy and still in her hand.

"One of their first advertising priorities is a corporate logo. They've not had the best of luck and their previous agency didn't have an in-house specialist. *We* do." He looked at her meaningfully. "So, would you be interested?"

The key sent electric shocks up both of her arms. Sarah bit her lip. "Do you really think I can do this, or. . . ."

"Or am I just trying to get a date?" Edward responded. He sighed. "This was why I'd asked for the date first. I guess it's true about office relationships." He stood straight and looked her directly in the eye. "Sarah, I would like you on the Keyes and Rhodes team, no matter what."

The key tingled in her hand. Hell, *she* tingled! "Then perhaps a date isn't such a good idea."

Edward sighed again. "You're absolutely right. Are you free tomorrow at ten?"

Distracted by the shock waves emanating from the key and his sudden about-face, Sarah said, "Beg pardon?"

"Are you free at ten a.m.? Ms. Keyes, Ms. Rhodes, and their junior partner Mr. Wingate will be here in Meeting Room 2. I'm sure they would appreciate knowing that our trademarks specialist is on-board."

"Then I'll be there," Sarah said. The key's emissions changed, from shocking pulses to a subtle nuance. It felt warm like a cup of hot cocoa on a winter's day, or a mother's embrace, gently stroking her hair, with a hint of spice, of an almost sexual pleasure radiating upward from her hands through her arms and into her whole being. The sensations caught her off guard. She swallowed hard. "I—I'll be there."

Sarah glanced at her watch. She had time.

Marva answered on the first ring. "Yeah?" she yawned into the receiver.

"Are you just getting up?" Sarah looked at her watch. Seven-thirty.

"What of it?"

Sarah bit her tongue. Marva could be pugnacious in the morning. After thirty years she should know better. "Sorry, Marv, I'm in a hurry this morning."

"What's the big deal?"

"Well, lots, actually. Uh, the store we went to yesterday? I can't find it listed in the phone book, the operator doesn't have a listing, I can't even find it on the 'net. It's like the store was never there."

"Don't be silly."

"Well, do you have a number? Address?" Sarah asked.

"Yeah, sure," Marva yawned. "What's the big deal, Squeak?"

Sarah took a deep breath. If there was anyone she could tell about the key, it would be her sister. "You know those keys, from the basket?"

Marva yawned and mumbled something vaguely affirmative.

"Did, did your key *do* anything?" Listening to the silence on the other end of the phone, Sarah held her breath and crossed her fingers. "Marva? Still there?"

"Uh, yeah." She sounded fully awake now. "What do you *mean* when you ask me if my key did anything?"

Sarah could hear Marva scrabbling through her purse on

the other end of the phone. "I just wanted to know if your key did anything."

"My key has been sitting in my purse since I bought it. What happened to your key, Sarah?"

"Ah, well, oh I forgot, I've got a meeting this morning—"

"Sarah Jane Parkinson, I will come down to your office and clobber you if you don't tell me what happened to your key *right now*!"

"Don't get all worked up. I really don't have a lot of time, but, it was weird. I just dusted it and read the inscription and then there were fireworks and Edward came to my office and the key kept tingling and it hurt when I wasn't going to accept his offer, but then when I did—*whew*! It was incredible, Marv!"

"Are you talking about Edward, as in that man from lunch?"

"Who? Yes, but this key—"

"*You* took Edward's offer and *then* what happened? Where did you go?"

"Oh, we didn't go anywhere. We were in my office."

"Your cubicle!"

"Oh!" Sarah felt the scarlet heat of a blush rising from her toes. "Marva, I didn't mean that!"

"No?" She sounded disappointed.

"It's supposed to be a key to success, Marva, not something to help my love life."

"What love life?"

Sarah bit her lip again. She could argue the point, but she wasn't about to win this war. It *had* been too long since she'd been on a date. "That isn't the point. I'm talking about the key."

"Right, your key to success. Go on," Marva said.

"You sound like a psych—" Sarah stopped. Her *key to success*. Edward had never come to her cubicle before and when she hesitated—Sarah rubbed her palm, feeling the unpleasant vibrations again. "Marv, it's my Key to Success!"

"Yes, dear, we've been over that."

"No! I mean it's *really* my 'Key to Success.' It's like magic, Marv."

"Squeak, sit down." Marva sounded impatiently patient. "You sitting down now?" She didn't actually wait for an answer but went on. "Okay, now, when I take you to a *magic* shop, it's magic. The thing about magic though is that it's, well, a spiritual thing. There aren't really big flashes of light and electric shocks."

"Yes there were."

"Sarah, you're beginning to worry me."

"I can't help it. I told you, fireworks went off and everything, right there in my own little cubicle and then Edward came over and he's never done that before and then he asked me to be on his team for a new client. He wanted me, especially *me*."

"Well, *duh*!" Marva snorted. "Squeak, you've been working at that job for years. You're an expert, a specialist. I've told you before, they don't appreciate you enough. At least now someone's giving you a break. If it happens to be an incredibly hunky man that you'll have to work side by side with for weeks, well, I'm sure that's no tragedy either."

"That's true, about Edward, I mean. But there really were fireworks, Marva, really, Honest to God!" Sarah looked at the clock. Eight a.m.! "Listen, Marv, I gotta go, but honest, this isn't a joke! There *were* fireworks and I mean coming from the key. The key felt all jumpy and buzzy like I had hold of an electric wire, except when I thought Edward was just flirting with me and I wasn't going to accept the offer, well, then the shocks made my whole arm hurt, but when I accepted, well, that was almost as good as—it was almost as good as—"

"Sex?" Marva said.

Sarah sighed. "Yeah. I gotta go, we'll talk tonight." She slammed down the receiver, snatched up her purse and ran for the door. It seemed like only the space of a breath and she was standing before the chrome and glass doors of the agency.

The doors were a shock of reality, breaking her from the

fog of thinking about magic. She stopped and touched the key hung by a gold chain around her neck. She wasn't ready to go in yet. She needed to compose herself, gather her wits about her before venturing into the big league.

Sarah turned right abruptly, heading into the public rest rooms. She took a seat in front of the make-up mirror in the lounge and tried to slow down, breathing deeply. The key began to thrum quietly again. It felt like a warm little heart-beat just over hers.

"I hope this McGuiness fellow can get his people to-gether soon. I'm not about to miss my court date. The judge was furious about rescheduling for the defense."

It was impossible not to hear the woman. *No matter how polite you are,* Sarah thought, *you just can't help but over-hear what other people are saying in the restroom.* Maybe it was all that tile, she didn't know, but one thing she did know was that they were talking about Edward.

"All I want to hear is something novel for a logo," said a second voice. "That would get us started. With this case, we're going to make a splash, and we need to be ready. We need to look sharp and aggressive."

The first voice replied, "But we also need something that says we have more than five years of practice in our own firm—"

Sarah checked her makeup briefly and left. She had made some notes last night and some of them were about to pay off. She just needed to show them to Edward first.

"Ms. Parkinson!"

Sarah stopped and turned. The receptionist waved two neon messages at her. The key warmed. She took a deep breath and snagged the notes from the young woman's hand. "Thanks, Jenny."

She glanced down at the messages as she headed for her section of Cubicle Hell. The top sheet was a note from Marva, brief and to the point: "Going to shop. Will call." The other was a note from Edward. As she had already de-duced, Keyes, Rhodes, and Wingate were early. The key felt like a warm, soothing balm against her chest. Surprisingly, she didn't have her normal case of nerves. She *knew* what she was going to do and how she was going to do it.

"There you are!" Edward said. He was close on her heels. "Keyes and Rhodes—"

Sarah showed Edward the message. "Are already here. They want something fast. Don't worry. I'll join you in a minute."

"What? I know it's been awhile since you made a presentation but—"

Sarah stopped, turned and smiled. She patted his shoulder. "Relax, Edward. Everything will be just fine. I drew up some things last night before I left."

Edward visibly relaxed. "You're a trooper. Five minutes, Meeting Room Two."

"Maybe six minutes, I need to copy a couple of things, but I'll be right in." She divested herself of coat and purse, grabbed a reference book and printed the file she had sketched out last night while waiting for her pulse to return to normal.

Edward and a short dumpy gentleman in his forties rose as she entered the room. Ms. Keyes and Rhodes looked up expectantly. They were sharp-eyed women, dressed and coifed perfectly. Ms. Rhodes was the more flamboyant of the two; her neckline was ever-so discreetly low and she wore a teal and scarlet scarf with her two-tone gray suit. Ms. Keyes, on the other hand, looked hard, clean and cold, like a shark.

Pleasantries aside, it was Keyes who struck first.

"So, do you have anything for us or will we have to come back?"

"Sarah was brought on last night, after our meeting, she—"

"Thank you, Edward," Sarah murmured and gently took over. The key felt like it glowed. She rose and handed each of them a folder. "Mr. McGuinness explained that a logo was crucial to your plans. As he's explained, I've been specializing in trademarks, logos, and such for the past several years. You'll find a couple of options that might suit your needs there in the folders."

Ms. Keyes opened her folder. Her brow arched. "Heraldry?"

"Yes, combined with modern elements, it shouldn't be too hard to combine family heraldic patterns so that you have something vaguely romantic and old-fashioned. The newer elements, the icons, will be what makes the difference, gives the look an edge. . . ."

Sarah sighed and leaned back in her chair. It had been too long since she had made a presentation. She felt sapped; the key, nestled between her breasts, felt warm and soothing.

"There you are!"

She looked up to see Edward leaning into her cubicle. "I can't believe you, Sarah. You were amazing in there—and less than twelve hours after I asked you onto the team! They've given us the contract."

Sarah smiled, basking in the afterglow. "I thought they might."

"So, how did you do it?"

She closed her eyes and touched the key. "Magic."

DIME STORE RINGS

by *Michelle West*

Michelle West is the author of a number of novels, including The Sacred Hunter *duology and* The Broken Crown, The Uncrowned King, The Shining Court, Sea of Sorrows, The Riven Shield, *and* The Sun Sword, *the six novels of* The Sun Sword *series, all available from DAW Books. She reviews books for the on-line column* First Contacts, *and less frequently for* The Magazine of Fantasy & Science Fiction. *Other short fiction by her appears in* Knight Fantastic, Familiars, Assassin Fantastic, Villians Victorious, *and many more anthologies.*

IT'S NOT my shop. Let me say that first. Not mine, never has been, never will be.

But yet it *is* my shop. Always has been. I don't know about the will be part, though, and that's why I'm writing this.

I wanted to keep things vague; to make that old store an every store, part of an everywhere that would make people think about things, pause for a moment, remember. But I realized that that would be cheating; wouldn't be fair. After all, it's *my* store, and it deserves a little more than a gloss of general words, a little gift of sentiment.

Let me describe it now. It faces out onto Queen St. West, one peculiar wedge in a row of buildings that were old before I was born. The years haven't been kind to its facade, and the deep green paint has a coat of dust and grime that darkens it without quite robbing it of color. But the windows are clean and clear, and they stretch from my knees to the edge of a carved wooden overhang.

On the inside, it has tall, tall ceilings, fifteen feet, maybe a little higher, and they've been buried under layers of junk. I think the ceiling might have been tin, or something metallic, once upon a time, and if new owners came to lease it— or buy it—it would probably have those ceilings again, restored at great cost, made shiny and new for people who love new things. But it doesn't have them now.

The floor is made of old boards beneath older carpets, and you can tell where a person is standing by the sound the floor makes; can tell if they're browsing, or walking quickly past the shelves and drawers, the little pockets of cheap toys, the old poster rack, enamel long since chipped and cracked. There's a trap door that sits someplace just before the three steps that lead to the back of the store, which is far enough from the windows that it's almost always a shade too dark, and every so often the owner will move boxes and display stands and put his shoulders into the task of lifting it.

Beneath it, stairs descend into the basement, the storeroom, a place marked clearly STAFF ONLY, although of course there aren't any signs.

The door is made of wood and glass, and nestles between two large bay windows, each window the proud owner of a large, gold-tinted word: Magic Shop.

Sometimes there are flowers outside, but not in the winter. In the winter, the steps, covered in astroturf, are also dusted with snow, with frost, with the salty dirt of slush spewed up by passing car wheels.

It's in the winter that I used to come to this place.

I followed my father, both of us bundled in scarves and hats and mitts made for us by my grandmother; a matching set. I loved them, then, even though the wool was scratchy and rough, because they so clearly marked us as family, as two: Father Daughter. My mother was not less loved, but she was home, wife to a house and the responsibilities of feeding and clothing us during the long, long hours my father spent at work or on the road.

It's not fair to her that I treasure the moments I spent with my dad so deeply; I know this now, as an adult with an adult's responsibility, and adult's caged life. But what's fair and what's real are often separated by a little bit of guilt.

My father's. Mine.

He used to take me to see the Christmas windows on Queen Street, at the old Simpson's building. He used to take a whole afternoon off work to do it, and we would look for presents for my mother, just the two of us; he would make her part of our private outings.

But he did it, I think, to give her a break.

It doesn't matter why he did it. We would take the bus, and people would smoke beside the cracks of open windows—if they were considerate. The bus driver would count change from the silver metal tubes he wore at his waist when he let us on. Often there weren't two seats together, and those were the best times, because my father would take the single seat and perch me on his lap, and we would chatter endlessly.

"What will we buy your mother for Christmas, bug?"

"Something really pretty."

"Like a pretty dress?"

"No, something *really* pretty."

"*Ah*. What, bug, is *really* pretty?"

"She likes flowers."

"I know. But flowers are harder to find in the winter, and they just die."

"She likes me!"

"She already has you."

"Can we buy her a diamond ring?"

And he would smile, a bit of a sad smile, and he would say, "Why don't we look?"

I never got my father anything for Christmas when I was young. Christmas was my mother's time, and ours; we were the pilgrims who came back to her clean little shrine with our offerings.

"Can we get hot chocolate?"

"Yes, bug."

The bus would roll on to the subway, and the subway would take us all the way to the heart of downtown, the place where lights flourished beneath the darkening winter sky. My father had old cameras, and many of the pictures he took with them are scattered about my house, some in frames, and some in the drawers of my desk, faded into sepia with time. He's never in those pictures; I am, wrapped head to toe in woolen coat and rubber child's boots, my hair tucked under grandmother's hat, my eyes peering up above the surface of scarf.

But when I see me, I see him, and I remember him.

The Simpson's building was a fine old building, with huge windows and displays that put the lights at City Hall to shame. There were reindeers with blinking noses, and elves, their small feet shoved into shoes with curlycue toes; there were matronly old women—Santa's wife and her elfin helpers—and workbenches across which small trains came to life. There were snowflakes, larger than my face, hung from string so fine they seemed suspended in air, absolved of gravity's accusation. Sometimes there were crowds as well, other fathers with their children, and mothers, or, young couples whose hands seemed eternally joined at the palm.

Sometimes other children were in prams with big heavy wheels. Because I was too short to see past them, my father would hoist me onto the perch of his broad shoulders; I was princess of the world then, my scarf dangling in his eyes, my hands above the hat that hid his bald spot, protecting it from the winter wind.

But Simpson's was expensive.

It's funny, to say that now.

We lived in a house with a television that had been donated to us by my grandparents; an old black and white box that had long since stopped working. My father took out the picture tube, and my mother made sock puppets for me, and

I would be the whole of our family's entertainment, surrounded by the television's old wooden walls.

Food was expensive; clothing was expensive if you didn't make it yourself. The toys that I dreamed of owning were also expensive. We didn't have a lot of money.

We have money now—not more than the neighbors, and certainly not enough to put us in the grand manors that hide in Rosedale and Forest Hills—and we have color televisions, new computers, two telephone lines; we buy CDs and DVDs and the books that catch our fancy; I don't even know how to use a sewing machine because store-bought clothing is often so much cheaper and time is also so scarce.

But then, we had little, and after we had gone to see the windows and look at the beautiful elegance of Christmas displays, we would trudge through the snow up to Queen Street. There, we would pause in front of the Magic Shop. And there, if we were lucky, we would find something beautiful enough for my mother.

The very first Christmas I came here—or that I remember coming here—comes back to me every time I open that old door, its skewed sign clearly stating the hours. There's a bell, a tarnished brass bell, that rings loudly when the door pushes against it. It always rings. It rang then. I loved that sound, and I remember standing in the door, the door's edge slippery in my mitts, opening and closing it while I looked up at the mouth of the bell, its metal clapper.

This Magic Shop was no Wiccan haven, no incense-heavy New Age retreat; it carried no herbs, no spices, no charms against evil, no symbols of love, no books about the greater Gaian mysteries. It wasn't that kind of magic. Instead, it had things that we could afford; tin cars, small soldiers, little horses and wagons, and jewelry.

It also had cups, and plates, and cards; bows and ribbons, paper; I think it had old forks and knives, spoons, tarnished dishes. It had ornaments for our tree, and a great angel for the treetop. We bought that, because I thought it was so beautiful; it was colorful, and the angel's face was white, her lips red as a rose, her eyes a lovely, deep blue. Her hair was golden; mine was black, black as night, black as a small Japanese girl's hair is black. I wanted golden hair, and angel wings.

It's hard to remember everything else the store contained; they've long since disappeared from the shelves and the cases. In their place are windup toys, kites, pinwheels, plastic swords and shields. But there are always angels for the tops of our trees, and I know now that those angels are tacky and cheap. I can tell it just by looking, even though they are kin to the one that I treasured for years.

But the one thing that hasn't changed is the jewelry. It's not real, of course. And when I look at it, plastic diamonds and rubies, plastic emeralds, soft blue edges so easily worn and broken, I feel two things clearly: disdain and longing.

The old man behind the counter has changed as well. His clothing is newer, and his face is paler, lined around lip and eye and over the edge of a beard that has whitened and thinned; he is slender, but his shoulders are stooped by the burden of age and the changing face of the economy. I don't know his name. I have never known it.

He smiles when he sees me. It's a quirky smile, but it lifts the age from his face, as if it were a veil.

"I haven't seen you in a long, long time," he says.

I'm almost surprised. But not really. He's not an elf, and he's far too thin to be Santa Claus and, besides, it's not Christmas. "I've been busy."

"I know. Everyone has. Have you come alone?"

It's such an odd question. But it's a fair one; I've never really come here alone before.

The world changed when I wasn't really paying attention. Color television. Computers. New buses to replace the old ones; new streetcars, new subways, new tickets. New names for old roads, gentler winters. I can't remember when we last had to worry about putting food on the table, although I know that both my parents gave up the dream of finishing school to do just that. A different world.

"What can I do for you?"

"I don't know." I linger a moment in front of the old case, seeing it with new eyes, seeing it with old ones.

He stands up, his trousers shedding folds. His legs are long, even if his shoulders stoop. "I should let you look around, then." He smiles. "If you want them, I have angels."

Just like that, a little smile in the corner of his lips. I expect him to say something about price, something that fixes them, gives them a value that can be easily grasped. But he says nothing; he waits for me.

The old store smells of dust. Of pine, of lemon, of pipe smoke. A cat peers around the edge of the counter, its tail flicking to-and-fro, as if my feet might move and catch its attention, inviting it to pounce. I don't know why I came here.

But I *do* know why I came.

My hands touch glass as I kneel in front of his old, gaudy display.

Can we buy her a diamond ring?

Why don't we look?

And that year, that year we found emeralds, rubies, sapphires; we found amethysts and topaz and aquamarine; we found a golden crown, a princess tiara that would never fit my mother's broad forehead. We found them here.

I remember it so clearly I can see my father's shadow standing just past my shoulder, and I want to weep. Tears come easily in the odd places, the corners of the world.

"You bought the sapphire," he says unexpectedly.

I laugh. It doesn't sound forced. "You remember that?"

"Because blue was her favorite color."

"Yes. And because you had no diamonds."

It was all blue glass of course; perhaps blue plastic. Memory is kinder than reality, it always has been. We make our memories; we knit them together out of disparate events; we define ourselves by what we make.

"How much was it, do you remember?"

"Twenty-five cents," he tells me, with a genial smile. "And you paid with one dime, two nickels, and five pennies. Your father let you count them."

"And it took me three tries."

He nods. "Three is a magic number."

"We bought an angel as well."

His smile dims. "I remember. You thought you wanted to be one."

"My father said I was."

"You never believed that."

I laugh. Sort of. "No, I never did."

"You wanted to be white."

It's such a shock to hear that, at a remove of so many comfortable years. It brings back other memories: the schoolyard taunts, the gleeful epithets, the shadows on my parents' faces. Their fear for me, their desire that I somehow fit in. The silence of their language, their parents' language, a language denied me by the choices they were forced to make. "Maybe. Maybe then."

"Now?"

"I just want to be me."

"Good." He claps his hands and the dust moves around the motion, like a cloud or a veil. "Tell me about the sapphire."

"You gave me a box."

"Yes."

"And paper. We wrapped it together, my father and I. I was afraid it wouldn't fit her finger." I was, although it had one of those cheap little bands that could be pulled or pushed to fit any hand.

"And did it?"

I nod softly. "She loved it," I tell him, because it's true.

"Because you chose it, and she knew what it meant to you."

"Because of that."

"And?"

"I. . . ." silence, now.

There is a magic in childhood that slowly fades. Time hurts it, truth changes it, experience makes it something other than what it appeared to be. Magic is all in silence.

"No," he tells me, as if I have spoken the words out loud.

I might have, kneeling before this case, the cat at my feet. "Silence is a way of hoarding things, and there are some magicks that die when hoarded, like cut flowers die."

"Flowers die anyway."

"Yes. But leave them, and they linger longer. Your father never liked them as gifts."

"I never gave him flowers. I never gave him anything."

"Ah." He comes round to the front of the case, shuffling; I hear the *thump* of something heavy and I see that he walks with a cane. It's an old cane, stained dark and pocked with deep scars, but its handle, beneath his wrinkled fingers, shines like gold. I can't tell what it is; some bird's head, or perhaps something serpentine. His palm covers it with care.

"The sapphire?"

I look up and I notice that his eyes are blue. I mistrust that blue in older eyes; cataract color, something that speaks of age, of blindness, of inevitability. But his eyes are lively; he doesn't squint.

"She wore it," I tell him quietly. "Around her little finger. On her left hand." Just that.

He frowns. "And that's why you've come back?"

I don't know what to say. It's funny. I've learned with time that I can stand almost anything. I can speak of every humiliating thing I've ever done and I can even smile when I do. But I protect the things I value. The things I've come to love, the scattered, fragile memories.

"Yes."

"You don't have to tell me what happened," he says quietly, "but I'm afraid I can't help you if I don't know what you're looking for."

I am *not* comfortable with this discussion. I could tell this man all about my own life, but my parents' life isn't my own, and I feel as if, in speaking of that time, I give them away. They're as much mine as anyone can be. But when I look up, trying to think of a nice way of saying that, I can't. He invites confidences. This store, with all of its little knick-knacks, its crowded, glorious junk, invites more.

I tell him, "I love my parents. A lot. It was different when they were younger. When they were my age."

"A different world," he says quietly, leaning forward to pat the cat at my feet, coming closer to me in the process, wizened, old, wise.

"When I gave her the ring, in that little box, it was the last gift she opened. I was *so proud* of it. I was so certain that she would love it. That it would make her more beautiful." Looking at the mounds of trinkets he's hoarded, I can almost wince, but I smile ruefully instead. "She was beautiful, to me."

"It's a rare mother who isn't beautiful to her children."

"And she put the ring on, and. . . ." All my childhood. I don't know what to tell him. "This sounds silly, but—"

He touches my hand. Just that.

"She grew younger."

"Younger?"

"Not young like I was, but younger somehow. And she smiled, and she turned to my father—not to me—and she said, 'Can you hear it, Hiroshi?' and he looked at her as if, as if he were seeing her for the first time. I didn't understand it then. Not really; I understand it now."

"What did she hear?"

"I don't know. I didn't hear it. But my father took her hand and he held it as if it were the most precious thing he had ever touched, and he smiled at her."

"You weren't jealous?"

I laugh. "Yes, of course, but—but no. They started to *dance*. My father never took my mother dancing. I mean, not that I can remember. They never went out anywhere. They never went out to dinner or anything like it—she *lived* in that house. Our house. But that day, that morning, when he took her hand, I thought. . . ."

I can't tell him anymore.

I thought they were in love. I thought she was a princess, and he was her prince. I thought, when they started to dance, that they must be in love forever.

"I wanted to touch them," I tell him quietly. "I wanted

them to pick me up and dance with *me*. But they didn't; they had eyes for each other, and whatever music it was they heard, it was only for them."

"That must have made you sad."

Children can be so selfish. "I was, a little," I tell him. "That year, I was. But only a little. She looked so happy. She almost never looked happy."

"Ah." He stands. "And today?"

"I wanted . . . to find . . . another ring."

He makes his way back to the countertop, and the cat deserts me; I am crouched on the rickety floor of his store, and all of childhood has passed me by.

"Children see things differently," he says quietly. "Why did you come today?"

"I. . . ." I wanted to be that child again. For just a minute. I wanted to enter this store and see that ring, and see it not as junk, not as a cheap trinket of plastic and glass, but as something so beautiful and so perfect, I could carry it back to my mother as a gift.

"You aren't a child anymore," he tells me sadly. "And children can pay the price for such wonder without even re-alizing what it is they give up when they do."

He's not talking about money. We both know it. But I don't know what he *is* talking about. I place my palms on the flat of the glass top and lean toward him. "I'd pay any price you ask," I tell him, "if I could find a ring just like that one again."

"Well, then." He smiles and takes a key from his pocket. "I have something for you."

He opens the cabinet and reaches in, and out of the mountain of junk jewelry, costume jewelry, things that are not and have never been real, he takes out a ring.

A diamond.

"I only have one," he tells me gently. He places it in the palm of my cupped hand. "One ring, and no boxes."

"What price?"

"This?" He smiles. "Inflation," he says, "makes every-thing more costly."

I reach for my purse and he takes one dollar and twenty five cents. He writes a receipt in his strong, slanted hand, and he gives me my change.

She wore that ring faithfully for years. I tried to buy her a real one, when I was old enough to work, when I had money. A sapphire. A gold band. And she accepted the new ring, even smiled when she lifted it from its velvet box.

But there's a magic in childhood. A magic in the things that are seen only through the eyes of children. She took the gift, understood that I meant something by it. It didn't fit her finger nearly as well and, because it was real, the gold was hard and, in the end, we had to have it remade.

I was embarrassed by the dime store ring. That's the truth. Embarrassed by the place it held in her collection, her meager collection, of things given her by her family over the years. We were not the poor family that we had once been, and the city of Toronto had opened its doors to us, slowly shedding the burden of a history that was too painful for my parents to speak openly of.

But the new ring didn't have the weight and the authority of the old one, and it was to the old one that she turned, time and again, until the day it broke.

It should have broken sooner. That's the truth. It was of shoddy make. How could it not be? Twenty-five cents, twenty-five precious cents, did not a lasting item buy.

But it broke the day my father died.

Significant, that, if you believe in such signs. The blue glass gem, worn and scuffed with time, fell off the tin band, its patina of so-called gold long since faded. My mother wept when it broke, quiet tears, but it was hard to tell if they were for the ring or for the loss; she said very little. She was there for me, and I was heartbroken, and she made room for *my* tears, and left little for her own. I was selfish. I admit it. I wanted my *mother*, when my father died; I did not want a woman with grief of her own, and a private, personal sense of loss.

She was not a strong woman, not in the way we use the word now. She did not argue, did not assert herself, did not present herself to the outside world as if she were a small dragon; I did that. But it was my mother who phoned the funeral home, and my mother who phoned the papers to place the obituary notice; it was my mother who slaved over the stove in the kitchen, making the food that would feed people kind enough to come to the funeral and remember my father with her.

I tried to help. But every act was a reminder of the lost years, the things that were now left only to memory, the death that made those memories so bitter.

And after my father's death, after the guests had left, after I had helped her clean up a house that would always be empty, she was alone. I had friends, of course, and I suppose she had some, but she had let so many of them go when family had come, and although they returned to offer food and comfort, they could not quite reach her.

None of us could.

That was three years ago. Three years, three Christmas trees, three shrouded winters. It was hard to go shopping that first year because it was the first year I had done so without my father. We made no treks to the wilderness of the retail world, and we conferred over no gifts, no clothing, none of the small musical instruments that she often loved; we touched no books, discussed no Santa Claus. I went alone. Alone was not a good way to go.

But my mother had never made a place for herself in our annual pilgrimages; or perhaps we had never made a place for her. I didn't know how to start.

The ring is in the box. Not a box from the store, but a box I found elsewhere, one solid enough to hold a real ring. A different one. I wonder what she'll think of me, carrying this trinket, this meager offering. I suspect she'll be polite because she always is.

Polite and distant.

She fell two and a half years ago, and she broke her hip,

and although surgery was done, the hip was never quite the same. She shuffled, where she once walked, and she couldn't navigate the stairs well. I had a chair installed on the stairs, one that she could sit in; she could move between the floors of the home we had always lived in, but even that became more and more of an onerous burden.

So after I buy the ring, I find a small tree. An artificial one. The nursing home that is now her dwelling doesn't approve of real trees in the antiseptic rooms that house the occupants who wait there, living out the passage of years. Waiting, I think, to die. I hate to think that. I hate the place.

But I go. I go because if I don't go, no one else will. I want to be a good daughter, but I don't know what that means anymore; my job occupies most of my waking hours, and I can't afford to lose it.

I don't know what I would have thought of this place when I was a child. I don't know if I would have come to it in dread, or if I would have seen with a child's eyes, and a child's desperate sense of need. I don't know if I would have had the courage to cross the threshold of swinging glass door, pass the gauntlet of nurses stations, walk past the old men and women who sit, confined to their wheeled chairs, their stares vacant, their hands outstretched as if any hand—any hand at all—will provide strength and sustenance.

But I am always glad that, walking this gauntlet, I do not see my mother. She has made her room her home, and she seldom leaves it; she waits for me to come, to help her into her chair, to take her out into the sunshine in the good weather and into the arboretum in the winter.

Today is not different. There is a tree in the hall, and it is so heavily decorated its branches sag with the weight of adornment. The nursing home has arts and crafts, as if its occupants were children—as I was once—who must be directed, occupied, taught to use glue and scissors, paintbrush and crayon.

I hate it here.

I ask her if she is happy, when I see her, and she smiles and tells me she's fine. But she's lying, and I have come to understand it in a way that defies the outer shell of the platitudes she offers me.

If she had been angry with me, I might have dealt with it, confronted it, made my excuses. But she has never offered me something as simple as resentment; she understands that my life is made of its own demands: work, and more work. She always understood work. She understood it in the long, empty weeks when my father was on the road, and we were the only people in the emptiness of our house; she understood it when he came home late, left early, pursued the demands of his job as if it were his sole calling.

I don't know if I would have been so understanding. I don't think that I am capable of it. Maybe that's why I never married; I could not imagine being cooped in a house, waiting quietly with a young daughter for a man whose return was never guaranteed.

She waits now.

She still waits.

Today, I walked beside my father's ghost, and the old memories were so painfully strong I turned to ask him time and again what he thought my mother would think of the item I held in my hands. He wasn't there, of course, and my memory didn't provide an answer, just a terrible silence. A reminder that childhood ends.

But I found my way back to the old store, and I stood in front of the old case, and I felt, for just a minute, I felt as if all the old, vanished things were once again some part of my life. And I thought of that ring, that old ring, and that single day.

I could almost see things as I saw them then. Almost. And I grasped for them as desperately as I have in years.

To come here is to forget, and I don't want to forget.

The nurse I am most familiar with smiles when she sees me. She likes me because I'm not above changing the bed, bathing my mother, helping with the things that in theory are already paid for.

In return, she keeps an eye on my mother; she tells me of

any falls or mishaps; she calls me when she thinks things are going as well as they should.

And how well should they go? How well can they, here?

But I smile when I see her. I nod, I ask after her sons, her husband, her dog. I make small talk while I hold, in my hands, a small wrapped gift.

For my mother.

Let me see it as I saw once. Let me see it, not as something that cost a dollar twenty-five in an old, weather-beaten store, but as that elusive ring that we hunted for, my father and I, in the streets of a long-vanished Toronto.

My mother is sitting in bed. She looks up when I enter. Her face is bruised.

I walk to her quickly and take both of her frail hands in mine; they weigh nothing. She tightens them, and they feel like baby hands, like hands that are far too weak to hold things. Even mine. I touch her hair, her face, seeing liver spots and wrinkles around eyes that have shrunk with age.

I hug her, because I always hug her; she allows this before she pulls away, shoving me gently with the turn of a slender shoulder.

I start to tell her that I brought a tree, but it's so self-evident the words desert me, and I busy myself setting it up, putting its small stand on the dresser table, unfurling its fake, green branches, its slender point. Too small, that point, for angels. Too small for anything.

"I've arranged for an ambulance," I tell her. "You'll come home for a few days and stay with me. For Christmas."

She nods and smiles. It's the only time I wish I had children. Because children see the universe in such a different way they almost can't allow for age. All infirmity is in the stubborn way they learn to walk, to speak, to reach for things that are just beyond their grasp. And she would be captivated by them, because she always has been; she would take some measure of the youth they can't even see and treasure it.

Instead, she has me, and I am beyond that. I don't fit in her lap; I don't fit in that tiny, perfect world.

And yet it is as child that I have come.

"I brought you a present," I tell her, awkward now that the work is done.

She looks at me, looks past the word, and smiles. "I'll open it when I come to your house."

I find myself at the shop again on the day the ambulance is to bring my mother home.

The old man raises a brow when I enter his store, shaking snow from the shoulders of my coat. Caught out, I apologize; the water has already melted down the runnels of cloth folds, adding to the stains in his ancient carpet.

"I want an angel," I tell him.

He nods. "The ring?"

"Not yet."

Nods again. He gets up, the cane supporting his weight, and I bitterly wish that such a cane could grant my mother the freedom of the life that she knew. As if he can hear me, he frowns.

"She's not a child," he tells me.

"I know."

He shakes his head, almost sadly. "You are."

"I'm not a child anymore."

"You are her child. And if you can't find that, you'll never see clearly enough."

"To what?"

But we both know the answer to the question. I'm afraid. I'm afraid, in this place, and I have never been afraid here.

No, no, that's not true. When I first came I was afraid that I wouldn't find what I wanted to give her. A different fear.

Or is it?

I wander the shelves, looking for angels. Failure then had never seemed so profound, perhaps because it was always such a distant possibility. My father had been at my side, his presence an unspoken promise of success.

I never thought I would do this alone.

"Nothing you like?"

The old man is standing at my shoulder, standing where my father might have stood. I should resent him, but I don't. "Nothing I think she'll like."

"Why is that?"

"She has pretty particular tastes."

"She didn't, when you were young."

"She did," I say ruefully. "*I* didn't."

"No. You were certain that where you saw beauty, she would see it; and you were so certain, so earnest, that she couldn't help but see as you saw." A pause.

"You want too much from her," he adds quietly.

"Now? Hardly. It was when I was a child that I wanted everything from her."

"Did you?"

"Yes. Everything, because. . . ."

"Yes?"

Because she *was* everything. She, my father, our home.

"Want everything from her," he tells me gently. "Want everything for her."

"I do, and she has—"

But he lifts an old hand; it hovers inches away from my lips, denying the passage of words. Of time.

He seems taller when he pulls his hand away, and the store seems brighter somehow. Maybe it's because I'm crying and water changes the passage of the light that reaches the eyes.

Maybe it's because, beneath the dusty racks of plastic covered ornaments, I find something that is so like the angel we bought years ago, I touch it without self-conscious thought; I say, "this one," and it means something I thought I had lost forever.

I want everything to be perfect.

I cook and I clean, and I move the tree from place to place—not that there are many places to move it. In the end, of course, it perches where it always did: in front of the mantel of a fireplace that we never used. This house, empty of father and mother, is mine now, and I am afraid to sell it; afraid to let it go. But it is mine by extension; mine because it was theirs.

I find my father's old pipes, and I pull one out. Its bowl is carved in the shape of a bearded man's face. It was not his favorite pipe but it was mine. He stopped smoking years ago, but he kept these, and I love them. I love the times he stood in the door of my room, tobacco embers glowing, the scent of their burning a wordless reminder that someone watched over me.

I find old slippers that I have never quite gotten around to throwing out. Funny; I got rid of many of the other things: a computer that was four years old and, by any standard of technology, ancient; the empty fish tank; the scads of old, squat ties; the old suits. But the slippers, the bathrobe, the pipes—I couldn't bear to part with these.

Nor could I part with the boxes of ancient Christmas glass, the old orbs that we—he and I—would take out together and put up, one by one. I decorated the bottom of the tree and he reached for the top, and in the background my mother would play the piano or sing the songs of the season, her voice an amateur voice colored everywhere by the tone of her great affection for tradition.

When I'm finished, and it takes some time, I remember the angel. I rush back to the bags that I left at the foot of the stairs. . . . and find that the angel is gone.

And when I return to the living room, she's there, on her perch, her false golden hair, her glitter-speckled wings, presiding over the treetop. She looks so pretty there, her face white as porcelain in the distance, her white cloth dress stiff as linen. I wouldn't have had the words for these things as a child.

It is into this room that I bring my mother. The bed is in the dining room; the stairs are simply too difficult for even the two of us to manage. The piano is silent; I do not think she will sit at it or play it, and I miss the sound of her voice:

that young voice, that voice that could carry a tune without quavering or tears.

Her eyes widen when she sees this tree, so different from the small boxed monstrosity that I thought might offer comfort in the nursing home. She loved the tree, although she never joined us in dressing it.

I offer her tea, and then, although I know it's not suggested, I offer her the shortbread cookies I baked, the tin cookie cutters I used another artifact of a childhood search for season. She takes both, holding them carefully above her thin lap, her eyes watering.

She said, "You found the angel."

I don't have the heart to tell her that it's not the same one. Because, for just a moment, it *is*.

I tuck her in. I want her to tuck *me* in, and I almost ask, because I think it will make her smile. But I don't, just in case. I kiss her forehead and she turns to smile, not at me, but at the tree that will be in her sight for the whole short holiday.

My arms are tired; she is not light, and I have borne her weight since she entered the house. I have her walker tucked away in one corner, since she doesn't use it much, and I have a chair, a wide, comfortable chair, at the foot of the tree. I only have one; I'll sit on the floor, as I always sat.

But there are almost no presents beneath this tree, and no stockings pinned to the mantel; there's no promise of Santa Claus, no threat of his loss if my behavior isn't quite up to the standards of Christmas Eve. I remember believing in Santa Claus, and the crushing reality of his lie escapes me.

In the morning, she is waiting for me, sitting on the edge of her bed. I don't know how long she's been up. I ask her—I shouldn't—if she's seen Santa Claus. If he ate the cookies we left out for him.

We didn't, of course; I haven't done that in years. But she smiles and nods. I take her hands in mine, intending to help her up, and then I kneel in front of her, and I bury my head in her lap, and I lay there, cheeks against the folds of her nightgown, weeping.

And she folds her fingers through my hair, gently stroking black strands back from my face, waiting in the silence of this motion until I can gather myself. It takes a long time. I don't want to move. I don't want to relinquish this momentary haven, this homecoming. No one else is there to witness it; no one will tell me that I have to grow up; that I have to be strong because I *am* the stronger one now.

Not even my mother.

When I stand up she waits for me, and the smile she offers me is a smile I have not seen in years. Not a Christmas smile, but something deeper and more enduring. I remember it when I see it; it cuts me deeply, but it causes no pain. I wonder that I could forget it, that I could ever forget it.

I help her to the tree. Or she helps me. It's hard to say which is true; this is the first Christmas that we've spent in a house that isn't really hers anymore.

But she takes her place in the chair, waiting patiently, and I bring her the gift that is small enough to nest in the branches of the tree. She opens the box slowly and carefully, peeling the tape away, taking care not to tear the paper. She never liked to tear paper; I remember that now, although I certainly loved the sound of the hidden being revealed.

She sees the box and sets it in her lap, gazing at it almost thoughtfully. I want her to like it. I want her to like it because we were searching, so long ago, for diamonds, and this is the first one I've found.

She lifts the lid of the box, and her face lights up in a smile, and this smile, this one I know. I hold my breath as she pulls the ring from the box and, for just an instant, that ring is the most beautiful thing I have ever seen: a gift for my mother.

She puts it gently on her finger. Her ring finger.

And I wait. And wait. And wait.

For what? For magic? For an instant I falter, and then I bite my lip. No. Not here, not today, not now. It *is* beautiful. It is a treasure. It is for her.

Her eyes widen.

She stands, her legs shaking beneath her, and she smiles, not at me, but at a spot beyond my shoulder. I want to see what she sees, but I don't want to lose sight of her face.

"Can you hear it?" She says, and my eyes tear. Because I can't. I can't hear a thing. She tilts her head to one side, and the gray hair that curls in short, dry strands around her neck seems to darken, to take shadow, the shadows of tree in early morning, light curtained against outside glare of winter snow.

"Hiroshi, can you hear it?"

I don't answer.

I don't answer when she rises from her seat, lifting her hand and touching . . . nothing. I don't answer when she leaves the chair, the confinement, the trappings of age and experience and a life that she lived in the only way she knew how.

But I feel something like envy, and something far older than that when she begins to dance. I don't know old dances well, but I know from the faltering steps she takes that she is not leading this dance. Her eyes are crinkled at the corners, and they are dark and wide, her lips are full; for an instant she is a young woman, and the frailty of age is the frailty of early love.

I want to watch her, and I want to leave her to the only gift that I have brought. I am torn between these desires, and they are both so strong; I want to run to her side, to wedge myself between her and the nothing that she dances with, to *see* as she sees.

But I can't.

Instead, I rise and I go to the kitchen, and I make tea because she drinks tea in the morning. I open the cookie tin, I reach for the milk, and then I stop because I hear a much louder noise.

I run.

She has fallen, and in falling, she has caught the tree; it lays beside her, fallen companion, glass ornaments shattered against the bare wood of the floor.

My father is not there. If there is music, if there was ever music, it is silent. She is silent.

I walk slowly, as if in dream, and I kneel by her side, and I know before I touch her that there is nothing in her that can respond to that touch.

The Magic Shop is closed now.

I don't know if it opened for Boxing Day; I don't know if it opened after. When I went back to visit, the doors were locked, and a sign in the window, sprinkled with the legalese of an annoyed owner, claimed the contents of the store in return for rent arrears.

If it weren't on the inside of the glass, I would tear it down. Not because I'm angry; I'm not. But because I want the windows to look as they did when I stood much below the serif fall of golden letters. Because I want to see, in that mirrored surface, whether or not I am six years old, and my father is beside me, wearing rough woolen mittens, a rough scarf, an old coat.

Instead, I see the notice, the words, the progress of time and commerce. I'm alone now. I know it, but I think it will take a while for the truth to sink roots, become as real as that notice, as the changing of the street, of all the streets that I used to walk through.

I start to turn, and I see that there *is* a shadow in the glass, and I look down to see the long, slender form of a cat. It crosses my feet and then decides to perch there, and after a moment, I bend and pick it up.

I wait, and wait, and wait; people pass by on their way to one sale or another. I have an appointment with a funeral director in an hour, but an hour seems like an eternity to a child, and I don't fear to miss it.

But the old man doesn't come.

And as the minutes pass, as the air grows colder in the light of sun stretching toward the horizon, I realize that he won't.

The cat waits patiently for as long as a cat can wait, and then it reaches up and bats the side of my cheek.

And I think I understand what it's saying, although I've never spoken much with cats before.

"Thank you," I tell the old man, wondering if he can hear me. Wondering if he walked away to the distant strains of a different music.

Wind fingers the door chimes, wresting music from them. "I'll take care of her," I tell the old man, and I take the cat with me, leaving the store behind.

GRAILS

by Bradley H. Sinor

*Not long ago Brad Sinor ran into someone he hadn't seen for
several years. The friend asked if Brad was still writing.
Brad's wife, Sue, said "There's still a pulse. So he's still writing." His short fiction has appeared in the Merovingen Nights
series,* Time of the Vampires, On Crusade: More Tales
Of The Knights Templar, Lord of The Fantastic, Hor-
rors: 365 Scary Stories, Merlin, Knight Fantastic, *and*
Such a Pretty Face.

IF HE could have had anything just at that moment, anything in the world, Jared Santee would have wanted a cigarette followed by a drink, several of them. Oh, they were
available, an all-night convenience store for the former and
any bar could help with the latter.

Only Jared knew that he wouldn't, That would be a sign
that she had won, since he hadn't had a drink in six months
or a cigarette in more than two years.

Instead he just stood in the doorway of the abandoned
building and stared out at the street. His thoughts, and they
were many and varied, for he couldn't find the comfort of
forgetting right now, raced from one to another. Always
though, they came back, back, to one image: Laura. Her
laugh, the feel of her hand in his, the provocative promise
her smile held as they walked along the beach. The images
almost made him forget the constant arguments over his lack

of a steady job, his dabbling in everything from sales clerk to security guard.

But all that was gone now.

The sudden screeching of tires, as an old pickup came too quickly around the corner, brought Jared back to the present. As the truck headed off toward the docks, Jared caught himself almost expecting to see another one coming after it in hot pursuit.

"You've been watching too many old movies," he said and suppressed a tired chuckle.

Jared looked around. He vaguely recognized the street, somewhere in the old city district. It was mostly warehouses, with a few decrepit apartment buildings mixed in. What few business there were had long since been locked up behind the protection of rolling steel shades.

"Jared, Jared, Jared," he muttered. "You're getting far too morose for your own good."

The green glow of his watch read two-fifteen a.m. Four hours since he had walked out of his condo on the west side, not three minutes after he had walked in it. Instead of the greeting he had expected, the kind that had awaited him since the day a year ago when Laura had moved in, he found only a single sheet of typed paper waiting for him, pinned to the purple hippo they had used to leave messages for each other.

I'm leaving. Don't try to find me. I don't love you. I don't want to see you again.

"It's not like you're the first man to ever get a Dear John letter," he said to the night. The words did little to do away with the deep gnawing ache in his gut.

There was a single word painted on the wall near Jared; repeated over and over again. Each iteration was a different color, each one a different style, all repeating the same word. WHY?

"Why not?" he muttered and drew a deep breath, letting it go slowly as if it were cigarette smoke. This was not the moment for deeply universal philosophical questions. Jared had enough of his own, and right then they all boiled down to the exact same question the unknown graffiti artist had posed.

Why?

He left the doorway and continued down the street. Jared had no idea how far he'd walked, or for how long, when he heard the crashing sounds coming out of an alley. Standing just where he could see him, Jared spotted a small man, perhaps four feet tall at the most, who wore a black dusterlike jacket that swept the ground. There was something almost feral in the way he held himself. In his right hand he held what for anyone else might have been called a long dagger, though for him it was a sword. A sword that had blood along its surface.

"Yeah?" he demanded when he saw Jared.

"Sorry to bother you." Jared backed slowly away, afraid.

"Well?" the little man demanded again.

"I heard the disturbance and thought that I'd see if I could be of any kind of help," Jared told him.

"Nope, though I appreciate the offer, I got everything under control for now." The small man gestured farther back in the alley.

Two bodies lay a dozen steps away. Jared had the feeling he knew where the blood on the sword had come from. They were clearly corpses. Nothing living could be forced into the unnatural positions Jared saw. One of the dead bodies looked like it had lizardlike skin. The other seemed to have odd protuberances on its back. Wings? Jared drew closer, intrigued by what he saw. Just what had he stumbled into here?

"It's none of my business, but you've got me curious about something," asked Jared.

"What?" responded the little man.

"Them," he gestured toward the bodies, not entirely sure that he wanted to know the answer. "Who are—or should I say were—they?"

"A couple of pains in the ass." The little man grinned. "Low-level enforcers for a local entrepreneur who claims I owe him money because of the outcome of some recent sporting engagements."

"Are you saying they work for a bookie?" Okay, at least this had a touch of something familiar.

"If you must use such a coarse term," said the little man. "Yes, a fellow by the name of Blaylock."

The little man took a long silk scarf out of his sleeve and began to carefully clean his weapon. When he was done both the weapon and scarf vanished beneath his coat.

"Well, I guess there's nothing that I can do," said Jared. "I'll be on my way."

Before Jared could turn away, the little man looked up and down the street and began to stroke his chin. "You know, now that I think about it, if you wouldn't mind, I could use a bit of a favor. And no, before you ask, it doesn't involve lending me money."

"That's a relief."

"Well, I was just on my way to deliver a package." From another place under the jacket he pulled a small parcel. It was wrapped in brown paper and sealed with clear plastic tape. "Don't worry. It isn't drugs. I was taking this to an antiques dealer over on Garibaldi Street. Realistically speaking, I think I may need to disappear for a while, at least until I can straighten things out with those fellows' employer. Problem is, I did promise to deliver this package and it needs to get there ASAP."

"So what's in it?"

"I told you not to worry about that, it isn't anything illegal. Plus I think I can make it worth your while to run my little errand."

Three coins hit the ground at Jared's feet. Heavy and yellow. Krugerands, that was his first thought. But when he saw the profile of Miss Liberty on one side and a double-headed eagle on the other he knew that wasn't what they were. Each one was in pristine condition, just as shiny and bright as the day it had been struck, way back in 1883.

"I don't know. . . ." Jared began, but realized that he was alone.

"Damn," muttered Jared. He picked up the package and read the address. Grails. 127 Garibaldi Street.

"Grails?"

Why?

As he walked, Jared kept remembering the graffiti-painted wall and its multiple depictions of that question. Once he had gotten himself oriented, Jared realized that he wasn't that far from Garibaldi Street. Only a matter of a few blocks to the west and then another dozen or so to the south.

The farther he went the more run-down the area became. No bright history now decaying away here; it felt like a place that had started out blighted and despairing.

"M'boy, what have you got yourself into now?" Jared's common sense said that the best thing for him to do right now was to just set the package down on the ground, leave it and the coins, and go back home to his condo.

Yeah, that would have been the sensible thing to do. Certainly a lot more sensible than walking down a deserted street in some god-forsaken section of town, doing a favor for some escapee from a bad road show company of *The Hobbit*.

Though there was that bloodstained sword. . . .

Not to mention Jared's incurable curiosity. . . .

Maybe that's why I don't just dump the goods and run home, mused Jared. *There are times when a person just doesn't want to do the sensible thing.* He had no doubt that Laura would say that this was yet another one of his damn fool ideas and he was getting himself deeper into trouble with every step he took. That had been the thesis for many of their arguments over the past few months.

He spotted Grails from a half block away. At first glance there was nothing particularly outstanding about the store, except for its very existence in this neighborhood. It looked like any one of hundreds of small businesses that Jared had seen over the years, a small, storefront, family-owned operation that was more than likely just getting by.

The most extraordinary thing about the place was that it

appeared to be open at this time of night. A convenience store or a gas station open in the middle of the night was one thing, but a place called Grails?

A good part of the store's window was taken up with intricately detailed lettering that formed the store name. Jared could see display cases just inside, but not what was in them. In the lower right-hand corner of the window was a small plastic sign that read "Open, Please Come In."

Jared touched the door handle. The metal was cold. When he turned it and pushed the door, the hinges groaned loudly, announcing his entrance.

"Hello?" he said.

No answer.

Given the neighborhood, he had been expecting a junk shop, or perhaps a pawn shop where local thieves could fence their latest acquisitions. This was neither. Banks of neon bulbs hung close to the ceiling, their light almost painfully bright in the night.

A number of counters and wall shelves displayed a variety of items: swords, Indian masks, reproductions of paintings, watches of various kinds, even electronic gear ranging from Gameboys to computers, some so ancient a pile of punch cards and vacuum tubes lay next to them. Clearly this was no ordinary shop. Though Jared wasn't quite sure what it was. . . .

"Welcome to Grails. Can I help you?"

The voice was just another one of the things that Jared could add to the list of things that had surprised him since he moved here from Baltimore. The speaker was a woman, with short brown hair, dressed in black jeans and wearing a cut-off Mozart T-shirt that left her midriff bare. She stood just behind him, but he hadn't heard the sound of her approach.

"Yes, good evening," Jared answered, feeling awkward as soon as he heard those platitudes coming out of his mouth. "I'm sorry to be bothering you this late. Although I'm more than a bit surprised to find your shop open at this time of the night."

"We're open when we need to be," the woman said, her voice touched with a "don't make foolish comments" tone.

"Okay, that's cool. Look, I—"

That was when the side door came flying open. A human tornado, in the form of a tall thin woman with short blonde hair and glasses perched on the end of her nose, came rolling through it, so furious she seemed to be spitting piss and vinegar with every step.

"You!" The target of her ire was definitely not Jared. He was thankful for the fact that he had never laid eyes on her before.

The young woman shook her head, a sad smile on her face. "Another satisfied customer," she whispered to Jared, and turned to greet the new arrival. "Is there a problem, Ms. Lansdown?"

"A problem! A problem, she asks! Yes there's a problem! That damn brooch that you sold me is the problem! You said it was just what I needed to add that little bit of something to my new outfit and blow away the producers on the new series! It was supposed to cinch my being cast!"

"No, Ms. Lansdown, I didn't say anything about it assuring your getting the part. I just thought it would compliment your outfit," said the brunette.

"All that producer did was proposition me! It made me so mad I dumped a platter of lasagna on his head."

"I'm sorry about that."

"You bitch! I told you what I wanted! Grails is supposed to give me that!" The Lansdown woman grabbed the other girl by the shoulders, clipping the edge of a display case. Both of them went tumbling to the floor.

Jared watched the two women for a minute. Then he grabbed the Lansdown woman, mainly because she was the one on top, and hauled her onto her feet. Trying to hold her was a struggle; she kept twisting and turning. But with every step he forced her farther toward the front of the store.

"I think you better go somewhere and cool off, lady," he said forcing her out the door. "Come back later, when I'm not around!" The door slammed behind her as she left, still muttering under her breath.

"Since you got rid of her, the least you can do is offer me a hand up," said the other woman.

"Oh, sorry." Her grip was tight and strong. Jared had a feeling that had the recent fight come to fisticuffs she would have come out the winner.

She straightened her shirt and brushed her hair back into place. "I never promised her that the brooch would be what she wanted. I just said it was what she needed and, in the long run, I think it was. I'm pretty sure, in a couple of days, she'll get a call from a casting director who saw her little performance with the producer, and who wants her to audition for a sitcom."

"I don't understand."

"It doesn't matter . . . I'm sorry I didn't get your name."

"Santee, Jared Santee."

"My name is Tanith Zachary. Now, understand that I do appreciate your stepping into help. But there wasn't any need. Here at Grails, we do occasionally get unhappy customers. It wasn't anything new."

"All right." Jared nodded. "I wasn't planning on coming here tonight anyway. In fact, until a little while ago, I didn't even know Grails existed."

"Really? That happens sometimes, Mr. Santee. So, welcome to Grails. How can I help you tonight?"

"It's more like I'm helping someone else out," Jared offered the package to her. "I ran into this little guy a few blocks from here. He asked me to deliver this to you."

Tanith's face went pale when she saw the package. "Who gave you this?" she demanded. "Is he still alive?"

"Yes, he's still alive, at least he was about fifteen or twenty minutes ago. I never got the guy's name, but he was a little guy in a longish coat."

She ran her eyes up and down Jared. "About four feet tall, most of it solid attitude?"

"Yeah. A poster boy for attitude, in fact."

"Rupert!" she muttered under her breath. "There are moments I wonder why I don't kick his butt from here to San Francisco!""

"Look, he was okay. Some . . . things had jumped him and. . . ."

She held up her hand. "Wait, you need to be telling this to my father."

"Okay by me, I guess. Did you say the little guy's name is Rupert?"

"Yeah. Got a problem with that?"

From her tone Jared had the feeling that Rupert wasn't the only one who had a large dose of attitude. "No! Shall we go talk to your father?"

Jared was completely lost.

Tanith led him to the back of the store and down a narrow hallway. Their route soon passed through room after room, down some staircases, up others, through more hallways than he thought he had ever seen in any building; more, he was sure, than should have been in the old building that housed Grails.

Some of the rooms they passed were obviously storage areas, with narrow walkways between huge crates, the light so dim that he could barcly see Tanith a few steps ahead of him. Other rooms held the weirdest assortment of items that Jared had ever seen, from a gargoyle statue with a clock in its belly to costumed dummies wearing outfits that would have been contemporary during Prohibition. In one he saw an ornate coach and was certain that there were horses' whinnies coming from the far corner of the room.

In the center of yet another warehouse-sized room, filled to the brim with still more packing crates, sat a big mahogany desk and file cabinets; on its inlaid top was a laptop computer centered on a large blotter, right next to an old-style Royal manual typewriter.

Sitting behind the desk was a man, his red hair streaked with odd gray highlights. He didn't seem to notice their arrival, as he was reading a comic book and had a pair of headphones wrapped around his ears.

"Dad," Tanith called out. When the man didn't respond, she stepped up next to his chair and pulled his headphones off.

"Oh, hello, dear," the man said nonchalantly. "Is that young man your date for the evening?"

"Hardly," she snapped. Jared could feel the sting in that one word and didn't particularly like it.

"Sir," he said to Tanith's father. "My name is Jared Santee. I'm not really sure just what is going on here. I was asked to do someone a favor by delivering a package to your store. Just as soon as your daughter saw the package she got highly agitated and said we had to come talk to you."

"Well, this is unusual." He extended his hand to Jared. "Forgive me, Mr. Santee, my manners are lacking sometimes. My name is Nathan Zachary. Let me welcome you to Grails. As you might have guessed, my daughter and I operate a rather unusual store."

"I'll say," said Jared.

"Dad, we really don't have time to give him the ten-cent tour. Look at that." She gestured at the package.

Zachary pursed his lips as he held it to the light. "Not good, not good at all," he said. "Is Rupert alive?"

"As I tried to tell your daughter, this Rupert, as of a few minutes before I walked into your store, was very much alive. He was looking a little disheveled, but he was very much alive." Jared was getting a little tired of repeating this litany.

"Disheveled? How so?"

"Apparently he'd had a run-in with a couple of guys who worked for some bookie by the name of Blaylock."

"*Ahh*. That doesn't surprise me, then. Rupert's gambling is nothing new," nodded Zachary. "Did Rupert give you anything else besides this package?"

Jared fished the coins out from his pocket.

"Would you look at that!" said Tanith. "Rupert turning loose of money? If he's done that, then he's scared, really scared."

"Knowing Rupert, he's probably been trying to draw to inside straights," said Zachary. "That'll get you every time."

"Speaking of money, where is this Rupert getting mint-condition Double Eagles," asked Jared. "Aside from the gold's value, do you understand how much each of those coins is worth, just as a collector's item?"

"Quite a bit," nodded Zachary. "Let's just say that Rupert has access to those coins and a lot more like them. Of course, getting him to turn loose of any is a major production. Though he goes through paper money like it's water."

"Dad, I think this is Rupert's way of saying he knows he's in big trouble. I think he's sending for help."

"I have to agree." A spasm of coughing ripped through Zachary. "Forgive me, it's a combination of asthma and malaria that acts up on me every now and then. I'm afraid I'm not in any shape to do anything about Rupert. Of course there have been times when I would say that he wasn't worth the trouble of saving."

"Dad, he's family," Tanith said. "We have to do something. Leave it to me. Nice to have met you, Mr. Santee. Hopefully you can find your way to Grails again sometime."

She was gone before Jared could say anything. Her father just shook his head and sat back down in his chair.

"She is as stubborn as her mother was."

Jared couldn't take it. Before he could stop himself, he yelled, "What in the name of all creation is going on here? What is this place? Who are you people?"

"It's funny you should use that particular phrase, Mr. Santee ... all creation. You might say, it fits Grails. This store is, shall we say, a central point for things, things that people have lost and want back. People come here because they need to find their way here. My daughter and I try to help them find what they are seeking. Sometimes they don't even know what they're looking for."

"That's a little too *Twilight Zone*-ish for me. Are you saying this is where all those socks that always disappear end up?"

"Sometimes." Zachary laughed. "Before you ask, I have

no idea why it happens or how it works. It just does. People come here looking for something. It might be major or minor, but it is important to them. They will find what they need at Grails. Always. It might not be what they want, but it *will* be what they need. Tanith and I, along with my late wife, have always tried to help the people who come here."

"And Rupert is one of those people?"

"He came in the door about twenty years ago and quite surprisingly kept finding his way back. We get very few repeat customers. I think he sort of needed a family, and that's what he got with us." As he spoke, Zachary opened the package up and removed a leather-covered jewelry box. Inside was a silver necklace that held a green wire-wrapped stone that reflected the light into a rainbow. "Rupert helped us raise Tanith, even suggested her name. I guess you could say he's kind of like her godfather," he said and began coughing again. "Gads, I hate it when my own body is acting against me. Look, I'm afraid that Tanith may need help. She's as stubborn as her mother and would never admit that she needed help, even to herself. I know I have no right to ask, but I'm going to anyway. Is there any chance you might be willing to go with her?"

For no reason that Jared understood, he nodded. "Why not? If I get myself killed, it will fit with the rest of the things that have happened to me tonight."

"Take a wrong turn on your way out?" asked Tanith.

Jared shook his head.

Her father had been quite detailed in giving him the necessary directions and Jared'd had no trouble in finding the dressing room where Tanith was preparing to leave. Tanith had exchanged her T-shirt for a sweatshirt and was in the midst of putting on a vest made of what looked like Kevlar armor when he walked in.

Why was he doing this? That was a damn good question. Jared didn't have an answer and he didn't think that he'd get one anytime soon. But he knew that nothing would stop him from going with Tanith tonight.

"I'm exactly where I need to be," he said.

"Look, I don't have a whole lot of time and I sure don't want to have to be baby-sitting you tonight. If Rupert has gotten himself involved with who I think he has, then it's going to get a mite rough out there," Tanith told him.

"You mean that bookie, Blaylock."

"Exactly. You stand a pretty good chance of getting very dead tonight. So why don't you take off?" she said.

When Jared just stood there looking at her, Tanith shrugged. "Okay, fine. Come, then. It's no skin off my nose!" She went over to a small cabinet and began to go through several of the drawers, pulling out a number of items that she slipped into her pockets. "Look in that closet over to your left. I think you'll find some body armor that will fit you."

Indeed he did. The armor wasn't all that heavy, not like conventional Kevlar, but it had a sturdy feel to it and helped to bolster his confidence. This whole thing was crazy. He'd definitely gone down the rabbit hole and was falling deeper every second.

"Are we going to be needing guns?"

Tanith shrugged and gestured at a set of drawers. "If you feel the need," she said. "Third and forth drawers over on the left. Ammo should be in the back."

There were half a dozen pistols of various sorts in the top drawer, ranging from revolvers to automatics. Jared picked a Glock. He found a matching ammo clip that fit snugly into the gun's butt; two others just like it went into his pocket.

Tanith handed him a sheathed Bowie knife, the twin of the one hanging from her own belt. "In case we need to work quietly."

"Am I correct in assuming that you have some kind of idea where Rupert may have gone to ground? He did say that he would be needing to disappear."

Tanith laughed. "Rupert has his own definition of things. His idea of making himself scarce means going to a different bar than the one he normally hangs out at or getting his meals at a Chinese joint rather than an Italian place. I'm pretty sure I can find him."

As he followed her, Jared found himself with the oddest feeling that they had forgotten something. It was a nagging sensation that wouldn't let go. But he just couldn't think of what it was.

"Having second thoughts?" asked Tanith as they passed the desk where her father had been sitting. There was no sign of Nathan Zachary.

"No. Flashes of intuition." Jared darted into the office. The wrapping paper was exactly where the elder Zachary had left it, though it took a moment to spot the necklace. Only the thin silver chain was visible, hanging over the edge of a plastic police riot helmet.

Jared grabbed the necklace, and the nagging feeling slipped away as his fingers wound through the chain. He joined Tanith at the door.

"What are you waiting for?" asked Tanith.

"Nothing. I think we're ready now."

"How nice of you to say so."

"Look, if you want me to take you for a midnight stroll, just tell me. Maybe next time we can leave the armor at home and I can bring you flowers."

"Shut up," Tanith whispered.

They had been on Rupert's trail for just over an hour. He'd visited a pool hall, an all-night diner, and a twenty-four-hour liquor store. They'd been just behind him every time but still hadn't caught up with him. Jared couldn't help but notice that Tanith was getting into a fouler and fouler mood.

He wasn't having fun yet, but he was still too curious to abandon the chase and go home.

Finally they came to Harridan Park. The park was built five years before, with the idea it would be the centerpiece for the rejuvenation of this part of the city. Only it had been mired in bureaucratic bickering since the original contractors had gone bankrupt.

At night, the only people who dared to enter the park were either desperate or dangerous: the homeless, addicts, predators of various sorts, gang-bangers, and a few others who preferred that their business not take place in the light of day.

Jared followed Tanith into the park and hoped that they looked dangerous enough to hold their own.

"There's just a chance he might be here." Tanith said. "He says it reminds him of Ireland."

"Rupert is Irish?"

"He likes to think he is."

Before Jared could say anything more, he spotted Rupert. The little man was standing near a park bench, about fifty feet away from them, busily rolling a cigarette. Several abandoned butts lay on the ground, suggesting that Rupert had been there for some time.

"There he is!" Jared said. "Let's grab him and get out of here."

"No, wait. I've got a bad feeling about this."

A man, dressed in a western shirt, jeans, and wearing a baseball cap, stepped up beside Rupert and spoke. They were too far away to hear what was said, but the little man's face had gone pale when he realized he wasn't alone. The newcomer produced a lighter and held it close enough to light Rupert's cigarette.

"Well, well, well," said Tanith. "We may have had a bit of luck after all. When you said it was Blaylock who had laid off Rupert's bets, I thought it was the old man. Instead it looks like we're dealing with Junior, his number one son."

"Is that good?"

"Matter of opinion. Maybe." She pulled a stone out of her pocket and pushed it into Jared's hand. "Hang on to this. Squeeze it when you need to. It will let you see things the way they really are."

Jared did as he was told. The scene before him shifted immediately, like some weird movie special effect. Rupert looked the same, but there were some changes in Junior. His hands were now covered with fur, as was his face, which had taken on a distinct wolflike appearance.

"Are we talking werewolf bookies here?" he asked Tanith.

"Lycanthropes, that's the proper term. But werewolves will do. Young Mr. Blaylock doesn't like to work alone. Look back in the bushes," whispered Tanith.

There were two other men standing some distance back from Blaylock. Even at this distance, Jared could see their wolflike features.

"So, do we call a dog catcher?"

"Hardly." Tanith looped her arm around Jared's waist. "Put your hand on my ass and try to act like we're the only people in the world. With a little bit of luck, we might live another ten minutes. Just be ready to act when I say so."

"I think I can handle that," he whispered. Right then, it occurred to Jared that he hadn't thought of Laura for some time. That didn't bother him in the least. The pain of her rejection was still there, deep in his gut, but it was something that he would deal with later. He suddenly knew that he could.

If Rupert recognized them, Jared didn't know. The little man had dropped his cigarette and started rolling another one. This time around his hands were so shaky that he could barely get the makings out of his pocket.

Jared could see, out of the corner of his eye, Blaylock watching them as they passed. When his attention shifted back to Rupert, Tanith launched herself at him, driving her shoulder hard into his chest. The collision was enough to send Blaylock stumbling backward. Before he could do anything, Tanith kicked him hard in the knee. He rolled around on the ground in agony.

Jared leveled his gun at the other two.

"You've got to be joking," one of them said.

"Silver bullets." Jared said. "At this distance I can't miss. I'll rip whatever I hit to shreds."

"One of us could take you if we both charged you."

"Maybe, maybe not, but I'd sure as hell blow one of you

away. Maybe both, if I'm fast enough. You ready to take me on?"

Tanith had her arm around Blaylock's neck, her big Bowie knife against his throat.

"Now, listen up, fur-face. This blade is solid silver, blessed by three different popes, two chief rabbis, a voodoo priest and a whole bunch of other people who would just love to see me use it to skin you alive!"

"You bitch! I'll rip your guts out and pan fry them," Blaylock screamed. "Do you know who I am? Even if you manage to get away, I can promise you that you won't live long enough to see the sunrise."

Tanith pulled the edge of her blade along Blaylock's throat. A tiny trickle of blood followed it. "Trust me on this one, dog breath. I'll live a lot longer than you, if you don't cooperate."

"I'll grind you—"

"Offhand, Junior, I would say that she's got you where she wants you. Personally, I'd try negotiating with her, if I were you."

A gray-haired man dressed in an elegantly cut silk suit stood next to the park bench, holding a black wooden cane with a silver cobra head in one hand. Where he'd come from, Jared had no idea.

Jared squeezed on the stone that Tanith had given him. When he looked at the man again, he saw the image of the biggest, meanest-looking wolf that he had ever imagined. This werewolf made the others look like ninety-eight pound weaklings.

"Father! She's using some sort of witchcraft to get an unfair advantage over me. I can handle this whole thing," growled the younger lycanthrope.

"I really wonder why I brought you into the business. Maybe I should have financed that bluegrass band you wanted to form. Oh, well, hindsight is twenty-twenty." The older Blaylock pointed his cane at Rupert. "I have a breakfast appointment with the mayor. So let's see what we can do about bringing this whole thing to a peaceful conclusion. Rupert here is hardly worth a fight."

"I barely know him," said Jared. "And I agree with you."

"Hey," yelled Rupert. "I just asked you to do me a little favor and you insult me!"

"Shut up, Rupert," said Tanith.

"Look I'm just defening my reputation. I'm the one who is being insulted."

"Shut up, Rupert," Tanith, Jared, and the elder Blaylock all said at once.

"How much does he owe you?" asked Tanith.

From inside his jacket the older man produced a small account book. "Let's see, rounding off a few numbers, it comes to just over fifty thousand. Rupert, did you really start placing bets on girls' volleyball?"

"Hey, I had some insider information."

"But you lost."

"A run of bad luck. It can happen to anyone."

"Shut up, Rupert," said Tanith. "How about we trade you? I'm willing to take Rupert's IOU's for the life of your son."

"I suppose you realize that, knowing this little reprobate, he'll be back making bets by this time tomorrow."

"That's then, this is now. So will you do it?" asked Tanith.

"All right. It's a deal. Maybe this will teach my pup to be a bit more selective on whose bets he takes. But I will require something else as well, a token payment in lieu of what Rupert owes me."

"Such as?" asked Tanith.

Jared acted on a hunch, pulling the necklace he'd taken from Zachary's desk out of his pocket. The stone was glittering even in the dim light of the park. It felt like the right thing to do. "Will this do?"

Blaylock walked closer, looked at it for a moment, and nodded. The jewel vanished into his hand with a single movement.

"Come along, Junior. Your two friends can follow me as

well. Tanith, would you please give my best regards to your father? Tell him I'll see him Thursday."

The Blaylocks were gone, as soundlessly as they had come. Jared slipped his gun into his belt and turned to Tanith. "Your father knows that guy? What's Thursday got to do with it?"

"That's when they play pinochle."

The eastern horizon began to glow a ruddy red, though stars still held sway in the rest of the sky. Jared had the feeling that in daylight this part of town would only look worse than it did at night.

After they left the park neither he nor Tanith said anything. Rupert, on the other hand, had a number of things to say, on a number of subjects. Most of them boiled down to the fact that he was one of the nicest guys in the world, extremely misunderstood, and the world did not appreciate his genius. After a block or two Jared had pretty well tuned him out.

When Tanith finally spoke, he heard her quite clearly.

"Why?"

"Why what?"

"Okay, smart-ass," she said. "I'll rephrase the question. Why did you do it? Go with me, I mean, and end up risking your neck to save Rupert? Why are you here?"

Jared had been asking himself that, as well. Oh, there were any number of pithy one-liners he could toss off, such as "Why not?" or "It seemed like the thing to do at the time," but those weren't right.

"You went because you've known him all your life. What did you tell your father? 'He's family?' I guess I went because he needed help and I felt I needed to do something for someone else. That's about the only answer I can give you," he said.

"It'll do."

"Well I, for one, am glad that you knew to pack the valuables and some silver bullets," Rupert said.

"Yeah, how did you know about that stuff? Especially the

silver bullets? You didn't know anything about the lycan-thropes until we got to the park."

"Oh, that," laughed Jared. "Who said I had silver bullets in my gun?"

"You did," said Rupert. "I heard you tell those two pug-uglies."

"I lied."

The strands of one of Beethoven's early symphonies drifted out of speakers set back from either side of Nathan Zachary's big mahogany desk. He leaned back in his chair, eyes closed, and savored the music. It had been one of his wife Elaine's favorite pieces; on their first wedding anniversary he'd taken her to a concert that featured it.

"God, I miss you so very, very much, sweetheart," he whispered.

"Are you getting sentimental again?"

"Shut up, Rupert."

The little man sat in a papasan chair just to one side of Nathan's desk. When Nathan finally opened his eyes he noticed that Rupert had picked up the wine bottle and was shaking his head as he looked at the label.

"What's the matter?" asked Zachary.

"Really, Nathan, the '63? You've got a lot better vintages in your cellar than this. I should know. I helped you stock it."

"Stop being such a wine snob; it's a perfectly good year. Just pour us a drink and answer my question," he told the little man.

Rupert poured several inches of wine into two glasses and passed one across the desk. "You had a question?"

"Yes. Don't play smart-ass on me. Are you sure?"

"Of course I'm sure," said Rupert, smiling. "Jared said he 'felt' that he 'needed' to be there to rescue me and that he 'needed' to take the necklace along. Sounds just like what you've been wanting."

Nathan hoped that the little man was right. The proper person "knew" what a particular visitor to Grails "needed."

Not what they wanted, but what they needed. That was the key. The key to Grails. Nathan had always described it as an itch at the back of his neck, one that he couldn't scratch until he found just the right item.

"I've been wanting to retire, now that Tanith is old enough, but she needs someone to help her run this place," said Nathan. "So I think I'm going to offer Mr. Jared Santee a job here. I don't know much about his background, but I have a feeling this place might fit him to a tee."

"Tanith is going to love this. The last time I saw them they were fighting like cats and dogs," said Rupert.

Nathan smiled. "Sort of reminds me of when Elaine and I were first married. Who knows? This may not be what my dear daughter wants right now, but I have a feeling it is exactly what she needs."

Both men laughed.

MIGHTIER THAN
THE SWORD?

by Josepha Sherman

Josepha Sherman is a fantasy novelist and folklorist, whose latest titles include Son of Darkness, The Captive Soul, Xena: All I Need to Know I Learned from the Warrior Princess, *by Gabrielle, as Translated by Josepha Sherman, the folklore title,* Merlin's Kin, *and, together with Susan Shwartz, two STAR TREK novels,* Vulcan's Forge *and* Vulcan's Heart. *She is also a fan of the New York Mets, horses, aviation, and space science. Visit her at www.sff.net/people/Josepha.Sherman.*

BLAME it on the editor. Or the story. Or the deadline.

Right, there's a good excuse. I mean, isn't that always the problem when you're a freelance writer? Deadline. Good name for it, too—particularly on a Sunday—morning, or barely so, when you've been typing up a storm all night and suddenly the damned computer crashes.

Right. Sunday morning, crack of dawn, and no way to get that less-than-24/7 tech help. And that blasted deadline, Monday Nine a.m. Or Else, staring me in the face.

Or, rather, the hair, since right now I had my head buried in my hands and was silently swearing, all the time thinking, *I knew I shouldn't have taken it on, not with so little time.*

Okay, this wasn't getting me anywhere. I had the whole

story plotted out in my mind, and so what if I couldn't get it onto the computer today? I could at least write down the story and get to one of those rent-a-computer places tomorrow morning at the, yes, crack of dawn, type my fingers off, and that would be it. Sleep, after all, was for wimps.

Yeah, right. I could do this.

I could? Pen? Pencil? I rummaged frantically through the piles of paper all over my desk. Nothing. Pen holder? Empty. Desk drawers . . . blast it, I had to have a pen in there somewhere!

Did I? You get into the computer habit, you forget about the low-tech stuff. And I'd had one of those wild cleaning frenzies a month ago, throwing out things with the abandon of someone who doesn't have the room for much stuff. Pens might have gone out with the trash.

All right, I told myself, try the less obvious places. I live in a brownstone apartment, in a second-floor walk-up, which means quirky space converted from something larger: In my case, an office/living room cut from a Victorian parlor facing Eighty-third Street, and a hallway leading straight back to my miniscule bedroom facing a backyard garden. I hunted up and down the length of the place, looking fiercely through kitchen drawers, closets, purses, and tote bags. . . .

More swearing. Unless I could somehow write the blasted thing in lipstick.

Okay. Wait. No need to panic. I couldn't exactly go hammering on apartment doors at this hour, demanding a pen. But there were stationary stores outside, and one of them had to have pens, yes, and enough paper for a trilogy.

Gulping down the last of my now-tepid coffee, running on adrenaline, I grabbed purse and coat, galloped down the brownstone's stairs, down the narrow hallway, down the outer steps, and hurried out into the dead quiet of early Sunday morning in New York, shivering in the chilly air of March. Eighty-third Street might as well have been in a small town for all the life I saw, so I hurried over onto usually hectic Second Avenue.

Not even a taxi, just a yawning, middle-aged guy, newspaper under his arm, walking a too-perky poodle.

Not a store open yet, either. One said, "Eleven a.m.," another said, "Closed Sundays," a third, "Reopening Soon." I was on the verge of racing after the dog-walker and begging a pencil from him.

Whoa. Wait. The corner of Eighty-second Street caught my eye, and I turned onto the street. *Aha.* One of those funny little sub-sidewalk stores, tucked into what once was the servants' entrance of another Victorian brownstone. I hadn't noticed it before, but there are plenty of those half-hidden stores in the area, and they aren't always easy to spot.

I bent over to look. Lots of stuff in the window . . . junk store masquerading as an antiques shop. . . . No, I corrected silently, straightening, not with all those pentagrams and weird little multiarmed statues. Make it New Age Shoppe, rather, or Magick—definite "k" on the end—Store. That was the name, all right: The Magick Store.

But it was open. Maybe I could find some Sacred Mage of Whatever pens in there.

Yes, there were the requisite creaky iron steps down. Yes, there was the requisite whiff of incense wafting out of the door to meet me. And of course there would be the stereotypical little old man behind the counter. . . .

No, there wasn't. She was tall, fashionably thin, blonde, and ageless, dressed in something definitely pricey and decidedly non-New Agey, and she looked downright displeased at the sight of me.

"You?" she snapped. "You are why I opened the store at such an unearthly hour?"

Nice act, but I wasn't in the mood for early morning theatrics.

"Yeah," I said, "I'm nothing before my coffee, either. I don't suppose you sell—"

"Pens? Not usually. But if I must, I must. Take it."

"It" was a pretty standard-looking ballpoint, sleek purple, no advertising or brand name, nothing special. But how had

she known I wanted—*Don't ask*, I told myself. There were
lots of tricks that could be pulled to fake psychic powers.
"Okay," I said warily. "What do I—"

"Just take it. You will know when to use it. And how. You
should have studied your building's history more thoroughly
and noted the date. Now go away." She rubbed a hand dramatically over her eyes. "The store is now officially closed."

I had the feeling she'd push me out the door if I didn't
leave. Okay. I'd found myself a crazy.

A crazy who'd somehow known I'd needed a pen. And
what in hell was that about my building? "My" building,
hah. As far as I knew, the place had been built in the late
nineteenth century, and that was about it. And the date, well,
March 3ʳᵈ, the anniversary of the day I'd moved into the
building three years back. So?

Heh. She'd just pulled a trick on me, all right. Any
brownstone in a city this age had to have *some* history about
it. So what? This was New York. We, as the saying goes, see
weirder things in our breakfast cereal.

Besides, if the pen wrote, who cared how nuts she was?
I tried to thank her, but she just waved an impatient hand.

So I hied me home, back up the stairs to my apartment
and that maddeningly dark computer, hunted up some un-
used paper, and settled down to write.

I'll sum up what happened next in one quick sentence,
leaving out the profanity: the pen didn't write.

The computer, however, when I turned it on in a fit of
desperation, suddenly did.

These things happened, I told myself, frowning at it. A
loose connection somewhere? Even though I'd tightened
every cable and checked every plug several times over,
maybe the vibrations of a passing truck had done the trick.
As I stared, the screen remained reassuringly bright and the
cursor blinked normally. At last I shrugged, tossed the useless pen aside, and got to work. Save early and often, and all
should be well.

But as I tried to concentrate, I found myself thinking,
Your building's history. . . .

This was ridiculous. *I* was being ridiculous. But, dammit, now she'd gotten me curious. With a sigh, I pushed back from the computer desk and went hunting for my copy of the *Illustrated History of New York*. Leafing through the dog-eared pages, I found . . . nothing about this building . . . nothing about this street, for that matter, other than, yes, most of the buildings on it did date to the late nineteenth century. Working class residences. Nice, ordinary homes. With a snort of disgust at myself for my gullibility, I went back to work.

Yes, but the book was basically a summary. What else could it be for a city this size? Couldn't expect to find every house and every story.

Whatever story there might be about this place. . . .

Dammit!

Saving the few words I'd managed to write, I went in search of Mr. Edwards, the landlord. He wasn't in, having a life of his own, but his wife was. A plump, cheerful, gaudy, brassy-blonde woman of miscellaneous middle years, she was delighted to see company. Or rather, she was delighted to see a Real Live Author. She was the one who'd persuaded her husband that having a Literary Person in the building would give it class.

Right.

We exchanged the expected "Don't want to bother you," and "It's no bother."

"Come in, my dear, please."

Come in, I knew, and get flooded with gossip. I really wasn't interested in the affairs or lack thereof of the other tenants, so I stayed planted in the doorway, refusing to be drawn any further. "I, *uh*, just wanted to ask a few quick questions."

"Oh dear. Is something wrong? My husband?"

"No, no, I just meant, I was curious about the history of the building."

Wrong thing to say. If she couldn't gossip about living tenants, Mrs. Edwards was perfectly happy to gossip about long-dead ones. Some of the ghostly stories she chattered at me, I recognized from those popular ghost books you can find in any bookstore, others were clearly being instantly cobbled together from her own imagination. Were any of these weird and sordid tales of adultery, murder, and wandering spirits the truth? I really doubted it.

And I was wasting precious time.

"That's, *uh*, very interesting, Mrs. Edwards." I began edging back from the doorway. "And I thank you, really. But I, *uh*, I'm afraid I have to get back to the computer. Deadline, you know," I added dramatically.

Aha, the magic words. Mrs. Edwards hastily waved me away, and I just as hastily scurried back up to my apartment and locked the door behind me. Sanctuary! My head was busy with tag ends of ghost stories, but I resolutely settled down to writing the story that, curse it all, *had* to be finished on time.

Half-done. Bathroom break. Stop for a quick mouthful of cold pizza and a flashback to college days. Back to the computer. And—

No, blast it, I was *not* going to start writing a ghost story! Back to the story that *had* to be finished.

Getting dark in here. I switched on the desk lamp and got back to work on—

No! No ghost stories! Back to *the* story! *The* story, which didn't have any lost souls in it, or vengeful spirits, or—

"Dammit!" I snapped.

Back to the story, yes . . . going along well . . . yes. . . .

I sat up, blinking, stiff in every muscle. Finished, by God! Finished, and it wasn't later than, *hmm*, eleven forty-five p.m. of course.

Yes, and now I realized that I was famished. I made myself a sandwich of turkey, a roll, and some not too wilted lettuce leaves, and gobbled it as I went over what I'd written. Pretty good. Very good, in fact. I could get it out tomorrow and be content.

I was still too keyed up to sleep. What the hey, I'd go on-line, see what I could find about the building.

Not much. I did find the precise year when construction

started: 1883, for what that was worth. Most of the block dated to then, it seemed. Nothing more, nothing really interesting.

Except for a murder.

I sat up straight. Well, what do you know? A story that could have come straight from today's headlines. Only this one dated to 1903. Abusive husband, wife who finally couldn't take any more, and a handy kitchen knife. Of course, in those days, there wasn't any such thing as clemency due to "extenuating circumstances," or whatever they called it; the wife had probably spent the rest of her life behind bars. A little unnerving to think it happened in this building, but, hey, during over a hundred years of occupation any building is going to have contained deaths, births, and every other aspect of human life.

Okay, enough of True Crime. Now, for dessert, I'd let myself sketch out a ghost story or two. Maybe use something of what I'd just read: nasty guy . . . turn of the century . . . the sort who'd abuse his wife just because. And she killed him . . . and. . . .

And suddenly I realized that it was dark in here. Really dark. I looked up, blinking in surprise. The lamps were all on, but they didn't seem to be giving very much light.

Con Edison brownout?

No. The darkness actually seemed to be growing and, in the best of horror tradition, growing from behind me.

Oh, come on, I don't believe in—

I swiveled in the chair. And froze. Maybe I didn't believe in things that went bump in the night, but Something was definitely in the apartment with me, and spreading that darkness, Something that was almost a shape. A not-quite-human shape, or maybe that was a no-longer-human shape. I felt hatred—cold, contemptuous hatred—radiating from it.

But what is it ? Where did it come from? I've lived here three years, and there's never been—

"All right," I snapped, and my voice almost didn't shake. "Who or what are you? And what the hell are you doing here?"

"It is the third day of the third month of the third year," a voice that was deep and utterly without humanity told me.

Three threes, my mind gibbered at me. Magic number, that triple three, at least in folklore, lots of power if you believed in such things. But what did it have to do with me?

Oh, no. Not possible. I couldn't have summoned it. How? Just by living here for—for three threes? Or by writing—

Oh, hell. Too coincidental not to be the answer. "You're the husband, aren't you? The wife-abuser from 1903."

The Something didn't answer me, but such renewed hatred spread out from the darkness that I knew with a certainty that was downright atavistic: No mere ghost, nothing that banal. What had been human was at the heart of the Thing, yes, but in this city of so many lives and so many deaths, there's got to be a lot of Darkness. And Darkness had grown about the revenant—a hundred years of Darkness, just waiting for the right summons.

I did summon it. Damn, March 3rd, the third month, I've been here three years and—oh, Lord, the murder took place in March, too, and I'll just bet it happened on the same date. And I was even writing about it.

Writing!

The pen!

The woman in the Magick Store, saying, *"You will know when to use it. And how."*

"I'm not afraid of you!" I snapped at the Darkness, fumbling for the pen. *Oh, yes I am.* "We have laws now; you'd be in jail and—and—"

Hell, where was the pen? I'd thrown it aside when I couldn't get it to write. But I'd better find it, and fast, because the hating darkness wasn't listening to my gibbering. It was oozing forward, coming closer, growing, and when I belatedly tried to scream for help, my voice sounded as muffled as though a blanket was over my mouth. The pen, dammit, where was it?

My frantic fumblings made me overbalance. I fell off the computer chair with a *thump*, knocking over the wastepaper basket, and scrambled backward as the darkness loomed over me, dripping down toward me. Damn! That was the computer desk at my back, trapping me. There was nowhere to go, and the hating darkness was chilling my mind, my thoughts.

But my hand brushed something.

The pen!

With a shout of effort, I brought it up, stabbing at the darkness as if it was a knife.

The pen left a slash of light in the air, as though the air were paper.

"You will know when to use it. And how."

The inane thought rushed through my mind, *No wonder it wouldn't write on plain old paper!*

The darkness swirled back, confused. But it didn't vanish, and I–I–I was a writer, dammit, a professional, not some silly wannabe. I should *know* what I'm supposed to write to get rid of it!

But how—

What—

Whoa, wait, what if. . . .

Yes! The sudden inspiration blazed through my mind. Not write, *un*write!

Frantically, my hand shaking, I began to unwrite the story of abuse, of murder, unwriting it back to innocence. The darkness recoiled, raging and shrieking, but I kept unwriting, the words blazing gold in the air, peeling the darkness away line by line, unwriting the hatred, while all around me the darkness swirled and screamed. I unwrote the screams into silence. I unwrote the rage into calm. I unwrote the darkness into light. I unwrote and unwrote and unwrote layer after layer, back into the safe, normal, sane world of my apartment. . . .

And with a shock that made me gasp, I woke, still on the floor, still with my back to the computer desk, still with the pen clutched in my hand.

Sunlight was stabbing in through the half-drawn blinds. There wasn't the slightest shadow. And the pen, when I tried a tentative scrawl, did nothing.

Stifling a groan, I struggled to my feet, flexing my aching hand. That had not been a dream. Hallucination? From what? The gas was off, the sandwich had been perfectly normal.

"All right, then," I said. "All right."

A quick change of clothes, a quick swipe of a brush through disheveled hair, and I was off and almost running. The Magick Store wouldn't be there, of course, and then I'd be off to the local Home for the Bewildered, because what other solution was there?

But to my shaky relief, the Magick Store was there. And open. I entered nervously, not sure what I was going to find.

"You survived." The woman looked elegant as ever, but the new day clearly hadn't sweetened her sour manner. And she still looked downright displeased at the sight of me. "You have returned the pen? Excellent."

She snatched it from me before I could move, and started toward the back of the store. "What happened?" I called after her plaintively.

"You summoned it. You banished it. And yes, your building is safe again. Go home."

There was the unmistakable sound of a door slamming and locking.

I went home. Sent off the deadline story by FedEx. And tried not to think about pens, or ghosts, or Magick Stores. Pretend none of it had happened.

Yeah. Right.

THE CURSE OF THE ITCH
OR
FINNEGAN WAKES

by Bill McCay

Bill McCay's editor-in-trouble Bob Lang has had one previous adventure, "Matchbook Magic" in the DAW anthology Vengeance Fantastic. *Like the hapless Lang, Bill has lived in Greenwich Village, worked in publishing (editing juvenile mysteries, among many other things), and like his protagonist, Bill invested his comics collection in what turned out to be a break-up gift. Unlike Lang, Bill is a published author, with five books carrying on what happened after the movie* Stargate, *three novels written with Marvel Comics' Stan Lee, and several weeks on The* New York Times *Paperback Bestseller list, thanks to his* Star Trek *novel* Chains of Command, *written with Eloise Flood. As for Mags Finnegan, any resemblance to real people, living or dead, is sheer wishful thinking.*

"COME ON, Lang." Mags Finnegan grabbed my arm. "Let's check it out."

I had no intention of crossing Arbor Street. Not that I knew what was coming. Or rather, what I thought was coming, while unpleasant, was very different from what came.

How many times had I turned onto Arbor and walked

past the Eldritch Shop? I'd passed that corner for the last ten years, ever since I'd started coming to Greenwich Village from beautiful outlying Queens. In that time, I had gone from a despised "bridge and tunnel person" to an honest-to-Pete Villager—and seen a lot of changes.

Back when, the Eldritch Shop had been a little piece of the nineteenth century hanging on in the face of the second millennium. The store, the green-patinaed bronze dragon sitting behind its dusty window, the frizzy-haired owner with the elbows out of his gray sweater—they all looked as if they'd been there forever. You could find enclaves like that all over the Village: streets where time had seemingly stood still. In some places, you almost expected to see horse-drawn cabs come around the corner.

For the Eldritch Shop, though, time had come at a run. Oddly enough, the first change had actually brought me around more often. The space had been subdivided. Now a comic shop appeared beside the curio store.

At the time, I collected comics and used to hang out there with the usual crew of misfits, presided over by Monk, the guy who ran the store. I always promised myself I'd use him as a character—he had a face right out of a comic book: a forehead that receded even faster than his hairline; a fringe of stringy, dust-colored hair; and a prognathous jaw. I just make average height, and Monk barely came up to my shoulder. But he could sling around four-foot-long boxes full of comics as if they weighed nothing. When I shifted full boxes like that, it reminded me that books are merely re-processed trees—and I was trying to move the trunk.

Even with the crash of the comics market, I'd still stop in just to yack, to pick up an issue of one of the few titles I still followed, sometimes to sell. But we'll get to that later. The Eldritch Shop and Monk's Comics seemed to coexist peacefully enough. Workmen had rearranged the old brass letters that had spread across the whole store into three lines over the curio shop's door. They made an odd but pleasant contrast to the psychedelic lettering on Monk's place. I'd pass by for a glance at the bronze dragon in one window, and the overmuscled heroes or half-dressed heroines in the other.

But time continued double-timing on, and the space was subdivided yet again. A joint that sold French fries—excuse me, *pommes frite*—held the corner, with the curio shop and Monk's jostled even closer together. Monk's Comics became Monk's. There was barely room for the word Eldritch to fit over the other shop, scrunched into two lines. The budding editor in me had been offended by the way they broke up the word: "ELDR" in one line, "ITCH" in the other. It only got worse as some of the letters disappeared. The important evening we passed the place, the shop sign read, EL ITCH.

Time had apparently caught up with the sweatered owner of the Eldritch Shop. The green-scaled bronze dragon was gone, and most of the shop seemed in the process of being emptied into a big rubbish dumpster in the street. I was inclined to stay well away from this act of Village real estate rape.

Not so Mags Finnegan. Mags—Margaret Mary Finnegan—came into my life back in high school. Once upon a time, we'd stood on an overpass spanning the Long Island Expressway, staring toward the Manhattan skyline and swearing that one day we'd live there. She was going to be a theatrical mover and shaker, and I was going to be somebody in publishing.

You know how some couples have "their song"? Mags and I had a poem, a six-stanza dialect confection by Strickland W. Gillilan called "Finnigin to Flannigan." It was about a shanty-Irish railroad foreman pushed to write briefer reports. Mags thought that, as a would-be editor, I'd appreciate it.

For me, though, the Irish-joke last lines sort of summed up our whole relationship:

> *Off agin, on agin,*
> *Gone agin. —Finnigan.*

As we went to college, we were "off agin," and Finnegan was gone: she picked a school on the West Coast to be rid of me. Sophomore year, she turned up at my university. Well, we did have a good drama department. We were "on" through a lot of college, in spite of the fact that I was shoehorned into a tiny Village apartment with two other guys. Thanks to her transfer, Mags had another year after I graduated. That's when things went painfully "off agin."

It was right before her birthday, and I'd seen the perfect gift: a delicate silver filigree necklace that had turned up in the window of the Eldritch Shop. Turned out Mr. Frizzy-in-the-sweater wasn't quaint. He was a snotty old soul who really dragged me over the coals. You'd think I was getting married instead of trying to set a price on a piece of jewelry.

The amount he quoted was way beyond what an editorial assistant could afford, so I liquidated the best of my comics collection to raise the cash. They really were the crème de la créme; I can't help but notice these titles have held their value after the crash and have even gotten more expensive. Not that I saw much profit. There's a big difference between what a shop owner like Monk charges the customers and what he pays.

The result of my sacrifice? Instead of being delighted, Mags got really upset when she saw the necklace. About a week later, I understood why. Finnegan and I were "off agin."

I tried to cope by losing myself in my work—not exactly easy, when your job is copyediting the adventures of Fizzy Farnum, Boy Detective. But playing the workaholic was better than brooding in the Sty in the Sky, the fifth-floor walk-up apartment I shared with the roommate from Hell. My roommate may actually be in Hell now, for murderously misusing arcane knowledge and opening one of those doors where mortals aren't supposed to fool with the knob.

The result was that the Sty was now my personal mess. I was living alone, barely able to afford it thanks to a recent raise and some freelance gigs. And, at least tentatively, Mags was back in my life. This was a girl with confidence enough for five. I couldn't help watching—and enjoying—the swagger of her hips as she strode over to the bin outside the defunct Eldritch Shop. Then she climbed in.

I blame her Scenic Design instructor at college. He was always sending his class out for Found Objects to spice up the drama department's sets. "Found Objects" is a highfalutin way of saying "garbage": objects found dumped on curbsides, in trash bags, or, yes, in dumpsters.

My girlfriend, the Dumpster Diver.

Mags ignored my protests as she rummaged through the debris: taxidermy samples leaking their stuffing, books disintegrating after being torn apart for their illustration plates, dust-covered store fixtures. If the bronze dragon had been in there, I might have joined Mags. I'd come across a picture of the beast in one of my freelance copyediting jobs. Turns out it was a Viennese bronze from the turn of the century—the last one—and worth something.

Blocking about half the dumpster was a dirt-crusted, discolored set of bookshelves. Mags heaved them out of the way in a move the Incredible Hulk would have envied. Joints on the old piece of furniture popped, and something came arcing out.

Mags snagged it on the fly.

She held out what looked like a smooth nugget of amber about the size and shape of my thumb. "This would make a nice pendant."

"Or paperweight." I couldn't help my tone. She was still standing in the stupid dumpster, for Chrissakes.

Mags' fingers clenched on the stone as her lips puckered. "Shut up, Lang!"

I went to reply—and couldn't. My mouth wouldn't open. All of a sudden, I was reminded of an old cliche: "His tongue clove to the roof of his mouth."

Oh, wonderful—more weirdness. While I struggled with being suddenly struck dumb, Mags was doing her best to keep the argument going; she liked nothing better than a good fight. In spite of her enthusiasm, though, she couldn't do it single-handed. Our evening together ended shortly thereafter, with Mags berating me for my childish silence.

She got no argument—and no answer—from me.

I headed back to the Sty in the Sky. Not for the first time, I cursed the architect who so ingeniously designed the stairs to take up the least amount of valuable floor space, turning each flight into a dark, narrow exercise space only slightly less steep than those rock-climbing thingies you see in up-scale gyms.

Between scaling five flights and walking home from my midtown office, no wonder Mags loved my legs.

Only slightly winded, I reached the fifth floor landing, entered my apartment, went to the bedroom closet, and began sorting the laundry piled on the floor. Looks like I'd put fresh sheets on the bed in vain. I sighed, tried to say something, anything. No luck. Whatever Mags had done to me stayed in effect even when she wasn't around.

So I gathered up the clothes and stuff and headed down to the twenty-four-hour laundry. Nobody talks in there, anyway.

Returning with three bags smelling of fabric softener, at least I felt I'd accomplished something. That delusion of adequacy was quickly deflated: I heard the phone ringing in my apartment as I was making my final ascent. Bags dropped, jockey shorts tumbled down the stairs as I ran to get the door unlocked. My toe caught on a worn spot on the rug, and I nearly pitched flat on my face. Somehow I managed to scramble to the phone just before the answering machine picked up.

Stupid move. I should have left it to the machine. I still couldn't talk.

Mags was on the other end. "Lang? Is that you? Answer me!"

Something came unstuck in my mouth, and words came out. "Mags? What—?"

"Where were you?" she demanded. "I've been calling for almost an hour."

"Doing the laundry."

That got a laugh out of her. "Guess that beats cleaning the bathroom."

"Next on my list," I replied, working to keep her in a good mood while I tried to figure out the rules here. "Are you still holding onto that doodad you found?"

"Got it right here in my hand." Mags' voice grew sharp. "Are you going to give me more grief over it?"

"No, no," I assured her. At least I knew why I was talking again. The doodad worked over the phone.

The rest of our call was short and pretty disjointed. Distracted as I was, I was always a cue behind. A little late, I realized Mags had called to hear an apology. She cut short my fumbling attempts at conversation with a tart, "You are a fool." Then she hung up.

For an annoyed Mags, that was almost a fond farewell. And I had learned a little about the magic doohickey she'd picked up. I hadn't felt any compulsion to give her grief when she asked me, nor did I feel any more foolish after having her call me a fool. Interrogative and declarative sentences were safe. Imperative ones—where she gave a direct order—weren't. When Mags demanded that I shut up, I'd shut up.

This wasn't good. Mags always had a temper, and a lot of rhetorical abuse comes in imperative form: "Get lost." "Take a flying leap."

I'd hate to see what would happen if she told me to get bent. And how about all those riper, Anglo-Saxon commands?

I sank into the half-sprung armchair by the bookcase; Mags had dubbed it "The Comfy Chair." We'd spent some pleasant hours sharing this space. Now I shifted the chair to reveal the picture hidden behind. It was in an acrylic frame, jammed into the row of books, about eye level for a seated person. A photo of Mags, shot by a shutterbug friend who'd recruited us as models while he taught himself portrait photography.

Mags looked a little self-conscious, but nonetheless managed to convey a bit of a swagger, even sitting down. Her half smile had a satirical edge, her big gray eyes a hint of challenge. Two wings of short black hair swept down from her brows. Her features were a bit too bold to be called pretty, but there was definite beauty there.

"Mags, what am I going to do with you?" I sighed.

During the times Mags and I were off, I'd spent a lot of time conversing with this picture. I could see the breaks in the photo emulsion from the time I'd crumpled the picture in anger. They remained, no matter how carefully I'd smoothed the photo out.

Now, between that damned stone and her quick mouth, Mags could probably crumple me up. How do I keep winding up with people like this in my life?

Maybe that comment she made about me being a fool worked after all. It took a couple of days for me to figure out that what I needed to do was separate her from the magic dingus. And there was an easy way. To make up with her, I'd offer to have the stone set as a pendant. Then the jeweler would "lose" it, and I'd get something else to replace it. Hell, if need be, I'd call her up with the damned thing in my hand and tell her to forget all about it.

Unfortunately, my brainstorm came a little late. When I called Mags, she was already wearing her new geegaw. "I told the jeweler what I wanted, and he took care of it right away," she told me.

Surprise, surprise.

Mags was in an unexpectedly sunny mood. Things were going very well for her at work. Upon graduation, she had managed to get a glorified gofer's job with a Broadway producer. The pay was even worse than my starting salary, but theater people were willing to kill for a chance at this gig, not for the donkey-labor, but for the possible contacts.

When Mags told me she'd gotten a promotion and a raise, I was pleased, then suspicious. How had this good fortune come about?

Mags burbled on about convincing a theatrical diva to go along with something her producer/boss wanted to do. "Difficult" should have been this woman's middle name. Around

Mags' office, this star had been dubbed "Vulva Toadstool." But she had meekly gone along with whatever Mags wanted her to do.

People have based careers on less than this. There's a real Hollywood agent who rose from the mailroom to the top of his agency after he punched a mega-star in the eye. The big guy was impressed: everyone else in the agency was afraid of him.

Although Mags had a hefty punch, she didn't need it. Her new piece of jewelry could convince people to twist themselves into pretzels if that's what she desired.

Job pressure kept us both on the phone rather than face-to-face for the next week.

Even without seeing Mags, though, I could sense she was changing. . . . and not for the better. Her voice was peremptory, whether she was picking up the call or making it. And she was full of complaints about the weird behavior of the people around her.

Strangely, neither she nor her victims had connected the weird behavior with her new pendant. Well, maybe it wasn't so strange. I'd only learned to accept at least one impossible fact before breakfast only after it had been crammed down my throat; the fact, that is, not the breakfast. When my roommate discovered magic, it had taken me long enough to believe.

Mags had much shorter patience when I tried to edge toward the subject. "Are you as nuts as the rest of the people around here?" she demanded, her voice getting shrill.

"You've got to admit it's a weird coincidence," I persisted, feeling like the point man in the minefield.

Mags' explosion was just as dangerous. "Oh, drop—"

I managed to slam the phone down before she finished that particular phrase. One friend who was able to make folks drop dead on command was enough for me.

After that fiasco, there was no talking to Mags, and I was getting nowhere talking to her picture. What I needed was someone who knew something about magic. I'd tried once before, attempting to reach out to my roommate's teacher.

Unfortunately, I'd need a Ouija board to communicate with him. Same thing went for the owner of the Eldritch Shop. Was there no one I could learn from?

I smacked myself for missing the obvious yet again. Maybe I didn't know Mr. Frizzy Hair, but I knew his neighbor.

Monk.

I took an afternoon off, heading down to Arbor Street and the comic shop. My timing was excellent: nobody was in the place except Monk. Assorted bangs and crashes came from the vacated shop next door, where a sign announced the imminent arrival of the Pillow Parlor, featuring hand-stuffed creations.

You really can find a store for almost anything in the Village.

Monk perched on a tall stool behind his counter, gnawing on the end of a pencil as he scribbled, scowled, and scribbled some more. His odd, moss-colored eyes dismissed me after a glance. I wasn't a paying customer, at least, not enough of one.

"How's it going, Monk?" I asked.

He slammed a big, spatulate hand on the piece of paper where he'd been writing. "Been figuring how much longer I can keep this dump going." His voice came out in a raspy growl. "With luck, it looks like three months, unless I switch to hand-stuffed French fries."

He bared big, yellow teeth in a mirthless grin. With that kind of trouble, I guess he'd have no ears for mine.

Then Monk surprised me. "So what brings you here on a school day, kid?"

I took a deep breath. "I need to find out some stuff about the fellow who used to own—" I hooked a thumb toward the former magic shop.

"If you wanted to pick up something you had on layaway, I think you're out of luck," Monk said.

"No, I need the story on that guy—"

"Arminius," Monk interrupted.

"Was that his name?" I shook my head. "Pretty fancy for someone who wore the elbows out of his only sweater."

Monk shrugged. "Latin for Herman. It was the fashion when he was young."

"I edited a book about this Dutch guy who did that Latin bit with his name. Passed it on to a town—" I closed my mouth with a snap. That Dutch guy had lived back in the sixteen hundreds. If that's when Arminius was young, well, it would put him way past Medicare age. This was just getting too weird to discuss. But I had to talk to someone. . . .

Monk watched my mental struggle. "Just spit it out, kid. Can't be any more bizarre than a lot of other stuff I've seen."

"Want to bet?" I asked. Then it all came out, Mags, the dumpster-diving, finding the stone, what it had done to me, to the people she worked with, to Mags herself. I braced myself for the disbelief I expected to see in Monk's eyes. Instead, he looked . . . pissed off.

He cut me off with a word that sort of slithered past my ears—too many sibilants. A cuss word in some foreign tongue? No, this was stronger language than I'd ever imagined. Monk had been glaring at his calculations when he muttered this Word. The edges of the paper curled and began to smoke.

Monk stopped the incipient blaze by smacking the smoldering corners with his oversized paw. Little bits of charred paper fluttered in the air as he turned his glare on me. "You mean to tell me that crazy broad you go out with has got hold of the Eye of Desaar?"

"The what?" I had to force the words through a suddenly tight throat. At least I didn't squeak.

"The Eye of Desaar," Monk repeated, the way you do for the feebleminded. "It's a focus, a focus for power."

"And this Arminius—"

"Was a wizard," Monk finished for me. "Been around here—well, when he first settled, Greenwich Village was still a town outside of New York."

That had to be before the Revolution. "You're telling me he had magic, and that stone, and wound up being pushed into a corner of this old store? Guess he wasn't a real estate wizard."

I got another surprise as Monk took my feeble joke personally. "Oh, he was wizard enough, kid. You ever wonder where I got my name?"

"A nickname," I fumbled, not wanting to make a comment about his looks. "Like the guy in the old Doc Savage stories."

"It's short for *Homunculus*, Lang. You know what that is? More Latin: 'a little man.'" Monk gestured at himself. "Arminius made me down in the basement here. The name was his idea of a joke. I'm a homunculus."

I managed to shut my mouth before I babbled something brilliant like "Don't ask, don't tell."

My brain seemed to be spinning its wheels like a cartoon character desperately running in place over the abyss. Once again, the solid, rational assumptions of my life had dissolved underfoot. I was in the world where secret cultists killed by merely pointing a finger, people did the oddest things because of a three-inch chunk of stone . . . and wizards built store clerks in their basements. Worst of all, all of this seemed to make a horrible kind of sense. Monk's size, the feeling he'd been made from mismatched parts, the slightly creepy vibe he gave off. . . . Sure, he really could be not quite human. Where else would he fit in except behind the counter of a comic shop?

It's a universal joke, even among the misfits of the comics industry. Ever see a comic artist's take on the store owners who sell his products? The shop guys wind up looking like troglodytes. Or maybe you've caught the big, fat sociopath of a comic shop owner on *The Simpsons*? And that's supposed to be a gentle satire.

"Arminius made you," I repeated brilliantly.

Monk nodded. "Sank a lot of his power into the job. He still owned the shop in those days. Figured he could break it up and use me to sell something more profitable than the dusty crap he'd accumulated over the years."

"But . . . comics? Didn't he know?"

Monk shrugged, a slightly disgusted look coming over his lumpy features. "Arminius was always piss-poor at scrying the future. Not that he'd ever admit it."

My head began to hurt. "I'm still not getting this. Here's a guy with the wisdom of centuries, who can make his own business partner. But you're implying he couldn't even manage to hold on to this place."

That got a roll of Monk's moss-colored eyes. "There's a problem with probing the wisdom of the ages, kid. Taking care of everyday business seems a bit . . . mundane."

I remembered my struggle to buy Mags' necklace from Arminius. "Yeah. I think I know what you mean. But he had that Eye thing to make people do what he wanted." My memory replayed the image of the stone popping out of the old bookcase. "Or did he lose it?"

Monk shook his head. "He hid it. Wanted it to lie fallow."

"Fallow?" I repeated like a dim-witted echo.

"It had to discharge." Monk leaned across the counter. "You saw it. What color was the damned thing? Did it look like a moonstone?"

I stared. "More like amber, I would say. Definitely a deep yellow."

The homunculus frowned. "That's bad."

Clammy hands seemed to clutch various internal organs. Mags was wearing this thing! "Bad how?"

"It interacts with the user's will," Monk said. "There's an effect on the stone, and on the person who uses it. Unless you've spent a couple of lifetimes building up your power and knowledge, the Eye of Desaar can be dangerous without the right safeguards. You've got to keep it apart from you except when you're actually using it. That's what Arminius was doing. He'd charged the stone up with a couple of big Makings way before I came along."

"So it's got to cool down?" Then that bit about keeping the damned thing apart hit me. "Suppose you're, *um*, like wearing it?"

Now I got the disbelieving look from Monk. "How long has this girl had the Eye like that?"

"Almost . . . a week?"

Monk nearly flew from behind his counter. "I think we'd better see your friend, kid—and quick!"

We ran, not walked to Eighth Avenue and hailed a cab. During the ride up to the West Forties, Monk cross-examined me about my contacts with Mags since she'd acquired the Eye of Desaar.

"And how did she sound the last time you spoke with her?"

"I don't know, kind of wound too tight."

He nodded. "Not surprising. If she's been wearing the Eye—getting every little wish or want—her will must be spread incredibly thin. I'm amazed she can stand it."

But then, he didn't know Mags. "Spirited" is one way to describe her. Less charitable folk have used words like "willful."

We arrived at West Forty-fourth Street—of course, I got stuck paying the meter—then rushed down the block. To get to the producer's office space, you went through the side door of a theater building and headed for the third floor. The choice was stairs or New York's slowest elevator, and I already had my climbing shoes on.

Monk and I were halfway to the second floor when the migration hit us. Mags' coworkers—everybody in the office, including the big boss—thundered down the stairs, almost tripping over themselves. The weird thing was the disoriented, almost vacant, look on their faces.

"Definitely the work of the Eye," Monk muttered as we clung to the banister against the storm of moving bodies.

I nodded, remembering all too well Mags' war cry when she was trying to get work done among all those loud-mouthed drama students: "Everybody clear out so I can hear myself think!"

As we approached the office door, Monk paused for a moment, as if he were testing—or tasting—the air. "Yeah. Tight. Spread very thin."

Suddenly I found it hard to breathe, and it wasn't from

the two measly flights we'd climbed. Hey, he was talking about the girl I loved. "What can we do for her?"

"Push her," Monk said decisively. "She can't hold on to the Eye much longer. I don't think we can overload it. But we can overload her."

"And?" My whole skin seemed a little too small for my body.

He gave me an impatient look, eager to get on with the confrontation. "Think of her connection with the Eye as a rubber band. She's stretched pretty tight as it is. We force her a little more, and *zip!* She snaps back."

I was thinking of the less happy ending for rubber bands: *rip!* They snap apart.

It's not as though I had a choice. I followed Monk as he opened the door and entered the office. Even to my decidedly unmagical senses, there was a palpable tension in the air. Mags sat at her desk, one hand rubbing her forehead, a look of baffled anger on a face that had gone beyond bold, the bones of her skull showing through too-taut flesh.

She looked at me as if the act of concentrating her gaze made her brain hurt. "What do you want?" she demanded.

"Just happened to be in the neighborhood," I desperately vamped, waiting for Monk to do something impressively mystical.

"Jeez-a-loo," he burst out helpfully. "The Eye! Take a look at that sucker!"

My gaze went from Mags' face to the pendant framed by her open collar. I recognized the size and shape of the stone she'd rescued from the dumpster.

The color was another thing, however. The doodad had gone from amber to bloodstone, a peculiar, pulsing brown-red. Whoever Desaar might be, he, she—or it—seemed to be suffering from a horrible hangover.

This thing didn't look like a gemstone. It looked like a blood blister in severe need of lancing.

Fury overwhelmed my fearful concern, and I turned on the little man. "You came here to do that?"

Mags' first reaction had been to raise a hand to her eye. I

remember my mom, who suffered from sinus headaches, using the exact same move.

Short-fused Mags cut right to the chase. "I don't know what you're talking about! Get out of here!"

Her anger seemed to lash me like a spray of icy sleet, a blasting whirlwind that drove me back toward the door.

"Fight it!" Monk rasped.

It took everything I had, but I managed to brace myself against the force raging against me.

Mags' eyes snapped to Monk. "You get out, too!"

Monk staggered, but, weirdly, the pressure on me faltered, halved. Now I saw what Monk had been trying to tell me. Mags' will was going out through the Eye of Desaar, spread out among who knows how many people? Unaware, these victims were controlled. But now, knowing what was going on, I could resist the diluted force of Mags' will.

"What are you still doing here?" Obviously, Mags had gotten used to having people jump at her orders, even if she didn't know why they were doing it. "Out! Out! Get out!" She actually made shooing motions at us.

It would have been funny, except I found myself being flung back again. Seems when Mags really concentrated on someone, the Eye upped the voltage. I fought it, I had to, for Mags. It hurt, but I made myself stop, then managed a step forward.

Grunting with the effort, Monk did the same. "Looks like you aren't getting your way, *huh*, girlie?"

"Shut up!" Mags yelled at him.

Monk made a gurgling sound, but that was it. *Know that one*, I thought. *Been there, done that.*

But what if Mags had yelled for Monk to drop dead?

"Mags!" I shouted. "I'm sorry! I hate this! Please! I love you!" Her lips worked, and for one second, I saw my Mags: the sometimes silly, always sassy young woman I knew and loved before this goddam Eye of Desaar popped into our lives.

"Lang!" she cried, tears in her eyes. "My head's being torn apart! Make it stop! Please!"

It was the hardest thing I ever did. What I wanted to do was take her in my arms and tell her everything would be all right. But, heaven help me, I had to keep her giving orders until she snapped.

"*Laaaaaaaaaaaaaaaannnnnnngggg!*" Mags sounded as if somebody were driving a spike through her head.

That's the way I felt.

One final shriek, and Mags collapsed onto the desk, a doll with all her strings cut.

I leaped forward. Should I check for a pulse, or go for that cursed piece of jewelry? With a gentle arm around Mags, I raised her up, reaching toward her throat.

A Mack truck plowed into me, sending me flying. Mags followed, although she didn't bounce as far. Something snagged on my fingers as we parted company.

Then I hit the floor—hard. Whatever was in my hand skittered across the rug. When the stars cleared, I saw what it was: the chain that held Mags' pendant. Beside it, like a little bloodstain, the Eye of Desaar lay on the gray industrial carpeting.

And there came Monk, big spatulate hands outstretched. "Get away from it!" he yelled.

For a second, I thought he was just warning me. Then I saw the wild greed on his face.

"It's mine!" the homunculus yelled. "That bastard Arminius hid it from me. He said I could never handle the power, that the Eye had to be drained. I waited ten years, and he said it would be at least another ten. Too dangerous, he said. Well, it was too dangerous for him!"

Monk's eyes were on the Eye of Desaar. I swung my legs around, catching him right across the shins. The homunculus hit with a crash. Then both of us were scrabbling along the floor.

Don't let him get his paws on you, the thought ran through my mind with cold clarity. Those knobby, powerful hands and arms could probably crush me.

My longer legs, however, beat Monk, pushing me a little

bit ahead, so my fingers were the ones to touch the Eye of Desaar—and clench around it.

"Mine!" Monk howled, spewing froth. "Kill you!"

I twisted aside, the gemstone seeming to pulse within my fist. "Oh, dry up!" I said in annoyance.

For a second, I felt as if I'd stuck my toe in an electrical socket. I'd forgotten I had the Eye of Desaar in my hand—and I'd just given an order, however rhetorical.

A bad order, it seems, to snarl at a homunculus. Monk convulsed on the carpet, no longer reaching for the Eye or for me. He began to shrink in on himself, but it wasn't a case of flesh sinking to reveal bone. Instead, his human features dissolved—and a vegetable nature began showing.

Monk vanished, and what looked like a cross between an oversized broccoli stalk and a mandrake root now occupied his clothes. Then it looked like something that had sat too long in the back of the fridge, falling in on itself, growing smaller and smaller, until all that was left was a set of old clothes and one hell of a lot of dust.

It was like something you'd see in a cheesy sci-fi movie. Then the reality of it hit, and reaction set in. What is it about me that seems to attract murderous nuts, even if they come to unfortunate ends?

My legs were too shaky to support me, so I scooted across the rug—avoiding the mess that was Monk—to get to Mags.

She was so very still and pale. I couldn't seem to draw breath myself until I saw the shallow movement of her shoulders.

I couldn't help myself. I wrapped my arms around her, holding her lax form to me, my fists clenched so tightly that damned stone was biting into my palms.

"You've got to get better, Mags." I'm sure my tone of voice sounded more like pleading than imperative, but that electric jolt ran through me again.

And Mags stirred and murmured in my arms.

I laid her down gently. There were things to do before

Mags came around. For that matter, the now-freed staff might return.

Scouting around, I found the supply of trash bags and filled one with Monk's clothing and shoes. Those Fizzy Farnum mysteries came in handy: there were several tricks I'd learned to keep from leaving fingerprints. The dust I just scuffed around the office—hope nobody in the place has allergies.

So there I stood, with a trash bag full of evidence in one hand . . . and the Eye of Desaar in the other. As if aware of my regard, the blood-red stone sent a tingle through my hand—a reminder of power. I had the world in my palm: Mags would slavishly adore me. I could be the most powerful editor of all time, bending writers, publishers, even media moguls to my will.

Hell, I could kick over this editing gig and become an author myself. I mean a *published* author. No editor would ever refuse my books. No rewrites. Every reviewer who counted would give me raves. . . . I looked down at Mags. She was beginning to recover her color, and some softness was returning to her features. But I remembered the tightly drawn, pale, half-mad face I'd confronted when I came through the door.

With an irreverent toss, I sent the Eye of Desaar spinning into the air, then caught it. I didn't have the will Mags had. This sucker would probably eat me up in two days. So, what to do?

First step, get downstairs. Second, find a trash basket to dump the bag of clothes. Then I headed for Eighth Avenue. Right before we'd pulled up on Forty-fourth, I'd noticed a new building going up—or rather, the hole in the ground where the building would eventually rise. Cement mixers were pulling up as we'd passed; they were laying the foundation today.

Still clutching the Eye of Desaar, I walked past one of the chutes where cement was flowing into a two-story deep plywood form. Nobody was looking. I tossed the stone into the glutinous flow and watched it disappear.

The eyesore to come would be around at least twenty years, maybe fifty. I could only hope that by then, the Eye would have discharged itself.

Belatedly, I realized I'd forgotten something while I'd had the world in my palm. I hadn't told Mags to forget about that damned pendant. With luck, she might have been too out of it to remember Monk and myself, or how the wretched thing had disappeared.

But I have no doubt she'll be looking for a replacement pendant. And where am I going to find the bucks for a decent piece of amber?

Damn! I don't even have a place to sell my comics anymore!

THE ASSASSIN'S DAGGER

by Kristine Kathryn Rusch

Kristine Kathryn Rusch is an award-winning fiction writer. Her novella, The Gallery of His Dreams, *won the Locus award for best short fiction. Her body of fiction work won her the John W. Campbell award, given in 1991 in Europe. She has been nominated for several dozen fiction awards, including the MWA's Edgar award for both short fiction and novel, and her short work has been reprinted in six Year's Best collections. She has published twenty novels under her own name and sold forty-one total, including pseudonymous books. Her novels have been published in seven languages, and have spent several weeks on The* USA Today *Bestseller list and The* Wall Street Journal *Bestseller list. She is the former editor of prestigious The Magazine of Fantasy and Science Fiction, winning a Hugo for her work there. Before that, she and her husband Dean Wesley Smith started and ran Pulphouse Publishing, a science fiction and mystery press in Eugene. She lives and works on the Oregon Coast.*

ASSASSIN'S Dagger. The Dagger of Hassan ibn-al-Sabbah. A *fidayeen* dagger. Talia pressed her stylus against the screen of her Palm Pilot and squinted at the tiny type. This was no way to do research.

She leaned her head back against the train's plush seat and rubbed the bridge of her nose with her thumb and forefinger. The man across from her was staring at the French countryside as if he had never seen fields filled with cows and centuries-old barns before. Next to him, a petite woman read a book about the Resistance. And on Talia's left, a man concentrated on *Le Monde* as if he were going to be tested on its contents.

No one watched her, but she kept her PDA turned toward the window anyway. After the mess in Penzance, where she'd had to close the Cornish Magick Shoppe pending further inquiry, she didn't want any more trouble.

Besides, the wounds on her arm were finally beginning to heal.

She sighed and wished she could call Marc-Alain Chartier from the train. But the questions she had to ask weren't questions mundanes should hear. Chartier had awakened her that morning, and she hadn't thought to ask him then.

"We have trouble," he said, after identifying himself as the manager of *Le Petit Château*. "Someone has returned a dagger."

"You're not supposed to be selling black arts equipment," she'd mumbled into the phone, without lifting her head from the satin-covered pillow the Hôtel Intercontinental had provided. The lights were out and she was sprawled sideways on the king-sized bed, enjoying her first eight-hour sleep in nearly three weeks.

"I didn't," he said.

"Then they couldn't've very well returned it, could they?"

She'd been about to hang up, already making a mental note to ream out someone in Corporate Publications for listing both her name and cell phone number under troubleshooting, when Chartier said, "We've had to close the shop. I'm not sure, but I think we could have an Assassin's Dagger."

That woke her up and, ultimately, had gotten her on the next train from Paris. She wheedled part of the story out of him: He'd come in that morning, saw the dagger on his counter with a small handwritten receipt attached. The receipt had the seal the store had used throughout most of its nine-hundred year history, long before Abracadabra, Inc. folded *Le Petit Château* into its corporate mantle.

A note left near the door explained that the dagger's purchaser wanted a refund in full—545 French francs—without interest or penalty. The money was to be left in an envelope just inside the door two nights later, and "the entire incident would be forgotten."

Chartier didn't know what incident and he didn't have access to old French francs. He also knew enough about Assassin's Daggers to stay away from the one on his counter. There was no way to tell—without an expert opinion— whether or not the thing was still lethal.

Talia wasn't sure how she counted as an expert opinion. She knew about Assassin's Daggers, of course, and she'd studied them in the Magicks of Antiquities section of the British Museum. But she'd never disabled one. To her knowledge, no one alive had.

And then there was the problem of the dagger's identification.

She studied the tiny images on her Palm again, wishing for a larger screen. Sometime in the past, she'd downloaded twenty-five books on every topic her work as a corporate troubleshooter for Abracadabra could possibly cover. Fortunately one of those books had been on lethal objects of enchanted worlds. But the text was in seventeenth century Church Latin, a language whose subtleties had never been one of her strong suits, and she'd managed only to confuse herself more than help herself.

She knew that there were three types of daggers often labeled an Assassin's Dagger, and they all had different powers and purposes.

Legend said that the Assassin's Dagger had its origins in the Middle East in the twelfth century. Named for a Muslim religious sect that specialized in assassination, the daggers could kill on their own.

Unlike the sect, however, the daggers often killed indiscriminately. Their targets were magically assigned: one specific victim or two, or an entire host of victims who happened to be in the dagger's vicinity. Once the dagger fulfilled its mission, however, it was dormant until some other mage programmed in a new set of victims.

If, indeed, what Chartier had found was an Assassin's Dagger, he was right in calling corporate. No telling how many people could have been hurt if he hadn't closed and locked the door to his shop.

He had done the right thing, and now it was up to Talia to do the same. She had to figure out if she was facing an Assassin's Dagger, a Dagger of Hassan ibn-al-Sabbah, or a *fidayeen* dagger. Or a hoax, designed to cut into the profits of the corporation's best performing provincial store.

Talia shut off her PDA and gave her eyes a rest. She couldn't do much more until she got to *Le Petit Château*. Then she'd begin the process that made her the very best magical business troubleshooter in the entire world.

Le Petit Château was about five miles from the train station, far enough that Talia decided to rent a car and check into her hotel room before finding the store. The city, small by American standards, was a major commercial port. Bombed in World War II, most of the architecture was wretched late twentieth-century steel and glass, but a small segment of the medieval metropolis survived.

A castle—*le grand château*, Talia supposed—flanked the large river that brought most of the industry into this part of France. The castle had been built in the thirteenth century, and three of its four towers were intact. Newer buildings stood off the courtyard—buildings built in the sixteenth, seventeenth, and eighteenth centuries respectively—and dwarfed the ancient walls. But the castle still had an air of magnificence that dominated the entire area.

Talia's hotel room overlooked the castle, the river, and a huge cathedral which had been built in the fourth century and added onto by each succeeding generation. She loved Europe and the sense of history here that had not existed in her Michigan hometown. She had been about to quit Abracadabra, Inc. when they transferred her to Europe, and her discontent fled.

It was almost as if the continent itself enchanted her, romanced her, fed all the lonely places she hardly admitted existed—especially to herself. She didn't dare think about it, or she would quit. Her job left her with no time for anything more than casual friendships and short stops between crises—not to mention the occasional emergency zap to the corporate offices in Salem, Massachusetts.

There were a few hours of daylight left, barely enough for her to get started. For a moment, she toyed with crawling into the comfortable double bed that dominated the high-ceilinged room, but knew she didn't dare. She would never forgive herself if something happened to the dagger that night.

She needed to go down and at least inspect the scene.

The walk was an easy one but took longer than she expected. *Le Petit Château* was in the medieval metropolis which hadn't looked large on the map. But she got lost on the windy cobblestone streets, many of which didn't seem to have names at all. Eventually, though, she found the store, recognizable from the photographs she'd seen in the corporate offices, only a block from the castle itself, visible from the drawbridge, although she hadn't seen it the first time she passed.

The high arched windows stole their shape from the cathedral's famous stained glass. The rounded front door mimicked the castle's main entrance. The displays were tasteful and touristy at the same time. Mixed among the mass-market tapestries and books on the castle's history were glass wands and delicate potion jars.

The average tourist would see only an attractive shop with a few odd items, but the magic-born would know this was a place that they could call home.

Police barricades blocked the entrances, though, and made it impossible to press up against the window's glass.

Talia couldn't see inside, so she was not able to catch a glimpse of the dagger as she had hoped.

She wandered around the building, finally finding the main entrance—another arched door—this one recessed against the stone walls, intricate carvings embellishing the arch like they did in so many of France's cathedrals. Only these carvings didn't depict religious scenes. Most of them showed magical instruction: an elder mage teaching a complicated spell to his apprentice—although sometimes the carvings showed such a spell going wrong.

"You can't go in," a male voice said behind her.

She turned. A slender man, his hair a light brown, sat on the stone wall that protected the road from the moat. His hands rested at his sides and on the thumb of his left hand was a signet ring with the same symbol on it that was on the sign above *Le Petit Château*.

"Marc-Alain Chartier?" she asked.

"Yes," he said. "If you have come to ask me for advice, you can see that I am dispensing none this day."

French was usually a formal language, but somehow, he made it seem even more so.

"Actually," she said with a smile, "you asked me for advice."

His mouth thinned, and she thought she saw annoyance in his expression. "Talia Miller of Abracadabra, Inc.?"

She nodded.

"I though you had stood me up."

Sometimes people expected her to magically transport everywhere. If she did that, she would deplete her magical reserves, reserves she often needed for the challenges that awaited her at these provincial shops.

"I got here as quickly as I could," she said. "The train from Paris takes two hours all by itself."

He slipped off the wall and walked toward her. He wasn't much taller than she was, although his slenderness lent him extra height. He wore the uniform of the intellectual Frenchman: black pants, a light shirt, and a black leather jacket.

"Have you experience with an Assassin's Dagger?" he asked.

"Some." She hadn't moved from her place beside the barricade. "Have you?"

"Only what I've read."

"What have you read?"

"That it's misnamed. It should be called the Dagger of Massacre."

She nodded. "It can be used that way."

"The *fidayeen* would not approve of a dagger used in such destruction." He spoke as if he were personally familiar with the sect that had brought the concept of assassination to the world. "They believed in killing a man face-to-face."

"With a dagger," she said.

"With a dagger." He nodded once in acknowledgment.

"There is a *fidayeen* dagger," she said. "It looks much like an Assassin's Dagger. And so does the Dagger of Hassan ibn-al-Sabbah. Are you sure you don't have one of them?"

"I haven't heard of these daggers," he said. "What do they do?"

He'd answered her question, and she wasn't sure she wanted to answer his. She crossed her arms and leaned on the wooden barricade. It felt flimsier than the ones she'd leaned on in the U.S., but she didn't move.

"How long did this shop sell dark arts?" she asked.

His eyes narrowed. "What makes you think—?"

"You said it was a return," she said. "Only those who practice the dark arts would have an Assassin's Dagger. I'm going to help you, but only if you're honest with me."

He crossed his arms, his posture mimicking hers. "What makes you think," he repeated, pointedly pausing in case she interrupted him again, "that I know the history of the store?"

"I've read all of your files, Monsieur Chartier. You owned this store until we bought it out. You could have quit then, but you chose to stay on, to manage, so that your customers would have continuity."

He smiled then. It accented his sharp features, made him seem somehow younger, and even more intelligent. "You didn't read closely. I worry about that if you're going to neutralize our dagger."

"The store has been here for nine hundred years. It is said that the store once had so much power, it rivaled the cathedral. Only an influx of clerics prevented this town from being overrun by witches."

"Witches." He sneered as he used the term. "Do you believe in such things?"

"I believe there is evil, yes," she said. "And I believe it takes different forms. Which is why I asked you, and I'll ask again, when did *Le Petit Château* stop trading in the dark arts?"

She was beginning to worry that he hadn't answered that question because the store still trafficked in dark matter.

His smile faded just a bit. "There are many kinds of evil. Not all of them are magic."

He said that as if he expected her to intuit more from the statement than he had actually said.

"So you are still practicing the dark arts then?" she asked.

"My name is Marc-Alain Chartier," he said. "My father was Marc-Albert. You misread your files, Mademoiselle. The person who sold to Abracadabra, Inc. was Marc-Albert, not Marc-Alain. My father left with the profits. My mother and I coped as best we could, but I was forced to work here so that we could pay our bills."

"Forced?" she asked. "An odd word for economic necessity."

He shrugged.

"I'm sure Abracadabra, Inc. can find someone else to manage the store if it's such a burden for you." She shivered. The sun was setting, and the air was growing chill.

"I merely told you this because you assumed I knew the history of the shop. I do not. My father would have, and he is long gone."

"So you can't tell me when you stopped selling materials for the dark arts," she said.

He shrugged again, a single shoulder, such a small and eloquent gesture. "The receipt is one hundred and fifty years old. So sometime between then and now, I would think."

"You got close enough to see the receipt?"

"I have a small magic," he said.

"And what spell would that be?" she snapped. "I would think any spell done in the vicinity of the Dagger might risk setting it off."

"It is a scientific spell," he said, reaching into the pocket of his leather coat. He pulled out a small pair of opera glasses. "Amazing the things you can do with a few pieces of glass and some metal."

"Amazing," she muttered. "Let me borrow them."

She extended her hand. After a moment, he gave them to her. The metal was warm from his fingers.

Talia climbed over the wooden barricade and went to the door of the shop. The interior lights had come on—or maybe they had been on all day—illuminating the narrow shelves. She didn't need the opera glasses to see the magic case set directly in the center of the store. It had tiny rare items inside, from a bone thimble (guaranteed to protect a person's good fortune) to a Madagascar reflecting stone (designed to counter evil spells).

On the other shelves, mixed in with the candies from Brittany and the chocolate from a nearby shop were more potion bottles, all empty, their stoppers beside them. If there were potion bottles, then there were herbs somewhere, perhaps up the stone steps that disappeared into darkness at the back of the store.

She peered at that darkness, knowing she would have to investigate it before she left. Most herbs were harmless, but few white spells were cast with them these days. Herbs and potions had become the province of the dark arts, perhaps because few dabblers had the patience to learn something as subtle as spell-mixing.

Talia could see Chartier reflected in the window. He

hadn't moved from his place near the barricade. He watched her, his eyes dark with intensity.

She turned her attention away from him, back to the store itself. The counter, covered with glass displays containing items she couldn't make out, stood against the right wall. The cash register—an old-fashioned electronic model, the kind that had come a few years before computers—was not corporate regulation. She remembered seeing the proper computer reports for *Le Petit Château*, and wondered how they were generated.

The center of the counter, where the customers placed their wares, was closer to the other windows than the door she was looking through. Still, she could see a dagger resting on a blotter, and a receipt hanging off the ornate gold hilt.

The receipt had been tied on with a black ribbon. It had been written on parchment and, Chartier was right, there was an obvious seal still attached.

The note remained on the floor near her feet, but inside the door. She thought it curious that Chartier hadn't brought that outside with him.

"When you found the dagger, you called the police?" she asked without turning. Her fingers played with the opera glasses. So far she couldn't see enough of the dagger to know whether it was anything out of the ordinary at all.

"I called a man I know," Chartier said.

"A policeman."

Chartier didn't answer her.

"Who knows what type of store this is."

"Everyone in town knows what kind of store it is."

"Really?" This time she did turn. "They all know that you sell real magical items here?"

His lips were pressed together, his eyes even darker. He seemed to resent her presence even though he'd been the one who called her here.

"Of course not," he said after a moment.

"But the policeman does."

"He's bought from me," Chartier said.

She nodded. That was the admission she wanted. So Chartier claimed not to be much of a mage, but he had a policeman in his pocket, enough in his pocket that he could use his authority to close the sidewalks around the store if need be.

Curious. Most magic shops tried to keep their main purpose hidden from the authorities. This one did not.

She brought the opera glasses up and focused on the receipt. Threads ran through the paper, ragged edges, and proper absorption of ink showed that it was, indeed, parchment. But it didn't look like it had aged. Even the ink seemed fresh: still black, not brown as ink more than a hundred years old often turned. The seal, done in wax, looked like it was still soft to the touch.

Perhaps the receipt had been protected against the elements, or perhaps the receipt itself had been spelled, either when it was first written or when it was brought to the store. Either way, she didn't like it.

She turned her attention to the dagger. She still couldn't see the blade, but she could make out details on the hilt.

It seemed ornate for a Middle Eastern dagger. The metal—she still wasn't willing to admit it was gold—had a handle that curled downward, making it easy to grip. The handle itself seemed to have writing on it, or perhaps some sort of design. The glasses weren't powerful enough for her to make out the etching.

Perhaps the dagger was nothing at all, just a false alarm sent by an ignorant shopkeeper.

She would have to check her books, though. She'd been led to believe that the alchemy involved in forging an Assassin's Dagger had been lost. If it hadn't, then any kind of dagger could be used for anonymous treachery.

She scanned the items on the rest of the store's shelves, at least the ones she could see up close. Even with the opera glasses, she couldn't penetrate the darkness in the back. She also noted that none of the display windows opened onto that space either.

That was a violation of Abracadabra policy. No hidden

rooms, no secret passages, no dark and dingy spaces. Magical shops could not hide their purpose; that led to mundane fears and official closings, sometimes even public recriminations or worse, violence arising out of fear.

Abracadabra, Inc.'s purpose around the globe was to supply magical supplies to magical users while minimizing the fears of the nonmagical. It seemed like a simple proposition, but so many of her troubleshooting assignments came because someone violated that basic principle.

"See anything?" Chartier asked.

Too many things, but she didn't tell him that.

"I can't see it clearly from here."

"That's the best view you'll get from outside," he said.

She nodded. She wasn't ready to go in yet.

"Tell me," she said as she turned toward Chartier, "what would you have done if this return hadn't been for a lethal item?"

He froze. Just for a second, but she noticed it and wondered about it. Then he shrugged. "We have never had a return."

"Not in all the years of your business?"

"No," he said.

"Not even in the beginning?"

"No," he said.

She nodded, wondering if he knew that he had contradicted himself. He claimed to know nothing about the history of the store, and yet he said there had never been a return.

"You know that Abracadabra, Inc. does not allow returns on magical items," she said.

"I know."

"And we certainly wouldn't allow one on something that had been in someone else's possession for 150 years."

"It is not as if I had a choice," he said.

"But you do have a choice. The customer requested a refund, right?"

Chartier nodded once, as if the idea annoyed him.

"Are you going to give it to him?"

"Wouldn't you give a refund to a person who bought an Assassin's Dagger?"

"Out of fear?" she asked.

He nodded again.

"I never give in to intimidation," she said, turning back to the store and putting the opera glasses to her eyes again. This time she read the receipt.

It was written in a calligraphed hand, lots of flourishes, but the words were clear: *One Assassin's Dagger with instructions* and a price, written in francs. The date on top of the receipt was 24 Novembre 1851—during the reign of Napoleon the Third. She didn't know the history of French money, whether francs were even in use then or what they would have been worth. She had no way of knowing if the receipt was a hoax or not.

Not yet, anyway. But she would find out. She always did.

"The note said the person would come for his refund tomorrow?" she asked.

"Tomorrow night," Chartier said. "After we close."

Closing was something else the store wasn't supposed to do. Abracadabra's stores were open 24/7, even in remote villages. It was a policy that worked, since so many of the magical refused to buy their supplies in the daylight.

"I think the best thing to do would be to wait until tomorrow night and speak to the person who wants the refund," she said.

"We can't do that." He sounded alarmed.

She brought the glasses down, crossed the barricade, and handed them to him. "Why not? The corporation will cover your expenses. It would be the best way to handle the entire mess."

"Maybe for you," he said. "I have regulars. Customers I've cultivated for years who rely upon me. I don't want them to get into the habit of going somewhere else."

"There's somewhere else to go?" she asked.

"Look," he said. "This is an informal place. Someone might get in, and the dagger—"

"You mean like they did last night."

His gaze met hers. Then he nodded, but the nod seemed uncertain.

"Do you have any idea how this person got into your store?"

"It's a simple spell, really, one that opens locks."

"Then it's even simpler to guard against."

Color touched his cheeks. "We haven't had to before."

"It's corporate policy."

His lips thinned. "As you can see, the corporation's policies don't always work here."

"They would have if you'd implemented them. Then I could have stayed in Paris." Her words were harsher than she had expected. She sighed. "I'm tired. I'm going back to my hotel, freshen up, and do a bit of research."

"You're not going to finish this tonight?" he asked, sounding worried.

"Anyone who goes into a strange magic shop at night is a fool," she said.

"It's not strange," he said, "at least to me. I'll go in with you."

She gave him a small smile. "You're the one who received the dagger, Monsieur."

"So?"

"How many enemies do you have?"

He looked startled. "None, I think."

"Do you feel confident enough about that to step into the shop with the Assassin's Dagger on the counter, a dagger that may or may not kill you?"

He squared his shoulders. "It didn't the first time."

She nodded. "So that makes you safe. I thought you told me you didn't go all the way into the store."

"I read the note. I saw the dagger. I left."

"Dropping the note inside," she said. "In your haste."

His lips thinned. It was clear that he didn't like her. He wasn't making much of an effort to hide his feelings. For some reason that bothered her. She wanted him to pretend politeness, to keep up a sort of fiction that she was more than a solution to a problem he couldn't handle himself.

"Maybe you're not clear on how these daggers work exactly," she said. "They're dipped in the potential victim's blood. When the victim comes close enough for the dagger to sense him, the dagger will attack and continue to attack until he's dead."

"I know that."

"Then perhaps you didn't realize that you may not have gotten close enough to the dagger for it to sniff you out."

"Or perhaps the dagger has been used up, its power gone until someone dips it into the blood of a new victim."

"Perhaps," she said. "Are you willing to risk that? Because I'm not."

He looked inside the store, as if he could find his answer in there.

"You seemed worried enough when you called me this morning," she said.

"Nothing has happened all day." He continued to stare through the windows at the illuminated interior.

The store did look homey and warm, the kind of place she might like to own some day. She'd had opportunity, but she'd never taken it. She'd always been worried that life as a small town shopkeeper might be too dull for her.

"Nothing has happened because the dagger has been sealed inside. If it is truly an Assassin's Dagger, we can place it in a box and that will neutralize its danger."

"And if it is not?"

She shuddered. She couldn't help herself. "If it is the Dagger of Hassan ibn-al-Sabbah, it will quest until it finds its target."

"Then why hasn't it burst out of the store?"

"The Dagger of Hassan ibn-al-Sabbah is more subtle than that. It's almost as if it has a mind of its own. It waits until its victim is alone and relaxed. Then it strikes."

"I've never heard of such a thing," he said.

"These are powerful ancient magicks," she said, "their creation lost to time. And, thank heavens, they are rare. But I would not spend the evening alone if I were you, *Monsieur* Chartier."

"I waited for you alone on the street this afternoon."

"In a public place, in the daylight," she said. "Some say the Dagger of Hassan ibn-al-Sabbah was designed by Hassan ibn-al-Sabbah himself, the man who founded the *fidayeen* in 1090. He had strict codes about assassination: the assassin must be willing to lose his life in service of his cause—"

"Like the suicide bombers," Chartier said.

"No," Talia said. "Not at all. An assassin never killed himself. Hassan ibn-al-Sabbah believed it was against Islamic law. But the assassin could expect to be captured and to die at the hands of his captors. Some say that Hassan ibn-al-Sabbah did not like losing so many good men, so he invented the Dagger."

"Which would have been against Islamic law as well," Chartier said. "Magic."

She nodded. "Which is why we consider these stories legends, not truth. But we must always assume some truth in legends. I prefer to believe that a rogue follower of Hassan ibn-al-Sabbah invented the Dagger and perhaps even the *fidayeen* dagger—"

"What's the difference?"

"I'm not sure of all the differences," she said. "I will find that out before I go in. But I know that the Dagger of Hassan ibn-al-Sabbah is the most determined of all of them, and perhaps the most powerful. It and the *fidayeen* dagger share one other trait in common: they only target one individual. It is the Assassin's Dagger that can be the most lethal, modified to kill anyone in its path—as many as fill a room. Fortunately, it is the easiest to capture."

"I do not see why you don't try tonight," he said.

She was getting angry. She didn't like to be pushed, particularly by a small town mage who couldn't even follow the rules of shop ownership.

"I already told you," she said. "Besides, I am not careless enough to loose this thing on France."

"But it could be harmless."

"It could be," she said.

"But you don't think so."

"As I said, make certain you have company this evening." She nodded her head toward him. "I will meet you here at nine tomorrow morning. If you know any talented mages, bring them with you. And bring me a list of families who have shopped at *Le Petit Château* for more than a generation."

"I do not have—"

"Good evening, Monsieur Chartier." She walked away from him while he continued to protest. She had a lot of work to do, and she had let him badger her into giving herself only fifteen hours in which to do it.

Although it wasn't entirely fair to blame him. She did want to be done as quickly as possible. Even if she waited for the note-writer to return, she would have to confront the dagger at some point. She would do the research, and see where it brought her.

Sometimes these magicks were not as simple as they seemed.

Talia might have gotten her job because of her magical talent, but more and more her tools were technological. She spent the next few hours searching the internet and speaking to other experts on her cell phone.

She paced her stone hotel room, leaving the floor-to-ceiling windows open so that she had a view of the castle and the cathedral and, by extension, the shop. If something went wrong, she might see it.

It took her only a few taps of her laptop's keyboard to learn that France did indeed use the franc as currency in 1851. The franc first appeared in the Hundred Years War, but didn't become the standard currency of France until 1795. Somehow it remained through all the upheavals of the nineteenth century, even though the coins differed.

She wondered if the note writer wanted to be paid in francs of the period, which would have been worth considerably more than modern francs. And then she realized the oddity. Francs were nearly worthless currency. They still existed, and would for perhaps another year or so, but they were being replaced by the Euro. Just a few months before, France switched over to the Euro and while people could continue to pay for items with francs, they would get their change in Euros, something Talia found so confusing that for the first two months of the new system, she only used her credit card.

She had a hunch either the receipt or the note was placed in the store as a diversion. Her hunches were usually right. They'd saved her from the attack of a dark mage in Vienna—somehow she had known he thought her the threat to his store, not Abracadabra's buyout—and they helped her locate the nest of dragons' eggs beneath the shop in Lucerne.

This time, her hunch told her that the dagger wasn't an actual return. It was placed in the store as some sort of threat.

But she wasn't sure what kind of threat it was. Was it a warning or was the dagger armed and lethal? Was it aimed at someone in particular? And was it really an Assassin's Dagger or someone's idea of a hoax?

After seeing the hilt, she was leaning toward hoax. When she returned to the room, she'd looked at photographs of the only known Assassin's Dagger, and it did not have an ornate hilt. Neither did the drawings of the Dagger of Hassan ibn-al-Sabbah or the *fidayeen* dagger. They were plain tools that looked even more innocuous because of their simplicity.

But she kept in mind that legend claimed fifty Assassin's Daggers had been created. She had no reason to believe they all looked the same. After all, they'd been charmed somehow, whether in the forging or afterward. They might have been made to look different purposefully, perhaps because the daggers were going to different parts of the world.

The hotel did not have room service, so she had to interrupt her research to get some dinner. She went to a nearby bakery for freshly baked bread and some madeleines for dessert. Then she went next door to the grocery store, and bought two different kinds of cheeses and some salami. She returned to her hotel with her purchases, made herself a simple feast of salami and cheese sandwiches, washed down with bottled water, and continued her work.

She used her series of passwords to log into the corporate records. Abracadabra, Inc. kept files and histories of all of its stores. *Le Petit Château*'s records contained sales figures for the past twenty years, broken down by month, but little else. There was a notation that the store had been in the same location for nine hundred years and that its worldwide fame would help Abracadabra, Inc.'s legitimacy. But there was no profile of Marc-Alain Chartier, nor much mention of his father. It was as if whoever had written this expected the reader to already know the history of *Le Petit Château*.

Maybe if she were a European mage, she would. She'd seen records like this in America, mostly for the Massachusetts stores. Many of them had stood on the same ground since the early seventeenth century and most mages knew their histories as well.

But the history of *Le Petit Château* bothered her, mostly because of the hints she'd been getting about the dark arts. One of the things she liked about Abracadabra, Inc. was the way it avoided any contact with the dark arts. She wouldn't have been involved with them if the dark arts were even part of the focus. She abhorred black magic and part of her job as troubleshooter for Abracadabra, Inc. was to make certain that the dark arts had no influence in the business whatsoever.

She didn't like the fact that she couldn't find simple answers to the questions she had. And the answer she sought the most proved the most illusive. She found out how to trap an Assassin's Dagger, but not how to disarm one.

None of her books had that information. Neither did the websites she visited. The way to stop an Assassin's Dagger (besides boxing it and hoping it would never get out of that box) was lost, just like the way to make it was.

She put in several calls to experts on the dark arts within Abracadabra, Inc. She also left a message with Cedric, the curator of Magical Antiquities at the British Museum. No one called her back. Of course, she was trying to reach them all after hours. They'd probably call her the following day, when she was dealing with that dagger.

At one a.m., she had gone through all the materials she brought and all the internet sites she could think of. She felt no closer to solving this dilemma than she had when she started. In fact, she felt like she had raised even more questions.

She set her travel alarm, then lay back on her bed, her hands tucked beneath her head. Maybe she should just close *Le Petit Château*. She had the grounds for it: past history in black magic, possible black magic connections even now, improper cash registers, lying on monthly reports (after all, if they weren't using the proper computerized cash register, then they weren't giving completely accurate reports), and having hidden or closed-off rooms.

But this store would be more difficult to close than the werewolf-infested shop in Lockerbie or the shop in Leeds that was selling virgin's blood, a prime ingredient in black magic spells. It had taken her weeks to get the permissions to close those shops, and they didn't make the kind of money that this shop was making.

Eventually, the Leeds shop reopened under new management, but the shop in Lockerbie never did. The werewolves had destroyed most of the customer base, and Abracadabra, Inc. decided that the shop was too remote to attempt rebuilding.

All in all, she'd probably closed fifteen stores, many of them in outlying areas of Europe, most of them with long magical histories. The influence of the dark arts seeped into the buildings, and she could sense how horrible the past had been. She was following company orders, but often the locals didn't see it that way. They expected her to resolve problems in their favor, not shut down stores that had no real hope of survival.

Sometimes she did resolve problems in favor of the shopkeeper. She'd done that just last week in Cardiff, when she'd discovered an imported pixie who had gotten trapped under a bookshelf. It didn't speak Welsh and the shopkeeper refused to acknowledge any words spoken in English—even, apparently, the word "help."

Once the pixie was freed, all the bad problems affecting the store were resolved, and the shopkeeper swore he wouldn't import living beings for sale again. Talia had sent a recommendation to headquarters, banning the sale of all live creatures from Abracadabra stores, but she had been turned down. It seemed that, as long as the creatures were fundamentally good and not considered human, they could be sold should a shopkeeper decide to do so.

So many tricks to the job. She thought she had seen them all until that dagger appeared.

And now she was uncertain about her next move, for the first time in her career.

Talia awoke to the sound of church bells. For a moment, she thought herself back in Michigan on Christmas morning. She was cold enough and she felt that same scary sense of anticipation.

But all she had done was leave the window open while she slept, and failed to cover up with one of the thin blankets the hotel provided. The church bells came from the cathedral, probably ringing early mass.

It didn't take her long to shower and change. She checked her e-mail while finishing the last of her bread; she'd received a lot of responses to her questions, but no one knew how to neutralize an Assassin's Dagger.

It apparently had never come up before.

The morning was clear and cold. The sky was a pale blue, and the cathedral, outlined against it, looked majestic, dominating the scene the way it had for centuries. Even the castle seemed dwarfed by it.

Talia walked quickly, her supplies bag over her shoulder. Inside were her usual tools: a wand, spellbook, and electronic incantation translator. She also carried an iron box big enough to house a dagger. Her research had told her how to capture the dagger, but she would have to keep the box closed at all times, or it would escape.

Usually her box held some of her casting relics, but she put them in a plastic container. She wasn't sure plastic could hold an Assassin's Dagger, but she knew the box could.

Her laptop was over her other shoulder, and her cell phone in her jacket pocket. She felt weighed down by all the equipment she brought, but she didn't dare be without it. She wanted to check out that dagger before nightfall. If the note writer planned an attack, he might do it then, expecting Chartier to be waiting for him.

Talia would be waiting instead.

This time, she didn't have any trouble finding the shop. The road seemed straighter, more familiar. This part of the city had a particular odor she was beginning to recognize: the rotted scent of the scum covering the castle's moat. She wondered why no one had bothered to clean it up, particularly something this close to the shops.

She would insist on it when she wrote her follow-up memo to Abracadabra, Inc. Pond scum, particularly old and lusty varieties, was often used in the most vile spells.

She arrived a half hour early so that she could survey the scene and perhaps take action without anyone there. But as she walked up the last stretch of cobblestone, she saw a crowd of people outside the door.

Most were elderly and some were wearing robes decorated with half moons. One man had a long white beard and thin white hair. If she hadn't known better, she would have thought he was a mundane, a pretend mage trying to look like Dumbledore or Gandalf the Great. Some of the women were pressing their fingertips together, incanting.

A shiver raced up her spine and she ran the last few yards, her equipment jostling, bruising her.

The barricades had been moved aside, blocking the street instead of the store's entrance. Chartier bent over that entrance, an old-fashioned gold key ring in his right hand.

"Stop!" Talia shouted.

He unlocked the door anyway, and reached inside, grabbing the note. She thought she saw a movement deep within, but she didn't stop to analyze it. Instead, she said a quick kinetic spell, forcing Chartier outside and the door closed.

"Hey!" he said in unaccented English.

That stopped her. She hadn't expected him to speak English at all. He hadn't so far, even though he had known she was an American.

"You have no right," she said, pushing her way through the crowd, all of whom were staring at her as if she were the one who had done something wrong. "Especially with all of these people here. Someone could have been killed."

"They were reciting a 'protect' spell," he said.

She snatched the note from his hand, then took the key. "A lot of good that did you. I blew right through it with a spell of my own. Assassin's Daggers have even more powerful magic."

"I thought you didn't know anything about them."

"I know more than I did," she said. "And the power of magic often comes from age. Or haven't you been taught anything?"

Color ran up his cheeks. The people around them didn't seem too concerned by the conversation, but perhaps that was because they had continued in English.

"Get them out of here," Talia said.

"They have the right to be here." Chartier crossed his arms and leaned against the door.

"They have no rights," Talia said, "and neither do you. You're just an employee and I have the ability to fire you here and now."

"I wouldn't do that," Chartier said.

Something in his tone caught her attention. She looked up and saw coldness in his eyes. It had been there all along, but it seemed to have grown, to have taken over his entire face.

"Why not?" she asked.

"Because they stand with me." And as if proving his words, the people gathered around him.

Inside the shop, the dagger floated upward.

"Get out of the way," she said.

No one moved.

"The damn dagger's alive," she said. "Get away from the windows."

But they didn't. Instead, Chartier smiled. "Look at the note," he said.

She frowned, not understanding. The dagger floated closer, moving slowly, as if it had all the time in the world.

"The note," Chartier said again.

She stuck the key ring over her wrist and opened the envelope. The paper inside was empty.

"You lied to me," she said.

He smiled.

"Why would you—"

The dagger burst through the window, shattering glass onto the cobblestone. Somehow the glass missed the people in front of it. The dagger floated through them, and straight at Talia.

"Jesus," she said, suddenly understanding. The dagger was meant for her.

It picked up speed as it came forward, heading directly for her heart. At the last moment, she swung her laptop forward, and the knife pierced it. She flung the laptop at the scum-covered moat.

She had only a few moments. The people beside Chartier were reciting a chant in unison, something foul and dark. She uttered a quick protect spell, hoping it would work against them, and knowing it wouldn't do a thing about the dagger.

Then she reached inside her supplies bag, and removed the box. She dropped the bag to the cobblestones as the knife, freed of the laptop, floated over the stone wall.

This time, she ran for the knife, holding the box open. As the knife came toward her, she slammed the box around it. It took a moment for the knife to lose its momentum. She felt it strain toward her even as the iron protected her. Then the struggle ceased.

"What's this all about?" she asked.

"Our shop," Chartier said. "My father had no right to sell you our shop."

"He didn't sell it to me."

"But you're the one who interferes."

The box rolled in her hands. The knife clattered inside. She had been wrong. The receipt had been wrong. Of course it wasn't an Assassin's Dagger. It was more sophisticated than that.

They had put that label on it to lead her astray.

She was facing either the Dagger of Hassan ibn-al-Sabbah or a *fidayeen* dagger, and she didn't know how to disable either one.

The crowd watched her and Chartier watched her, his eyes shining with anticipation. He wanted her to die. She had no idea why; she had never met him before. But she could feel the power of his hate.

The box swelled. In a moment it would explode open. She flung it as if she were a quarterback, and it soared, spinning, just like a football, until it dove down and landed in the center of the scummy moat.

She couldn't spell the knife, but she could spell the box, the moat. Hands trembling, she reached for her supplies bag.

"Nothing will help you now," Chartier said.

She ignored him. Her supplies bag grew hot. She removed the relics she needed as the bag scalded her skin. She could smell singed skin, and more than once she had to slap out fires that started on the fine hairs of her arm.

Relics, and her spells book. She didn't dare take out her incantation translator. She couldn't get one word wrong, because she didn't dare let the spell go dark.

Her cell phone started ringing, breaking her concentration. She had an urge to throw the plastic thing into the moat with the box. The scum was bubbling where the box had gone in, huge gaslike bubbles that seemed to come from underground.

She lined up her relics, grabbed the wand, and opened the book to a spell in the center. She started to read, wishing she didn't have to. Her only flaw as a mage: she never could memorize the hard spells. The book slammed closed.

She opened it again, but it slammed closed again. She glared at the people behind her. They couldn't spell her because of her protection shield, but they could spell the damn book. She grabbed it, pulled it against her and tried a third time.

And, a third time, it slammed closed.

More bubbles erupted from the moat. She was running out of time.

Maybe she had read enough. After all, it wasn't like she'd never done this spell before. She raised her arms, started reciting. The book skittered away from her, sliding up the stone wall, and then over, heading for the moat.

Damn them for distracting her. Like the phone which was still ringing.

She shut it all out, all but the bubbles in the moat, and continued reciting. Inside the green bubbles, she thought she saw a flash of silver and gold. Her heart started hammering.

She was out of time.

Snow burst from her wand, streaming for the moat. The silver thing—clearly it was the dagger—sliced up from the bottom, carrying more slime with it. Apparently it had gotten trapped in the scum.

The snow hit the slime, and then a huge cracking sound filled the air. The moat froze over with a deep glacial ice. The spell hadn't quite worked the way she wanted it, she hadn't planned on the glacial ice, but she was happy with it. The knife was trapped inside.

The knife still vibrated, sending cracks across the surface. She uttered a continual reinstate, and the cracks receded. Every time it seemed like the knife would break free, the ice trapped it.

The people behind her chanted some more. They could be doing one of a hundred counter spells. Quickly she clapped her hands together, doing a spell she'd done fifteen times in her career.

"To headquarters!" she snapped and everyone, including Chartier, disappeared.

For a moment, she stared at the empty storefront. Then she collapsed against the cobblestones, exhausted, her powers used. She certainly hadn't expected anything like this.

Her cell phone was still ringing.

She pulled it out of her pocket, flipped open the receiver and snapped, "What?"

"Oh, dear, is this a bad time?" Cedric, the curator from the British Museum asked.

"It is—but I—how are you, Cedric?" She had a million things to do. She had to explain to Abracadabra Corporate Headquarters why she had just sent them a crowd of people from France. She had to make certain that knife was neutralized. She had to see what else was in *Le Petit Château*.

"Quite fine, quite fine. I can ring you later if need be."

"No," she said, leaning against the stone wall. "Now's good."

"Your message said you're having a problem with an Assassin's Dagger?"

"Well, now I'm pretty sure that it's the Dagger of Hassan ibn-al-Sabbah or a *fidayeen* dagger."

"Truly? I'd love to see one. Where are you?"

She told him.

"Oh, my God," he said. "Describe the dagger."

She did.

"That can't be Middle Eastern," he said.

"That's what I thought, but it's acting like a *fidayeen* dagger."

"Then the rumors are true."

"Rumors?" Maybe she wasn't having this conversation. Maybe she was dreaming, after all. Maybe she would wake up and walk to the shop and everything would be as it was the night before.

"You know that many believe the Assassin's Daggers were created during the Crusades to discredit and perhaps even use against the *fidayeen*."

"I'd heard that."

"Well, they had to have been created somewhere."

She sat up. "You think they were created here?"

"There is an old magic shop there, goes by the name of *Le Jardin Noir*. Have you been there? Near the castle?"

"No," she said. "The shop near the castle is called *Le Petit Château*."

"Oh, that's right. They changed it just after the war." He meant World War II. There was no other war in this part of Europe. "Very nasty place. Very nasty. Built on the site of an ancient garden, near an old cathedral. The dark mages took over that cathedral for a time, decided to use magic to save the Christian world."

She rubbed a hand over her face. "This is the center of dark arts in France?"

"Perhaps in Europe."

"How come no one told us that?"

"Abracadabra? Someone probably did, but you Yanks always believe the best of people. The name change probably convinced your hierarchy that everything was all right. After all, it was sixty years ago—practically an eternity to an American."

She let that slide. "How do I neutralize the dagger, Cedric?"

"Find the spell," he said. "If they did create the daggers, the spell has to be there somewhere. I say, though, where would they have gotten your blood?"

She half-smiled. "From any one of a dozen shopkeepers, all of them dark, all of whom I put out of work."

"Oh, right then. Need me to come out there?"

"Not yet," she said. "But I'll let you know."

She flipped the phone closed and stood. The key ring was still attached to her wrist, and her possessions were still on the ground, but her supplies bag had burned up, and her laptop was gone.

She was on her own: no props, no technology.

She hoped there weren't any more daggers waiting for her inside.

But there was only one way to find out.

*   *   *

The shop had a faint odor of mold, the smell of age. The floor was made of stone, uneven, and tilted slightly toward the center of town.

Talia locked the door behind herself and walked as quietly as she could across the store's carpet. Nothing attacked her from the shelves or growled at her from the cases. Out front, at least, the store seemed completely normal.

Except for the receipt lying on the counter. She picked up the parchment, and it crumbled under her fingertips. Spelled, just like everything else. Done for her benefit and no one else's.

If she had been less cautious, not quite as good at her job as she was, she would have walked into the store yesterday afternoon, picked up the note on the floor and not even noticed the dagger as it sped toward her. She would have been dead before she perceived the threat.

A warning to Abracadabra? Perhaps. A simple operation, taking out one of their most valued employees, and warning them that more would die unless *Le Petit Château*, and maybe some of the other shops she'd closed, were set free of their corporate chains.

What had Chartier said? There was more than one kind of evil in the world. He probably saw Abracadabra as an American corporate evil, using money to eliminate his family's past. Which it had. But Abracadabra hadn't forced his father to sell. The old man had done that all on his own, and left with the profits.

How many times had she heard that in her career?

The walls got smoother the farther back she went. The stone was very old, worn, and the mold smell grew stronger here. She wound her way up the tiny staircase, found a locked, grated door, and used the key ring to open it.

Then she stepped inside a magic den unlike any she'd ever seen.

The stench of moat slime overpowered everything. Potions sat on shelves so old that the stone had blackened with time. A fireplace in the corner looked like it dated to the Romans, and some of the tools on the far wall seemed even older.

Recipes were written on the walls, on parchment yellowed with age, on tablecloths in a substance that looked suspiciously like blood. She found books filled with spells, all of them dark, and she saw vials filled with foul things.

She went through room after tiny room, until she found a more modern work area. And there, she saw a modern test tube, stained but empty, labeled with her name and her blood type. It had been shipped from Penzance.

Talia shuddered. Apparently Chartier and his friends had not just been acting for themselves, but also in revenge for the other dark stores she had closed.

Beside the vial, she found a recipe written in Latin. Fortunately, not Church Latin, but the more arcane version used for spells. This she could read.

It was the spell for creating a *fidayeen* dagger. She didn't touch the parchment, knowing better this time. She just read, amazed at the simplicity of the spell, and understood.

She finally knew what she had to do.

By the time she'd neutralized the dagger and thawed the moat, it was early evening. Her phone had rung incessantly, and she had finally turned it off so that she could focus on the task at hand.

Then she spelled herself to Abracadabra headquarters. Chartier and his troop were already gone, banned from their magical headquarters, and stripped of their abilities to shop at any of Abracadabra's stores.

That would limit some, but not all, of the group's magical abilities since Abracadabra was close to a complete monopoly on magic shops. But that was the extent of Abracadabra's powers, and there was no magical tribunal to appeal to.

If Chartier and his group wanted to continue fighting Abracadabra with dark magic, they could. Only now Abracadabra was warned.

As was Talia. She had done her job. More than her fair

share, in fact, since she actually found the long lost recipes for the *fidayeen* dagger, the Dagger of Hassan ibn-al-Sabbah, and the Assassin's Dagger. She also found several other lost spells, and an entire history of dark magic from the Crusades forward that had existed only in legend before.

Abracadabra offered her a reward, and she had only one request.

She was tired of traveling, tired of solving someone else's problems, tired of having no friends and no real life. She wanted to sleep for a week and then she wanted a nice quiet place to call her own.

She asked to take Chartier's place at *Le Petit Château*.

Her request, of course, was granted. Provided that she follow all of Abracadabra's rules. And since no one knew them better than she did, she was happy to oblige.

She mentioned this to Cedric, when she called him about her discoveries. He didn't seem as happy for her as she had expected.

"I worry about you," he said. "Your life has been so exciting up until now, and you're trading all of that for life in a small town in France."

"And a magic store with a hell of a history," she said. "One I'm sure that Chartier and his friends won't let go of so easily."

"You expect fights?" he asked.

"I hope for them," she said. "They'll keep life interesting."

And then, when she finished talking to him, she spelled herself back to the store.

It seemed smaller than it had just a few hours before, and dingier, as if some of the life had gone out of it. She supposed it had: she had taken all of the old potions, spells, and recipes to corporate headquarters so that they could be destroyed.

She had a lot of rebuilding to do, starting with the displays and the interior. She had to banish the mold smell and open up the ancient back rooms to sunlight. And she had to get a computerized cash register to comply with the corporation's regulations.

Small things, but important ones. Things that would make *Le Petit Château* completely hers.

Like a new name. She was toying with *Enchanté*, but she wasn't certain yet. The name would come as the store changed, grew, developed.

Like she would.

She smiled to herself, her exhaustion gone. She'd finally made a change.

It was about time.

THE SERPENT
OF THE LAKES

by Mel Odom

Mel Odom is an Oklahoma-based author who has written nearly a hundred novels that span the spectrum from science fiction to gaming to young adult to mystery. Among his recent books are the well-reviewed fantasy novel, The Rover, *several books in the* Buffy the Vampire Slayer *and* Sabrina the Teenage Witch *series, and the novelizations for the films* Vertical Limit, Tomb Raider, *and* Blade.

WEARING buckskin breeches, his chest painted red, the warrior stepped unannounced from the forest, a shadow lifted from the shifting fog only by throwing the tomahawk at Taregan. The weapon flipped and the sharp steel head glistened.

Burdened by the weight of the buck deer across his shoulders, Taregan staggered for an instant, then twisted and dodged. The spinning weapon chopped into the brush behind the young brave as he dropped the deer.

"We have an enemy among us!" The painted warrior melted back into the fog-bound forest.

"Who?" Another man's voice rolled through the trees a little farther away.

Taregan folded into the brush as his father and his grandfather had taught him. Since he had been a young boy in the tribe, he had been trained in the paths of the warrior and the hunter.

"An Algonquin."

Feeling the rough tree bark at his back, Taregan listened to the soft footfalls of the hidden warriors. Taregan wasn't prepared to make war; he'd been hunting to provide for his family and the strength of the tribe.

"Is the Algonquin alone?"

Listening to the man's voice, Taregan knew the timbre was different from the first two. Three enemies moved through the forest.

Taregan slid his deer sinew bowstring from the pouch at his waist, looped an end of the string over one end of the bow and dropped that end to the top of his moccasin. With practiced ease, he bent the bow and finished stringing it. Taking shallow breaths, he offered a silent entreaty to Bear, the spirit totem of his tribe, asking for patience and for strength to kill his enemies and warn his people.

"He's alone," the first warrior replied.

Wary and alert, tracking the warrior's voice, Taregan slipped an arrow from his quiver. He kept the bow low and out of sight as he hunkered down and moved through the brush.

"He's just a boy," the warrior said, and Taregan knew the man intended to hurt and frighten with his words, just as the man intended to kill him if the chance presented. "He's not old enough to be much of a warrior."

Taregan wore fringed deerskin leggings, a breechcloth, and moccasins. The sash around his waist held his toma-hawk at his right hip and the scabbarded scalping knife at his left.

The first Erielhonan warrior slid through the forest and stopped at a fallen tree. Taregan recognized the tribal enemy from the painted marks his foe wore. A chill trembled through the young brave. The Erielhonan sometimes carried poisoned arrows into battle.

Cautious as a beaver leaving the water to travel treacherous dry ground, the Erielhonan man rose from behind the tree.

"Has the coward fled?" one of the other warriors demanded.

Lifting the bow and drawing the arrow fletchings back to his jawline, Taregan stepped from the trees. The Erielhonan warrior turned to face the young Algonquin brave.

The Erielhonan man started to yell, but Taregan released the bowstring. The arrow darted as swift and lethal as a diving hawk taking a fish. Following the chipped flint arrowhead through the Erielhonan warrior's throat, the ash shaft sank to the turkey feather fletchings.

The warrior fell, clawing at the arrow in his throat.

Taregan remained low to the ground, like a rabbit evading a hunting eagle's sharp claws. The swirling fog took him in as he nocked another arrow to bowstring. Here in the deepest part of the forest, the shadows remained thick and dark even under a noonday sun.

Taregan ran parallel to the crest of the last hill before the lush river valley where his tribe had built their village even before the time of his grandfather's grandfather. During that time, the Algonquins had warred with the Erielhonans over the ease of access the land provided to the river. Neither tribe claimed ownership to the land, which was an unheard of concept until the coming of the white man from the great ocean to the East and the strange lands beyond; but the sachems of both the Algonquins and the Erielhonans believed their gods had blessed them with the rights of hunting and fishing in the area. They could not live in peace.

Until now, the Erielhonans had reluctantly stayed away from Taregan's people. As the young brave scanned the fog-shrouded forest around him, he wondered what had upset the balance between the tribes.

Even as quietly as he traveled, Taregan frightened a young doe from hiding. With awkward grace on too-long legs, a fawn with a spotted rump followed her mother down the hillside away from the men. The young brave froze, knowing if the two Erielhonan warriors had much experience they would do they same. Movement attracted a warrior's eye when he stalked the death ground.

"That was a deer," one man said.

"I saw her," the other warrior said. "Perhaps when we finish this day, we can track her."

"We already have the deer the boy left us."

"We will take the other deer as well, to prove to the old ones how good the hunting is in this land."

Listening carefully, Taregan placed the two warriors. One was behind and the other was uphill, between him and his home. Moving with quiet ease, the young brave traveled along the brush line. No leaf shivered to mark his passage.

Taregan approached the crest of the hill at an oblique angle, taking advantage of the thick brush. The ground, softened from the heavy rains only two days ago, shifted beneath his moccasins. If they caught his trail, he knew they could follow him.

As he went, Taregan's mind wrestled with the questions raised by the presence of the Erielhonan war party. If the group had only been a small band of hunters, they would have marked themselves with hunter's paint instead of war paint. In the before time, before today and before the white man had come into the land and spread like a disease, the Erielhonan had not painted themselves so garishly. But they had found in their trading and in their warring with the Europeans that vivid paint colors and symbols struck fear into the hearts of the newcomers.

And if these Erielhonans made up a war party, had they come to murder lone Algonquin hunters? Or were they only a few of a much larger group?

The cover provided by the brush ended midway up the hillside. In time past, the river had sheared through the small valley on the other side of the hill from the deeper valley. The current had sloughed off part of the hillside, leaving a deep, crooked scar of bedrock.

The barren strip of land offered no protection.

Taregan halted behind the brush with an arrow nocked and the bow across his knees. The fog swirled like capering spirits across the naked strip of land. Rabbits, mice, and squirrels might never leave one side of the forest for the other and live out their whole lives there, knowing they risked exposure to predators if they crossed the barren strip.

Scanning the forest on the other side, Taregan knew the area was a good place for an ambush. If he'd had the chance, he might have used the place as such.

Nothing moved. No birds sang. The feathered and furred forest folk knew that death walked among them.

If Taregan had known his family and his village were safe, if he had known that Kaliska—the young woman he had offered his heart to—was safe, he would have hunkered down into the woodlands and forced the Erielhonan warriors to seek him out at their own risk. But he didn't know those things.

Offering a prayer to his gods, Taregan touched the deer-skin medicine bag on his cougar-claw necklace. The young brave hoped that all the skill and luck his grandfather had woven into the medicine were still strong.

Taregan exploded from the brush, driving his legs hard against the soft ground, feeling his moccasins sink in the soft earth till he reached the unyielding bedrock. The other side of the forest offered protection less than thirty feet away.

The Erielhonan warrior emerged from the sheltering girth of a white-barked poplar with a bow in his hands and took deliberate aim.

Never breaking stride, Taregan shifted his aim and let his own arrow fly. The arrows crossed each other in mid-flight. Before Taregan could drop the bow, the Erielhonan shaft took him high in the upper chest. His own arrow skidded off a branch over his enemy's head.

"He is here," the warrior yelled.

As he dropped the bow to one side and the pain and fear of his wound seared his mind, Taregan lifted the steel-bladed tomahawk from his sash. He pushed through the pain, watching as the Erielhonan warrior dropped his bow and reached for the tomahawk at his side.

Only feet from his enemy, Taregan leaped and collided with his opponent, driving them both to ground. Taregan felt the arrow in his shoulder snap. His arm felt sluggish as he rolled to his feet. Pain gnawed at the edges of his conscious mind.

Sliding the tomahawk's shaft through his fingers, he gripped the end of the handle so his blow would be most powerful. He stepped toward the Erielhonan warrior, who had come to his feet as well and blocked the tomahawk blow.

Taller and thicker than Taregan, the Erielhonan warrior disengaged his tomahawk and stepped forward. A cruel grin twisted his lips.

Taregan retreated, blocking his enemy's merciless blows, then stepped to the left, lowered his tomahawk and caught the Erielhonan warrior's lifted right foot with the underside of his blade. Taregan yanked upward, pulling his opponent's leg backward, turning and setting himself, sweeping a high kick to the back of his opponent's head, tripping him and driving him to the ground. Before the Erielhonan warrior could push himself from the ground, Taregan smashed his tomahawk into the back of the man's skull. Bone crunched. The Erielhonan shivered and lay still.

Rising at once, Taregan transferred his tomahawk to his left hand, then pulled the broken stub of the arrow through his shoulder. The shaft had gone through his flesh and scraped bone, but he knew that he would live and heal.

"Where is he?" the surviving Erielhonan demanded.

"Your friend is dead." Taregan took a fresh grip on his tomahawk. Cold, gray tendrils of fog swept in as if drawn by the warm blood running down his upper body.

"You will die, too, boy," the Erielhonan shouted. "Our shaman has made peace with the Serpent of the Lakes and joined the monster to our struggle against the Algonquin. Even now a war party journeys to your village."

Kneeling, Taregan grabbed moss from a nearby tree. Gritting his teeth against the burning pain, Taregan shoved moss into the two wounds the arrow had made. He hoped the arrowhead had not been poisoned. The moss would leave scars, but for now the wounds were plugged to slow the bleeding.

Ever watchful, the young brave made his way to the hilltop and ran, stretching out his stride the way his father had taught him when they had run wounded deer to ground. The fog chilled his skin, but fear fired his heart.

"Run, boy," the Erielhonan warrior yelled. "Run, but you're too late." His mocking laughter filled the emerald green forest around Taregan.

When Taregan first saw the wooden palisade that protected the village of his people, the young brave thought he had arrived in time to give warning. Then, beneath the fog layers, he saw the line of bodies that led from the slow river to the spit of land where the Algonquins had built their longhouses. Warriors and women and children sprawled across the muddy bank of the river. Surviving warriors ringed the inside of the village palisade, and the young brave knew he'd been spotted.

"Taregan," a warrior called.

Drawn in shocked horror to the site of the bloody battle that had left bodies strewn over the riverbank, Taregan ignored the call.

"Taregan," the man tried again. "Come inside. The Serpent of the Lakes may return."

But Taregan stepped through the corpses of the men, women, and children. Helpless tears blurred his vision. He struggled to wipe them away so he could search for the face he dared not find. Carrion eaters, crows and possums and crayfish, worked the bodies of the dead, and sometimes Taregan had to wave his arms and drive them away.

"She's not there, Grandson."

Hopeful then, and ashamed of his reaction because he dared feel that way when so many had died, Taregan looked at the old man standing farther up the riverbank.

"Kaliska is alive, Grandfather?" Taregan asked.

Silver streaked the old man's hair braids, and time had

wrinkled his face and stripped much of his strength from him. He clutched a stout spear carved with medicine signs in his gnarled fists that had served him during war in times past. These days, though, he leaned on the weapon for support.

"I don't know if Kaliska lives, Grandson," Ahanu replied. "Only that she is not among those dead here."

Fear quaked through Taregan. He gazed at the pale blue of the river, at the dead faces he saw so clearly beneath the water. Around him, green brush and plants festooned the rich brown earth. Higher up on the hills, a field held tall stalks of corn and vines laden with squashes. The blue sky cradled the warm sun. Sweeping across the riverbank, the gentle breeze carried the sweet fragrance of flowers and grass. If he closed his eyes, Taregan felt certain the day would seem like any other he had spent on the riverbank.

"Where is Kaliska?" Taregan asked.

"The Serpent of the Lakes took her," Ahanu said, "as he took three other young women from our tribe."

All the stories Taregan remembered hearing about the ancient monster rattled through his mind. At the bottom of the deep lake the Europeans had named after the Erielhonan tribe, shortening the name to Erie, the Serpent of the Lakes lived in a longhouse built from the bones of his victims. He controlled the waves and waterways of the lakes. He came to the surface only to accept tribute from the tribes that traveled or fished the lakes and even the rivers that fed them, and that tribute was always measured in human lives.

By all accounts, from tribes that told stories about the Serpent of the Lakes, he was a monster. He was man-shaped but three times the size of the tallest warrior. His skin was scaly like a fish, and dark green like a soft-shell turtle.

"No one tried to save her?"

"Those who tried," Ahanu said, "lie stretched out on the ground before you." He walked through the bodies and stopped at the water's edge. "Here are Kaliska's father and two brothers."

Grieving for the men he'd known all of his life and for all

the others that had been lost, Taregan stared at the bodies. If Kaliska had accepted the offer of his heart, these men would have been his family. Horrible wounds showed in the flesh of all three warriors. They hadn't died easily.

The old man returned to Taregan and took his un-wounded arm gently in his hand. "Come, grandson. You have come a long way and you are wounded. Let me tend you, then we will talk of what we must do."

Heavy-hearted and numb with loss and fear, the young brave allowed his grandfather to lead him away.

A nightmare woke Taregan, yanking him from slumber to coughing shudders and a thundering heart. He shoved the bear robe from him. Cold sweat covered him and soaked his clothing.

"Easy, Grandson," Ahanu whispered from Taregan's side. The old man sat cross-legged beside him in the dark-ness that filled the longhouse. He held eagle feathers in both hands and clenched a pipe of tobacco between his teeth.

From his training, Taregan knew the eagle feathers warded against evil spirits that brought only restless sleep or none at all, and the tobacco smoke appeased the gods and drew favor.

"I dreamed a medicine dream, Grandfather," Taregan whispered hoarsely.

"Maybe it was only the fever," the old man said, handing him a hollowed-out gourd that contained the thin broth of rabbit stew the women had prepared earlier.

"I must find the longhouse of the Three Sisters, Grandfa-ther," Taregan said in a hoarse voice.

Ahanu looked away from him, turning his attention to a bowl of rabbit stew beside him. "You must eat, Grandson, and keep up your strength."

Grudgingly, Taregan accepted the soup. "We can't wait. More of our people will die when the sun comes up."

"You don't know that."

"The Erielhonan people won't rest until they have claimed our village as their own." Taregan's voice broke as he continued speaking. "And I won't allow the Serpent of the Lakes to keep Kaliska. I love her. If I have to, Grandfather, I will confront the monster on my own as I am."

"You would die." Ahanu's eyes shone like obsidian, flat and lifeless. "I have buried my son, Taregan, after he died in my arms. And I buried his wife who was like a daughter to me when the sickness took her. Would you have me bury my only grandchild as well?"

"Would you rejoice in having a grandson who lived only in shame?" For a moment, Taregan thought the old man would stare him down. During their life together since his father's death when Taregan was only a boy and his mother's death only a short time later, the young brave had seen Ahanu turn aside even the sachem's fierce gaze.

"Tell me of your dream, Grandson," Ahanu said in a soft voice.

"It was about the Three Sisters."

The three goddesses had come into the world and brought corn, barley, and beans to the People. The Three Sisters had shared the secret knowledge of how to grow the crops with the women of the tribes, ensuring the women power and prestige because the men were proud and sometimes lazy.

"What of the Three Sisters?" Ahanu asked.

"You've told me many stories of their longhouse, Grandfather," Taregan said. "They keep weapons with powerful medicine there."

"So the tales say," the old man agreed.

"I must go there and ask for the loan of some of their medicine." Taregan had never even considered going in search of the Three Sisters' longhouse before. Only death awaited those who tried to take from the Sisters.

"That would be a fool's quest to travel unprotected through the forest in these times."

Feeling the fever burning within him, seeing his body glisten with sweat, Taregan leaned back against the bark side of the longhouse. He looked away from his grandfather and at the families sleeping around them. "This evening,

Grandfather, our warriors left the bodies of the dead out on the riverbanks for predators because they feared attack."

"The Serpent of the Lakes might decide to return at any time," the old man said. "We must protect those that live."

"Grandfather," Taregan said, "we can't protect them. At best, we can only offer those around us a lingering death if the Serpent of the Lakes returns."

"Perhaps the monster will not return."

"There's no reason why the monster shouldn't." Curling his hand into a fist, Taregan laid the fist over his thundering heart. "Our family has been tied tightly to the medicine of our tribe. You have always told me this. As warriors, my father, your father, and his father's father's father before him fought monsters and men to keep our tribe safe from harm."

"Yes." The old man bowed his head. "All those stories are true, Grandson. I am shamed, for I am afraid to lose you."

Taregan placed his hand on his grandfather's narrow, bony shoulder. For the first time, Taregan noticed how frail and withered the old man had become. Fear, as Ahanu had always told him, somehow made a man smaller.

"If I do not follow my heart in this, Grandfather, then you have already lost me."

Ahanu nodded. "In the morning, then. The dead will draw the predators tonight. Now, eat your stew and let me pray over you that the fever may leave your body. You will need to be strong, for the way is not easy."

Taregan ate the stew in quick bites and hoped that the warm broth stayed down. The whole time, his grandfather prayed over him, burning tobacco and waving the eagle feathers. When he finished the stew, the young brave passed the bowl back to his grandfather, then pulled up the thick bear robe, hoping to sweat the fever out before morning.

The young brave's last waking thoughts centered on Kaliska, but he dared not think them too deeply because he didn't want to dwell on what the Serpent of the Lakes might already have done to her.

*   *   *

Sweat poured from Taregan as he strode up the mountainside, following the narrow game trail through the dense brush. Red furred squirrels scampered among the boughs, watching Taregan and his grandfather. Occasionally, the squirrels tossed nuts and chattered threateningly. Birds swooped under the leaves and branches, and sometimes burst through the emerald canopy to seek the blue sky. Rabbits had gotten scarce the higher up the mountainside they'd gone, but Taregan had found sign of deer and foxes.

Ahanu labored farther down the game trail, leaning on the feathered war spear he carried. He wore a bear robe against the chill that lay over the forest.

Taregan had tried to talk his grandfather out of accompanying him. Ahanu's strength, however, proved surprising, and his reluctance to accept his grandson's help would be a thing of legend, an elemental force.

"Perhaps we should rest for a time," Taregan suggested when the old man reached him.

"No." Ahanu looked up the mountain. "We are almost there. If you look hard, up to the left, you'll see the mouth of a cave." He pointed.

Taregan scanned the mountainside, then noticed a deep shadow under an overhang. The cave wasn't far away, and it seemed that he was already somehow closer to Kaliska. "Are you sure you can climb there, Grandfather?"

"Of course," the old man replied. "And you will need someone to make the medicine to open the way to the Three Sisters." Without another word, Ahanu took the lead.

A short time later, they stood in front of the cave's mouth. Taregan's nose wrinkled at the sour stench of animal infestation that shortened his breath.

"Light a torch, Grandson," Ahanu said.

"Are you sure this is the way, Grandfather?" Despite his misgivings, Taregan dropped the deerskin pouch he and the old man had packed in the early hours of the morning for the trip and rummaged inside.

The old man stood resolute before the cave mouth with

his bear robe pulled tightly around him. "I have been here before. I would never forget."

Taregan struck sparks from his flint and steel several times but couldn't get the pitchblende torch to light. Gently, Ahanu took the unlighted torch from Taregan's hand and strode into the cave. As soon as he passed the threshold, the torch lit explosively.

"Ah," the old man whispered. "We are welcome here. Otherwise the torch would not have lit."

"A welcome is good," Taregan said, though he wasn't sure.

"Not always." Ahanu continued forward, ducking a little to avoid collision with the low roof.

At first, Taregan believed the cave was small and low-ceilinged throughout, but gradually the narrow tunnel opened into a more respectable cavern. Ahanu straightened and held the flaming torch high.

Leathery rustling sounded among the stalactites jutting from the ceiling.

Bats, Taregan realized with a chill. He'd rarely encountered the creatures in the forests, and never within a cave that he knew to be infested with them. The thought of being covered by the tiny animals as they clung to him and fought him left him with cold dread.

"Ignore them, Grandson," Ahanu advised. "The bats won't bother us if we don't bother them."

"We're invading their cave, Grandfather," Taregan said. Uneasy, gaze darting along the upper regions of the cave constantly, he followed the old man.

"This cave isn't theirs," Ahanu disagreed. "As we belong to the land, so do the bats belong to the cave. But this place is special, Grandson. This place is kept sacred by the Three Sisters."

Taregan's fingers raked the barren floor of the cave. A few gnawed bones covered the uneven surface amid the dirt and guano-stained rocks. Nothing about the cave looked sacred.

Ahanu kept walking, following a tunnel that had been invisible even with the blazing torch. Water glistened along the wall to Taregan's right, letting him know some of the stream's bounty coming from the mountaintop passed through the rock. Pools caught and reflected the torch his grandfather carried.

"This place," Ahanu said in a soft voice, "was set apart for the People by the Three Sisters only a little while after the Earth was formed upon the turtle's back. This is a place of great medicine."

Thinking of Kaliska, filled with the pain of her absence, Taregan hoped so. His thoughts tracked back to the last morning he'd seen her. Young and shy, she'd hesitantly shown him the new deerskin shirt she was making for him, letting him admire the beaded patterns and designs she was adding. He'd promised her that he would bring meat back for the tribe, and she'd promised to have the shirt finished by then. And then he'd asked her to marry him. His request had surprised them both. She'd turned away from him and not answered.

Now, he might never know that answer.

He offered a quick, silent prayer that nothing had happened to her, and that the Three Sisters would give him the path to the Serpent of the Lakes and the means to destroy the monster.

The tunnel ended only a little farther on. A narrow dagger of land thrust out into an underground pool, which glimmered pale green under the influence of Ahanu's torch. A charred pit that held the burned husks of coals occupied the end of the land.

Bat wings fluttered overhead as Taregan followed his grandfather to the water's edge. Despite the lack of wood or fresh coals, the black pit that contained the remnants of the campfire lit as soon as Ahanu touched the torch to it. Yellow-tongued flames leaped up from the fire pit and spun glowing orange embers through the air.

Ahanu sat cross-legged at the side of the fire pit. "Sit, Grandson."

"Where is the longhouse of the Three Sisters?" Taregan

asked. "I don't see a way out of this cavern other than the way we entered."

"You are not meant to. Now sit." Turning his attention from his grandson, the old man doffed his bear robes and rummaged through the beaded leather pouch he carried at his side.

Reluctant, thinking of Kaliska in the clutches of the Serpent of the Lakes, Taregan sat on the other side of the fire pit from his grandfather. The pouch was Ahanu's medicine bag, cleverly sewn so that a number of pockets were available inside. Firelight flashed against the gems and rocks that had been stitched onto the worn leather.

Ahanu chanted, his words a hoarse, rasping whisper above the undercurrent of noise trapped inside the cave.

Taregan recognized only a few of the words and knew that his grandfather spoke the ancient spirit words of warriors preparing for battle. He followed Ahanu's lead and repeated the words he knew.

Leaning forward, Ahanu dribbled powder and bits of dried crushed leaves over the fire. The flames reached for the leaves and powder like a wolf freed from a trap. Bright purple, orange, and blue flared around them and brought out medicine symbols carved deeply into the cavern's stone walls.

The light-green water trapped and held the colors from the powders and leaves even after they had burned out above the fire pit. The colors spun and whirled beneath the pool's surface. As the powders and leaves burned, smoke rose in a cloud around the blazing fire pit. Warmth seeped into Taregan bone-deep, and the heady scent of tobacco and other herbs filled his nostrils. His senses reeled and he knew his grandfather's medicine was strong.

In the next moment, Taregan spotted something alive and moving beneath the pool's surface. He dropped his hand to the tomahawk at his waist.

"Be still, Grandson," Ahanu whispered.

Under the pool, the blurred shape swam through the fuzzy colors, then reached for the pool's rocky edge with a webbed paw. Black fur slicked back by the water, the beaver held onto the pool's edge. Cautiously, the creature pushed up and looked at the two men sitting on either side of the fire pit. Using one paw, the beaver raked his whiskers, brushing away water droplets that glistened like worked silver in the firelight.

The beaver shot a curious look at Taregan, then looked at the old man. "Welcome to my home, Ahanu."

"Thank you, Beaver," the old man replied. "I came in the hopes that you would see me."

"You will always be welcome, my friend." Hoisting himself up, the beaver crawled onto the rocky land and waddled over to the fire. He was fat but had a proud carriage about him. Balancing on his flat tail, Beaver held his paws out to the fire.

"I treasure your friendship," Ahanu said.

Were it not for the elongated round face and the creature's small size, Taregan thought Beaver could have passed as a tiny man in a hide robe.

"As I treasure yours." Beaver returned his attention to Taregan. "And this must be your grandson. He favors his father, and you."

"Yes," Ahanu replied. "Taregan, this is Beaver."

Taregan nodded. He felt thickheaded and slowed.

"Beaver has always been my chosen spirit guide," Ahanu said. "The tribe follows Bear in all things, but when I work my medicine, Beaver has been my teacher." The old man reached into his medicine bag again and took out a few morsels.

Beaver smelled the proffered morsels and his eyes flashed in the firelight. "Honeyed acorns."

"Yes," Ahanu said. "I always keep some put back for you. I only wish that I was still well enough to make the trip up here more often to leave you more."

Beaver captured one of the morsels in a webbed paw and shoved it into his mouth. "Perhaps now that Taregan has been here he can bring me such delicacies."

Taregan had to clear his throat twice to speak after his

grandfather glanced at him. "Of course, Beaver." Even as he spoke to the creature, amazed in spite of all the stories his grandfather and father had told him about encounters with spirits during their adventures, he had trouble believing what he saw.

Waiting politely, Ahanu offered more morsels to Beaver.

The animal spirit took another treat, but turned his attention to the old man. "What brings you here, old friend?"

"We came seeking a favor, Beaver. Taregan seeks an audience with the Three Sisters."

"Why?"

In a quiet voice filled with emotion, Ahanu related the events of the Erielhonan warriors' attack on the Algonquin village while aided by the Serpent of the Lakes.

Beaver scratched his whiskered chin in thought, and his claws rasped audibly against the leathery toughness. "The Erielhonan people have drifted far from the old ways."

"They've been trading too much with the newcomers," Ahanu said.

"The unbelievers who think they can own the land and control the winds," Beaver said. "If they are able, the unbelievers will take the People far from the things they have been taught. The People will learn to think of themselves as things apart from nature, which will lead them to self-destruction."

Ahanu nodded.

"Beaver," Taregan said, interrupting.

The creature looked at the young warrior, and irritation showed in the black eyes on either side of the wedge-shaped head.

"The Serpent of the Lakes has my wife-to-be," Taregan said. His own words shocked him; never before had he spoken of Kaliska as his wife-to-be. They were in love, and he had always thought of them as that. But he assumed that she would return that love, and that her answer to his question would be yes.

"You could find another," Beaver suggested.

Taregan glanced at his grandfather, but the old man kept his face impassive.

"No," Taregan said.

Beaver cleaned his whiskers again. "That is a very self-ish view of the world, boy. You would deprive your tribe of a distinguished lineage. You and those that have gone before you are born warriors. And you can talk to some in the spirit world when so many of the people have given up believing."

Taregan hesitated for a moment, steeling himself against the beaver's fierce gaze. All his life, his father and grandfather had trained him to be respectful of Beaver, Bear, Turtle, Fox, Raven, and the other spirits. But the stories he'd been told also indicated that the spirits, although powerful, oftentimes shared the views of the People, their strengths and their weaknesses.

"There can be no other for me," Taregan said.

Beaver slapped his flat tail on the rocks in annoyance. The wet smack echoed throughout the cave and disturbed some of the bats above.

"Seeking out the Serpent of the Lakes could mean your death, boy," Beaver snarled. "Many of your tribe have already learned that."

"There is no other choice I can live with."

Beaver shook his wedge-shaped head. "So young, and yet so certain. Ahanu, couldn't you have trained the whelp any better than this?"

"Beaver," the old man said, "I did the best that I could."

"My grandfather has no responsibility in this," Taregan said.

"Of course he does," Beaver snapped. "He brought you here, didn't he?"

"If I had known of this place, I would have come on my own."

Beaver smacked his tail again, causing yet another rustle of leathery wings above. "And you would never have found this place. Nor me." He paced about upright, waddling on his short back legs.

Ahanu offered more treats, but Beaver ignored them.

"Seeing the Three Sisters is not an easy thing to hope for. Since giving the People the gift of barley, corn, and beans, and teaching the women of the tribes how to cultivate and care for the crops, they haven't had much to do with this world."

"I have to rescue Kaliska," Taregan said. "Nothing else is acceptable.

After studying Taregan for a moment, Beaver reached into the fire pit and took out a brightly glowing coal. The fur and flesh of his paw didn't burn or even singe. He pushed the coal toward Taregan's face.

Unflinching, Taregan waited, feeling the heat of the coal against his forehead and cheeks.

Beaver halted the coal only inches from Taregan's face. The animal spirit shoved his head forward in a challenging manner. His black eyes searched Taregan's face. "Do you love her that much, boy?"

"Yes," Taregan answered without hesitation.

"Enough to die for her?"

"Enough to fight for her," Taregan said. "I don't plan on dying; I plan on winning."

Throwing back his wedge-shaped head, Beaver laughed, then turned away and took one of the morsels from Ahanu's hand. "He is most definitely your grandson."

"Yes." A slight smile played on Ahanu's face. "What shall we do with him?"

"Keep him with you. He has portent."

"He is in love. You remember love, don't you, Beaver?"

"A worthless emotion," the animal spirit snorted.

"The most powerful thing ever made by the spirits," Ahanu countered.

"A mistake we made when we first began to conceive of the People."

"Love is the only thing that truly sets us apart from everything that has gone on before us. If not for love, we would be no more than the animals that exist in the forest and swamps and lakes. Love is the greatest gift the spirits ever granted the People."

"Love is weakness."

"Love is strength also. You can't have the one without the other."

"You would let him go?" Beaver asked. "Knowing that he will face the Serpent of the Lakes if he is able, and perhaps die?"

"He gives me no choice."

"You could stop him."

"Easier to stop the wind," Ahanu said.

"Then it shall be." Beaver whirled without warning and hurled the glowing coal he still carried in one clenched paw.

Desperate, Taregan tried to leap up and dodge out of the way at the same time, but the lethargy slowed him, made him behave as though he was moving through thick mud. The burning coal came closer, until he could pick out the different glowing surfaces that spun around.

Then the coal exploded in a fiery shower.

Taregan expected to be consumed by the leaping flames. Instead, the flames wrapped around him, blinding him with their brightness.

"Be safe, Grandson," Ahanu called out, but his words slid away as dizziness swam through Taregan's head.

Taregan's senses returned slowly. Cold mud burned into his left cheek, and rain slapped against the right side of his face. He blinked his eye open and found himself lying on a riverbank under a leaden gray sky.

His grandfather and Beaver and the cave were nowhere to be seen.

Brown streaks showed in the gray river, proof that the current tore at the earth and wore it away. Thick forest hung over the river from the banks on both sides. The sky held whirling black and gray storm clouds.

"Are you going to sit there all day?" a grumpy voice demanded.

Taregan fisted his tomahawk and followed the sound of the voice.

A large snapping turtle regarded him from the river's

edge. The creature lay half in and half out of the swiftly
moving water, rocking gently in the fierce current. The dark
green shell was as long as Taregan's arm from shoulder to
fingertip, and nearly as wide. Mottled gray-green skin covered the creature's thick, bulbous head and feet.

"Who are you?" Taregan asked.

The creature wiped at the curved beak that framed his
mouth. "And who would you think I'd be?"

Taregan glanced around the riverbank. "Where is
Beaver?"

"Beaver passed you on to me," the turtle replied.

"Why?"

"I can take you the rest of the way to the longhouse of the
Three Sisters." The turtle clambered out of the water, leaving a wide track in the mud behind him. "Do you know
me?"

"You are Turtle."

The curved beak of a mouth almost smiled, mocking
Taregan. Turtle cocked his head at the end of his long neck
and focused one orange eye on Taregan. "Of course I am
Turtle. There could be no other such as I." He lurched forward, lifting himself on all four legs so that his shell cleared
the mud.

Soaked to the skin and cold, Taregan followed. He gazed
through the dank and forbidding forested lands. The forest
was the gloomiest place the young brave had ever been, and
fear vibrated within him. Then he felt guilty. Surely the
hardships Kaliska and the other women were experiencing
were much worse than any discomfort he was going
through.

Low as he was, Turtle had no problem with the brush and
trees that Taregan had to fight his way through. Turtle simply slipped through the forest as if following an old and familiar trail.

"Are you always this clumsy?" Turtle demanded.

"The way is hard," Taregan protested.

"Only because you have eyes and you choose not to see."

Turtle kept lunging ahead, not even leaving a quivering leaf to mark his passage.

Challenged by Turtle's harshly spoken words, Taregan paused and studied the path the animal spirit chose.

"Look to the side," Turtle advised. "You can never see what lies directly in front of you when you are looking for it."

Cocking his head, Taregan narrowed his eyes and used his hunter's vision, tracking the forest through his peripheral vision. Then, as if fog had lifted from his vision, Taregan spotted the trail Turtle followed. The young brave moved into step with Turtle, following a different but similar path.

The going became easier.

Turtle wasn't as much of a talker as Beaver had been. Quietly and without discussion, they made their way through the uphill country till they arrived at a solitary longhouse in a small clearing beside the river. Built of young saplings bent and shaped while still green and fresh-cut, and covered in bark sections that had been sewn together using thread made of animal hair and bear and deer sinew, the longhouse looked no different than those of Taregan's tribe. But the young brave felt the power of the place resonating within him.

Without pause, Turtle plodded out of the forest and into the clearing toward the longhouse. "Come on, boy, if you would rescue this girl that you profess to love so much."

Tomahawk in hand, Taregan stepped into the clearing.

As Turtle approached, the door opened suddenly and a beautiful woman stuck her head out. Her hair was black as the night and she wore a deerskin skirt with beadwork designs of flowering cornstalks.

"Turtle," the woman said, stepping back and holding the door open. "Welcome to our home."

"Thank you, Sister Corn," Turtle said as he crawled on into the longhouse. "I bring Taregan. He is of the Algonquin people, and grandson of Ahanu."

"Enter, Taregan," Sister Corn said. "Be welcome in my

house as your father was and his father before him, and all
their fathers before them."

Heart beating rapidly, Taregan stepped into the house and
put his tomahawk back at his side. The dome-shaped roof
showed curved saplings as they would in any home his tribe
might make, and piggin' strings held meats and bags of veg-
etables from the rafters. A neatly laid fire occupied the center of the longhouse. Baskets lined the walls and held herbs
and bones.

"Sit." Sister Corn waved to a place by the fire.

Taregan sat, but his eyes wandered covetously to the war
lances, shields, tomahawks, knives, bows, and quivers of arrows that lined the walls. Several other items, some of them
things that he felt certain he recognized from stories his
grandfather had told him, hung on the walls as well.

Turtle sat up on his back legs and shell, then held his
forepaws out to the fire. "Ah, but this is a welcome place
you have here, Sister Corn. I do enjoy my visits."

"I am glad." Sister Corn retreated briefly to one of the
woven-hair sacks, then returned carrying two flat cakes. "I
have only honey-dipped corncakes to offer you as guests.
Had I known you were coming, I could have given more."

Turtle accepted his cake graciously. "No, this is plenty. I
would crawl long distances for the corncakes you and your
sisters make."

Sister Corn nodded and sat. "Thank you." She lifted her
black eyes to Taregan. "Is your corncake satisfactory?"

Taregan looked at the untouched food on his hand. He bit
off a piece and chewed, finding the flavor delicious. "Yes. It
is the best I've ever eaten. I'm sorry, but my mind is elsewhere." He wasn't sure about the protocols involved in
speaking to the Three Sisters. In the stories his grandfather
had told him, the People were always represented by the animal spirits to the great spirits.

"Are you ill?" Sister Corn asked. "If so, I have some
herbs and poultices that may cure you."

"Young Taregan has no physical sickness," Turtle said.
"His heart is sick."

Concern touched Sister Corn's beautiful face. "Are you in love with one who does not return your love then, Taregan? Or perhaps you are so ambivalent about love that you can't pick from those that catch your eye? I have potions and herbs that can help you."

"No," Turtle said. "Taregan's troubles are much worse. The Serpent of the Lakes has taken his true love."

"That is a terrible thing," Sister Corn agreed. "Better to mourn her and move on to your next love now."

"Mourn her?" Taregan couldn't believe it. "Kaliska is not dead." Surely as much as he loved her, he would know if such a terrible thing came to pass.

"If the Serpent of the Lakes has her," Sister Corn said, "then she might as well be. You'll never see her again."

Taregan started to stand, but Turtle quickly rested a foreleg on one of the young brave's legs. Turtle's strength proved to be too much, surprising Taregan greatly.

"Taregan can't live without her," Turtle said.

Sister Corn shook her head sorrowfully. "It is only a feeling, Turtle. He is young. The feeling will pass."

"Beaver sent him to me," Turtle insisted, "and asked that I bring him to you."

"Beaver should not have done that."

Turtle quietly continued eating his corncake. "Beaver felt he had no choice. This is true love."

Sister Corn shook her head. "Beaver is a romantic and soft in the head."

Taregan couldn't believe that the beautiful woman would think that irascible Beaver was a romantic.

"Beaver also knows true love when he sees it," Turtle said.

Sister Corn made a face. "You're just as bad as Beaver, Turtle."

"Perhaps," Turtle admitted.

"All of this talk of love is nonsense," Sister Corn protested.

"One day," Turtle said patiently, "you will know love too, Sister Corn, and you will know what you are missing."

"A bad case of heartbreak and foolhardiness evidently," Sister Corn said. She gazed sternly at Taregan. "Why would you ask Beaver to bring you here?"

"Everyone knows the longhouse of the Three Sisters holds incredible things," Taregan said. "You offered me love potions only a moment ago."

"That's because men and women who come here always ask for such things. But you come here seeking more than that." Sister Corn's words were a challenge.

"Yes," Taregan answered.

"Even though a course of action like this may mean your life?"

"Freeing Kaliska from the Serpent's clutches will mean my life," Taregan replied. "Without her, I will have much less in my life."

"But you will still have your life."

"It won't be the same."

Sister Corn sighed deeply and looked back at Turtle. "You tried to talk him out of this?"

"Beaver did." Turtle finished the last of his corncake. "But you see how he is."

"Allowing him to pursue the Serpent would be sending him to his death," Sister Corn argued.

"I will go without your help," Taregan said politely. "If I must."

"Foolishness," Sister Corn said.

"Foolishness is not my chosen course," Taregan said. "I sought out you and your sisters first." He nodded at the walls of weapons and things containing big medicine and powers. "I know I will need help fighting the Serpent."

"He will," Turtle said. "Perhaps we should ask your sisters here to talk with us."

"No," Sister Corn said. "That won't be necessary. They are as foolish about love as you and Beaver. I have what Taregan needs." She rose and walked to the wall, taking down a fisherman's net with care, then turned and brought it back to Taregan.

Trying not to show his disappointment in Sister Corn's choice, Taregan accepted the net.

"Don't look at the net so glumly," Sister Corn advised him. "It is an old net, filled with great medicine. With this net, one of your ancestors fished the stars from the skies and caught the Moon as it passed to light the night so that the People wouldn't walk in darkness when the Sun had finished his day."

Taregan gazed at the woven net in awe.

"If this net can catch stars and the Moon," Sister Corn said, "it can surely catch the Serpent of the Lakes."

"Thank you," Taregan said in a hushed voice.

"I have one other thing you may borrow," Sister Corn said. She returned to the wall and brought back a small pouch. "Don't open this till you reach the river. This pouch contains a canoe that you will need to reach the Serpent's longhouse."

"Thank you," Taregan said again.

"You shouldn't thank me," Sister Corn said. "I'm probably only sending you to your death."

Later, after Turtle had excused them from the Three Sisters' longhouse, Taregan stood once more on the bank of the tumultuous river. He opened the pouch and saw the tiny canoe within. The canoe was framed of stout ash and covered by stretched deer hide that was light and waterproof.

"What's wrong?" Turtle stood on the riverbank beside Taregan.

"The canoe is too small."

"Take it out."

When Taregan took the canoe from the pouch, the boat grew to full size on the riverbank. The young brave stared at the canoe in wonderment. Besides being river worthy, the canoe also held pouches of food, a bow and quivers of arrows, and a spear.

Taregan looked at Turtle. "Are you coming?"

"No," Turtle answered. "I am a reluctant warrior at best, and I have no place in this."

"How do I find the Serpent of the Lakes?"

"Follow the river."

With skilled ease, Taregan shoved the canoe into the water far enough that the current would take it, then leaped aboard. He took up one of the paddles and used it to guide himself out into the middle of the river.

"Good-bye, Taregan," Turtle called. "May fortune favor you."

Taregan turned and took a last glance at Turtle, looking past him to the longhouse of the Three Sisters. He wished that he had more to show for his visit than the fragile-looking net Sister Corn had given him. Doubt filled his heart, and he couldn't help but wonder if she'd given him the net so he would fail. He turned and faced the river, stroking with the paddle to get himself right with the current again.

Only a little farther on, the river current filled with white-water rapids. Taregan's muscles ached and strained with the effort required to keep the canoe upright. The white water ringed broken fangs of rocks that thrust up from the shallow river bottom, and the current was so fast that the young brave knew if he ended up in the cold water he would drown.

The icy spray chilled his face and occasionally blinded him. Without warning, the canoe caught on something submerged in the river and turned crossways. Before Taregan could correct his course, the canoe started for a copse of jagged rock that would destroy the craft and leave him to die in the water if the impact didn't kill him. He fought with the paddle desperately, but to no avail.

At the last instant, a huge hairy paw with fierce claws grabbed the canoe's prow and prevented it from smashing against the rocks. Worn and exhausted, Taregan watched in disbelief as an enormous brown bear clambered aboard the canoe. The bear reached for one of the paddles and took his place in the prow of the canoe. His weight helped settle the canoe into the racing current.

"Row, Taregan," the bear growled over the roaring river.

He wrapped his massive paws around the paddle's handle and stroked with fierce vigor.

Shaking off the exhaustion and surprise that overwhelmed him, Taregan rowed, digging the paddle deep into the river and pulling hard. The canoe sped through the broken fangs of the river mouth, jumping and jerking like a green-broke mustang.

Taregan's teeth chattered as he fought to keep paddling. To fight against the pain, fatigue, and fear that he felt, he thought of Kaliska, remembering the way her black hair shone in the full sunlight and of how she never seemed to tire of him talking about places he'd been to and men he'd seen.

The white waters only worsened. Thankfully, Bear seemed better able to handle the swift current than Taregan was. The white-water spray blinded him, thick as fog and burning like knife blades raking his eyes. Then they were through the worst, shooting on past the broken rocks and out into the lake beyond.

Shoulders heaving as he strained to get more air into his aching lungs, Taregan gazed behind the canoe. In direct counterpoint to the leaden gray sky that had hung over him on the journey downriver, only clear blue sky appeared over Taregan now. White terns coasted on the gentle currents over the huge lake.

"Stand ready," Bear rumbled, turning his massive head back and forth to survey the great lake. "This isn't over."

"You are Bear?" Taregan asked.

"Yes," Bear growled. "I came to aid you, Taregan, as I have aided the fathers of your father in the past. The Serpent of the Lakes has transgressed against my tribe, and that can't be allowed." He reached into his fur and pulled out a mighty war spear festooned with eagle feathers dyed a brilliant vermilion. "Beaver sent for me at the same time he sent you to Turtle and the longhouse of the Three Sisters." He looked at the young brave. "Did you get what you needed at their longhouse?"

Taregan pulled up one end of the net. He had tied the net

around his waist when the river had first started becoming turbulent. "They gave me this net."

"Good," Bear growled.

"There were many other fine weapons on the walls," Taregan said. "That's why I wanted to visit their house."

"When the Three Sisters choose to help someone, they usually know what is best."

"A net seems a poor choice as a weapon against the Serpent of the Lakes."

"Only to you," Bear replied. "To the Three Sisters, there can only be one choice, and that one must always be the right one. That net has heavy medicine woven into it." He looked down into the water, then back at Taregan. "Can you swim?"

"Yes."

"Good," Bear said, "because we must swim to the Serpent's longhouse." The animal spirit stood in the canoe and fell into the great lake. Only a moment later, he bobbed up and looked at the young brave expectantly. "Well?"

After only a moment's hesitation to tie his weapons to him more securely, Taregan stood and dove into the lake. He surfaced and looked at Bear floating easily beside him. "What about the canoe?" Taregan asked.

"The canoe will be fine here till we return," Bear answered. "Come." He upended himself and dove deep into the lake.

Taking a long breath, knowing from the stories that his grandfather told that the Serpent of the Lakes' longhouse lay at the bottom of the lake, Taregan dove as well. He had to swim hard to keep up with Bear as he dropped beneath the waves raking the surface.

Bear remained ahead of Taregan. The animal spirit dove toward the lake bottom fearlessly. After only a short distance, the light stopped penetrating the depths, leaving only darkness that stretched out long and ominous before them.

The pressure closed in over Taregan and his lungs burned. Still, he managed to keep himself from breathing. But after a dozen more swim strokes, he knew he couldn't make it. Panic set in and he glanced back up toward the surface.

"No," Bear growled. He caught the young brave, the big claws poking into Taregan's arm. "You can breathe here. I promise. Just open your mouth and try."

Unable to hold his lungs back, Taregan drew in a deep breath, having no strength to try to stop himself. Surprisingly, he managed to breathe. The air entering his lungs felt thick and sluggish. But he could breathe.

"Above or below the water," Bear confided, "I know much strong medicine."

Heart still beating rapidly, Taregan nodded. He made himself remain calm. Only moments later, he saw a bright spark below and to the left.

"It's the longhouse of the Serpent of the Lakes," Bear said. Together, they swam toward the pale amber light that grew larger.

Light as a feather in the buoyancy of the lake, Taregan landed in the lake-bed mud. As the tales had always told, the Serpent's longhouse was built of human bones. The structure sat only a short distance way, clinging to the muddy ridge that rose up from the lake bed.

Horrified at the thought of how many victims the Serpent of the Lakes had claimed in order to build his house, Taregan stared at the gray-white bones. Leg bones, arm bones, hands, skulls, and ribs were interlaced to make the walls and the roof. The Serpent's longhouse was the largest structure Taregan had ever seen outside of a European ship.

"You don't have to do this," Bear growled beside him. He waved a massive paw at a school of curious fish that had come to inspect him. Light from the Serpent's longhouse glittered across the fish's scales as they scattered from Bear's paw.

"I must free Kaliska," Taregan said.

"Even if you succeed in freeing her and the other young women," Bear said, "the Serpent will only return along the river to wreak his vengeance on your tribe."

"Then I must also destroy the Serpent." Looking at the large house made of human bones, Taregan only then began to realize how huge the task was.

"Can you believe in the medicine Sister Corn gave you in the net you carry?" Bear asked.

"I must," Taregan answered.

"Good." Bear clapped the young brave fiercely on the shoulder. "Believe in yourself also, Taregan, as your grandfather and father have taught you." Without another word, Bear swam toward the Serpent's longhouse.

Taregan followed, kicking his feet to keep up with Bear. Some of the tales his grandfather had told him of heroes flashed through his mind, as well as some of the encounters in battle other warriors of the tribe had told him. In all of those stories, the fights had been fiercely won or lost, and the prodigious courage of the heroes was talked about at length. Taregan didn't feel the courage of a hero filling him, not even knowing Sister Corn had given him the net with great medicine woven into it.

As they swam over the final hill before the Serpent's longhouse, Taregan spotted the ship lying on the lake bottom. The vessel was of French origin. The young brave recognized the distinct tattered red and blue flag flying from the ship's mast. A great black hole showed in the hull below the waterline.

Few stories existed to tell of the Serpent's attacks on the vessels he chose to bring down, but Taregan saw canoes and small riverboats the Europeans built and used to travel the waterways across the land they called America and the People simply called home. The doomed craft stood out starkly against the light-colored sand illuminated by the Serpent's longhouse. Taregan swam over the graveyard of boats and canoes and the solitary ship.

Bear dropped down to the lake bed in front of the Serpent's longhouse.

Taregan floated down and joined Bear in front of the door. Like the house, the door was made of human bones cunningly fitted together. Skulls peered at Taregan from amid a pattern of arm bones, leg bones, fingers, and toes. Great fang marks scarred the gleaming ivory. Small fish swam in and out of the hollow eyes and open, broken-toothed mouths of the skulls.

Bear laid a paw on the door. Immediately, the skulls tried to bite him. The animal spirit spoke words that were old and filled with medicine. The skulls quieted, then the door opened.

"I know some of the Serpent's tricks," Bear whispered.

Taregan followed Bear into the huge house. Everything in it was three times as tall as a man might have needed, and the young brave remembered his grandfather's description of the Serpent.

The young brave trailed after Bear through the long, high hallways that made up the Serpent's longhouse. Inside the longhouses of Taregan's people, no walls existed to keep the People apart. Perhaps the Serpent's walls served only to bind the bones and keep the roof from falling.

Blown glass jugs that Taregan knew had to come from the Europeans held finger-length glowing fish. The fish provided the light that filled the Serpent's longhouse. Some of the trapped fish had died and floated at the top of the jugs, proof that the Serpent preyed on the fish folk as well as travelers across the lakes and rivers.

Taregan passed two rooms filled with ironbound chests that he guessed the Serpent had taken from European vessels he'd raided.

"He keeps their gold and silver," Bear stated quietly, "because it amuses him to walk among them as one of their kind. Their gold makes him welcome among them."

Taregan knew from the stories his grandfather told that all of the totem spirits possessed the ability to appear human. Now that he thought about it, he wondered what Sister Corn really looked like. Then his thoughts fled as Bear opened the third door and he spotted Kaliska inside.

Kaliska sat on her knees on the bony floor and looked up at him with frightened eyes. Her face and body held the curves of youth and beauty, and seeing her with gold chains binding her wrists made Taregan's heart ache. The other three young women were with her, all of them frightened and chained.

The women drew back from Bear as he entered the room, evidently thinking the animal spirit was some horrid monster the Serpent had sent.

Taregan rushed past Bear. "Everything is all right," he told them, dropping to his knees in front of Kaliska. "I have come with Bear to rescue you and take you from this place."

"Taregan," Kaliska whispered softly. She reached for him with her bound hands and succeeded only in clutching his face in her fingertips. "You can't save us. The Serpent told us we would die of drowning if we tried to leave."

"Bear," Taregan said softly, his eyes never leaving Kaliska's. "The Serpent's power keeps them safe here in his longhouse, but what will happen when we leave?"

"My medicine will protect them," Bear replied. "Just as I have protected you." He started toward one of the young women, who shrank back from him. His claws flashed and the soft metal of the gold chains parted, freeing her hands though she still wore the loops around her wrists.

Taregan used his tomahawk to shear through the cuffs, driving through the gold and biting into the bones that made up the floor.

Once all four women were freed, Taregan took Kaliska by the hand and led her from the longhouse. Kaliska and the others hesitated at the doorway, but Taregan talked to her, drawing her across the threshold. Once she found that she could still breathe, the other women followed her.

"What are you doing?" a grim and terrible voice demanded.

Kaliska drew back against Taregan as a deep, dank shadow fell over them.

Looking up, Taregan saw the Serpent of the Lakes floating in the water above them.

The Serpent's upper body was man-shaped, possessing two arms and a broad chest, but they glinted with tiny scales. His features were chiseled and proud, handsome. Only the gill slits in his neck marked him as something other than human. Dark hair with blue highlights drifted in the lake currents across his shoulders. Black, piercing eyes bored into Taregan. Below the waist, though, a long, sinewy serpent's scaled body trailed out, the tail coiling and snapping in obvious irritation.

"Swim," Taregan said, shoving Kaliska into motion. He drew the tomahawk and knife from his waist, aware that Bear had set the other three women to swimming as well.

"I'll have them back," the Serpent declared, hefting a huge war lance, "and I'll have your bones to build my house." With a flick of his serpentine tail, he swam toward Taregan.

The young brave dodged, throwing himself into the water and swimming. If he'd been on dry land, the leap might not have taken him from the monster's path.

The Serpent thrust his huge war lance at Taregan. It missed and went into the lake bed, burying the bone point deep. Before the creature could free his weapon, Taregan swam toward the Serpent. The Serpent raised a hand and Taregan slashed at the exposed palm with his tomahawk. The steel edge bit deeply into the Serpent's scaled flesh. Blood poured from the wound, creating a dark fog in the water.

Roaring in pain, the Serpent freed his lance from the lake bed and swept it toward Taregan.

Before Taregan could dodge, the spear crashed into his ribs. Dazed and out of breath, he flung himself backward again, landing on the lake bed and stirring up a cloud of silt that choked him and stung his eyes and lungs. A glance up showed him that Kaliska and the other women continued to swim. He hoped that Bear's medicine would protect them.

The Serpent came at Taregan again, sliding sinuously through the water. The monster drew back the long spear again and thrust it forward. Unable to completely get out of the way, Taregan brought up his knife and tomahawk, catching the spear between the crossed weapons and turning it aside. The bone spear point crunched into the lake bed again, scattering silt, gold coins, and bones.

Before the Serpent could strike once more, Bear swam through the water and came up behind the monster. Bear latched hold of the Serpent's head, wrapping his back legs around the monster's neck, holding on with one of his forelegs, and slamming the Serpent's head with the other. Bear's great claws sliced deeply into the monster's head, sending more blood flying.

"Bear!" the Serpent cried. "That is you!"

"Of course," Bear replied, striking another blow. "You attacked my people, Serpent. People who were under my protection. You knew when you did that I wouldn't allow that act to go unpunished."

The Serpent shook his large head, sending clouds of blood to muddy the water. Bear's savage blows left great wounds behind. "You should not have come here, Bear. I rule these lakes and all the waters of this land."

"Until this day, perhaps," Bear said, and he struck again.

Recovering, his senses still reeling, Taregan took a fresh grip on his weapons. He leaped up and swam through the water as the Serpent turned his attention to Bear sitting astride his shoulders. Getting close enough, Taregan thrust his knife into the monster's belly and tried to rip it across to allow the intestines to slide free.

With a mighty roar, the Serpent dropped his spear and reached up for Bear with both hands. As the monster's hands seized Bear, the fingers elongated into harsh claws that dug deeply into Bear's body.

Bear yowled in agony but fought fiercely to cling to his opponent. In the end, though, the Serpent's strength proved to be greater and Bear was pulled from his perch.

"Perhaps I can't destroy you, Bear," the Serpent said, "but I can hurt you so badly that you leave this place." The monster held Bear in his two hands and squeezed.

"Taregan," Bear wheezed, the breath nearly gone from him. "Use the net that Sister Corn gave you."

Only then, remembering the net, Taregan dropped his

tomahawk and knife, pulling desperately at the net wrapped around his waist. Even as he freed the net, the Serpent glanced down at him.

"So, whelp," the Serpent snarled, "the Three Sisters gave you one of their precious keepsakes." He flicked his tail out, slamming it into Taregan.

The young brave almost blacked out at the impact, and remained barely aware of the water rushing by him. But he had dropped the net. Desperately hanging onto his consciousness, he watched as the Serpent threw Bear's body from him. Bear bled nearly as much as the monster even though he was less than half the Serpent's size. Bear struggled weakly to take up the battle again, but Taregan knew the creature was nearly spent.

"Now," the Serpent said, facing Taregan with flashing black eyes that held hints of green, "you're going to die." He lunged at the young brave.

As Taregan watched, the Serpent changed from his half-man shape into a full snake, even longer than the ships the Europeans sailed across the lakes. The net drifted through the water from where Taregan had been, settling slowly toward the lake bed.

Empty-handed, Taregan faced his foe, heart beating, hoping that Kaliska and the others reached the surface without drowning, hoping that Bear could maintain his medicine a little longer so he didn't drown as well. The Serpent opened his cavernous mouth, exposing fangs longer than Taregan's arm.

Sliding through the water, Taregan managed to put his hands against the Serpent's snout and evade the monster's attack. Catching sight of the sunken European ship, Taregan swam toward it, mustering his last reserves.

In the water, the Serpent's great strength and speed also worked against him, sending him shooting far past Taregan. Coiling, spinning through the water, the monster regrouped and pursued the young brave.

Only a short distance ahead of the enraged monster, Taregan swam in through the ship's broken hull. Not having ever been on a European ship before, the young brave thought he might get lost, but once he was inside the great gullet of the vessel, he spied a small hole at the top of the ship. The ship rocked when the Serpent struck the vessel, and the sound of cracking timbers filled Taregan's ears. By then, though, the young brave had aimed himself at the hole.

Passing through the hole, knowing the Serpent was close on his heels, Taregan turned back immediately for the net he'd dropped. The last folds of the net only now finished drifting to the lake bed.

Inside the ship, the Serpent wasn't able to make the sharp turn. The vessel rocked again as the monster battered the hull. Also, the hole Taregan had swum through was too small for the Serpent's gargantuan body. The monster had to smash his way out, which only slowed him a little.

But the time was enough.

Lungs burning, looking at Bear's body floating limp in the lake current and wondering if the animal spirit was in the process of returning to the world he lived in when he wasn't in the land of the People, or whether Bear might even be dying, Taregan hoped that the medicine that allowed him to breathe underwater continued.

And he hoped that the medicine Sister Corn had said was in the net truly was. Moving quickly, aware that the Serpent was once more bearing down on him, Taregan scooped the net from the lake bed. He turned to face the monster.

"Stand steady," Bear whispered from nearby.

"I thought you were dying," Taregan said, watching the giant snake streak toward him.

"The Serpent can't kill me," Bear said. "Stand steady and let your arm and eye be true."

As the Serpent neared, looking as sleek and deadly as an arrow in flight, Taregan cast the net. Floating toward the Serpent, the net opened. Unable to stop, the monster struck the net and became enfolded in the woven strands. Like a live thing, the net wrapped the Serpent tight, drawing every last coil and twist of the monster's body inside, making the scaly flesh bulge on either side of the strands.

Bound securely, the Serpent drifted in a writhing heap to the lake bed.

Angry and hurting, remembering the bodies of the friends and family he had seen the previous day at the village, Taregan swam toward the Serpent's spear thrusting up from the lake bed. The young brave took up the spear and turned back toward the monster fighting the binding net.

Bear seized Taregan's arm. "No," Bear commanded. "You can't kill him."

The Serpent roared in anger and frustration, unable to break the net.

"He killed my people," Taregan said.

"He killed *our* people," Bear corrected. He slid his hand from Taregan's arm to the spear and gently worked the weapon from the young brave's grip. "But you can't kill him, Taregan. Just as every bird and beast on the land serves a reason, whether as prey or predator, so too does the Serpent serve the lakes. He can remain here, forever bound in the net Sister Corn gave you, and he can fight the net. But for all his great strength, he will never get free. The net is filled with powerful medicine."

Taregan looked down at the fierce creature and knew that he would have felt bad about killing a foe that was so helpless.

"Come," Bear said. "Leave him here. Such a fate will be harder to suffer than death. Here on the lake floor he will tire and weaken. The People that fish and travel these waters will be safer for what you have done."

"That's not true," the Serpent shouted from the lake bed. He grunted and groaned against the net. "I will save up my power, Bear, and I will strike through the lakes. They will not always be safe to travel. I will continue to take canoes and boats and ships. Not even the largest will be safe from me during those times."

"Perhaps," Bear replied, but he didn't look at the Serpent. Bear's eyes rested on Taregan's, holding the young brave's gaze.

"Sister Corn wanted her things back," Taregan said.

"She will understand the necessity of this," Bear replied. "Come. Your grandfather will be worried."

Turning from the Serpent, trapped and nearly hidden by a cloud of silt he'd stirred up from the lake bed, Taregan swam up with Bear. As he neared the surface, he saw Kaliska and the other women sitting in Sister Corn's canoe, gazing worriedly into the lake.

Kaliska helped Taregan into the canoe, then all of them braced the vessel as Bear clambered aboard as well. Kaliska held Taregan tightly for a moment, and he felt the love they had for each other, a thing so strong that he knew he would never doubt it.

"One day," she whispered to him, words for his ears only as Bear commanded the other women to start paddling, "I will tell your sons how you and Bear came to save their mother from the Serpent of the Lakes."

THE HAND WHICH GRACES

by Gary A. Braunbeck

Gary A. Braunbeck is the author of the acclaimed collection
Things Left Behind, as well as the forthcoming collections
Escaping Purgatory (in collaboration with Alan M.
Clark) and the CD-Rom Sorties, Cathexes, and Human
Remains. His first solo novel, The Indifference of
Heaven, was recently released by Obsidian Books, as was
his Dark Matter novel, In Hollow Houses. He lives in
Columbus, Ohio and has, to date, sold nearly 200 short sto-
ries. His fiction, to quote Publishers Weekly, ". . . stirs the
mind as it chills the marrow."

For Rod Serling

GRUBER'S was the type of neighborhood bar that gave
the great American institution its more quaint side: long
and narrow; bar on the right and small round tables on the
left; a comfortably scuffed polished-wood dance floor in between with a stage set against the far wall and an ancient but
functioning jukebox (whose selections leaned heavily toward old blues standards) off to the side. Gleaming brass
horse rails braced the opposite wall and the bottom of the
bar itself, while electric lanterns anchored on thick shelves
just barely wide enough to hold them kept an air of twilight
inside regardless of the time of day outside. The place
smelled of cigarettes, pipe tobacco, beer, and popcorn, all of

these scents mixing with the lemon oil used to polish the bar. It smelled somehow safe and welcoming, like a favorite scene from *Casablanca*.

Jack Gruber, owner, proprietor, and bartender *par excellence*, was the true embodiment of his profession. A little over six feet tall, with hair that was thinning and a long time white, his jovial bulk could be found behind the bar from nine a.m. until midnight, six days a week. He looked at his patrons through two sets of glasses: the ones that he wore, and the ones that he served.

On this particular night business was slow. Except for him, the only person in the place was a tired-faced, hollow-cheeked young girl who looked around twenty or so. She sat—*slumped* might have been the better word—at the end of the bar drinking a Coke. Jack's glance kept finding its way over to her. He thought if it weren't for the dark bags under her eyes and the way she kept shaking all the time, she might be kind of pretty. But she didn't return his glance, even when he served her, and all attempts that he made at conversation went unheeded; he thought it best to just leave her alone. Poor little thing. It always bothered him when people like her came in late at night; he knew that as soon as he closed the bar down they would go outside and be just as lost as they'd been before they found his place. He shook his head and wiped his hands on his apron. Didn't do any good to harp on stuff like that; it came with the territory.

He checked his watch: ten-thirty. No Sykes. That was strange, he was usually out front by now, setting up his little stand, barking passersby over, starting the show. A little magic for the evening. Jack wanted to laugh at his memories of Sykes' shows, but couldn't for some reason. Sykes wasn't the best specimen of humanity that Jack had ever met, but he was always honest . . . and usually on time. Every night he'd be out front doing the card tricks, pouring milk through a newspaper and turning it into water, picking people's pockets without them even being aware of it; where the hell was he? This was the first time in five years that Jack could ever recall him being late. He couldn't have a busy social calendar; there wasn't a big fan base for bum magicians waiting out there. Besides, Jack had to admit, he liked listening to the stories Sykes would tell him after the show ended.

The girl at the end of the bar ordered a beer this time, and Jack served it to her without looking at her eyes. That would only serve to depress him. Even if he knew what her problem was, he wouldn't be able to help. Wanting to help and having the means to do it were two different things, and without Sykes outside to drum up the last-minute business, the evening would be depressing enough in itself.

Just as he was putting some dirty glasses into the sink, he heard the sound of the front door opening and turned to see Sykes shambling in, looking as if he hadn't slept in days. His eyes were puffy and bloodshot and he needed a shave—more so than usual. But there was more to it than that; he was limping, badly. Like he'd walked away from an accident or something. Jack thought that maybe Sykes had gotten tapped by one of those crazy cabbies, but he didn't walk like the limp was new. He walked as if he'd been born with it.

Sykes hobbled up to the bar and took his seat with a great deal of difficulty. His left hand was jammed deep in his coat pocket. The coat he wore was incredibly bulky and far too hot for the weather they were having outside. His face was contorted and looked swollen. He wore his captain's cap pulled down over his forehead, shadowing his eyes so much that Jack could hardly see them now, except when the light from the bar would hit them and a quick sparkle would blink in the air. Sykes looked shrouded and worn-out.

"What the hell happened to you?" asked Jack, setting down a shot of whiskey. "Wait, let me guess—you finally checked out that new magic shop I told you about, right?"

"That . . . and a few other things."

Sykes picked up the glass with his exposed hand and downed the drink in one great swallow. He slapped it back onto the bar so hard it sounded as if he'd cracked it.

"One more," he said, clearing his throat. Jack filled the

glass again, never letting his gaze shift from the shadows beneath Sykes' cap. Something was wrong, he could tell. He'd known this man for too long.

"You gonna tell me what happened or not? You haven't been late for a show in five years, and tonight you show up without your stuff and looking like something that stepped out of an old horror movie. What's up?"

"You'd never believe me."

"Oh, trying for a little drama, are we? Look, I don't believe half the shit you tell me but that never stopped you before." Sykes looked up and for the first time Jack saw his eyes clearly. They weren't the same. It just wasn't because they were bloodshot . . . they weren't the *same eyes*: it was Sykes' face, but those eyes had come from somewhere else. They looked like a child's eyes; small and perfectly rounded, yet somehow disproportionate beneath the surface. If they were the eyes of a child, that child was very sick.

"What happened?" asked Jack, his voice cracking with impatience.

"Did I ever tell you my cat story? Did I ever tell you that one?"

"That supposed to be an answer?"

"Let me tell the story and you can judge for yourself."

"Go on." said Jack with a heavy sigh.

"Thank you." Sykes sat up as best he could and began his tale. It looked to Jack as if his back were hurt beneath the coat.

"I used to work in a supermarket when I was a kid. It wasn't a very big place, in the middle of this little neighborhood, but it always got a lot of business. I was just starting to learn some tricks back then, and every time the old ladies on the street would need a delivery they'd ask for me and I do a card trick or something when I dropped off their stuff.

"Well, they'd always ask me what the secret of magic was and I'd tell them what I thought." He laughed; a bitter, forced laugh.

"I was younger then, dumber, more at ease with myself. I'd tell them that magic was simple misdirection. Just a matter of making them look where I wanted them to when I wanted them to do it. Magic was all trickery and charades, you just had to know how to use it to your advantage. You let one hand grace the other with the secret, and while they're watching your left hand the right one is up to something."

"What's that got to do with a cat? Or why you look like hell?"

"I'm getting to that, be patient. You forget, a true magician must enhance his atmosphere."

Jack winked at him and turned to see if the girl at the end of the bar needed anything. Her face was buried in her hands and Jack could see that she was crying. Poor little thing; just leave her alone. He turned back to Sykes, who was launching back into his story.

"I was cleaning the beer cooler one afternoon—it had been defrosted the night before or something—and there was this big puddle in front of the door. It was the first thing that the customers saw when they came in so the boss wanted it to look nice. This one customer came in and pulled the spring off its hinges. The door slammed shut and the boss told me to leave it. I figure fine and I go on cleaning up.

"A few minutes later another customer came in and followed by this little gray cat. Cutest cat you ever saw, all furry and friendly . . . and hungry." He looked up, and the sparkle that Jack once recognized appeared for a moment, then was gone.

"It kept running over to the produce section trying to get at the apples and oranges. I thought whoever owned it must have kept it on one hell of a diet. Anyway my boss told me to get rid of it. I picked it up, kicked open the door, and threw it out. Now I threw it hard on purpose so maybe it'd get the hint and go back home. No such luck. The door started to slam shut and that thing was back over like a clap of lightning. Poor little thing never had a chance.

"The door slammed shut right on its neck. I was only a foot away and I heard it crack. Then somebody else came in and it fell out." Sykes ran a sweaty hand over his face, and when he spoke again his words were slow and deliberate.

"I opened that door and saw that thing choking to death. It just kept kicking and coughing . . . and it never closed its eyes. It just kept staring at me the whole time, like it was my fault or something. My boss made me throw it in the trash out back. God, I was sick about the whole thing: I didn't mean for it to happen, but. . . ." His words trailed off and he sat staring into his empty glass. He seemed honestly upset to Jack, who reached out and put a hand on Sykes' shoulder.

"It was just one of those things Sykes, they happen all the time."

Sykes lifted his head and chuckled. "I wish I'd felt like that at the time, but I didn't. I felt like a killer. I'd committed murder."

"No, you didn't."

Sykes raised his hand in the air and shook it. Jack shut up and let him finish. "After I threw it away, I prayed. I prayed that none of it had happened, that I could go back inside and start all over again, that the cat wouldn't be dead, that I wouldn't be a killer. I didn't expect anything to happen— which was nice because nothing did. I went back inside and started cleaning up my beer cooler again.

"A few minutes later a customer came in and that was when I noticed the spring on the door was back on its hinge. I asked my boss when he'd put it back on and he just looked at me and asked when it'd come off. I dropped my mop and ran back out to the trash and . . . what do you think I found?"

"No cat?"

Sykes nodded.

"I don't believe you."

"Told you you wouldn't."

Jack shook his head and refilled Sykes' glass. "So?"

"So," said Sykes, "I discovered something about magic that day. I discovered that every true magician has a third hand, a hand somewhere deep within himself that will only show itself when real, true, pure magic is needed. And that is the hand which graces the magician. That is the hand which gives him the power to do incredible things when the need is so desperate, so intense and all-consuming that nothing else can help. It's not a trick or an effect of misdirection then, it is magic, the mortal man's small miracle."

"That still doesn't answer my question," said Jack, smiling.

Sykes sat upright and, for a moment, almost removed his left hand from its hiding place. He noticed it and shoved his hand in all the deeper. "What all this means," he said, "is that every magician, no matter how much they use gadgetry and illusion and props, if the belief in magic is there in their hearts they can do the big thing, the grand thing. A miracle if you need a name for it, but it can be done. You only have to want it enough."

"Uh-huh," said Jack. "And I suppose you're going to tell me that you knew this after the cat, and that now you've got the power to perform miracles if need be." Sykes glared at him through the eyes that were not his, then turned his gaze toward the girl who sat at the end of the bar. She had fallen asleep, but she still shook from time to time.

"Probably a junkie or something," said Jack. "She came in here about an hour ago and ain't said a word since she sat down, except to order a drink."

"Mm," muttered Sykes, his gaze intensifying. "You still collect model ships? The little ones in bottles?"

"Why, yes! As a matter of fact I just picked up a new one today. It was over at a little curiosity shop on—" He stopped abruptly, his mind screeching to a halt then slamming into reverse, looking for an answer. ". . . How in the hell did you know that I collect model ships? I never told you that. How did you know?"

"The same way that I know that girl's name is Marcie Wilson and she's just found out she's pregnant by a boyfriend who's long gone. The same way I know she's lost her dancing job and is being evicted from her apartment the day after tomorrow . . . the same way I know you got a letter from your mother yesterday begging you to take her out of that god-awful nursing home."

Jack stared at him. About the girl, sure, it could be bullshit, but his mother's letter . . . ?

"How did you know that?"

"The hand which graces," replied Sykes. "The hand which graces. Its shadow is passing over me this evening."

"Oh, now we're going back to the dramatics, are we?"

"You're getting upset, aren't you?"

"Damn right I am. You come in here looking like you got run over by a bulldozer, you don't do your show outside and get me some extra business, and all you do is sit here and tell me stories about cats and third hands and how you know all these things about me and Marcie down there, and you have yet to answer my original question."

"And that would be?"

"What the hell happened to you?"

Sykes smiled then, and Jack knew that his old friend hadn't changed a bit. This was all some joke that Sykes was playing on him, and now he was going to get hit with the punchline.

Sykes pulled his left hand from his coat pocket and slapped it onto the bar.

Jack's breath caught in his throat.

It wasn't a hand at all. Maybe it had once been a hand, but what was on the end of his arm now was nothing more than a fleshy stump with three crooked stems slithering out of it. Maybe they were fingers, maybe not. It was where it should be, but it wasn't a hand at all.

"Jesus," Jack whispered.

"It started when I stopped by that new magic shop to get some sleight-of-hand gags. I mean, sure, they have a section that caters to 'that sort of thing'—that's what the owner of the shop said: '. . . that sort of thing. . . .' Like I was asking for the kiddie porn section or something.

"Anyway, I got some new cards and coins and a few other things and, as I was at the counter paying for them, this guy behind the counter, the owner, he starts giving me ten different kinds of grief about the difference between real magic and 'parlor tricks.' Starts talking to me about the

Goddess and Gaia and white sorcerers and I don't remember what all. I told him that what I do doesn't hurt anyone, so where's he get off being so damned offended.

"You know what he said to me? Looks me right in the eye and says, 'Ever since you were a child and saw what real magic could do, you've been trying to recapture some part of it but haven't been able to, and a lot of you has died because of it.'

"I don't know how I knew *he* knew, but he was talking about the cat. And you know what? He's right. At that moment, when I saw that cat was alive, I felt . . . I don't know, a part of the *Mystery*, y'know. Like maybe I'd gotten a glimpse at something bigger than anyone can ever imagine. And I got to thinking about how I . . . I never been too bright, okay? I admit that. I dropped out of school, never really had a home, and all I know is magic. But I always thought that was okay. Except when I got to thinking about today, I realized that somewhere along the way, I *gave up* trying to recapture that moment with the cat and just . . . settled. Being faced with true magic scared holy hell out of me, so I resorted to a lifetime of parlor tricks.

"This guy behind the counter, he gives me a couple of charms and herbs to take with me, to '. . . bring back some of the wonder,' he says. I stuck the crap in my pocket and didn't give it a second thought; I had shows to do tonight.

"I was over in the children's wing at the hospital. I do a show there twice a week, and if I ever need medicine or medical attention someone looks the other way when it comes time to bill me. I had just finished my act when the doctor who's in charge of the shift comes over and asks me if I'd go up to the delivery floor and do something for this one guy who's still waiting for his wife to give birth. It seems that this guy's wife was having a pretty rough time of it and the doctor thought it would help keep his mind off things. I said sure thing, no problem, always happy to oblige.

"I got up there and launched into my act." He pointed to-

ward his glass and Jack filled it again, wondering why Sykes
was drinking so heavily.

"I was halfway through the milk transformation routine
when this guy falls asleep on me. Now at first I was insulted.
I mean, I know I'm no frigging Houdini but I can't be *that*
bad. Then I look real close at this guy and I see the grease
on his face and clothes. I see the wrinkles under his eyes and
I see the calluses on his hands. I was putting all of my stuff
back in the case and all of a sudden, these crazy damn
thoughts start rippling through my head." He downed the
drink in one swallow, winced, and went on.

"I get to thinking about this Polish guy named Dozel
Yates who grew up in a prison camp and saw his family
killed by Nazis. I think about Dozel Yates who survived the
Holocaust to come to this country in 1950 and start his trade
as a carpenter. I think about Mary Yates who's lost two babies at birth and who's in the delivery room trying to have
her third and probably last child. I think about Dozel who's
tired and doesn't have much money and wants nothing more
than to have a wife and child who are happy and healthy so
his wife doesn't cry all the time and won't make love with
him because she's afraid to have babies.

"The next thing I know this nurse walks up to the glass
and knocks on it and Dozel is awake. He walks over to the
glass and the nurse brings the baby over. The nurse is named
Jennie and she's new and wondering if she's doing the right
thing. Then Dozel gasps and Jennie starts crying and all
these doctors and nurses come running in. It all looks a little odd to me so I walk over to the window and take a peek."
Sykes took the bottle from Jack and poured himself three
successive drinks, all of which disappeared down his throat
as quickly as they splashed into the glass. He set the bottle
back down and exhaled, but Jack could tell that his nerves
were still on edge.

"God," said Sykes. "I have never, in all my life, seen a
child that malformed. One leg was way shorter than the
other, its back was all twisted and bloated, its hand was
nothing more than . . . and the eyes. Its eyes looked at me

the same way that damned cat did: it looked at me like it was all my fault, like I should do something to change all of it." Then Dozel starts to lose his balance he's crying so bad, so I help him get into a chair.

"I thought about Mary and how she'll never let Dozel touch her again because all she produces is monsters. I thought about Dozel and how all of his suffering and hard work has come down to—" He shook his head and stared down at the surface of the bar. Jack didn't know what to do. He was still trying to absorb everything Sykes had told him . . . and the image of what had once been Sykes' hand was right in front of him if he doubted the story's truth. Then Sykes looked at him, got up from his bar stool, and removed his coat.

Jack wasn't one to recoil from unpleasant sights, but this one almost did the trick.

From his shoulders on down Sykes' body had only a passing resemblance to that of a human being. It didn't look like a man's body at all, just a series of bones and flesh thrown together in a heap with little regard or care. There were bone joints where none should have been, turns in the legs that didn't belong, something that looked like an extra collarbone. . . . Jack closed his eyes.

"Please," he said. "Put your coat back on." He heard Sykes' rustling, and he heard him sit back down. When Jack opened his eyes, his friend was crouched over his shot glass, as he was at the start.

"I prayed then," said Sykes. "I prayed to that hand which graces. I prayed that Dozel and Mary would have a strong, healthy son, and that the rest of their lives would be filled with joy and love and prosperity. I prayed that those terrible deformities on that child would go somewhere else." He downed another drink.

"My prayer was answered."

"But why you?" asked Jack. "Why didn't you just wish it away? Why wish it on yourself?"

"Because if you'd seen the look on Dozel's face when Jennie held out a healthy, perfect, beautiful baby boy, you'd know that there was no other way to make it all right. You should have seen him beaming, Jack, like the whole of his life had come down to this one golden moment. Don't ask me to explain it any more, I don't think I can." And so they were silent for a moment, Sykes staring into his scotch, Jack methodically wiping his hands on his apron, and Marcie, silently sleeping away her sorrow.

Finally Sykes said, "That's all been a good three hours ago. Since then, I've helped Marthe Fiorre find enough money to buy herself some food and a bus ticket to go live with her son in Maine. I helped a boy named Willie Benson work up enough courage to ask his girlfriend to marry him, and she said yes. And I stopped a man from going back to drinking. He was an alcoholic for eight years and has been on the wagon for four. He was confused and hurting because the last few weeks of his life haven't been so hot, but he suddenly lost the desire to drink." He pointed to the glass and Jack filled it again, understanding at last.

"I was walking down this way and suddenly I started thinking about Marcie Wilson and an old lady named Alice Gruber and her son who collects model ships."

Jack looked at Sykes and smiled. Maybe it was true, maybe the power could work like he said. But Jack didn't know if the price for a miracle was worth being paid. Poor Sykes.

"What are you going to do now?"

"Oh, hell, that's easy: I'm going to bring Marie's boyfriend back and make sure that he's got a good paying job, and I'm going to make damn sure that he asks her to marry him so that kid will have a home and a family that loves it. Don't worry, I'm not forcing anything that shouldn't be, he loves her, that I know. It's just speeding up a change of heart, if anything. What time is it?"

"About twenty after eleven."

Sykes nodded his head. "Anytime now."

And just then a tall young man with auburn hair walked into the bar. He looked toward Sykes and Sykes pointed toward the end of the bar. The young man's eyes brightened as he saw Marcie; he rushed over and lifted her head up. She was still sleepy and more than a little groggy from all the worry and tears, but it didn't take long for the recognition to register on her face. Her eyes lit up with more emotion than Jack had seen in her all night, and she threw her arms around the young man and kissed him. For a few moments they whispered in soft, excited voices, Marcie's eyes becoming clearer and more hopeful with each word. At last they kissed and started for the door. At the last moment Marcie ran back to the bar and threw some money on the counter, then ran back to her boyfriend and, together, hand in hand, they walked out of Gruber's bar and into their new life.

"They'll be happy," whispered Sykes. "They'll have a fine life together."

Jack stood silent, dumbfounded. In all his days at the bar he'd seen some dandy sights—knife fights and crap-frames, hookers and drug busts—but never anything like this. He looked at Sykes and was given, for the first time that evening, a wide, radiant smile.

"What about you?" asked Sykes. "What can I do for you, my dear and only friend? Would you like me to bring your mother here?"

Jack shook his head. "I couldn't. Damn, Sykes! This is all so incredible: I just. . . ." He rubbed the back of his neck. "I don't have the money to support her. I make just enough to keep the bills paid and food on the table for me."

"But you do get lonely, don't you?"

"Well, yeah . . . a little."

"Try a lot."

"All right, fine, but who the hell isn't lonely?"

"You a little tight for money, is that all?"

"Yes."

Sykes pointed toward the money that Marcie had left on the bar. Jack picked it up: a five-dollar bill, two quarters, and a funny-looking coin. He turned to Sykes and held the coin up.

"I give. What is it?"

"That," said Sykes, "is an 1865 Double Eagle. It's a

twenty-dollar gold piece and is worth somewhere in the neighborhood of fifteen thousand dollars on today's coin market."

"Wonderful, but what in the hell am I gonna—"

Sykes raised his good hand and silenced Jack. "You interrupt me too much. Just off Lexington Avenue there's a coin dealer's shop called Wades. He's an extremely rich gentleman, retired from the army, but he's getting a little bored with his shop, and he's decided that if something doesn't turn up soon he's going to close it down." His voice dropped to a whisper as he leaned in.

"He'll pay you cash on the spot. I know you, Jack, you're stubborn as hell and want to do it all yourself." He gestured to the coin. "You will. By this time Sunday your mother will be out of that dreadful nursing home and living here with you, not to mention that you'll have enough money to hire an assistant and start that model shop that you always wanted. The building next door, wasn't it?"

"Yeah," said Jack. Then: "*Yes!* With model cars and planes and—"

"Ships in bottles?"

"Yes, ships in bottles."

Jack walked over and leaned on the bar, closer to Sykes. "What about you?" he asked. "What are you going to do for yourself?"

Sykes raised his eyebrows, considering the question, and exhaled. "I'll tell you, Jack. I've been given one night, don't ask me how or why, but for whatever reason the fates have handed me one lovely night that I can go out there and take away all of the pain and loneliness and misery that I can. This is something that I dreamed about as a kid when I first heard that fairy tale about the genie and the three wishes. But to answer your question, I don't want anything for myself. Nothing at all, thank you very much . . . this is just fine."

"But afterward," said Jack. "What about tomorrow when you wake up and the sun is shining? What are you going to do then? I mean you're, you're. . . ."

Sykes smiled, patted Jack's hand, got up from his stool, and headed toward the door.

"By this time tomorrow, Jack, no one will even remember that I existed. I'm going to wish myself off the face of this Earth. I'll never be able to function normally again, and God knows that from tomorrow on, the rest of my life will just be a downhill slide. So I'm going out on a high note. It's my choice, my friend. I won't have to worry about looking back on this night with regret or longing. It's better this way." He produced a small plastic bag from his pocket and pulled from it something that looked like a cross between a leaf and a flower and a bush.

"This," said Sykes, "is a little something called Lethe's Bramble. Ever heard of it?"

Jack shook his head.

"It does a little trick with people's memories. I'd like to say 'You'll see,' but the truth is, you won't."

"I could give you a job here," said Jack. "I could give you a job, a home, a friend for the rest of your life."

Sykes raised his good hand, silencing Jack. "You've got to learn to stop interrupting people." And he laughed. "No, Jack. You'd tire of me after a while. I'm the type who outstays the welcome real fast, but not this time." He started to open the door when Jack called to him.

"Sykes!"

He turned in the doorway. "Yes?"

"What's it all mean?" said Jack. "Magic?"

"Magic?" said Sykes. "Magic is that power that dwells somewhere in the back of our dreams, that makes us wish that miracles were possible and that a mortal man could have the ability to grasp a part of eternity, if only for a moment. Magic is the total of all the mysteries we can't understand and the culmination of all the hopes we've ever thought possible. It is our last true miracle, and you know that it exists every time you feel the rain on your face, or hear the sound of children asking questions, or an old man laughing at a slightly off-color joke his nine-year-old grandson told at dinner. It is with us always, and it will comfort and protect us when the darkness arrives, holding our hand until the morning is in sight. It's the reason that we go on living, even in the face of hopelessness. It's the final mystery of the human heart, my friend. For it is there and only there that all true wizardry lies." He tipped his cap to Jack. "You take care. And stop interrupting people. Get a hobby, fer Chrissakes."

"I thought I did all right that time," said Jack. "You behave yourself."

"Why?" said Sykes, lighting a match and setting flame to the Lethe's Bramble. "I never have before." And out the door he went.

For just a moment, everything froze: a memory, an errant wish, a glimpse of a still-life painting.

Jack Gruber stood alone in his bar. It was almost midnight. He looked at the coin in his hand and tried to remember where he'd found it, then wondered if it was worth anything. Maybe he'd take it over to that coin shop on Lexington he passed every day on his way in. Might be worth a little something. Maybe he'd even go see his mom, as well. She'd probably ask him to take her out of the home again but what else could a body do, what with the money being like it was?

He turned the coin back and forth in his hand, then tried rolling it between his fingers. He'd seen someone do that once, just *flip-flip-flip* it through their fingers, easy as pie.

A voice, unbidden, its source a mystery, echoed in his head: *Get a hobby, fer Chrissakes.*

Maybe he'd take up magic tricks. Seemed a good way to pass the time. Might even entertain the customers. Could be good for business.

He tried flipping the coin through his fingers but dropped it on the bar.

"Fellah'd need a third hand to do some tricks," he said, then laughed as he scooped the coin into his pocket, wondering how in the hell he managed to get some of the ideas that came into his head.

THE FAIREST

by Von Jocks

Von Jocks believes in many magicks, especially the magic of stories. She has written them since she was five years old, although it took another twenty-five years before she started publishing. She now writes historical romances (as Yvonne Jocks), paranormal romances (as Evelyn Vaughn), and fantasy short stories as "Von" Jocks. She has also edited and contributed to two anthologies about witches: Witches' Brew *and* Words of the Witches. *When not exploring fictional dimensions, Von lives in central Texas with her cat Simone and her dog Kermit. She teaches community college English to support her writing habit, or vice versa, and only wishes research papers could be this much fun. Feel free to write her at P.O. Box 6, Euless TX 76039, e-mail her at Yvaughn@aol.com, or check out her website: www.yvonnejocks.homestead.com*

ZOE IGNORED her reflection in the store windows as she finished chaining her bike, then headed into the Magic Shop. She barely glanced at the taped-up flyers for upcoming spiritual retreats and Wicca 101 classes, a help-wanted sign, or the array of crystals displayed there. None of those were what she was after.

Inside, magicky music—a Synthesizer/Drumming/Nature Sounds mix—pulsed dramatically over her, the better to shift one's consciousness. So did a wash of good

scents like incense, candle wax, and best of all, books. But
Zoe didn't bother with the display of Tarot decks, or the god
and goddess—and wizardly cat—figurines, or even the
floor-to-ceiling bookshelves with labels like Astrology and
Past Lives and Ceremonial Magic. Her immediate needs required she ask at the counter.

Luckily, the clerk—an amiable-looking guy in his mid-
thirties, with long, wheat-colored hair and tattoos on his
bare arms—seemed familiar from her other visits. Not re-
member-his-name familiar, but at least remember-he's-not-
scary/loony familiar.

She lowered her voice, so as not to be overheard by other
shoppers. "Do you . . . ?"

The clerk leaned closer in response, like maybe he got
this a lot, and waited patiently. He was, she noticed, wearing
a simple ear cuff.

She had no choice but to ask it. "Do you have a bathroom
I could use?"

"Sure." He cocked his head toward the back of the store,
only a quirk of a smile revealing his amusement. Then
again, weren't pagany people supposed to be comfortable
with their bodies, and nature, and . . . stuff? "Hallway's behind that curtain, first door to your left."

Even in the cramped bathroom, washing her hands at the
pedestal sink, Zoe didn't think to check her reflection. She
focused on drying her hands, crumpled the brown paper
towel, and dropped it into its wicker trash basket. Then she
headed back into the Magic Shop proper, without bothering
to glance at herself.

Now she could savor her shopping experience.

She compared all twenty-four Tarot decks on display, especially the non-Tarot cards like the fairy decks and angel
decks and Shamanic-wisdom decks. The different artistic
styles were a marvel to her. She flipped through the T-shirts,
with their Celtic knotwork and their cute symbols and say-
ings. She admired the wire rack of greeting cards showing
gods and goddesses and unicorns and dragons, as well as
whales and porpoises swimming through outer space. She

lingered over new calendars for the upcoming year. In all of it she found works by her favorite artists, like Sulamith Wülfing, Robin Wood, Susan Sedon Boulet, and Real Musgrave. Variety. Beauty.

She'd ridden her bike here because the day was so beautiful, so she wasn't in a hurry. It took her a long, delicious while before she started shopping for what had actually prompted the trip.

Business.

Zoe had gotten a new secretarial job over a month earlier, enough paychecks ago to have finally caught up on old bills, not quite enough to start thinking about a bigger apartment, maybe a used car. Today was her day to splurge on the kind of work-environment supplies she couldn't get at Office Depot. The job was a great one, really: downtown where salaries were higher; in one of the tall, shiny office buildings, not four blocks from the light-rail station. But the energies in her open-sided "cubicle" were scattered, at best.

Not that Zoe was some kind of witch or magic user, to be noticing "energies." At best, she might label herself a New Ager. She knew her sun sign and rising sign, but the rest of her natal chart remained a mystery. She didn't own a Tarot deck, but she did have a set of Angel Cards and a box of Creativity Runes that worked similarly. She wore an inexpensive ring carved out of rose quartz, for good moods, but no crystal necklaces.

A dabbler, she knew just enough Feng Shui to put her paycheck in danger. Between that basic knowledge, and a folded copy of an article on the topic which she'd torn from a women's magazine, she figured she could get the job done.

But she took her time. She loved Saturday afternoons, not being at work. And she loved having an excuse to hang at the Magic Shop.

A scented jar candle labeled Clarity, that should help. But she sniffed all the different scents, from Harmony to Wild Nights, before deciding. A silken rope of brass bells . . . not that she had an office door to hang them on, but she could still display them near the entrance of her cube.

She decided on the green silk, though all of them—new and shiny—appealed. If only she could alternate.

She already had a clear vase at home, with a peace lily growing out the top and a long-finned, blue betta fish swimming gracefully around its roots; she would bring in that for prosperity.

And, oh yeah. It wouldn't hurt to hang a little mirror in the corner shadows, to keep the cubicle's *chi* moving.

Of course the Magic Shop had a selection of mirrors. Some of them were completely black, for better fortune-telling, but others came in cute shapes, set inside suns or stars. One round mirror, too large for Zoe's purposes, caught her attention. It had an Art Nouveau design around the edges, spirals and arches, half etching and half beveling. Admiring the pattern, she leaned closer to see it better. . . .

And a pretty face looked back. Wide, friendly eyes. Nice-sized nose. Unself-conscious mouth.

"Oh!" she exclaimed, then pressed her lips together and felt embarrassed at her own response. But not half as embarrassed as she felt when the pretty reflection pressed *her* lips together, too.

That was HER?

But she looked . . . *good!*

Zoe squinted her eyes for a better look. So did the face looking back at her. And it wasn't a weird illusion or something. This really was her.

Wow.

Zoe supposed there were women who enjoyed looking at their reflection, but she'd never been one of them. Not even in her late teens, when she'd been downright cute. Now . . . well, she still didn't frighten small children. She didn't cringe in horror from the necessity of, oh, washing her face, and she didn't choke on Crest if she caught a glimpse of herself brushing her teeth.

But in a world of pretty TV actors and fashion-skinny models, where sitcom characters actually considered thirty to be "getting old" and real-life teenagers got nose jobs for their birthday, where make-up was considered almost as necessary outside one's home as a shirt and shoes and any woman over a size 14 had to shop at a Plus Size store . . . well, Zoe just didn't fit that world. She was comfortably in her thirties, she wore a size 16, makeup made her face feel greasy, and her general strategy for coping with all that was just plain not to notice. So, except to occasionally make sure that she didn't have spinach in her teeth, or that her skirt was hanging more or less straight, or that her hair wasn't pulling an Alfalfa in back, she not only didn't look in mirrors very often, she didn't even think about them much.

Outside of Feng Shui, anyhow.

Now she peeked into the Art Nouveau mirror again, while bongos and croaking frogs wove themselves together with synthesized flutes in the music behind her. Her reflection peeked back out, wide-eyed but a little flushed at such a pleasant discovery. She didn't look like a TV actor, fashion model, or teenager with a nose job, clearly. But she looked . . . nice. Interesting. Clean, and friendly, and artsy. Her lack of makeup, mixed with a touch of sun from the bike ride, added a feel of athleticism.

Had she ever looked like this before?

It was probably the effect of the Magic Shop itself: the incense and music shifting her into alpha state. Maybe this is what the *inner* Zoe looked like. *Mirror, mirror, in the shop.* . . .

Or maybe she'd been damning herself with comparison. Maybe she watched too much TV or glanced at the covers of too many fashion magazines in the supermarket checkout line.

In any case, she smiled into the big, round mirror, and her reflection shone back at her.

Cool.

Then, because that particular mirror *was* too large for her cubicle, and she really didn't use mirrors enough at home to need anything beyond the old standard in her bathroom, she passed up the Art Nouveau mirror and found a palm-sized looking glass to keep the *chi* moving at work.

Zoe left the shop with her purchases. Afterward, for the rest of the weekend, she'd feel herself smiling for no reason.

Actually, she had reason enough. She was healthy—her doctor was happy with her weight, even if the department stores weren't. She had a beloved cat at home, and a circle of friends and family, and she had her drawings. Zoe had always loved art, ever since grade school. She filled her free time drawing, painting, and creating paper projects—mixing ink and pastels with printed computer graphics for a quirky, neo-medieval look she liked. Of course there wasn't much money to be made in it. She'd put aside money in savings, before her trip to the magic shop, to register for an upcoming fantasy con where she hoped to enter some of her favorite pieces. But it made her happy.

She stayed up late on Sunday night, shading a piece that showed a princess asleep in a dusty, cobwebby bower. On the painted bedpost hung a sign that said, "Press any key to continue." Then, because she got to sleep so late, she almost missed her morning train. But *almost* missed meant *didn't* miss; she made it to work on time—no harm, no foul.

Then she set about trying to adapt to her still-new surroundings.

And these offices were, above all, *new*, halfway up a tall, sleek building. The hallways were thickly carpeted, the computers were cutting edge, and each floor had kitchenettes with free coffee, tea, and cocoa, not to mention refrigerators to keep an employee's lunch and microwaves to heat it. She'd temped in far worse surroundings. The work, though not rocket science, required its own often underappreciated skills. . . . She firmly believed that plenty of middle managers could never survive as an administrative assistant. All in all, it kept her busy, passed the time, and paid her rent.

After a few cups of coffee, Zoe felt fine. Setting up the betta vase didn't hurt either. She enjoyed having another creature with whom to make eye contact anytime she liked.

And one who didn't bring demands for copies, calls, faxes, or letters with that eye contact.

She hung the bells by the opening that constituted the door of her gray, fabric-walled cubicle. She lit the candle on the open counter between her and the rest of the office. She hung the little, palm-sized mirror in the back corner, to keep any sludgy energy from getting stuck.

At one point, remembering the mirror at the shop, she peeked at her reflection, but all she saw were her eye and part of a cheek, the skin of which looked vaguely mottled.

Well, that's what she got for looking so closely. Still, her cubicle felt better and the week was off to a dandy start . . . until the three cups of coffee finally caught up to her.

Zoe headed down the thick-carpeted hallway to the Ladies Room, glad for the opportunity to stretch. The "powder room" was as plush as the rest of the building, with a mirrored antechamber complete with brocade-cushioned benches before one even reached the marble counters, pretty gilt fixtures, and mahogany-sided stalls. She grinned at the luxury of it, then smiled hello at the frumpy woman standing in the corner, then turned toward the inner sanctum—

And spun back, startled.

The frumpy woman, reflected in the mirrored wall, spun back at the same time.

It was her!

Zoe's first instinct was flight. She followed that instinct, straight into a gleaming, mahogany stall. The routine of physical necessity calmed her, marginally. When she approached the counters, the warm, soft water that flowed over her hands also helped, as did the rich smelling soap and the warm air of the hand dryer.

But when she dared raise her head from the sink and faced the track-lit mirror over the counter, she looked downright frumpy there, too. Was this the same woman she'd seen at the magic shop? Clearly it was; the Universe hadn't switched the actresses who played her or anything.

But contrasted against how good she'd looked this weekend. . . .

Zoe took a deep breath, pretended nonchalance, and tried stepping into the antechamber to surprise her full-length reflection. If this were a woman she was seeing for the first time. . . .

She wasn't impressed. At all.

She looked big, for one thing. Fat, despite her doctor's approval. Her hair, which she'd let fall loose, seemed to swallow her big face. She'd thought she had a good-enough tan to use minimal makeup—a glance of powder, a kiss of blush—but she'd been horribly, horribly wrong; none of her features stood out, and her shiny forehead made her look dirty. The chunky bead-and-bronze necklace that had struck her as multicultural and kitschy this morning seemed ridiculously cheap. The long, gauzy gypsy skirt looked clownish, too bright, inappropriate for even a temporary secretary in a company like this, much less someone who'd been hired full-time. And those sandals! Even if it was summer. Although she knew full well that she'd showered just this morning, Zoe thought her feet looked as if she'd been walking dirt roads, carrying crops to market.

Is *this* what she really looked like? God, how embarrassing.

Much of her enjoyment at her clean, rich surroundings faded beneath the reality of the dumpy nobody staring back at her. What good were such surroundings, if she didn't fit them?

No wonder she didn't like looking at mirrors!

She fled the powder room, retreated back to her cube and the uncomplaining company of the flowing blue betta fish, the control of knowing how to process data, words, and a twelve-line phone. Maybe the Feng Shui she'd designed by her workstation had helped; the sick feeling at the pit of her stomach, after an hour or so, *did* begin to fade.

She wasn't a complete loser. Even if she looked like one.

But really, she did look like one. All day, the same dumpy woman stared back at her over the powder-room counter, reflected off elevator doors, until five-thirty finally rolled around and Zoe was able to escape for her train.

This was, she decided firmly, a growth opportunity.

She studied the other women on the train, made herself notice what before had seemed like annoying minutiae—skirt lengths, whether their shoes were open or closed-toe—and resolved to fix this.

Early the next morning, at home in her cheerful apartment bathroom, Zoe nodded with wary satisfaction at the reflection she had created. She hadn't allowed herself to work on the art last night, specifically so that she could get to bed early and wake up well rested. Today, she'd carefully applied more makeup, a cream foundation under the powder, two similar shades of blush, blended together to better define her cheekbones. She'd lined and shadowed her eyes, brightened her lips. She'd pulled her hair back into sleek, gelled, businesslike obedience. She wore a navy skirt and jacket she'd borrowed from her best friend, and her only jewelry was a simple chain necklace with a heart pendant and two little post earrings; the quartz ring could stay in the drawer. She even wore pantyhose and the low heels she generally kept for parties.

"Pretty damned classy, don't you think?" she asked her cat, Wow'em, who lay with dignified tuxedo-cat grace on a forgotten towel. Wow'em didn't seem to care about Zoe's appearance but did voice her warbling disapproval of this early-morning-departure stuff. When Wow'em cried that way, mouth wide like a baby bird's, it reminded Zoe of the stray kitten she'd once found, alone and abandoned. She ached a bit for the kitten still lurking beneath the cat's sleek, black-and-white exterior, and made sure to give Wow'em a little extra loving and wet food as an apology for leaving so soon.

To get to the better job in the city, she needed to take the train. And that meant leaving earlier than she had back when she was working temp, part time.

Sometimes a person—and a cat—had to sacrifice.

On the train into the city, Zoe thought she spotted a guy checking out her legs. Clearly, the extra effort on her appearance had made a difference, right?

But something weird happened at work. Actually, two

things. One was that one of her coworkers, Jordann, complained about the scented candle. The unusual angle about that was, Jordan clearly *bathed* in her own chosen cologne, leaving a wake of CK Eternity for Women wherever she went and all but fumigating the elevators. But to each their own. Zoe was still new and didn't want to cause trouble. She still had nice energy in her cube with the candle unlit.

The second weird thing happened in midmorning, when Zoe walked into the powder room and saw the dumpy, middle-aged lady, now disguised as a businesswoman, staring back at her.

Had this morning been an illusion? She didn't look any better at all!

Her "sleek" hair now looked greasy. Her foundation seemed to have partly melted off her cheeks and forehead and settled into the edges of her eyes and mouth, and her blush had a garish effect, like a clown's. The silver-plated necklace now seemed as cheap as the plastic-and-bronze jewelry had yesterday. Her navy blazer and skirt might match in color, but definitely not in texture, and neither texture was particularly attractive.

She looked even more ridiculous than she had yesterday, even less real.

Her feet hurt from where the shoes pinched. Her thighs felt sweaty under the pantyhose. And now her stomach was cramping, either from her full-length, front-row reflection of reality or from the way the elasticized waistline of her skirt was cutting into her gut.

This was *so* why she didn't used to look at her reflection! Damn that mirror in the magic shop, for having seduced her into doing otherwise.

And now that she knew the truth, she had to do something about it.

Right?

When she finished the ROI project two days ahead of schedule, or when the boss said her editing of his letter was "excellent," Zoe momentarily forgot feeling bad. But that way probably led to laziness and denial. She eyed the other office workers in their navy, forest, wine, and chocolate suits, or their equally subdued sweater sets, and tried to figure out why she hadn't managed to come close to their air of competence. Whenever she went into the powder room, she forced herself to study the awkward, ill-composed woman in the mirror for comparison. She even stopped to face herself in the glass side of the building, as she left. To her guarded relief she didn't look quite so bad at that point. Then again, the sun was setting, so the light probably was kinder.

Still, she wasn't old *yet*—was she? Even if she *was* over thirty? Surely modern technology could at least help her achieve if not beauty then a margin of normalcy, couldn't it?

Now that she knew the truth, how could she *not* do something about it?

It meant losing another evening of artwork, and companionship with the cat, but Zoe dragged her best friend to the mall and got remade. She bought a sleek suit in the latest style, even if, to find a flattering cut, they had to buy it at a plus-size shop. Maybe she should start drinking diet shakes for lunch? She had her hair cut and styled, and she got a makeover. The woman staring back at her in the department store mirrors looked normal enough that she bought the makeup, even if that meant spending her fantasy con money.

The artwork was just a hobby anyway, right? This was her job. Hell, at eight hours a day—not counting lunch, breaks, or the commute—and five days a week, it was the larger portion of her *life*!

The last thing she did was have her nails done. Now even her hands looked like the other women's in the office. Even if that meant not touching the pastels, in case she messed the fake nails up before she even got in a single day of looking good.

She still broke one nail off, scratching behind Wow'em's ears, and her curse sent the poor cat skittering off into another room. But Zoe glued the damned thing—nail, not cat—back on, and resigned herself to being a little more careful.

She had trouble sleeping. Still, the next day at work, two

people told Zoe how nice she looked. That made her feel relieved—not good, really, just relieved. Even when the boss asked her to take down her silken rope of bells, since they didn't "project a corporate image," Zoe complied without complaint. She'd spent more on makeup the night before than she usually spent on clothing for an entire season. In contrast, taking down bells that couldn't be rung anyway didn't matter, did it?

But walking up to the elevator during her lunch break and wondering who the plastic broad in the suit was—then recognizing herself in the mirrored doors. *That* almost broke her.

Maybe she was hormonal. Unbalanced. But it wasn't *fair*. She had the right fingernails. She had the right hair. She had the right kind of necklace—until last night, she hadn't even realized that necklace styles came in and out of fashion, but now she did, and with earrings to match. She looked like half the other women in this office building, except . . . artificial. Why was she . . . ?

She . . . ?

Her heart almost broke to think it, but there was the truth. *Why was she ugly?*

She'd much preferred not thinking about her appearance at all.

"It was that damn mirror," she whispered, startling an intern from the mailroom as he wheeled his wire cart by. *That* was when this whole thing had started, wasn't it? The mirror at the magic shop!

Normally Zoe tried not to be a clock-watcher—she *was* one, absolutely, but she generally fought it. Today, she was unlocking her desk drawer to get her slim, stylish purse out before five-thirty even hit, so that she could be on her feet and out the door as soon as that happened. She caught the earlier of her usual two trains and could barely sit still during the commute.

It was the fault of the damned magic-shop mirror, and she was going to find out why! As soon as she got home she stripped out of her new suit, yanked on jeans and a T-shirt, and carried her bike downstairs. She rode hard, since the magic shop closed at seven, barely making it in time. She stalked past the flyers and signs and window displays to push into the store.

Into a rich scent of books and wax and frankincense, myrrh, copal.

Into the calming rhythm of ocean waves playing across the store's speakers.

"Hi, again," greeted the long-haired guy behind the counter. "We close in ten minutes."

"Thanks," she said, walking purposefully past the Tarot decks, the new calendars, the greeting cards—past Susan Sedon Boulet's shapeshifters and Sulamith Wülfing's frail waifs—to the back aisle where the mirrors were displayed against one wall. There, round and perky, sat the large one with its Art Nouveau styling. She glared into it. . . .

And a pretty woman with nicely cut hair, looking back out of it, slowly stopped glaring.

She wasn't ugly at all.

Oh, the business-sleek earrings clashed oddly with the T-shirt, but that just seemed curious, not ugly. She looked a bit flushed under the nice makeup, which Zoe hadn't bothered to wash off. But she had pretty eyes, an unembarrassing nose, a kind mouth.

After a careful glance toward the front of the store, Zoe used the loose hem of her T-shirt to wipe off her face, so she could see the truth without the expensive makeup. She didn't get it all off, of course—for that she would need her expensive makeup remover—but when she glared rebelliously into the mirror, she still didn't look any worse.

Deliberately, she reached up and mussed her hair.

The face in the mirror grinned honest amusement at the effect, which *was* funny—but not ugly. Not dumpy. Not in the least artificial.

She and her reflection stared at each other, stumped—and then a shiver skittered over her skin. It was the mirror, wasn't it?

It *really was magic*! Like . . . like Snow White's evil

stepmother's mirror or something. Except instead of telling her the truth, it just went on reassuring her that she was pretty, even if all the proof from the office reflections spoke to the contrary.

Lifting the mirror off its hook, she carried it to the front. "What's up with this?"

"With what?" asked the guy behind the counter as he glanced toward her from where he was counting the cash from the register.

"What kind of magic does it do?"

He blinked at her, his friendly face taking on a carefully nonthreatening expression. "It's . . . a mirror."

Oh *sure*. He would *say* that. "Then why's it on sale in a magic shop?"

"Some people use mirrors to scry," he offered slowly. "To see images of the future, or of other possible realities. The black ones are most popular for that, but to each his own, ya' know? This one had a cool design, so I figured some magic users would like it. Especially with those spirals."

Which didn't really explain anything, did it? "What do you see when you look in it?" challenged Zoe, and the guy behind the counter put his money back in the cash register and closed the drawer, as if to prepare for something to go way wrong—she suspected with her, not with the experiment. Then he looked into the mirror.

"I see Glenn," he said diplomatically. She assumed that was his name, since he didn't seem the least bit surprised by it. "What exactly do *you* see?"

I see myself the way I'd like to look, she thought. *The way I only seem to look in this mirror.*

But suddenly saying that seemed even more over reactive than the previous night's shopping spree. And asking whether the Glenn he saw was particularly good looking . . . that just opened doors she didn't want to walk through. "Are you sure there are no spells cast on this mirror? That it's not got some kind of enchantment on it?"

He grinned. "I know the sign says Magic Shop. But this

particular shop only sells the *tools* for magic. The magic itself comes from you and how you use them."

By now she didn't know what to believe.

"You . . . want to buy this?" asked Glenn.

"Yes. No—" She winced at her own idiocy. "I came on a bicycle."

"No biggie. If you live nearby, I'll take you and the mirror home. I drive the blue pickup out there, the one with the *Don't Follow Me, I'm Following My Bliss* bumper sticker. We can toss your bike in back."

Zoe hesitated.

"I don't bite," promised Glenn. "And I'm seriously hoping you don't, either."

That made her laugh. "I've been having a really weird week," she offered, apologetic.

"Trust me," he assured her, ringing up the purchase. "In this line of work, I'm familiar with weird. You're not it. So, stuff at work?" When she raised her eyebrows to question his almost psychic perception, he made a V with his fingers and pointed to his own cheeks with them. "You look tired."

Considering how late she'd been staying up, and how early she'd been waking, she wasn't surprised. "Yeah."

"Hey, I just thought of something." While they were waiting for the credit card swipe to go through, he came out from behind the counter and jogged to a bookshelf marked Magical Theory. Unlike the men Zoe worked with, Glenn wore faded, soft-looking jeans.

He wore them very well.

"Here," he offered, returning with a slim paperback which he handed her before he began wrapping the mirror in newspapers. "On the house."

The book was called *Mirrors, Water, and Windows—the Science of Reflections*, with a flash identifying it as part of the "Most of Magic" series.

"Take the word *science* with a grain of salt," he warned amiably, as the register chattered out its receipt. He passed the slip across the counter for her to sign. "Still, you seem to have a lot of questions, and that series of books is good for introductory stuff."

"That's really nice of you," said Zoe, giving him the signed receipt and taking her bag. And it was. *Really* nice.

In fact, *he* was nice—in a lanky, long-haired, tattooed way. Between the long workdays and hoarding her free time for art, when was the last time she'd really paid attention to men?

She noticed, on the drive home, that Glenn smelled of incense.

He was helpful enough to walk her bike to her apartment for her, and then considerate enough to back subtly away from the door, in case she worried that he meant to bully his way in as soon as she unlocked it.

"Let me know what you think of the book," he said. "I'm at the shop every day it's open."

"I will," she promised.

"Really," he said, with a half grin. "I'm not just saying that."

"Thanks." And she meant it.

He pointed at her front window, as if stalling. "Pretty cat."

Sure enough, Zoe's black-and-white pet sat there, watching the whole scene through calm green eyes. Zoe wished she could see what the cat did. No man would stall for the frump she'd been seeing in the workday mirrors, but the one she'd just bought . . . ? Which was real? "Her name's Wow'em."

Glenn laughed. "*Meow* backward, right? Like in that old commercial."

Zoe nodded. She guessed she liked him just fine.

"See ya," he said then, backing away.

And she carried her magic mirror inside.

So. A mirror. Magic, right?

Or maybe not.

Zoe hung it by her front door, where she could glance at herself on her way out. Even with hair sticking to her warm face after the moderate effort of drilling a hole and installing a molly screw, and her concern during that perilous moment of making sure the mirror's hanger had caught before letting go, her reflection didn't look half bad. By way of comparison, she ducked into her bathroom.

She didn't look so bad in the bathroom mirror, either. Of course, everything looked cheerful in her bathroom, with its rainbow shower curtain and plastic frog soap holder.

She went back out to the magic mirror. Same here as the bathroom.

That was the part that confused her. It wasn't like the reflection in the magic mirror belonged to Catherine Zeta-Jones. It was still her, complete with laugh lines and slightly crooked front teeth and even a hint—though thankfully only a hint—of a double chin. She was wearing an old T-shirt with the collar cut out of it, and funky earrings that looked like kitties dangling from her ears.

And yet she looked so much better here, the relief felt almost physical.

"I don't get it," she said to Wow'em, who'd settled comfortably on top of the discarded newspaper with which Glenn had wrapped the mirror. "Is it magic, or isn't it?"

Wow'em meowed her silent *meow*. She didn't know, either.

So Zoe got some iced tea and cookies, and settled down with her paperback instruction manual.

Who would have thought that theories about subjective versus objective reality and the nature of magic could be so gripping? She enjoyed the chapter on seeing reflected possibilities—both the future and past lives—but didn't feel up to lighting candles and turning out the lights to give it a try just yet. Why open a new kettle of magic when she might not have finished with her first course? Another chapter discussed the idea of reflections as portals to other realms, real *Alice Through the Looking Glass* kind of stuff, though it seemed this was mainly a metaphor for astral, not physical, travel. And then there was a long and surprisingly undry chapter on using mirrors to better know oneself.

The gist of it seemed to be that even mirrors didn't show the unvarnished truth, that people could face their own reflection with no less prejudice than they would look at an annoying neighbor or a beloved friend—but that this wasn't necessarily a bad thing. *"Perhaps a mirror's greatest power is that it lets you not just see yourself, but see how you see yourself."*

Considering the week she'd had, that seemed kind of depressing.

Each chapter had spells and exercises. After skimming them, Zoe set her cookies and the purring, comfy cat aside, and stood in front of her maybe magic mirror, book in hand as a cheat sheet.

She took a deep breath—then laughed, together with her reflection, at the idea of trying to do a real, magic spell. It took her awhile to compose herself, but finally she tried again.

> *"Mirror, mirror, on the wall,*
> *What's the fairest sight of all,*
> *Not for others, but for me?*
> *Show me now, so I can see."*

She wasn't sure what she expected. Mist, billowing into reflected view? Glowing lights? Maybe she imagined a complete shift of the image facing her to sometime, someplace, completely different, like a far shot of her someday autographing prints and posters at a Fantasy Con?

All she saw was herself, looking tired but intrigued, a little powdered sugar on one cheek. At least she didn't look unattractive, for once. But then, when had she ever, in this mirror?

Only when Zoe turned away did another shiver, like at the magic shop, skitter across her skin, giving her goose bumps. Quickly, she spun back.

The Zoe in the mirror looked curious, hopeful.

No answers there.

Zoe glanced at her clock—one of those silly birdcall

clocks, which she and Wow'em adored—and groaned. She'd stayed up too late, again.

Not the best track to improving her professional appearance.

The next morning, she dressed in a wine-colored sweater set like Jordan sometimes wore. She didn't have wine-colored shoes to go with it, the way her coworker would, but by wearing black earrings and necklace, she thought she managed to tie in a color theme that included her basic black heels. She still used her expensive makeup carefully. Then, with more anticipation than normally would be merited, she braved her reflection by the door.

In the magic mirror.

She looked tired. A little . . . regimented. Otherwise, not so bad.

As she picked up her purse, she noticed the paperback sitting on the chair and picked it up too. It would be fun to read more about magic mirrors during her lunch hour.

To her relief, a second glance in her own mirror showed her looking a bit more lively.

Much of the workday passed uneventfully except that, as usual, Zoe's powder-room reflection looked lousy. Maybe it was the lighting in there? She didn't know anymore. She wasn't sure she could care, much longer.

At least when she went home, she would probably look okay.

She microwaved her lunch, to eat at her desk, when the receptionist suddenly needed a break. It was while she was devouring food and the book that Jordan stopped by. Zoe sensed her presence even before looking up.

Her rice bowl suddenly tasted vaguely like perfume.

"*Uhm*, Zoe?" the slim, forest-suited middle manager said, by way of a conversational start.

Well, that didn't bode well. "What is it, Jordan?" asked Zoe, putting down her book like a little paperback tent on the desk surface.

"Are you sure you should be reading that up front? I'm not sure it gives a positive impression about the company."

Zoe stared at her. Of course, the company's impression *was* important. Especially to the company. And yet. . . .

Jordan shrugged. "Not that you can't read whatever you want, but maybe you can save it for the break room."

"Suzie asked me to cover the phones," Zoe reminded her.

Jordan cocked her head and widened her eyes with a little, *what can you do?* smile. The smile faded in the face of Zoe's *get out of my space* stare.

"I just thought you should know," Jordan insisted, petulant now. "What with evaluations coming up in three months and all. Best impressions."

Zoe said, "Thanks for sharing." But it didn't come out sounding particularly supportive which, since she was support staff and since Jordan wasn't completely wrong, probably wasn't a good thing. Jordan huffed off, and Zoe reluctantly put down her book.

The longer she thought about it, though, the angrier she became.

Jordan and her perfume fetish, complaining about Zoe's faintly fragranced Clarity candle. The boss telling her that the bells weren't corporate enough. Herself, spending how many nights not working on her art. And now her book? Next thing she knew, someone would come after the fish.

Maybe no amount of Feng Shui could combat a magic-free zone like this. It didn't seem fair.

By time Suzie buzzed in to thank her for covering the phones, Zoe was in a downright bad mood. She carried her empty dinner tray to the staff room trash can, then went by the ladies' room. She nodded a glancing hello at the bright-eyed woman already there—

Then stopped, let her head fall back in disgust, and slowly turned around. Because of course there was no other woman there, it was just her own freakin' reflection again. Except. . . .

She didn't look half bad.

She squinted, to be sure. The woman, cheeks flushed and shoulders squared, squinted back at her in challenge. Maybe it was the new sweater set . . . but Zoe didn't think so.

Watching her reflection, she carefully stepped out of her black pumps—and the reflected Zoe improved further.

She slipped the black earrings out of her lobes, then took off the matching necklace.

Better yet.

She ruffled her hair—and grinned. That was more like it.

Finally, like an anvil to the head, she figured out what all the mirrors had been trying to tell her.

Zoe was tempted to turn in her two-weeks notice then and there. Sanity interceded, so instead she stripped out of her pantyhose and padded, barefoot, back to her desk.

First, she put on walking shoes that she kept in the bottom drawer of the filing cabinet, from her and Suzie's occasional attempts to stay in shape by walking during their lunch hour. Then, she found the business card she'd been using as a bookmark while reading *Mirrors, Water, and Windows*.

"Hey, Glenn?" she asked, when he answered the phone at the magic shop. "This is Zoe, from yesterday evening. Is that help-wanted sign still hanging in your window?"

"You don't want to just buy it, do you?" he asked, the dread in his voice making her smile. "'Cause if you get my hopes up like this, and then just want to buy the damned sign. . . ."

"I'd like to interview," she assured him. "If you can give me thirty to forty hours a week, anyway." Wow'em would appreciate having her work so much closer to home, but she still needed her kitty kibble.

Glen said, "You're hired."

"You haven't even seen my application," she reminded him, feeling her smile widen.

"I own the store; I don't have to stand on formality. And you're the least weird person to have inquired so far. Please let me hire you."

She hesitated. This was *so* not how normal people decided their careers.

Then again, too many normal people made long commutes and wore corporate uniforms. And pantyhose. For those who wanted that, more power to them. But the others—

The others, like her, weren't being fair to themselves or their employers by pretending.

She wondered what they saw when they looked in the mirror. "When can I start?"

"Soon as possible. I'd like to get you up to speed so you can man the booth at the fantasy con next month, if you wouldn't mind attending."

Now Zoe laughed. She looked into the corner of her cubicle, where her small mirror reflected her part of her mouth, sending her laugh back at her with a sparkle of *chi*. She was starting to recognize the not-unpleasant shiver that whispered over her already. Possibilities. Following her bliss. *Magic.*

"I think I could manage that," she promised.

With or without mirrors.

A WINTER'S TALE

by Rosemary Edghill

Rosemary Edghill's first professional sales were to the black & white comics of the late 1970s, so she can truthfully state on her resumé that she has killed vampires for a living. She is also the author of over thirty novels and several dozen short stories in genres ranging from Regency romance to space opera, making all local stops in between. She has collaborated with authors such as the late Marion Zimmer Bradley and Science Fiction Grand Master Andre Norton, worked as a Science Fiction editor for a major New York publisher and as a freelance book designer, and is currently an Associate Editor for Swordsmith Books and a professional reviewer, as well as a full-time writer. Her hobbies include sleep, research for forthcoming projects, and her Cavalier King Charles spaniels. Her website can be found at: http://www.sff.net/people/eluki

ANY BIG city holds places you'll never find unless you already know they're there, as if what you're looking for determines what you'll see. You could pass the street the Snake is on a thousand times without turning down it. You could walk by the front when it's closed for the night (or, more likely, before it's open in the morning, as the Snake keeps *late* hours) and never suspect what's inside. When the doors are closed, the shutters are down over the velvet-draped display window full of swords and Tarot cards and "magic wands" and crystal balls, and the lights are out on the Mighty Wurlitzer jukebox that fills half the doorway, it's a pretty dull-looking place . . . unless it's the place you came looking for, the place you came to New York to find. Then it's the center of the universe, and you can't imagine how anybody could overlook it.

The Snake (not its real name) is one of the largest and most out-of-the-broom-closet occult shops on the entire East Coast, making its Manhattan neighbors, Mirror Mirror, Chanter's Revel, and The Sorcery Shoppe, look meek and tame by comparison. Its official DBA is, I'm pretty sure, The Serpent's Truth, and it is known to its intimates as The Sneaky Snake, or, more briefly, The Snake.

The Snake is in the lower East Twenties (which despite what real estate developers will tell you, is nowhere near the Village), and shares its street with the back of a parking garage, an S&M bar (that has a complex schedule of exclusions and name-changes I've never been able to master), a commercial photofinishing lab, a sleazy Greek coffee shop, and a store whose plate-glass window says "Novelties" and lies. You can recognize the Snake by its beyond tacky neon sign: a flaking neon walking stick with a bright green snake wrapped around it. When the sign's lit (rarely, as electricity costs money and Tris hates to spend it), the snake coils up and down the stick and flicks its tongue in and out.

To be fair, the sign was there before the Snake was, and is almost certainly the reason for the store's name, though over the long decades of its existence, the sign has lost all of the neon letters that spelled out its former business name. The lease on the Snake was signed back when real estate in this neighborhood was cheap, or as cheap as anything in Manhattan ever gets. I suspect it of having been a very long lease, if not an outright purchase, because any landlord with half a lawyer would have evicted Trismegistus—the Snake's owner, he of the scarlet cowboy boots and the deafening all-Elvis jukebox—had it been possible, yet Tris and an ever-changing mayfly succession of clerks continue onward unevicted.

You see, the Snake is not, and never has been, good press for what I, in moments of *hubris*, call the New York Occult Community, which includes pagans and witches and ceremonial magicians and Crowleyites and permutations of all of the above too numerous and inconstant to catalog. The Snake and much of its wares makes us look exactly like what some of us want to be seen as being—those people your mother warned you about—which is a cheap thrill for the news stations every October and one of the things that makes it hard for a lot of us to get visitation and custody rights for our own kids post-divorce. Just about all you can say in the Snake's defense is that it's been around a long time, and that it has done less harm to fewer people than televangelism.

And that it provides gainful employment from time to time for folks such as me, who might otherwise be reduced to the truly terrible prospect of becoming seasonal help at Macy's Herald Square.

My name is Bast, and I'm a Witch.

Once upon a time—just about before my time—to be a witch was to be custodian of a deep and ancient secret. Then, for about fifteen minutes or so as the popular culture reckons time, it was glamorous, which meant the label, if not the content, became adulterated and co-opted and applied to a number of things about as far from actual witchcraft as tofurkey is from sirloin. These days, to say you're a witch requires so much additional explanation about what you're not that most of us don't say much of anything at all. The old truths still apply: never argue religion or politics. Like the man said about teaching the pig to whistle, it wastes your time and annoys the pig.

And speaking of the truth, there are a few other things that are eternally true. One is that in publishing, the Christmas (gloss it how you will) holidays begin the day after Thanksgiving and continue until the first Monday after New Year's, during which time very little of import gets done. Two, it follows that as above, so below: if publishing isn't moving, Houston Graphics, my nominal day job (book production and design), is similarly dead. Three, it seemed just now as if everybody in all Manhattan and the five boroughs was out buying things they couldn't afford to give to people they didn't like, because they certainly weren't in their offices coming up with freelance design projects to offer to my small yet struggling freelance design company, High Tor Graphics.

Ergo, I was doubly unemployed. And as the capstone of it all, while people might be rushing into every other retail establishment in all of Manhattan to spend money, the one place they stayed out of in droves at this time of year was occult bookstores.

Which was how I came to be sitting in nearly solitary splendor at the Snake one Wednesday evening in the middle of December, watching an entirely unseasonable snowfall turn the street outside into something out of Currier and Ives.

Lark and I were intermittently huddled together around a small electric heater behind the cash register, since if the Snake ever had any form of heating, it has long since been removed to make room for more bookshelves. The checkout is on a built-up platform that raises it about eighteen inches off the floor, the reason being so that the person sitting behind the cash register can clearly see both aisles and most of the rest of the retail floor. From my vantage point, I could look down not only on the Mighty Wurlitzer, blessedly dark and silent in Tris' absence, but on an eight-foot-high plaster statue of the Goat of Mendes sharing wall space with the Snake's ecumeni-altar.

Directly facing the Siege Perilous is a counter-height jewelry case full of pentacles, bat earrings, and pendants made out of glass eyes and, beyond that, some taller cases containing crystal balls and ancient Egyptian meteorites and genuine Lady of the Lake chalices. At the back of the store are candles, floor washes, and Santería supplies; running the length of the long wall facing the checkout is the Snake's famous antique herb collection, displayed in even-more-antique flint-glass jars.

In between are the books. Wicca on the right, magick on the left, Rosicrucianism and what-have-you down the middle, plus anything else Tris thought he could possibly sell to tourist, novice, or advanced occultist: in short, the Snake was an Occult Shop of a certain vintage, a cross between a sideshow and a museum.

It was also a retailer's nightmare, because have I mentioned that if you stripped the store to the walls and removed every single shelf and bookcase, the selling-floor was approximately fifteen feet by thirty? Now take away half that for display cases, shelves, and the shaky freestanding bookcases running down the middle, add a thick miasma of incense and about thirty people at peak occupancy periods, and you'll know why shopping at the Snake on a Saturday afternoon and swimming upstream to spawn had a lot in common.

But I digress.

Tris certainly wasn't turning anything approaching a profit this evening, nor was it at all difficult to move around within the confines of the Snake. Nobody was here. I'd come down around noon when the shop opened, ostensibly to help Lark take inventory, and there hadn't been a customer in the store all day.

Lark had been a gift to Tris from whatever gods there are who watch over pagan retailers. Circumstances had conspired—as they say—to bring him East at about the same time the Snake's previous manager became permanently unavailable. Lark was looking for a job and had retail experience. Tris was desperate. It was a match made in whatever place matches like that were made in.

I'd spent the afternoon going through the books, pulling the ones too mangled for even Tris to sell them at cover price, and organizing the rest of them into what passed for order. By six I was pretty much done, huddling behind the space heater to thaw out. By then it had started to snow, and somehow the prospect of making my way several more blocks downtown to my marginally heated studio apartment was something I was reluctant to do. It certainly wasn't the prospect of spending several more hours in Lark's company that kept me here. Lark and I had been a mismatched item about ten years before. Neither of us had any real desire to put things back the way they'd been, but we continued to circle around each other with the wary attention of old lovers. In fact, at the moment we were engaged in a different sort of courtship dance entirely.

I'd left Changing, the coven in which I'd been initiated and trained, and finally come to terms with the need and desirability of running a coven of my own. I would need someone to run it *with*, and it seemed more and more likely these days that someone was going to be Lark.

It had to be admitted that Lark was more eager about the notion than I was, even though women outnumbered men in our corner of the Craft and theoretically he ought to have his pick of working partners while I should have to look carefully to find anyone at all. But the fact of the matter was that Lark came with history and dangerous emotional baggage that made a lot of folks wary of him. He'd been a guest at Changing for the last several months, but I knew he was looking for a permanent home.

The question was, could we transcend the scars old lovers leave each other to make that home together? And did I want any home at all?

Homes are fickle things. Peculiar as it was, in an odd sense the Snake was more home than my own apartment, so while I was brooding about my interior life, I figured I'd stay around until Lark, ever hopeful and ever stubborn, locked the place up around ten, which was the Snake's more or less normal closing time.

While I'd been going through the books, Lark had been dealing, in a more dilatory fashion, with the one-offs, singleton objects that had accumulated in the Snake down through the years, collected by Tris from who-knew-where. They were still here usually for a combination of reasons: they were far too expensive for a casual purchase; too big to display easily; and didn't really have any known application to any common pagan path.

The combination of all three was the killer: pagans and jackdaws have many of the same acquisitive instincts, but the pagan pocketbook is notoriously slender. At random intervals throughout the evening, Lark had appeared from the dim reaches of the Snake, brandishing his latest finds. Some we decided to consign to the window. Some he had hopes of selling to some antique store or junque shoppe, if he could manage to sneak them out of the store beneath Tris' radar.

There was, for example, the stuffed snowy owl. I wasn't even sure having that was legal. The obsidian-bladed sword (fragile, dusty, and expensive) had sat in the display case taking up room since long before I'd come to the Snake for the first time—every few years, Tris raised the price. There was a small brass cannon on a wooden base, bizarre for a complex number of reasons. Several painted leather masks in the Venetian style, which would certainly have sold if they weren't priced at eight hundred dollars each, topped the pile.

"Hey, look at this."

Lark came striding up to the front of the store. He was dragging a battered mailbag behind him. It was the sort in which the U. S. Mail ships bulk deliveries and always wants returned, and of course most people don't. Under his free arm, he was carrying a box, a silver-colored box about the size and shape of a small loaf of bread, with a domed top and a filigree surface. It seemed to be studded with jewels.

"Where did you find that?" I asked, coming down from behind the cash register and taking it away from him. It was heavier than it looked, though not heavy enough to be made out of solid metal. Probably metal over some kind of wood; the metal seemed to be actual silver. The crevices of the filigree were black with tarnish, and only the highlights of the geometric design showed clearly. I held it up to the light. The gemstones were real: cabochons of carnelian, pale amethyst, agate, rock crystal, lapis, citrine. Not mineralogy's A-list by any means, but enough to run the price tag up several hundred dollars, minimum.

"In the back—in the office, under the mailbag. Looks

like somebody hadn't been opening the mail for awhile."
Lark shrugged. A lot of Tris' sure-thing mathoms had ended
up there, hidden out of harm's way by the Snake's last manager. It looked like Julian had been hiding more than unsal-
able stock, and I hoped for Lark's sake that there weren't too
many overdue bills in that sack. "Gotta be for sale, but it
isn't stickered or anything."

I shook the box experimentally. Something inside it rattled dully.

"Maybe the invoice is inside," I suggested. Boxes always
sell well, and this one was large enough to hold even the
largest deck of Tarot cards or an average-sized athame. If we
could figure out an attractive price for it, Lark should be
able to move it.

I set it down on top of the jewelry counter and tried to
raise the lid. It moved a hairsbreadth and stopped—locked
from inside, somehow, though I could see neither catch nor
locking mechanism.

"Here, let me." Lark reached into his jeans and pulled out
a long clasp-blade knife. He'd fiddled with it in ways that
would make the hair of any self-respecting peace officer
turn gray; a wicked five-inch blade locked open with sound-
less fluidity.

"What are you going to do with that?" I asked nervously.
I told myself firmly that it wasn't any of my business what
Lark did with the Snake's stock; that if anyone were going
to meddle with it, he had more right to do so than I did.

"Get it open," he said succinctly, elbowing me out of the
way and sliding the point of the knife into the black line
where top and bottom of the lid met. He scraped the blade
back and forth, probing delicately, and I was insensibly relieved; apparently Lark had learned a little finesse since our
youthful days together.

At last he found what he was searching for. He twisted
the blade slightly, and then slid it all the way in, moving
some interior catch back and out of the way. The catch let
go, and Lark lifted the lid.

"No invoice, unless the bunnies ate it," he reported, peering in.

"What bunnies?" I said, in spite of all my better instincts. I looked over Lark's shoulder.

The inside of the box was unadorned pale wood: cedar, by the faint scent. In the bottom of the box lay what had been making the rattling noise, a cluster of rabbit's foot key chains, the cheap kind you used to be able to buy at any five and dime, threaded together by their cheap brass chains.

"*Huh*." Lark picked one of them up and dangled the lot. They looked like a cluster of weird hairy bananas; all of them were *au natural;* dark brown. "Well, I can sell these."

I picked up the mailbag and retreated, sitting down on the step of the Siege Perilous. I untied the knotted cord and pulled it open. It was half-full of envelopes, catalogs, and a couple of small packages, all, as far as I could tell, unopened. I put the packages aside to open last, and started rummaging through the rest. I had the odd unsettling feeling that something ought to have just happened but hadn't—but then, I have never had particularly fortunate experiences with severed animal parts worn as jewelry—with the people who make them, or the people who wear them.

Lark leaned back against the display case, twirling the severed bunny feet around his finger. At the best of times, Lark looks like a denim-clad Biker Jesus; he has long dark-blond hair, which, in defiance of the passing winds of fashion, he refuses to cut. At the moment, lit from beneath by the display case, he looked positively Mephistophelean.

"You know," Lark said broodingly, "just about anything could have been in that box."

"Severed hands, the Shroud of Turin," I suggested.

"No, really. Doesn't it look like it ought to contain something important?"

"Appearances can be deceiving." And we see what we want to see far more often than we see what's really there. That's why all the old folktales—which have such a kinship with magic, down at the bone—always hammer home the power of three. Look three times. See what's really there.

"Ain't it the truth." Lark smiled his crooked grin. He was charming. I am not easily charmed. "But, hey. This reminds me of a something that happened one time while I was still out West."

I regarded him warily. Lark is not above trying on a shaggy dog story or two if he thinks it'll fly, and there are times when his reminiscences hold more allure than others.

"The weirdest thing that ever happened to me . . . until I started hanging out with you again, anyway," Lark went on.

"Cute." I made a long arm and pulled the trash basket over within reach. It was metal, and warm from the space heater. Most of the contents of the mailbag were easily identified as junk mail. I took a handful and tossed it into the trash unopened, and kept digging.

"You ever heard of 'The Monkey's Paw'?" Lark asked.

"It's a story," I said. In fact, a story written by W. W. Jacobs in 1902; Houston Graphics designed an anthology of great (meaning public domain) works of horror and the supernatural last year and I'd caught the job, so in fact, I'd actually read it recently. In it, a woman grieving for her lost and dead son wishes on a monkey's paw enchanted by an Indian fakir. It has the power to grant each of three possessors three wishes. The woman soon uses it to wish her son alive and out of his grave again—though not, alas, whole and well. The last wish is expended, as wishes in such tales often are, in sending the son back into death and undoing the damage caused by tampering with the unknown. Though it's a work of fiction, the story is a classic fairy-tale type: be careful what you wish for, you may get it.

"It's real," Lark said.

"I could send you out for coffee," I suggested, pointing toward the snow. In a few hours, New York would come to a screeching halt, just as it does for the first snowfall every year.

"No. We had one at this shop I worked at. I think it worked, too. It did *something*, anyway. Or . . . anyway, I'll tell you what happened, and you tell me what you think. I've never been able to figure it out. Haven't thought about it in years, actually.

"When I was living out in the Valley, I used to work at a New Age shop called Dolphin's Dream. Ramona, the owner, couldn't keep staff to save her butt, with this whole Faerie Princess of the Mysteries gig she was always running, but she liked me. Hell, she even paid me, on time and in cash. I never contradicted her when she started going on about her power animals or her spirit guardians or all that crap. Or when she'd come wafting in around noon dressed like K-Mart was running a sale in the "Crochet Your Own Pope" aisle and she'd bought two, going on about how the Powers That Be had sent her a vision and she was going to have to be away for a few days to take care of something for the sake of humanity. I didn't bother to laugh in her face. I mean, she was pathetically trivial, but where would the point have been? As far as I could see, she wasn't hurting anybody else, if you didn't count firing any clerks who didn't take her astral missions seriously. And if she was deluding herself, she was still enough grounded on the Earth plane to keep Dolphin's Dream going. Ramona handled all the ordering, and she had a pretty good sense of what would sell.

"Dolphin's Dream was mostly cards, herbs, and crystals, with a little Tibetan Buddhism around the edges. Not like this place. Very Wicca-in-Ten-Easy-Lessons, with a lot of tie-dye and some gargoyles thrown in. You could go in there and pick up some nice meaningless silver jewelry, a couple of decks of Tarot cards, some cone incense blends with names like Midnight Enchantment and Diana's Moon, a couple of scented pillar candles that had been rolled in glitter, a blank book to record the details of your spiritual journey, and there you'd be, heir to the ancient mystical tradition of Avalon and Atlantis."

Lark's voice was neutral, but I could sense his contempt and frustration. The day-trippers would take their cotton-candy version of Wicca home, and when it had dissolved away to nothing in their hands would wonder why they hadn't gotten the fulfillment they'd been promised. They'd feel cheated, and vaguely dissatisfied, and think—if they ever got far enough again to pick up Phyllis Curott or Margot Adler—that the people claiming to get that much out of Wicca were deluded or lying.

Neither is true. The difference between that world and this is the difference between an afternoon's idle play and years of training and study and practice. It's a difference that lies in that which can't be spoken of, because it can't be put into words.

But as it is in fairy tales, you only get what you give.

"So you worked in a New Age shop?" I asked half idly, just to keep the conversation rolling. What else was there to do on a cold winter evening, besides opening ancient mail?

"Most of the stock was seriously fluffy, and Ramona didn't carry blades at all, but she had a couple of high-end items tucked away in the back of the store. Better blank books. Salt and water dishes. Some good cups. And a small line of the basics: frankincense and Gloria and cake charcoal and sea salt and plain jar candles; that kind of stuff. And she could put you in touch with craftspeople who could take orders for the usual sort of custom work. So Ocean Circle— my coven then—and just about everybody in the local area hung out there. It didn't hurt that there was a Starbucks two doors down."

Eventually, I was hoping, this tale would come to a point—or end—I didn't really care which. I piled the catalogs and magazines that had been in the bag under the desk to get them out of the way for the time being; I knew Lark would want to go through them, even if they were months out of date. Or even years. How long had that pile of mail been sitting there? And why? Not that it was any of my business, I told myself firmly.

Lark was undeterred by my display of disinterest.

"So one day, as usual, Ramona gets the call to run off and fight Evil again. The truly bizarre thing is, she never wanted to talk about her adventures when she came back, and you would have had to have met Ramona to understand just how wacko that was. While I sincerely doubted she was actually receiving telepathic calls from Guardian Spirits to run off and combat . . . well, whatever she was going off to combat . . . the point is, she was telling everybody she was, or at least she was telling me. So when she showed up again after one of these missions, it would have been nice to hear a little postmortem on how she whacked the Powers of Evil. But she never said a word. She also never had anything to say about why it was that the Powers of Evil required so much whacking. But hey, she wasn't paying me to wonder about things like that. She was paying me to tell customers whether a pink candle or a purple candle would balance the energies in their auras better, and to restock the shelves.

"Unlike this place, at Dolphin's Dream, it was easy to tell when you'd sold something, as Ramona was into the One Perfect Lettuce Leaf school of retail design. That meant I was going back and forth to the stockroom a hundred times a day to bring out more of whatever I'd sold the last one of and to arrange it on, I swear to God, little paper doilies on the glass shelves. A real bitch to keep clean, but the total effect was worth it in a Martha-Stewart-Does-Silver-Ravenwolf kind of way. Ramona's markups—on her fancy stuff, because she was too smart to do it on the basics where everybody comparison shops—was highway robbery. And the tourists loved the place. So stock moved through there pretty fast, and a couple of times a week we'd get shipments from the wholesalers to replace what we'd sold.

"Usually Ramona took care of that herself, she probably didn't want me to see how much she was gouging my friends and co-religionists. But on this particular occasion we'd been getting really low on candles before she was "called away," and it was going to be an especially long adventure against Evil this time, so she told me to open the boxes as they came in and, if the contents happened to be candles, to check them in and put them out and she'd take care of the details later.

"It was just her luck that this was the week the heavens

opened and all the back-ordered stock that had been circling the landing field decided to come in at once. I ended up unpacking and checking in a lot more than the candles in simple self-defense, because if I hadn't, there wouldn't have been any place to store the boxes. And of course, wouldn't you know that the moment she leaves, an Astral Memo goes out to the day-trippers that it's time to visit Dolphin's Dream, so I'm run off my ass every single minute. The place looks like it's been hit by locusts. I'm selling stock out of open boxes. Crazy.

"Anyway, in the middle of everything else, this one funny-peculiar shipment comes in. Funny, because like I say, I know the Dolphin's stock inside out, and the box contained three items that would never *ever* make it into a case at Ramona's.

"By the time it occurred to me it might have been a really good idea to hang on to the wrapping—it was covered with stamps and tied with string, and I didn't think the International Post Office went for either notion in a really big way, even in those days—it'd disappeared. Maybe one of the customers that day snagged it for the stamps. At any rate, I never saw it again. It came from whatever foreign place does triangular stamps, and if there's more than one, too bad.

"Inside the box—it was a Pet milk carton, if that's any help—and wrapped in scraggly cheap brown paper, were the things.

"One: a necklace of teeth. Some of them were human . . . unless animals get gold fillings. Some of them looked a helluva lot too long and pointy for that, so maybe they were human and animal mixed together. There were a lot of them, maybe a thirty-six-inch strand. The teeth were drilled through the root and strung on heavy waxed red cord. All of them were really white, like maybe they'd been bleached or something.

"Number two was an iron knife. It was about ten inches long, black iron, leaf-bladed, and forged all in one piece. The handle looked as though it had been beaten flat and then hammered over to make a hollow tube, then overbraided with some kind of dark brown leather cord. The whole thing was greasy—it'd soaked right through the wrapping. Good thing, too, since iron rusts like a sonovabitch.

"The third thing was a monkey's paw. I wasn't sure what it was, you know, it was all kind of black and hairy and shriveled, about three or four inches long. The end was sort of wrapped in the same kind of leather cord as the knife. The fingers had been bent into a *fica* before it dried up, so they were clenched into a fist, with the thumb thrust between the middle two fingers.

"There was no bill, no receipt, no invoice."

"This is the wrong time of year for a ghost story," I pointed out irritably. Lark looked hurt.

"I'm telling you the absolute truth. If you want to bring ghosts into it, that's your business. All I'm saying is that this was weird, and this is exactly how it was weird."

"That while you're all alone in this bliss-ninny New Age shop out on the Left Coast while the owner is off chasing cars or UFOs or whatever the hell it is she does on her off hours, somebody mails her a terribly meaningful box full of Clive Barker."

I was almost minded to go out for coffee myself at that point, because by now I was sure Lark was trying to sell me a bill of goods, but the snow was hissing down outside like somebody had opened a bag of granulated sugar in Heaven and I wasn't sure the Greek place was even open.

"So imagine how I felt," Lark said reasonably. "Because I'm staring down at this stuff rearranging my carefully ordered world and wondering if somebody's trying to curse Ramona and, if they are, if I've intercepted the curse."

Always a cheery thought. Even if curses aren't quite the flawless infallible push-button agents of destruction that popular fiction would make them out to be, they still aren't something you want to mess around with.

"So what did you do?" I asked, resigning myself to playing straight man in this shaggy-witch story.

"Oh, what any good Wiccan would do in an emergency.

Warded the hell out of it, got coffee, and called my High Priestess."

Unfortunately, so Lark's rambling explanation continued, Lady Cinnamon was unable to be particularly helpful, being as baffled as Lark was about why on Earth Ramona would have ordered these items for her store. She did come down to the Dolphin's Dream as soon as she got off work to help him stare at the items in disbelief, matters not being helped by the fact that Cinnamon was vegan.

"What would she want with a monkey's paw anyway?" Cinnamon had said. "Oh, *ick*. Was there a Customs declaration on that package?"

Until that moment, Lark assured me, it had not occurred to him that the monkey's paw was, in fact, a *monkey's paw,* much less a magickal cursed talisman. Once Cinnamon mentioned it, however, he started wondering about a number of things, like the legality of mailing human teeth internationally. And the fact that he hadn't seen a green Customs slip on the package at all.

But there wasn't much he could do about the objects, other than throw them out and pretend they'd never arrived, which he wasn't quite prepared to do, being in his own intermittent fashion a man of his word. So he and Cinnamon wrapped them up in one of the silk scarves from Ramona's stock, added a little frankincense, sea salt, and vervain, tucked the bundle into the stockroom, and then thoroughly blessed the entire store, stockroom and all.

Couldn't fault him there. It was what I would have done, when faced with bizarre incursions from an alternate reality.

"So then a few days later Ramona gets back, and has spinning kittens about the state the store's in, because of me unpacking the boxes and all. So I'm thinking that telling her about her package can probably wait until she's in a better mood, or at least tired out from redoing everything I've done. Besides, she's banished me from the store because I have unsynchronized vibrations, which apparently I get about once a month by her clock, and I'm already out the door before it occurs to me that I left the box full of horror movie garbage out of my report about how things had been at the store while she was gone."

"There's a point to this, eventually?" I asked, just to show Lark I was not being impressed by a good story. Which was, of course, all this could be.

"Yeah, well, I'm getting to that.

"It was still bugging me. I knew it was a mummified monkey paw, but I wasn't thinking *Twilight Zone*. Anyway, Ocean Circle was meeting that night, so I went on over to Cinn's house, and by the time I got there she'd told everybody about Ramona's package, and Rain or somebody knew the whole story about the real—or fictional, or whatever—monkey's paw. The way I got it, it was like Aladdin's lamp, except no genie and with a guaranteed bad ending involved if you messed with it. Death magic, you know?

"Now a lot of Ocean Circle were flakes, but even we knew the difference between fiction and reality. The trouble was, I was pretty sure Ramona didn't. I called the store the next morning to see if everything was okay there, and Ramona said she didn't need me to come in, which was a bitch, because it wasn't like I was on salary or anything, and if I wasn't there, I wasn't getting paid. I went down there anyway, because I figured I needed to tell her about the stuff, and if she threw me out, I could always go get a cup of overpriced Starbucks.

"Well, the place was full—it was a Saturday, and Dolphin's Dream usually did a good business on a Saturday—and just as I come walking in the door, I see Ramona behind the counter dropping something—and I was pretty damned sure I knew what it was—into some tourist's bag, and short of mugging them and running off with it, there wasn't a lot I could do about it. I hustled into the back room, and sure enough: the necklace, the knife, and the paw were gone. There was a little bit of sea salt spilled on the floor where Ramona must have unwrapped the scarf, but that was it.

"I looked around, but I didn't see either of the other things anywhere, not in the back, and not in the cases, either, but she'd had all yesterday evening and half the morning to do anything with them—even sell them. So I grabbed her as soon as I could.

" 'You sold the monkey's paw,' I said to her.

"She looked at me, and she had this weird little smile on her face. 'I am but a tool of Greater Powers,' she said back, which was nothing new and, actually, it made me feel a lot better about the whole thing. If Ramona was off on one of her Greater Powers delusions, this whole thing just had to be one of her setups, and I knew she didn't have enough occult power to light a birthday candle with a blowtorch. But the whole thing was still creepy as hell. I mean, *human teeth*? Jesus.

"So after that, everything was fine for about a month. Or at least normal. And then the monkey's paw came back. Only it was different."

I had to hand it to my boy Lark. He *did* know how to tell a ghost story, and he had that trained speaker's voice, the legacy of being a Drama major in far-off college days. Here we were, alone in the Snake on a cold winter's night, him going on with his tales of days gone by in tones of deadly reasonableness . . . how could it *not* raise a few hackles?

But I did believe in magic—changes in reality in conformation with the directed Will—not random drive-by hoodoo. Those stories are tales told by amateurs, tourists in our reality, confused and building upon old legends—and sometimes, rarely, dazzled by a brush with true Power that they have no context for interpreting.

"Different how?" I asked blandly, unwilling to let Lark see how well his campfire tale was succeeding.

"This time there was a ring on its finger. A regular boring mundane kind of ring, like you'd find in any jewelry store— gold, stones; diamonds and a tanzanite, I think; something trendy—but sized to fit a mummy-monkey finger. It was in the case in the back of the store with the expensive items, big as life and twice as natural. I knew it was the same damned monkey hand, though: the braiding on the cord over the stump was really distinctive.

"Now I knew Ramona had to know it was there. It was a

locked case; I had the keys to the store, but she had the only key to that case, and the case was locked that morning; I checked. What I couldn't decide was whether it was my business or not. Her store, her stock, you know? It wasn't like she was selling drugs or anything, that would at least have been illegal."

My boy Lark, connoisseur of the niceties of our legal code.

"What I couldn't figure out was what the hell she was up to, or what kind of little drama was going on in her head. Dolphin's Dream was not the kind of place that sold this kind of stuff, and like I said, Ramona had always had a really good handle on what sold."

"So you confronted her? Checked with Cinnamon?"

"Hell, no." Lark looked affronted. "I kept my mouth shut and my head down. The *last* thing I wanted was to start a witch-war. Dolphin's Dream paid my rent, or part of it, anyway. I was working part-time at the clinic, too, by that point, and cutting back my hours at the Dolphin."

The Family Planning Clinic, Lark meant, which employment'd had such disastrous long-term consequences for him.

"I tried to keep an eye on it, but it disappeared while I wasn't looking. And then—a few days later, this time—it was back."

"Another ring?" I suggested.

"Gold bracelet, right above the braiding," Lark said, deadpan. If he was faking all this, he was very good; he wasn't sounding scared so much as puzzled. And that was as it ought to be, if he were talking about events that had happened years ago and miles away. "One of those thin gold bangle kinds, and just like the ring, it was really small. Small enough to fit the monkey's paw; it couldn't have been more than an inch across, if that. Nice and snug, but it didn't look custom. It looked like a regular mass-market piece . . . that had *shrunk*.

"Okay, so that was too much. I nailed Ramona as soon as I could get her alone. 'What the hell is this thing and why

the hell does it keep coming back here?' 'Oh,' she said, 'so
you do believe. That's good. It's magic.' "

Lark growled, still cheesed-off with Ramona after all
these years.

" 'Well, magic is all very well and good, Ramona, but
what does it *do?*' I said, being reasonable.

"She looked me over, like she was trying to decide
whether I was worthy enough to tell. 'It grants wishes,' she
said.

"Now, I'd had a lot of practice not laughing in Ramona's
face, and I was . . . not scared, but really, really nervous
after a couple of months of having that thing pop in and
out . . . or not. Because either she'd found an endless supply
of identical monkey paws and a source for doll-sized fashion jewelry, or the same one was coming back with an added
memento each time. And practically speaking, you can't
manipulate the fingers of something that's been mummified
to get a ring on them without having them just break off. So
I didn't really know which explanation I liked better, and the
plain fact of the matter was that Ramona seemed to have
gone from simple nut to barking mad while I'd been out getting coffee one day. And if she was messing with the black
stuff—conjure, *maleficum,* you name it, you can take it
home—she was not going to stay just this weird, she was
going to get weirder. And not in a good way.

" 'So if it grants wishes, Ramona,' I said, really glad for
once that Dolphin's Dream didn't sell blades, 'how come
you're selling it to other people and not using it yourself?'

" 'Oh,' she says, 'it has to be charged first.' Like it was a
cell phone or something.

"And then she explained how she'd been able to get one,
but it'd been empty, so she'd had to have two other people
wish on it first, and their wishes had to get screwed up so
that their life-essences got sucked into the paw, so that it
would be all charged up, full of energy and ready for her to
wish on. And now, tonight, after she closed the store for the
evening, she was going to use it. And she unlocked the case
and took it out.

" 'Okay,' I said. 'I'm going for coffee. See you in a few.'

"I got my coffee, and I kept on going. I thought about telling somebody what she'd told me, but there didn't seem to be a lot of point. Being a bull-goose loony is not a crime, especially in Southern California and, I mean, you know."

He shrugged helplessly, and in fact, I *did* know. What could he say? What had she done, other than tell him a story so he'd look like an idiot the moment he took it seriously? At most, she'd offered him evidence that she wasn't wrapped any too tight and, like he'd said, lunacy wasn't a crime in and of itself.

But his story, whatever its point, wasn't quite finished.

"I was supposed to work that afternoon at the clinic anyway, and when I went in I asked if they could give me more hours, and it turned out they could take me on full-time, if I didn't mind not being paid for all the hours I worked: they could always use people to walk the clients in through the picket lines, and stuff. I kept busy. Too busy to think, which was fine with me. Thinking had just gotten me into trouble. I wanted a vacation.

"About a week later I heard through the grapevine that Dolphin's Dream was gone. Packed up lock, stock, and aromatherapy candles, and the store was for rent. Boom. Overnight. Nobody knew where Ramona had gone, or why. She was just . . . outta there. Everybody started shopping at Green Magick instead. End of story."

Lark stopped talking. He was done.

I shivered, aware I'd been sitting completely still for the last several minutes, holding a sheaf of unopened bills and invoices. I took a deep breath, willing the story-spell to break.

The story had no proper end, but reality rarely does. It is the province of fiction to tie up loose ends, to punish the guilty and reward the good, to join the lovers together and answer all questions.

"Your point?" I said at last.

"She was bats," Lark said succinctly, banishing ghosts of his own. "I didn't believe her. Magic doesn't work like that, except in the movies. She was . . . I don't know what she was doing, or thought she was doing. She was a flake, but I never told anybody, and I wanted to tell someone. And, you know. . . ." He shrugged. "Things like that ought to happen in places like this, not places like that. Drag a mysterious jeweled casket out of the back room and there should be something in it more exciting than half a dozen rabbit's feet, you know?"

"If it wasn't disappointing, you wouldn't know it was life. You want to call for a pizza?" I got up and stretched, carrying the envelopes over to the jewelry case to open them.

"Hey . . . presents," Lark said behind me, pouncing on the boxes I'd set aside.

The bills were just that—ancient bills, almost a year old—for phone and water and garbage and lights, which must have been settled since, as the Snake was still here and open for business. And duplicate invoices from several wholesalers, who were probably still screaming for their money. I piled them all neatly for Lark's future entertainment. Behind me I could hear the sound of shearing tape, and editorial noises from Lark as he inspected his discoveries. Then:

"Bast." Lark's voice was flat, in the no-color way of profound shock. I turned around quickly.

He was holding one of the boxes out to me. I grabbed it just before he dropped it.

It was the bottom half of a small box, about three by three by six, brown pressboard. It was half-filled with cotton, and nestled down in the cotton was something black and withered and curled. A hand, perfectly formed, almost adult-shaped but smaller than a child's. At the wrist there was a sterling bezel-cap through which was threaded a silver chain.

A monkey's paw.

I stared at Lark, for one furious perfect moment, certain that all of this tonight had been one long setup, that he'd found the thing earlier and told his whole story as one long elaborate gotcha.

"More exciting," I said. I regretted it the moment I saw the look on his face. He wasn't excited.

He was terrified.

That was what convinced me, because above all things, Lark is vain, and there is nothing pretty about terror. Besides, if this had been a setup, surely the monkey's paw he'd described would match the one in the box?

He held out the rest of the package to me, mute refutation of what he knew I must be thinking, begging for my belief. I looked at it. Typewritten address label. Domestic metered postage. Brown paper and strapping tape. I'd handled the package myself, taking it out of the bag. The tape had been *virgo intacta*. He'd never opened it before he opened it just now.

I set the box down beside the pile of bills. Lark came over to stand beside me, as if the need for human contact was more important than the need to stay away from the contents of that box. I put an arm around his waist. Both of us stared down at the mummified paw. I could feel him shake.

Was his story true? I think so, in its essentials: there *was* an occult shop called Dolphin's Dream, and Ramona did sell a monkey's paw. For the rest of it . . . I know what he says he saw, and it may even be what he thinks he saw. I know there are catalogs where you can buy all sorts of things, and that the places that sell them all piously insist they're sold merely as curios, or "for entertainment purposes only."

I also know that belief is the most powerful—and sometimes the most dangerous—thing there is.

"Let's burn it," I said. I went to get an iron cauldron off the shelf.

Lark nodded without saying anything, and went to get some charcoal.

Tanya Huff

The Finest in Fantasy

SING THE FOUR QUARTERS   0-88677-628-7
FIFTH QUARTER   0-88677-651-1
NO QUARTER   0-88677-698-8
THE QUARTERED SEA   0-88677-839-5

The Keeper's Chronicles
SUMMON THE KEEPER   0-88677-784-4
THE SECOND SUMMONING   0-88677-975-8
LONG HOT SUMMONING   0-7564-0136-4

Omnibus Editions:
WIZARD OF THE GROVE   0-88677-819-0
(Child of the Grove & The Last Wizard)
OF DARKNESS, LIGHT & FIRE   0-7564-0038-4
(Gate of Darkness, Circle of Light & The Fire's Stone)

To Order Call: 1-800-788-6262